D1114790

MacDONALD HARRIS

A PORTRAIT
OF MY
DESIRE

SIMON & SCHUSTER
New York · London · Toronto
Sydney · Tokyo · Singapore

SIMON & SCHUSTER
Simon & Schuster Building
Rockefeller Center
1230 Avenue of the Americas
New York, New York 10020

10 9 8 7 6 5 4 3 2 1

Library of Congress Cataloging-in-Publication Data

Harris, MacDonald, 1921–
   A portrait of my desire / by MacDonald
Harris.
      p.   cm.
   I. Title.
PS3558.A6468P67   1993
813'.54—dc20   92-27119   CIP
ISBN 0-671-74195-0

For Ginger, Pat, Jack, and Ann—
my best critics

I knew not what my fate was to be in this house; except that I had nobody to save me except myself.

EMILY SAYLEY,
A Memoir of a Gentlewoman (1802)

A PORTRAIT OF MY DESIRE

one

Killian, he said aloud.

This hurt when he did it. He tried it again: *Killian, Killian, Killian.*

He felt tears welling into his eyes. Her presence persisted in the house, lurking about him in the particles of air that hung in the room. It was a year now and he was still suffering from grief at the loss. He lived in a state of numbness, going through the motions of daily life mechanically. It was hard for him to make decisions or think clearly about things. Her ghost was with him night and day, as though he might go into the next room at any moment and find her there, speak to her or exchange some triviality of their daily life together. Coming across a book she had started and only half finished, with a bookmark in the middle of it, gave him a pang. He would wake up in the middle of the night and stretch toward her and find the bed empty. In a crowd at a party he would catch a glimpse of the back of a head or the edge of a skirt in a doorway, and his nerves would flash *her* for a fraction of a second before his mind told him it was only a momentary delusion. Sometimes he wondered if he really wanted to be cured of his grief. To be cured of it would be a kind of disloyalty to Killian, a sign to himself and the world that his love for her had not been absolute and permanent, and this was a conviction he clung to like a religious belief in the months after she died. He tested the pain now and then, by speaking her name aloud or opening the closet door to look at her clothes, as someone might test an abscessed tooth with his tongue to see if the hurt was still there, taking a secret and self-pitying pleasure to find that it was. *You are dramatizing,* he told himself.

He didn't know what Peter felt. He had never been on intimate terms with him. He was a difficult person to be on intimate terms with. He was intelligent and good-looking, a thin solemn boy with a shock of dark hair, and he did well in school. At home, in the gated community on the coast where they lived, he spent most of his time reading in his room or prowling around by himself at the beach. He was solitary and independent, and if there was anything wrong in his life, he didn't confide in Harry. He had been that way since he was a small child; if he cut himself or stubbed his toe he would limp around, concealing it as best he could until somebody noticed it and put a bandage on it. Proud! Harry was drawn to him with a deep instinctual love that transcended all these superficial details of personality; besides, he recognized a good deal of himself in Peter. Whether Peter felt the same toward him he had no way of telling. As for the absent woman whose phantom hung in the house, in the months since she had died neither Harry nor Peter had talked about her or spoken her name to the other.

Then there was Solange, a large and lithe orange-and-white creature with fixed ideas of her own. She had always been Killian's cat, she would allow only Killian to feed or stroke her, and her favorite place, when there was nothing better to do, was in Killian's lap in the white wicker armchair in the patio, under the ficus tree. When Killian came out to sit in the chair, to read or sip a cup of coffee, Solange would follow her and mount into her lap with the ease of a jungle creature, settling down with a hind foot dangling and her chin on Killian's knee. When Killian was in her final illness—the agony went on for a year—Solange turned restless and strange, would allow no one else to touch her, and spurned her food in favor of grasshoppers, which she found for herself in the garden; sometimes they made her sick and she threw up afterward, but she scorned any overtures of sympathy. After Killian died she continued in this same grim pessimism, declining affection and spending most of the day in a place she had made for herself in the azaleas at the bottom of the garden. They were a fine trio, the man, the boy, and the cat, a living demonstration that no matter how many people live in a house, it is not a family unless there is a woman.

One day that winter, when Harry happened to be sitting in the white wicker armchair, forgetting that it had been Killian's place, Solange leaped onto his lap and he felt the soft animal warmth coiled into his groin. He reached to touch her, and tears sprang into his eyes. Luckily no one was around to see this; Peter was at school, and he was alone with the cat in the patio. After this incident Harry didn't sit in the white chair anymore, and the cat left him alone. They withdrew into their former isolation, Solange in her cat-grief and he into his grief as a lover.

On the practical level, he began to realize that he couldn't go on permanently coping with things himself; the gap left by Killian was too great. Mrs. Manresa came in once a week to clean the house, with the aid of her non-English-speaking helper, but there were the bills and household accounts, the cooking, the grocery shopping, overseeing the work of the gardener, tending the houseplants, taking care of Peter's needs, and seeing to things like getting a sofa cleaned or calling the plumber about a leaky faucet. Sustained by sheer nerve, Harry had done these things himself while Killian was ill, at a considerable strain to his mind and body. But now that Killian was gone and a year had passed, there was a letdown. The energy of the crisis had left him; he felt empty and alone in the house, in spite of his awkward and intermittent, half-embarrassed affection for Peter. And besides, to go on doing these household things himself would be in some obscure way a betrayal of Killian, an attempt to pretend that she had not been essential in his life and that her loss had not been totally crushing, *that he could get along without her.* He could not get along without her. He needed someone to help, not a housekeeper exactly, and not a companion (the thought that he might marry again struck him like an icy blow to the heart), but someone who would do the things that Killian had done in the house, with the single exception of his personal relations with her. He could live permanently with his grief, but not with poorly cooked meals, unpaid bills, or the lurking feeling that Peter needed new clothes and someone had to go to the mall with him.

He ended by doing what he often did—it was so obvious that he wondered why he hadn't thought of it before—he asked his brother-in-law for advice. It always embarrassed him to do this, because Golo, in spite of his obvious friendliness and goodwill, had an elaborate bantering manner about him, as though he were acting out a parody of friendship, or portraying a friend in an amateur theatrical performance, that made Harry feel he was being made fun of in some subtle way. But Golo knew many things and had an apparently unending store of information about such practical matters of life—women, money, houses, cars, and travel. Besides, he had always seemed to have a particular affection for Harry, even though a slightly ironic one.

As he expected, Golo had the answer to his problem. He told Harry about an agency that specialized in home managers, as they were called. No question of these people being servants or menials, or one's social inferiors. Some were Europeans, some were college graduates, some were cultured suburban widows in reduced circumstances. It would not be cheap, but the figures that were mentioned were something he could afford. (Harry owned a small but successful art gallery and had also inherited money from Killian.) At the agency, an efficient woman named Mrs. Genesee described the position exactly as he had imagined it. "A home manager," she said with the prim friendliness of a television commercial, "performs all the functions of a spouse except those of personal relations." She was concerned to make this point quite clear. "Some people who apply to us have different notions," she said. Harry did not have different no-

tions. The last thing he wanted at this point in his life was
the distraction of personality or affection, the complicated
algebra of human relations. He imagined a hypothetical person who would come into his house, competent, neat, even
attractive, but performing her functions like a pleasant robot. He signed the contract with the agency and went home
feeling solaced, as though he had filled the void left in his life
by the death of Killian and at the same time built a monument to its holiness, to her absolute and final irreplaceabil-
ity. There would be no more women in his life, he would not
marry again, and the proof of it was that he had taken this
step, that he had arranged for this person, the home manager
(silly term), to come into his house and do the things that
had to be done.

When he got home the house seemed even emptier than
it had before. It was the middle of the afternoon, and Peter
wouldn't be home for an hour yet. The things in the house—
the furniture, the guest towels on the racks, even the art-
books on the coffee table—were exactly as Killian had left
them; nothing had been changed. Except for the pictures
that Harry brought home from the gallery, the house was
the exact expression of Killian's taste and preference. In the
kitchen her special treasure, her silver-lined copper pans im-
ported from France, hung in a row on hooks, polished at
intervals by Mrs. Manresa. They shone now with a special
burnish, it seemed to him, like objects in a museum, or the
gold and jeweled reliquaries that he and Killian had seen in
the church in Conques on a trip to southern France. The
house was a sacred place like the sanctuary of a church; it
was a museum to the memory of Killian.

In the bedroom there were two large closets: one for his
clothes, the other for hers. He opened the door of her closet
and switched on the light. Her clothes hung neatly arranged
in two ranks: on one side summer dresses, suits, the linen
trousers she had worn around the house and for shopping,
and on the other side winter clothes, an old raincoat, a tweed
skirt and jacket for walks on the beach. Her shoes were

neatly ranged on the shelf. Standing in the corner was an oversized red-and-white umbrella with a brier handle, bought at Smith and Sons in London. The closet smelled of sachets (*corrupt roses*, he thought) and of her odor, thin and pungent, with a trace of something like cinnamon. Feeling strange, he turned off the light and shut the door.

Facing each other across the large bedroom were two sandalwood dressers. He knew the contents of hers by heart. A drawer for underwear, one for scarves, one for sweaters, one for nightgowns, one for belts and handbags. He knew he ought to throw these things out and the clothes in the closet too, or give them to some charity, but he had never been able to bring himself to do it. Probably he should ask some woman to do it for him, a neighbor like Dawn Gilbert, or Dorothy at the gallery. In the top drawer on the right were her personal souvenirs and keepsakes. He opened it mechanically, as though sleepwalking, and touched a lacquered Russian box with foreign coins in it, a seagull feather from the beach, an old brooch, a Navajo bracelet from Taos, a bundle of his letters to her, tied with a faded ribbon.

The sound of the drawer shutting was unexpectedly loud in the silent room. Through the shutters he could hear the tissue-paper crushing of surf and the whisper of breeze in the eucalyptus outside the window. The room was mute, even though he endeavored in the darkness of his mind to make it speak to him. Its voices lay imprisoned in the walls, in the furniture and objects of the room, which were unchanged, exactly as they had been when the two of them had lived in it together. He still slept on his side of the big bed with its chessboard quilt, each night slightly and imperceptibly deepening the hollow under his body, while the depression on the other side remained the same. Here she had lain day by day between her trips to the hospital, her flesh shrinking on her bones, her mouth thin with pain, offering him like an emblem, like the skeleton of a snake, the scar blazing on her hairless head. Harry deliberately inflicted this memory on himself, but it was too much for him. He had forgotten; the sharp and unbearable pain was always the same when he allowed himself to think about it, but he had forgotten and done it again. He left the room with a taste like gall in his throat.

Outside, he stood for a moment in the hall. Through the moisture in his eyes the past caught him and was frozen; he was helpless in its grip. It was dusk, and at the stairway at the other end of the hall he saw the ghost of Peter's form; narrow, fragile, like a portrait by Modigliani, like a portrait of Harry himself as a child. For a moment he caught the glance, white eyes in a blank face, an anguishing, questioning specter: *Why don't you do something?*

two

The doorbell chimed softly, and when he opened the door Sylvia Jacquemort stood framed in the rectangle of white sunlight. Under these conditions, blinded by the glare, he couldn't see her very well and could make out only a dark silhouette so slender that it seemed painful. At the sides of her head were the shadows of a pair of oversized earrings. Her eyes gleamed like two broken pearls, and around them were a pair of circles the size of teacups.

"Won't you come in?"

"Thank you."

With the door closed he could see her better. She was dressed in black, with sheer white stockings. The circles around her eyes were large tinted tortoiseshell glasses, and the black porcelain loops suspended from her ears were exactly the same size, so that she seemed to be wearing on her head two sets of advertisements for her breasts, which were set close together and not much larger than the glasses.

Pricking her way in her spiky black shoes, she advanced across the floor of the entry, glancing at the walls paneled in redwood, the two miniature Giagiù bronzes, the Embry at the end of the room, and at Harry himself with a composure that implied that all this was perfectly natural, exactly what she expected, as though she were entering an ambience that had been created for her, and for this moment.

Harry, in the spell of his grief, was in a slightly sadistic mood. He was by no means sure now that what he was doing was a good idea. The notion that this creature, as elegant and pretentious as she was, could replace even a tiny part of what Killian had been to him, of what Killian had done for him, produced in him only a sardonic inward grimace of self-mockery. The idea of a home manager was a good one only in the abstract, not when incarnated in this quite specific person. Still, on with the task! As empty and futile as it was. He led the way past the Embry into the study.

Here, in the diffuse light that penetrated through the shutters from the patio, he examined her as best he could without seeming to stare. She was tall and very thin, with olive skin, in a sleeveless black dress that clung to her like paint and ended just above her knees. Her black hair was pulled back skintight. Her expression was prim and self-contained. Harry had the impression of a nervousness, something like a mild craziness, concealed beneath the surface of her composure, which might have been a handicap for another person but which she focused through some special power of the will into a force which she used to make happen exactly those things that she wanted to happen.

The study, like the entry, was paneled in redwood, and a glass wall faced out onto the patio and the hillside beyond it, covered with lush semitropical vegetation. Visible now through the half-tilted shutters was the ficus tree and under it the white wicker armchair with its yellow pad, Killian's chair. In the study were a large Italian leather sofa, on which Harry sometimes took naps, a small pantry, like a galley on a yacht, and a wall of books, many of them in fine bindings. There was also a desk, which Harry kept as neat and bare as a display in a furniture store. He saw Sylvia Jacquemort taking all this in.

Deciding at the last moment not to sit at the desk, he motioned to one of the two rosewood armchairs and took the other one himself. Sylvia Jacquemort sat down on the edge of the chair and looked at him expectantly. She carried no handbag or purse of any kind; he wondered with curiosity where she had put her car keys. For a few seconds neither of them spoke. He noted the heavily made-up eyes behind their tortoise circles, the pastel lipstick, the nails like tiny swords painted mauve. Her breasts, in contrast to the maturity of the rest of her person (she was perhaps thirty), were small and elfin, suited to the cup of a child's hand, not a man's.

"You're not exactly the kind of person I expected."

"What did you expect?"

"I'm sorry. I don't know quite what I mean. I need someone to take care of this house. I don't know exactly how to describe the job. The agency calls it a home manager." She looked back at him steadily, showing no expression. "I have a thirteen-year-old boy, Peter. Of course, a woman comes in once a week and cleans the house." Then he stopped suddenly and said, "But would you care for something?"

"Something?"

"A drink, or a cup of tea."

"Tea. But," she said, catching sight of the miniature pantry with its hot plate and leaping up on her spikes, "I'll fix it." She seemed to know by intuition where the tea and the teapot were, and how to work the hot plate. He remained in his chair, a helpless spectator to a drama which she had taken charge of, a miniature demonstration of her household competence.

"Where are the cups?"

"Below, on the left."

"Genuine china. Are they English?"

"Royal Doulton."

"You have nice things." She slipped the filled pot and the cups onto a tray and found some Carr's water biscuits in a drawer. He began to see her in a new light. At first her fashion-magazine elegance and her mauve claws, her *noli me tangere* air, had only irritated him. The idea of her keeping house and cooking for him and Peter was ridiculous. But this deftness with the tea things opened up a new vision of a competent Sylvia Jacquemort, who, without losing her aplomb or removing her raccoon-mask spectacles, would perform any task assigned to her like a princess in chains, with a lightly superior smile.

"There is the cooking. Peter and I don't require anything elaborate, but . . ."

"I have a diploma from an *école de cuisine*. If you'd like
me to stay around for a while, I could fix dinner for you and
your son."

"That won't be necessary."

He imagined Peter's perplexity when he found her in
the kitchen. Peter had been told that Harry was going to be
interviewing some people, but Harry wasn't sure he had
quite grasped what the situation would be. As a matter of
fact, he, Harry, hadn't quite grasped what the situation
would be. Never in his wildest thoughts, when he began
this, had he imagined he would be sitting in the study drinking tea with a creature such as this sitting in front of him.

"Tell me a little something about yourself."

"There's nothing to tell." She poured his tea, then her
own, but ignored the water biscuits. "I'm thirty-one. I was
born in Los Angeles. Now I live here at the beach. I speak
French and Italian. I have certain abominable habits; for
example, I'm lazy and like to sleep in the morning. I've
never married, because I believe marriage is an abject anach-
ronism. I don't see why a man and a woman can't do exactly
as they want without this absurd legal fiction."

"Your attitude toward sexual relations is quite your
own business. I don't care to hear about it."

"Just as you like. I have no sacred reticences, no secrets.
At the same time, I have no desire to tell you anything you
don't want to hear. I'm used to being on display. What you
see," she said, "is what you get."

He cast about for something to rattle her a little, just as
a test. "How would you react to the suggestion that you're
a little overdressed for the occasion?"

"The occasion?"

"For the interview."

"I'm on my way to somewhere else. I have an engage-
ment later in the afternoon. These are simply the clothes I
happen to have on." She shrugged, with a little tightening of
her mouth. He had got to her, just as he hoped.

"What did you mean by saying you're used to being on display?"

"I'm a model. That's really my profession. It's what I've always done. But I've done other things too. I've been a travel agent. A restaurant hostess, then manager." She delivered each of these statements with a pause between, sometimes a sip of tea. "Manager of a manicure parlor. Contributing editor of a women's magazine."

"Which one?"

"You wouldn't have heard of it. It failed almost immediately. I ran a modeling agency, which lasted about six months, and lost all the money which a dear friend lent me to establish it."

"A male friend?"

"You asked that we shouldn't discuss sexual relations."

He smiled; a point for her. "Why don't you go on working as a model?"

"Because I'm thirty-one. I don't care to do matrons. A good many of the models you see in magazines are heavily made-up thirteen-year-olds, did you know that? And then too, the anorexic look is out. I could always gain weight, but I don't have the frame for it."

"Then how," he pressed her delicately, "do you support yourself?"

"I hope to get this job."

That couldn't be clearer. He was beginning to be impressed by her. "Tell me why you think you should have it."

"I feel that I would fit in here," she said, looking around not only at the house and its furnishings but at Harry himself. "I don't mind saying," she went on, "that I'm a person of better than average taste, that I have more than an average number of accomplishments, and at the same time—I don't mind saying this either—I'm in a difficult position just now, there's nothing else on the horizon for me except this job, and if I don't get it I'll be reduced to taking to the streets. I don't mean *that*," she said, catching his expression, "just becoming an old frowse pushing a grocery cart down the sidewalk."

He tried to imagine her in this guise. "Thank you. You've been very helpful. I appreciate your candor," thinking as he said it that Sylvia Jacquemort was the last person in the world you could expect candor from, and doubting at the same time that she really had been candid.

She said smoothly, "I'll expect to hear from you."

She produced a pale mauve business card, which had nothing whatsoever on it but her name and an address and phone in the nearby town of Playa del Mar.

He found himself examining this with curiosity, then he began to wonder where she had carried it in her clothing, which had no pockets or folds. Perhaps among her other skills she was a sleight-of-hand artist. The card was faintly perfumed. Instead of putting it in his pocket, he set it gingerly on the edge of the desk.

"Oh, what an elegant creature."

Solange stalked lazily into the room, slid along the far wall, and looked at Sylvia Jacquemort without curiosity and without surprise. Then she twined around the woman's chair, looked at her again, and lowered herself slightly on her haunches in a way that Harry knew well; it meant that she was about to leap into the guest's lap. Sylvia Jacquemort stretched out her hand toward the cat.

A shock of panic struck Harry. He saw all at once a threat to the sacred memory of Killian, the sole mistress of Solange, as though the two of them were an Egyptian goddess and her feline totem.

"*Don't touch that cat!*"

"All right." She was startled.

"Why don't we go and meet Peter?"

She rose from her chair and followed him into the living room.

"He's probably in his room."

At the foot of the stairs, he was on the point of calling him, then thought better of it and started up the stairs.

Sylvia Jacquemort followed him, in a curious failure of her usual tact. When he reached the landing he turned around and caught her eye, and she stopped at a point where her head was just above the level of the upstairs floor, so she could look around and see if this part of the house was anything like the rest of it. It was much the same: redwood, black enamel, and glass. He went on down the hall, leaving behind him her decapitated head looking around curiously but dispassionately, as though she were examining exhibits in a museum.

"Perhaps I should wait downstairs," he heard her saying after she had got a good look at everything.

Peter wasn't in his room and he wasn't in the bathroom. Harry glanced into the master bedroom, although there was no reason for Peter to be there. Still, from his own childhood Harry retained an infinite belief in the power of children to have devious impulses and to explore places they weren't supposed to when nobody was around. He remembered a time when he was about Peter's age or a little younger and he had crawled into his parents' bed when they were out of the house, to receive some strange looks from his mother, when they returned, on account of the ineptly made bed he had left behind him. How wicked we all are when we are children, he thought, and how mysterious and desirable the world seems to us when we are on the brink of adulthood. He had no idea whether Peter felt anything like this. Peter wasn't in the master bedroom, of course, and the bed was still neatly made up as Harry had left it in the morning. This was another household task that he would have preferred someone else to do.

He went downstairs and found Sylvia Jacquemort waiting in the entry. "He's not here. I'm sorry. I wanted you to meet him. But that will have to be some other time." As he said this it struck him that he seemed to be offering her the job as a certainty; he should have said *that would have to be some other time.*

"Quite," she said in her short, clipped way.

Now that the interview was over she seemed eager to

get out of the house. She tap-tapped over to the door on her spike heels, and he opened it for her.

"I have your phone number. Goodbye. It was a pleasure meeting you," he told her.

He took her hand, which she held as though she wore gloves, even though she didn't. Smiling, she left without a word. He closed the door and watched her through the tall, narrow window at the side of the entry, half screened by an urn of papyrus. She disappeared down the stairs, then appeared again on the walk. Her car was a small black Japanese coupe. At the curb she bent over, reached into the front wheel well, and took her car keys from the top of the tire. Then she opened the door and slipped into the car with ease as though it were a trick by a dancer, keeping her white knees together in the narrow black skirt.

Harry waited until he was sure she was gone, and then he went off down the road in search of Peter. He was pretty sure he would be at the beach. He didn't have any friends in the neighborhood, and there were almost no children his age in Orange Bay, a cove named not for a local industry—the land was too valuable for orange groves—but for the quality of its sunsets. The road wound down the canyon and came out in the park, so called, a square of lawn with a clubhouse, clumps of oleanders, coral trees, and some wind-bent Torrey pines in it. At the end of the park was a low seawall, and beyond it was the beach. There was only a short stretch of sand, sheltered by sandstone cliffs on both sides. There was Peter coming out of the sea like some juvenile sea god, waves breaking around his waist, brine falling from him in streams. Harry now saw his oversized tee-shirt and faded pink shorts lying on a rock under the cliff. At home in Orange Bay he went barefoot winter and summer.

On the beach, neither of them spoke. Peter went directly to his clothes and pulled them on over his soaking-wet trunks. Then he pushed his wet hair out of his face and met his father's glance for the first time. He resembled Harry himself and not his mother. Killian had been aquiline, alert, and nervous; he and Peter were somber and self-contained. Peter had Harry's shadowy brown eyes, his skeptical mouth (his Pirate Smile, Killian called it, contending that there was something sinister in it), his dark hair, as fine as a girl's, which hung over his forehead. At thirteen he was skinny and elongated but almost as tall as Harry.

"I didn't know where you'd gone."

"You had somebody in the house."

"I told you a woman was coming to be interviewed."

"I know. I went out."

"You didn't have to leave. You could have stayed in your room. I had the idea that you might want to meet her."

Peter had no comment on this. They turned and walked together up the canyon, still without talking very much. Behind them the sun sank cold and bulging into the winter sea. The waves buzzed faintly, filtered through air that made everything sound crisp as though polished with wax. Peter left wet sandy tracks on the road behind him.

"Aren't you cold?"

Peter shook his head scornfully.

Harry looked around to see what there was for the two of them for dinner. After Killian died he had never really mastered cooking, because she had been very good at it and to do it well would somehow be a slight to her memory. He found some lasagne in a long box and peered into it as into a telescope. It looked all right. It had been in the cupboard a long time, but dried pasta never got too old. He brought some water to a boil and shook the dried yellow vanes out of the box into it; one live squirming worm came out into the pan, and a few gossamer wings of deceased bugs. He looked to see if Peter had noticed, but he was engrossed in his book at the kitchen table. Harry poured out the water, rinsed the lasagne, and started over again. They were living like residents of a tin-can barrio in Rio, in spite of their money. When the lasagne was soft he made a sauce with tomato paste and an onion, put everything into a baking dish, and clapped it into the oven. When it was hot he opened a bottle of chardonnay for himself and a raspberry seltzer for Peter. He wondered if he ought to offer him wine.

"I was sorry you weren't here this afternoon. Miss Jacquemort wanted to meet you." Actually she had given no sign of any such desire. What he really meant was that he wanted Sylvia Jacquemort to meet Peter, so that she would be impressed by his unconscious childish beauty, his good manners, his quietness, and his self-contained aplomb, which almost matched hers.

Peter looked up from his book, set it aside, and began eating what was set in front of him.

"What's she like?"

"She's very nice."

"Is she old?"

"No. I wouldn't say that. Not extremely young either." He imagined himself trying to describe to Peter her clothes, her cool aloofness, her earrings, her mauve talons. He was on the point of saying "About thirty," but for some reason he didn't. He said simply, "She seems to be a nice person."

Peter said, "You want somebody to replace Mom, don't you?"

Harry looked up sharply. Their eyes met, and for a moment they seemed to be hovering on the edge of some truth; then Harry broke it off.

"No, I don't. It's just that we need someone to look after the house and do some of the things that your mother did. I can't handle it all myself when I'm working."

"We have Mrs. Manresa."

"That's just the housecleaning. There are a lot of other things. Cooking, managing the household accounts, taking care of the laundry, going to the market."

"But she wouldn't have anything to do with me, would she?"

As a matter of fact, Harry had imagined that this person could be a surrogate mother for Peter in a number of ways he could think of. He said only, "She could go with you to buy clothes, and maybe she could help you with your school-work."

"I don't need anybody to do either of those things. At school I wear a uniform, and at home I wear this stuff," he said, sitting at the table in his orange tee-shirt and pink shorts, identical to the water-soaked ones he had taken off when he came up from the beach.

"Peter," said Harry, "there's something I've been thinking about. I've been thinking that it might be a nice idea if you called me Harry. You're older now, you're not a child anymore, and we're just two men living in this house together. Anyhow I don't care very much for the word 'Father.' It's not a title that I feel happy about applying to myself. It implies that I've got some authority and you've got to do what I say, and also that there's an obligation on your part to love me, and on my part to love you, not on account of any true affection but just because we're father and son and we're supposed to feel a certain way about each other. That's conventional and alienating and forces us both into roles we don't need to accept. I'd prefer for us to be just Harry and Peter, making decisions by discussing things on an equal basis and feeling for each other whatever we happen to feel. Are you following at all what I'm saying?" he asked, as Peter went on sitting at the table with his fork poised over his dish, watching him intelligently but in silence as he went on about this.

Peter said, "Oh, yes." Without committing himself as to whether he thought it was a good idea.

"And 'Dad,' " Harry went on, "is even worse. Not to mention 'Pop,' 'Pater,' and all the other versions from the funny papers. What *do* you call me, by the way? It's a funny thing, but at the moment I can't remember."

"Well," said Peter, "it's a funny thing for me too. I can't remember either. I think that mostly I don't call you anything. I just say You or find a way of saying things without calling you anything."

"So you too feel that it's awkward and that it would be

better if you called me Harry? Imagine," he put in quickly, thinking in the instant of this example and wanting to offer it to him before he made up his mind, "if I went around calling you Son instead of Peter."

"Oh, I think it would be fine if I called you Harry. We can do it any way you like."

"But you see," Harry explained gently, "I'm not asking you if you want to do it the way I want. I'm asking you if you want to do it *this* way."

Peter, after a moment's hesitation, said recklessly, "Well, let's do it, then." It was as though they were agreeing—Peter reluctantly, but giving in to Harry's persuasions—to experiment together with some dangerous vice.

Harry remembered something. Only a few moments ago, before the subject of names came up, while they were still discussing the idea of having someone in to take care of the house, Peter had referred to Killian as Mom. Surely he couldn't have. What had he said? He had said that he, Harry, was looking for someone to replace Killian in his affections. Had he said Mother? Had he said Killian? Had he said your wife? It was impossible, Harry thought, that he had said any of these things.

"Peter," he said, "do you remember, a few moments ago, when we were talking about the idea of getting someone to take care of the house, and you said that I wanted someone in the house because I missed Killian. I forget now how you put it, but you said something like that." It was the first time that this name had been spoken between them since Killian died.

"I did?"

"Yes, and I want to know how you referred to her. This is important to me. Did you call her Mom?"

"I don't know. I don't even remember what you're talking about," said Peter, totally without embarrassment, as though Harry had simply made a mistake or was confusing him with some other person who had made the remark he was referring to. But he *had* said Mom. Somehow this devious but harmless lie, this evasion, so much like those of

Killian's own, made Harry love him so much that he almost got up from the table and folded him in his arms.

"Anyhow," he said, "it won't necessarily be Miss Jacquemort. I'm going to interview some more of them next week. The agency is going to keep sending them until we find one that's right." He was pleased with himself for thinking of that *we*.

three

Velda Venn.

She was a woman with an unmemorable face. After she left he could hardly remember what she looked like, although her body stuck in his mind. She resembled not a slender birch (Sylvia Jacquemort) but a Greek amphora, a shape for women that had been fashionable in certain periods of history but didn't happen to be so right now. Still, she seemed to be a pleasant person, and anxious to please, although she didn't appear to have any special qualifications except for her ordinary woman's skills, her youth (she confessed to twenty-eight), and her cheerfulness. For the interview she had chosen to wear an emerald jersey with fine horizontal stripes that stretched around her bust in contours like an engineering drawing, a violet headband, and tight polyester trousers, the same color as the jersey but without stripes. Sandals, and a silver ring with a large piece of jade in it. Hazel eyes and pale skin, as clear as a baby's. Her hair, brown with lighter streaks, stuck out behind her head like a fan. From the other side of the desk she radiated a pleasant womanly odor, the smell of something baking in the oven and a trace of cheap perfume. She looked as though she had bought everything new for the interview, but at a discount clothing store. She was a plain woman, no two ways about it. Still, she put him at his ease because she was so obviously at *her* ease. Nothing seemed to perturb her. She sat there prattling away as though they had known each other for years.

She provided the necessary information about herself without his having to ask questions. She came from Tahitian Gardens, one of the less pretentious suburbs of Los Angeles. Harry had never been there, but you could catch a glimpse of it from the freeway: rows on rows of identical crackerbox houses in various shades of pastel. Her schooling: she had gone as far as a community college but quit after a year because she had to get a job. (He had never asked Sylvia Jacquemort if she went to so much as the first grade.) Then she worked as a preschool teacher, a trainee computer programmer, and an assembler in an electronics factory, but now she was out of work and drawing welfare. She came back again to her experience as a teacher, contending that this suited her exactly for the job.

"But you said you taught preschool. Peter is thirteen years old."

"It doesn't matter. Children are children no matter what their age. I could throw his clothes in the washer, drive him to school, and see to it that he does his homework. I know that's hard for a father."

This seemed like a disastrous idea. He tried to imagine Peter, with his aloofness and his fierce independence, knuckling under to her spurious cheerfulness.

"He goes to a private school. The van picks him up."

"A boy does need a mother."

Harry inwardly seethed. A phantom picture of Killian came into focus, superimposed on this silly creature with her spaniel hair and her gourd-shaped figure. "He needs a parent, and he's got one. I can take care of that myself, and I can do all these other things too. I've been doing them for a year."

"Then why do you need me?"

"I don't necessarily need you. You're one of several candidates."

"That's fine." Still, it was clear she was confident she would get the job.

Her romantic life. This too she offered voluntarily, prattling on in her way. She had married someone she met in the
community college and lived with him for two years—this
was when she was a preschool teacher. Then they divorced,
because he didn't provide—that is, he didn't provide money,
so she didn't provide sex. Harry didn't really want to hear all
this. Single again, she became a computer trainee, which
worked well at first, but as the course progressed it required
more math than she was able to provide. "I'm not good with
numbers; I'm a people person." Thrown out once again into
the world, she turned to assembling printed circuits, which
paid well but was monotonous, and you had to wear a white
head scarf, and the people to the right and left of her were
morons. Then she met a friend—a boyfriend, as she called
him—and lived with him for two years, which seemed to be
a kind of private limit of hers on the length of sexual relations, in an apartment in Electric Beach. He had a mustache,
looked like a well-known television star, and wore designer
jeans; she told Harry the name of the brand. When he left,
he took the car, their expensive stereo equipment, and their
collection of records. What kind of music, Harry hardly
dared to ask. Country western.

Her husband's name was Max, the two-year boyfriend
Vivian. Falling into a lazy trance, he found himself contemplating her Ingres body and the jersey with its fine lines like
the contours on a map. Her face he forgot even when she
was sitting in front of him, until he looked at it again to
remind himself. He roused himself to alertness.

"So you still live in Electric Beach?"

"No; when Vivian left I moved back to Tahitian Gardens because it's cheaper."

"Do you like it there?"

"It's a place to live. It isn't Orange Bay, that's for sure.
You've got a nice place here."

She looked around with undisguised covetousness at the
black enamel and redwood, the expensive works of art, the
books in fine bindings. "I'd like to live here." She actually
said this. But even Sylvia Jacquemort had told him she des-

perately wanted the job, all her chic and coolness slipping away in this anguished cry.

"Do you really think you could do all this? Take care of a house this large? Pay the bills, do the household accounts, plan the meals, do the shopping?"

"No problem."

"Can you cook?"

"Of course I can cook. I cooked for Max and Vivian. Imagine either of those two mutts doing it for themselves. And I cook for myself now."

"It's getting on toward six. Why don't you stay and fix supper for us. That way you can meet Peter and we can get acquainted a little better."

"A test of my competence," she said cheerfully.

"If you want to put it that way."

"Sure."

He showed her where the kitchen was and introduced her to Peter, who said, coolly and appraisingly, "Hello." While the two of them watched from their stools at the kitchen bar, she scouted around in the refrigerator and the cupboards to see what there was. After an hour she produced a glass baking dish of macaroni and cheese. She did go to the trouble of sautéeing some onions to put in it, and adding a spoonful of capers she found in the refrigerator, and she put the whole thing under the broiler at the end, which made a crinkled blackish crust on top. Harry mentally compared it to his own lasagne to see if he would do better by taking her on. Of course, macaroni and cheese was not as fashionable as lasagne, but she had done a better job of it. It was about as good as the food in a school cafeteria. For the salad she tore up the lettuce with her fingers, a practice Harry found disgusting, and she put the dressing directly on the salad instead of setting the bottle on the table, as they did in the family. For dessert she produced a trio of baked apples, which Harry hadn't even noticed her cooking; she had concealed them behind the macaroni in the oven.

Peter and Harry exchanged glances, but they ate it all without a word. Harry scraped the dressing off his salad with a knife. Peter said very little during the meal, although he glanced now and then at her frizzy hair and her buxom figure.

As a well-brought-up child he knew he ought to comment on the meal, but he found nothing to say about the macaroni. "What's in the baked apples?" he asked her.

"I always put butter and sugar in them, and just a pinch of cinnamon."

After she left, Peter said, "Tahitian Gardens."

"Don't be a snob, Peter."

Mrs. Bream.

He was not sure he had even caught her first name, if she had one. She was a blunt, no-nonsense kind of person, a professional English housekeeper; she came from Manchester, she said. She wore a linen suit and carried the jacket over her arm. Her long-sleeved blouse was starched, her shoes were sensible, and her hair was the color and shape of a thatched roof, with the part a little to one side. Harry guessed she was forty, but she would not have been much different at thirty or fifty. If she had a shape, it was effectively concealed by the suit and the crinkly blouse. She was a little larger than average size, and stiffly resolute; she held her mouth like someone who is about to reply correctly and respectfully but with a touch of tartness to some slur by her betters. It was clear that for Mrs. Bream her employers (she had had several others in the past) *were* her betters, but also that she felt she was entitled to exactly as much respect as they were, although of a different sort. She was used to respectability, to wealth, and to nice things. It was an accident of fate that she had been born into her station in life, and it was to her credit (her manner suggested) that she on the one hand accepted this station (not that of a servant, but not gentry either) and on the other hand was quite precisely aware of its privileges as well as its limitations and would insist on the former; it would be impossible to get her to function in any way like a domestic, by doing housecleaning, for example, but it was also not to be expected that she would usurp herself, become overweening, and demand to be present at the table when guests came to dinner, although she would certainly sit with Harry and Peter at ordinary meals. This sitting or not sitting at the table under various conditions, Harry began to see, would be a crucial point in his relations with the person, whoever it was, who eventually took this job.

Mrs. Bream did not offer to put herself to the test by cooking a meal for them, although she did, when Harry offered her tea, say briskly, "Let me help," and then did most of it herself, calling on him only when she couldn't find the switch to turn on the hot plate. Harry felt that it was he who had been put to the test in providing British scones for the tea—he had gone out and bought them when he heard her name, imagining her almost perfectly from this one syllable, and she served them, warmed in a napkin, without surprise and without comment. Peter too was present at this tea but not at the interview; he was called in after the talking was over, and appeared to Harry's surprise in a clean shirt, a pair of slacks, socks, and loafers. Mrs. Bream put her linen jacket over the arm of her chair, as though she were afraid that someone would steal it, or thought it would not be seemly of her to ask Harry to hang it in a closet. He wondered why she had taken it off—it was a mild day in December—but even so it was the one flaw in her otherwise perfect picture of an Englishwoman of a certain sort. During the tea Harry amused himself by making wild guesses at her first name: Eloise, Marcia, Florence, Mabel, Constance, Clarice, Ernestine, Emily, Harriet (that was very likely it), Nancy, Louella, Bernice. Or even something exotic, Vita or Carmen, borrowed from the privileged Edwardians, who allowed the lesser classes to use their names a generation or two after they were done with them. But if she came to preside over the house, she would always be called Mrs. Bream.

When she got up to go Harry saw her eye passing over the Embry at the end of the entry, a large colorful canvas of a Norman seaside resort, with sailboats, tricolor flags, and a wedding-cake hotel. "Do you like pictures?" "I do when I understand them." It was not clear whether she understood the Embry; there was certainly not very much to understand in it. She didn't drive, of course; she had been left by a nephew who, she said, would pick her up at the curb. Or kerb, as Harry spelled it in his mind. Her accent was Midlands, an attractive drawl that made her sound like a minor character in a public television drama. As she left, Harry and Peter caught a glimpse of the nephew waiting in his car. He was a pasty-faced youth with his hair all on one side and covering his eye, and the car was an old but clean Ford Escort.

In the empty house Harry and Peter looked at each other without speaking. Mrs. Bream was very likely the one he would hire, he thought to himself in this moment when he was still under the influence of her formidable and efficient temperament. He was uncertain whether he ought to discuss it with Peter first or just go ahead and do it. She would probably be a terrible cook in the English tradition, treacle puddings and overboiled vegetables, but she would be marvelous with Peter. He would grow up to be a gentleman with perfect manners, a little afraid of women. He had sensed this about her and put on decent clothes before he even caught sight of her.

Edna Colchis-Wincroft.

Although she pronounced her first name distinctly, he promptly forgot it and thought of her throughout by her last name, as he had Mrs. Bream. In this case two last names. Miss Colchis-Wincroft. Could he afford a housekeeper with a hyphenated name? Perhaps it was only a harmless badge of feminism. Of all the women he had interviewed, she was the most concerned with making an impression on him, with bullying her way into the job, into the security of a position in the house, into the privileged sanctuary of Orange Bay, where she felt she belonged, the most concerned with making it clear to him who *she* was. She had an air of cheerful connivance, of complicity, of some kind of common knowledge the two of them shared, although he wasn't sure what this knowledge was supposed to be. She entered the house not hand on hip exactly, but with a flair and a smile, cheaply but brightly dressed, something *dégringolée* about her, the air of a faded actress who had once played Hedda Gabler. Because of her lithe movements, he could not, afterward, remember her clothing exactly, but it seemed to be made of layers of paisley or some other Indian stuff, and to involve lace, scarves, rings, necklaces, and ceramic pins, one of them in the form of a miniature painting which he was able to recognize as Fragonard's *The Happy Lovers.*

"Suppose," he said to her lightly (he was almost enjoying this), "you give some account of yourself."

"Well, I have lived in *many* households as friend and companion, as a member of the family, one might say, both in this country and in Europe. As for children, I adore them." She spoke of the Westerhouts, who had wept, all of them, when she left, from the three-year-old Phoebe to the father, who was a corporate attorney. Why did she leave? he inquired. The dynamic had evolved to a point where it seemed better that she should leave. Perhaps Miss Colchis-Wincroft had wept too, but if so she didn't reveal this.

"Have you made your living in some other way as well?"

"My what?"

"Have you had other jobs?"

"Oh, heavens, yes—I'm not a child, Mr. De Spain. I've been around for some time, as you can see."

"Well, what were the others?"

"The other what?" He had the impression that she was treading water and thinking rapidly, trying to decide what to tell him about this.

"The other jobs."

"I've made my living in any way that I can, Mr. De Spain. I've lived in many houses, both in this country and in Europe."

"Where in Europe?" he pressed her.

"Well, in Nogent-le-Rotrou."

She must know what she's talking about, he thought. She couldn't have made up Nogent-le-Rotrou. "*Est-ce que vous parlez français?*"

"*Un peu.*"

"*Est-ce que vous vous sentez capable d'enseigner le garçon en français?*"

"I can't follow you when you talk so fast, Mr. De Spain."

It didn't matter. After all, he was hiring a home manager and not a French teacher. "Are you married?"

"Not exactly. I used to be, once."

He was not going to get any more out of her on that account. He left it there. He asked her about cooking.

Sensing, perhaps, that French was in some way important to him, she said, "Mr. De Spain, *j'adore la cuisine.*"

He suggested to her slyly that the word *cuisine* had two meanings in French.

"Oh, I adore it in both senses. I like to eat cooking, and I like to work in the kitchen."

She did know some French. She was clever and quick-witted. This might not be altogether a good thing; perhaps she was *too* clever. He had the feeling that she was concealing something from him, although he had no idea what this might be.

"And what do you do, Mr. De Spain?"

"I'm in the art business."

"Are you an artist?"

He found himself imitating her deviousness. "Not exactly. I work with artists."

"I'm sure we'd get along well. I was trained as an artist. I went to an art school in Houston. That's a part of my life that I'd just as soon forget, but Houston does have a perfectly good art school. And I've known many artists. I have to admit, Mr. De Spain, that my own work—I've done silk screens, lithographs, whatever you like—is not exactly earth-shaking and has not won very many prizes, but I've been told by teachers that I have the talent to be a professional artist. All that has been lacking is the opportunity.

When I was living in Europe with the Simons—she's the former Betty Rockefeller, you know—I made the acquaintance of the artist Ioann Vlach. We became very good friends. This led to a misunderstanding with the Simons—they misunderstood my relations with Ioann—and so I was no longer welcome in their house. To my dismay, Ioann betrayed me too. I think the Simons must have got to him. The next time we met, he scarcely seemed to know me. Ioann is very well known, but I don't think anyone can say whether he was an important artist or not. My own feeling is that a person of such dubious character—someone capable of betraying an intimate friend who trusted him—could never take his place in the ranks of truly important artists. He had a certain facility, that I can't deny. A technical facility. I'm going into this, Mr. De Spain, because a while ago you asked me if I had ever been married."

"Yes. I see," said Harry.

In the days that followed, these four forms drifted in succession past his inner eyesight, while he considered their qualifications and tried to imagine this one or that one installed in the position in the house. Sylvia Jacquemort. Velda Venn. Mrs. Bream. Edna Colchis-Wincroft. (He remembered her first name now.) In the first place, it was clear to him that Sylvia Jacquemort was out. She represented temptation—this was the very flat and bald way to put it if he was to be honest with himself. Peter had suggested that he wanted someone to replace Killian. This idea was so painful to him that in thinking about the home manager business, he rejected out of hand, not only with his mind but with every corpuscle of his blood, anyone who had the slightest trace of female attraction. To hire Sylvia Jacquemort would be to install in the house someone who flashed out at the world flagrantly with her femininity, someone who would bring into the house again some of the flair and fascination, some of the perfume of the erotic, that had gone out of it when Killian died. And that was only a year ago! He would be the laughingstock of his friends, and he could imagine

what Peter's reaction would be. He felt a hot shame as he
even considered this idea. To convince himself that it was
utterly out of the question, he imagined Sylvia Jacquemort
standing on a step stool in her spike heels to get down the
china from the cupboard, chopping onions and tucking up a
strand of her hair that had come loose, and carrying out the
garbage to the street, all in her black dress and her oversized
earrings. Of course, she might change clothes when she got
down to business in the house. He tried to picture her in a
cook's apron or a flowered housedress with a white collar. He
doubted if they even made flowered housedresses in her
shape.

Taking them in order, he went on to Velda Venn. A fine
solid cheerful person. On the whole, he preferred her account of her previous sex life to that of Edna Colchis-
Wincroft, although it was absolutely none of his business in
either case. She would probably do the work at first with a
heavy hand, putting out the wrong wineglasses and getting
his books out of order, but she was clever and would learn
fast. He found her spaniel hair, her bottle-shaped body, and
her cheap discount-store clothing more pitiful than repul-
sive. No, not pitiful, amusing. No, not amusing, touching.
Harry had enough social consciousness to realize that being
on welfare or living in Orange Bay was mainly a matter of
luck in life. Still, he shrank from the idea of taking this
garrulous drab, so cheerful and so full of herself, into his
house, into his family, into a permanent place in his life.
Peter would whisper "Tahitian Gardens" behind her back
and engage in ironies at her expense. They would eat macaroni and cheese. She would prattle on about her past as a
computer programmer, as an assembler of electronic circuits.
She would call people mutts and she would want to sit at the
table when they had guests for dinner. Still, he told himself,
anybody he took into the house was going to be a person and
not just a mute and odorless robot. Velda would do an ear-
nest job; she would strive to do her best. He inclined to
Velda, while he was thinking about Velda. At a certain point
he wondered whether her personal attractions, as meager as

they seemed, were not a factor in his thinking. He remembered the wavy lines that went around the convexities in her jersey and then came back together again. If this was so, then she was out, along with Sylvia Jacquemort.

Mrs. Bream. She was the one he should hire; there was really no question about that. He realized this as soon as he stopped thinking about the other candidates and their hypothetical or dubious qualifications and focused on this no-nonsense Briton with her thoroughly professional attitude toward the job. That was what he wanted, wasn't it? A professional. A home manager—silly term, part of the jargon of the agency, yet it described exactly what he wanted and needed. Provided with this new tool, this simple two-word expression, he applied it to Sylvia Jacquemort. The idea of Sylvia and the idea of home didn't belong in the same sentence. As for Velda Venn, she had no notion of how the home of a family in Orange Bay was supposed to work, how vastly more sophisticated and complex it was than anything she had ever known about families. Mrs. Bream would be surprised at nothing. She had lived in the houses of the rich and the not so rich, and she would understand that their lives could never be her own, but the mechanics of the house were something she could master. She knew how to make tea. She had no car, but her nephew could take her in his car to do the shopping. She would be sensible with Peter—that is, she would leave him alone. She would add cachet to the house in the eyes of the neighbors. The rest of them had their Mercedes and went on their trips to Nepal, but nobody had an authentic English housekeeper. Only a joke, of course; he chuckled sardonically, but he imagined the reactions of Henry Fang, Golo, and the Gilberts. Mrs. Bream would be clear about her status in the house. Ordinarily she would sit at the table for dinner, but not when there were guests; on such occasions she would be transformed into a kind of female version of an English butler. Harry was not quite sure how this would work, but he was sure it would be impressive. The service at parties, under her care, would be immaculate. Mrs. Bream it was, he thought.

Of course, there was always the Colchis-Wincroft woman. She was crazy, there was no question about it. She had no doubt started as a romantic, in her girlhood as an art student, but this had progressed to the point where her self-dramatization had become a mental illness. She showed every sign of being afflicted with self-referential delusions of grandeur, along with a persecution mania. All her Rockefellers and Westerhouts were products of her diseased imagination. She may have worked for certain people as a housekeeper or companion, but even in her own account of it this career had been a succession of disasters, because she had always allowed personal relations to get mixed up in it. As to her alleged affair with Ioann Vlach, she had probably seen his name in a magazine. Harry conjectured wildly, and with a certain grim amusement, as to what her own art would look like. Technically inept, and full of symbols. And this, it occurred to him, was a pretty good description of Edna herself. He laughed, a single morose bark. Still, she was not to be ruled out. What was he thinking? Edna was not to be ruled out? Well, nobody was to be ruled out. The four faces swirled in his thoughts, in his dreams, and he could not make up his mind. Of course, he could never remember Velda Venn's face. They were all women, and it was difficult for him not to imagine them as women. Should he hire a man? A cook-valet-chauffeur? The idea was ridiculous. In spite of his denials, it was a woman he was missing, and it was a woman he needed. Before his eyes brimmed the vision of Sylvia Jacquemort walking out to her car in the white sunshine, bending over to retrieve her keys from the wheel well, and slipping under her steering wheel with the grace of a dancer.

four

Harry was in the back room of the gallery helping Dorothy Gaspar uncrate a new Nagamoto that had been delivered that morning. The two of them pried off the end of the crate and, with infinite care, slipped the painting out of the Styrofoam sheets that padded it on both sides. Harry brushed off a few crumbs of white plastic foam that clung to the surface. Dorothy set it against the wall, and they both looked at it.

Yukio Nagamoto. *Cormorant Fisherman.* Wash and acrylic, 40″ x 40″.

On an aquamarine background, turgid at the bottom and paling to a papery white at the top, indistinct black shapes floated, like ink blots or smudges of smoke. Through these figures, thin incandescent filaments of red, orange, and yellow ascended at a slope to the left. These fine lines, always at the same tilt, like the angle of the earth's ecliptic, were in all of Nagamoto's paintings, as though his universe had slipped and was in danger of falling out of his mind, then was halted by some invisible nail or doorstop. The fisherman was only a smoke cloud, except for a precise tuft of beard and an angle of arm extended by his oar or pole. The canvas was fine linen, glued to a board as carefully crafted and fragrant as a Japanese house.

"I don't understand. Does the old man fish for cormorants?"

"No, the cormorants catch fish for him and bring them back to the boat."

"One of his nicer pictures. I imagine it'll sell right away."

"Yes."

"And we've sold three Embrys in a month. No, four."

Out in front, on the white walls under the bullet lamps, there were a half-dozen Embrys, large acrylics with tricolor flags, sunlight, parasols, a small white dog, poplars, sailboats, and sun glinting on the sea, done with the blurry precision of a gifted child. There were Nagamotos in the front shop too, one of round bridges and craggy mountains, another of a pair of peasant children in a rice field, both traced over with the sloping incandescent threads. A trio of Nelson Kells: New England country scenes with something uncanny about them. Giagiù bronzes, roughly cast figures as skinny as canes, with oversized feet and hands, the females with breasts like nut meats. Kati Modane: serigraphs of tennis players in a splashy expressionistic technique, white and blue with orange flesh. A few Paul Garvey seascapes of the local coast. By the door was the only joke Harry permitted himself, a Dadaist Mona Lisa with a mustache. It was not for sale.

As a matter of fact, Harry personally preferred the old masters to these currently fashionable contemporaries; his favorites were Carpaccio and Vermeer. (Embry's small fluffy white dog, which appeared in all his pictures, was borrowed from Carpaccio, a joke he shared with Harry.) Harry successfully concealed from his clients this secret of his preference for the classics, which came out only in a single crotchet: he refused to handle things that were not representations of *something*, even though concealed, distorted, or blurred, like the fisherman of Nagamoto with his birds. No auto enamel dripped onto boards, no rectangles drawn with a T-square, no red spots leaking drips onto a slapped-up gray background. This policy was indicated by the two words, in slightly smaller letters of silver leaf, under *xavier gallery* on the window: *contemporary representational.*

Harry specialized in the work of these half-dozen artists, the tried and proven workhorses of his business. Over the years he had introduced them into hundreds of living rooms, bedrooms, and studies along the coast. The gallery was not demanding and took only a couple of hours of his time a day. The real work was done by Dorothy Gaspar. She opened the place in the morning and closed it at night, and she dealt with the people who wandered in from the street to look at the pictures—lookyloos, she called them. If there were important clients, Harry came in to have coffee with them in the back room. On Saturdays an art student named Boy Canady sometimes subbed for Dorothy, or a crazy painter who lived in the canyon, Mordecai Steiglitz. On Sundays the gallery was closed.

Standing on a pair of stools, Harry and Dorothy lifted the Nagamoto into place under the bullet lamp. The Nagamotos were all the same size, and when one was sold the next one fitted into the same patent fasteners on the wall. Dorothy was a woman the color of fine vellum, with creases around her mouth and at the corners of her eyes, and straight black hair pulled back tight and fastened with a barrette. It was odd that she had worked by his side every day and he didn't even know how old she was. Somewhere in her forties, probably. Because he had spent the week interviewing candidates for the home manager position, he was filled with a sudden curiosity about her curriculum vitae.

"How old are you, Dorothy?"

"I'm forty-seven. It's no secret. My Social Security file is right there in the back room with the records."

"Yes, but you take care of all that. You've worked for me all these years, and I don't know anything about you. I don't even know where you live."

"The address is in the file too. I have a little house on Shadow Lane."

"And do you live by yourself?"

"Oh, Harry, just look at me. I'm the perfect picture of a spinster. An old maid out of a story. Looking under the bed for burglars and so on."

"Why didn't you ever marry?"

"My, you're full of questions today, aren't you? Because the ones I liked didn't care for me, and the ones who cared for me I didn't like."

Maybe, it occurred to him, he should persuade her to give up her house on Shadow Lane, which he imagined as a small shingled bungalow overgrown with bougainvillea, and move into the house in Orange Bay. She was as efficient as any of the rest of them, and she was without a trace of female coquetry. With this thought came another: that Dorothy Gaspar, of all the women he knew, was the only one who didn't have her head turned by his good looks. At least she gave no sign of it, and she had been working in the gallery for years. Perhaps she lacked some fundamental woman-impulse, the hapless instinct that seemed to bewitch all the rest of them as soon as they caught sight of him. All the better, if he could get her to move into the house and take charge of things. Of course, she would still have to go on working in the gallery.

They got down from their stools and stood looking at the Nagamoto. "It's funny you should ask me a question like that, Harry. I've never talked to anyone about these things. You know, it's started me thinking too. Why *didn't* I ever marry? It's so strange; life is so strange. When I was a girl, I took it for granted that I'd marry like everyone else. And then, as each one came along, I told myself, No, he's not quite it."

He heard her voice going on about the strangeness of her life, but he was hardly aware of what she was saying. He contemplated the picture keenly, professionally, through half-closed lids. "I like it better than the others, really. It's more mysterious. Not so specific. The brushwork is superb. Those bright-colored lines. I wonder how he does them."

"You know, I see now that the real reason I never married is that at a certain point I decided to devote my life to art. Isn't that silly?"

He realized at last that she was not just chatting, that what she was saying was important, at least to her. "And did you?"

"Did I what?"

"Did you devote your life to art?"

"That's a question I've never thought about either. I guess I did, since I'm here, aren't I? Handling these beautiful things all day long. Talking to people about pictures."

"You seem to be saying that you took this job instead of marrying."

She only gave a little shrug at this.

"Did you ever want to be an artist yourself?"

"Oh, yes. But I didn't have a scrap of talent."

What a banal story, he thought. It was the story of half the people who worked in art galleries.

The glass door was opened by a pair of people from the street. With the agility of a gymnast, Harry moved away from Dorothy and pretended to be a customer examining a Giagiù. This was a game they often played. If people came in the door while he was there. Dorothy dealt with them and gave no sign that the silent man with his back to them across the room was the owner of the gallery. He caught a sideways glimpse of the couple. A gentleman of fifty in checked pants, a blue blazer, and an ascot, and his wife in a fuchsia suit with a large white collar. Money, but they hadn't had it very long. Harry drifted away from the Giagiù and stared vacantly at a Nelson Kell. The couple had fixed their attention on a large Embry on the rear wall. Behind his back he could hear Dorothy explaining it to them.

"The artist isn't French, but he lives in southern France. No, they're not cheap," as the gentleman bent to look at the card stuck in the frame. "Embrys are very much in demand.

They're large pictures, you see. And they're done in acrylic. It's a synthetic medium. It dries fast." A moment later, thinking that this was perhaps not the best way to put it, she added, "It's much more durable than oils, and I think the colors are lovely, don't you?"

A murmur from the couple.

"For a more modest acquisition, at least to start, there are the Kati Modanes. They're serigraphs, you see, so they come a little less."

Another murmur from the couple. Why?

"Because they're smaller and because they're prints. People don't ordinarily think of prints as being so colorful, do they? Of course, the Modanes are limited editions, and only fifty are made of each."

Looking at the pictures, the husband held his hands clasped behind him. The wife had hair that was all on one side and fell over her eye when she bent to examine the Modane.

"It's done with three screens, you see. The orange, white, and blue are her signature colors. They go beautifully with a white wall. I'm sure your designer recommends white walls, doesn't he? Then you can add the color accents with your furniture and your pictures."

Dorothy was shrewd. If they had a designer, they would be flattered that she had seen they were that kind of people. If they didn't, she was giving them the information they needed to decorate their house correctly.

What's that, the husband wanted to know.

"That's a Nagamoto. It just came in today. And here on the pedestal is a Giagiù bronze."

The trio moved up to an arm's length of Harry. To judge from Dorothy's manner, he was a total stranger to her. He solemnly consulted his catalog. The wife, he saw, had now caught sight of him and was as stunned by his looks as everybody else was. It was a universal reflex. It didn't matter whether they were young or old. It struck him in this situation, seeing Dorothy in the novel guise of a stranger, that she was even plainer than he had realized before. She had the long chin and prominent nose of an intelligent camel, and the same large brown moisture-fringed eyes. Her voice was a low contralto; it might have been taken for a man's voice in the upper register. She had none of the common female reflexes of smiling too much, laughing at anything even remotely clever, or putting question marks at the ends of her sentences; only the oblique glance of one who was taught as a girl not to meet the eye of a man directly. The flap of her tailored suit, he saw now from his hiding place behind the catalog, had got tucked into the pocket at some time in the past; it was out now, but it was folded like a spaniel's ear.

The married pair listened carefully to what Dorothy was saying. The husband pursed his lips, the wife absently scratched at the strap of her underwear through her blouse. They didn't look very long at the Giagiù. It was either an Embry or a Kati Modane. Dorothy was suggesting to them subliminally that having a Modane on your wall was a very poor thing when you could own an Embry. Dorothy did not give the impression of a vigorous salesperson. She seemed kind, knowledgeable, and a little shy. It gave Harry pleasure to see his employee functioning so efficiently and shrewdly on his behalf.

Folding his catalog and turning toward the door, he was filled with a wave of good feeling for Dorothy, compounded partly of sympathy for her difficulties in life, her plainness, her loneliness, and partly of gratitude for her conscientious labors in the gallery, which made it possible for him to earn a good living from it while showing up only a couple of hours a day. What should he do about this obvious case of injustice? Offer to change roles with her? Trade her his redwood-and-glass house in Orange Bay while he moved into the bungalow on Shadow Lane? Exchange his grief over having lost Killian for her loneliness in not having anybody? The world was not made that way. She had wanted to be an artist. But she didn't have a scrap of talent, she herself said.

Harry looked out through the glass door onto Paseo. He

saw a shady street with flowers in planter boxes, tourists in
shorts, an elderly man walking his dog, expensive English
sports cars nosing along looking for parking places. Superimposed on this was his own transparent and ghostly reflection, an image that he knew well but always stared at when
it appeared before him, with a kind of morbid curiosity quite
free from vanity: high forehead, thin cheekbones, eyes set in
shadows, soft dark hair with a lock that fell over the temple
on one side. On the sidewalk outside, a young woman in
tapered pants and a poncho stopped and stared through the
glass at him. For a second she seemed mesmerized; then she
came to herself and went on. Being good-looking would be
nice, he thought, if you had a switch to turn it off and on like
a light or a little motor. But to have the motor running all
the time was a nuisance. He was thoroughly tired of it and
would have given it away to anybody who wanted it. It was
a kind of physical deformity, like a harelip or an amputated
limb. It meant you couldn't live naturally and simply, like
the rest of the human race; you always had to think of your
good looks and the effect they were having on other people.
And if you were a man, it wasn't something that you could
demand sympathy for, like the silly woman who says, "Oh,
I'm so pretty. I don't know what to do. I'm so pretty that
nobody wants to be my friend."

Watching the girl in the poncho disappear down the
street, he felt a sense of excruciating loss. Killian's apparition, even more ghostly than his own, appeared to him in a
flash on the inner glass of his mind: beaky and bird-nosed,
with an avian angularity; her freckle-mottled skin, her
Titian hair, which she wore an inch long and sticking out at
the sides so that it gave the impression she was wearing an
odd flat-topped hat, a medieval beret as in a Venetian painting. The elegance, the flair, of a natural aristocracy, of a
person who cared nothing for fashion and knew exactly who
she was. A rare antique; a unique and priceless object from
a museum. For an instant the two images, his own and the
dead woman's, were locked together in a filmy two-
dimensional embrace. He thought, *All those others I could*

have had, and I only wanted one. I got her and then I lost her. I don't want any of the others. He opened the door and went out onto a Paseo dappled with shade, savoring in his grief the aromatic voluptuousness of the eucalyptus in the winter sunshine.

five

Because there was a teachers' meeting at Pointz Hall, the school closed early and the van brought Peter home about three. Harry was at the gallery, and Peter knew he wouldn't be home until after five. In the year since his mother had died, the house was often empty in the afternoon when he came home from school, and he was free to roam around in it and engage in his secret indulgences. These rather strange pleasures were his sole entry into the world of the illicit and sensual, his taste of the forbidden. He glanced out the window to be sure Harry's car wasn't coming down the road, then he went into the kitchen.

He set out two slices of whole-wheat bread on the kitchen bar, took the butter from the refrigerator, and got the sugar bowl from the buffet. Then he returned to the living room and opened the liquor cabinet. A light inside it went on automatically. The collection of bottles glowed in the mahogany cave: Scotch with its black-and-gold label, Kahlúa red and yellow like a Mexican fair, elegant bronze cognac, colorless vodka, aquavit with its silver-and-blue label and its Swedish coat of arms, a polychrome selection of liqueurs.

He found the Grand Marnier and took it back to the kitchen. Setting down the bottle, he spread a layer of butter on the bread and sprinkled on sugar. Then he poured two spoonfuls of Grand Marnier onto the bread, with care to

keep it from dripping off the edges. The butter held the
sugar in place, and the sugar soaked up the liqueur. He fitted
the second piece of bread on top, cut the sandwich in two,
and ate it slowly and methodically, standing at the kitchen
bar. The three ingredients softened and blurred, one into the
other. The richness of the butter blended with the gritty
sweetness of the sugar, and flowing into it and penetrating it
was the dark orange flavor of the liqueur with its bite of
alcohol. At his epicurean pace it took him a quarter of an
hour to eat the sandwich. He washed the plate, dried it with
a towel, and put it away in the cupboard, and remembered to
replace the Grand Marnier in the liquor cabinet.

In his bedroom, which was redwood and glass like the
rest of the house, with a bunk bed in case he should want to
have a friend over for the night (he never had), he took off
his school uniform and put on shorts and a tee-shirt, leaving
his feet bare. He sat on the bed for a while, thinking, with
the sugary and piquant alcohol seeping slowly into his veins,
then he got up and went down the hall to his parents' bedroom, now only his father's. Or Harry's, as he remembered
to think. The shutters were closed and allowed only the
faintest hint of light to penetrate. The presence of the sea
was a murmur like crushed silk in the distance.

Peter stood for a while, allowing the mysterious and
forbidden atmosphere of the bedroom to sink into him. He
had never in his life been here, when his two parents were
together in this room, although it was the place where the
most secret and important part of their life was enacted.
There was a presence here, a numen. He felt that the shadowy strangeness of the room was dominated by the presence
of his mother. *Killian.* He imagined what it would be like to
call her that to her face. It was an odd name, not like the
names that other children's mothers had. He had always
been conscious of that. He crossed the room to the one of the
two sandalwood dressers that he knew was hers. He opened
a drawer and sank his fingers into the softness of scarves, the
forbidden luxury of underwear, the nubbled fragrance of
sweaters. His fingers trailed absently over a leather button,

and he shut the drawer. Then he stood motionless for a while, with his back to the shuttered window.

His grief was still a stranger that he treated with a gingerly caution, keeping it at a distance and never looking directly into its face. From time to time he tested it warily, as he had just now by opening the drawers of her dresser and touching her clothing. At the bottom of his memory, unexamined but always lurking, were her ravaged and wasted body, her hairless head, her mute hopeless look as she had embraced him from the hospital bed in those final days. These were things that lacked reality for him. They had happened, but now they were only in his mind, in a place where he could lock them away in darkness. What presented itself to him now was an emptiness, a void. There was a place that needed to be filled in his soul, but there was nothing to fill it, and there never would be.

Before him was the bed, imposing and luminous, with its headboard carved from some rare Oriental wood. On it was a spread of large black-and-white squares, like an oversized checkerboard, and two gigantic pillows. After some thought he took off his clothes, pulled back the bedcovers, and lay down exactly in the shallow depression left by his father's body in the bed.

He pulled the bedcovers up to his chin and lay for a few moments savoring this novel situation. The elongated concavity, the footprint made in the mattress by Harry's body over many years, from a time before he was born, fitted his body neatly. With a rigid gesture of the will, of the imagination, he became Harry. The mental picture of his own body acquired mass and power, grew the shadow of a beard, the axillary hair, the slightly frightening sausage of the penis. His groin prickled with small stiff wires. He lay thinking, *This is how it is to be him, to be Harry.*

Then, with an agile twirl, he rolled to the other side of the bed.

Killian.

Now he became her. The thing he made in his mind was not Killian herself, the Killian as he had known her, but the

woman that Harry had known and possessed. (The word
mother occurred to him, and he threw it away as though it
were a white-hot piece of metal.) He imagined a dark chan-
nel at the center of his body. A warm slug crept into it,
looking about curiously and ruthlessly with its single blind
eye. This was what it was like to be her. He lay looking at
the ceiling.

After a while—it was only five minutes, but he almost
fell asleep—he got out of bed and meticulously smoothed
the wrinkles out of the covers. Then, still naked, he fluffed
the pillows and pulled the spread over them. His father, who
made the bed himself, did it only carelessly. Had he left the
odor of his curiosity in the bed? His body had no odor, not
like Harry's or the others. He put his shorts and tee-shirt
back on, went downstairs and glanced at the clock, found it
was four o'clock, and went out of the house into the slanting
yellow sunshine.

He followed the road up the hill and away from the sea.
Across from his own house was the Gilberts', a pretentious
place with a tiled bluish-green dome on top. The next house
up the road, hidden in dense landscaping, belonged to the
Bengtsens, who kept to themselves and were said to be connected to shipping companies in Sweden. Then there were
the Hassads and the Rileys. The road curved, and from the
sunshine he passed into the shade. Through an overarching
tunnel of pines he came out into the sun again and climbed
up the lawn to a large stone house with a flat roof. The yard
was overgrown with unkempt landscaping; the tiny fires of
bougainvilleas flared in the thickets of green. A puglike stone
lion had fallen onto its side on the lawn. Peter entered the
house through the unlocked door of a kind of potting shed or
screened-in porch at the side.

He found Henry Fang in the large room at the front of
the house, with sunlight streaming in horizontally through
the dusty windows and playing on the motes floating in the
air. He was sitting at a table, writing in a large book, like
Faust in his study. Henry Fang was an old man, probably an

octogenarian, Peter thought, with a face like an ancient parchment that has been wrinkled and folded until its wrinkles have become part of its substance. His small black moist eyes were almost hidden in the wrinkles. His sparse gray hair was clipped short, and his spectacles were halfway down his nose. He didn't look up when Peter came in. He went on writing in his book and remarked in his slow, reedy voice, "You're home early, I see. You always show up here looking like a ragamuffin. Like a street urchin. Do you select your costume deliberately, or do you just put on the first thing that comes to hand?" He himself was wearing what he always wore when he was home, a brocaded robe folded high around his throat and a pair of straw slippers.

Peter sat down in his usual place before the table, in the black lacquer armchair with persimmon cushions. It was too big for him, and he lounged in it like a beggar on a throne.

"I don't like my school uniform."

"I've seen it. Flannel pants and a shirt with some kind of coronet on it, as though you were all princes. Why not the traditional blazer?"

"Pointz Hall is an experimental school. They don't do things the same way as in other schools."

"What are they teaching you there nowadays?"

"French. Italian. History. Physiology. Paleontology."

"What are you reading in Italian?"

"We read Dante last term."

"In translation?"

Peter's smile indicated a lofty contempt for this notion. He recited in his thin, girlish, but slightly ironic voice.

> "Così andammo infino alla lumera,
> parlando cose che 'l tacere è bello,
> sì com'era l' parlar colà dov'era."

Henry Fang laughed silently. Still smiling, he made another entry in his book, in purple ink with an old-fashioned fountain pen.

Peter's curiosity, one of his strongest qualities, overcame his natural aloofness. "What's that you're writing?"

"My journals. Like Gide, I record everything that comes to my attention. It may seem trivial to others, but it is important to me. And perhaps posterity may find it of interest."

Peter looked at him skeptically. Then he rose from the chair and moved around to the back of the table. A playful ballet took place between the old man and the boy: Peter tried to look into the book, Henry Fang tried to prevent him, but it was clear that he intended Peter in the end to see what he had written.

Peter de Spain came again this afternoon. An inquisitive child, with a devious manner, yet not unfriendly. His personal beauty, like his father's: a peril. Does he understand this? He quotes Dante, from memory, on the subject of private things that shouldn't be revealed to outsiders.

Peter exchanged a glance with the old man; his face was expressionless. Below this he read:

Like Gide, I record everything that comes to my attention. It may seem trivial to others, but it is important to me. And perhaps posterity may find it of interest.

Peter tried to read higher up on the page, where Henry Fang had been writing when he came in, but the old man clapped his spotted hand over it.

With a smile he said, "*Cose che 'l tacere è bello.*"

He took up an enameled box from the table and offered Peter a cigarette. Peter took one, and Henry Fang lighted it for him with a silver lighter. It was a Muratti Ariston with an ivory tip. It was very mild.

"A woman's cigarette. When you are older you can have a man's."

"What are they?"

"For example, Gauloises Bleues." He took out a crushed pack from the recesses of his gown and slipped one into his mouth. When he lit it an acrid odor as of sage and manure, not unpleasant, filled the room.

He drew on it with savor. After a while he took it from his lips, exhaled the smoke, and asked agreeably, "And is your father still grieving?"

Peter eluded this too personal question.

"He wants me to call him Harry."

"And not father?"

"That's right."

"Your teachers at school would probably say that he is rejecting the role of father."

"I think he just wants to be friends."

"And fathers and sons can't be friends?"

"I don't think he thinks so."

Henry Fang considered this. "What do the two of you do by yourselves? Living there in that house all alone."

Again Peter's answer was oblique, but it still revealed too much. "Harry thinks we need somebody to take care of the house."

"You mean, a Mexican lady to sweep the floor and so on?"

"We already have that. Mrs. Manresa."

"What then?"

Peter said nothing.

"I imagine he's lonely."

There was a silence while the two of them drew on their cigarettes. Henry Fang said, "Well, I won't pry into your family affairs. You've come over for another movie, have you?"

Peter nodded warily. He only half understood this wily and malicious old man, who was, nevertheless, a strange kind of friend, his closest friend in the world; he had no friends his own age.

"Well, go ahead, then. Shut the door, because Mama is wandering around the house."

Carrying the half-smoked cigarette, Peter went downstairs to the recreation room. He shut the door, as Henry

Fang advised. This room was paneled in cedar that gave off a sweetish medicinal smell, and there were Oriental art objects, vases and lacquer boxes, on the tables; everything was dusty.

Because of the slope of the hillside, this basement room had a pair of clerestory windows opening into the garden. From the collection on the shelf he selected a black plastic box and slipped it into the mouth of the machine. There was a pause, a flicker of dancing dots, and a strip of numbers going by too fast to be read.

LOVE ALOHA STYLE

Peter sat down cross-legged on the floor with an ashtray next to him. After he drew on the cigarette, he left it in the ashtray. A thin thread of smoke ascended in the airless room.

There was the sound of Hawaiian music and of surf washing on a beach. Two young women in miniskirts descended from a plane and laughingly accepted leis from a brown girl in a sarong. They were followed by another girl, only a little older than Peter, in a schoolgirlish dress, who accepted a lei with an uncertain smile.

The three girls were on the beach in bikinis. Two men in swimming trunks jogged by, caught sight of them, wheeled around, and came up, showing their white teeth against their tans. They looked first at the older two, then at the girl who was hardly more than a child. One of the women spoke in a fakey contrived voice, like an old-fashioned gramophone.

Our kid sister.

More grins in the tanned faces. The two older women laughed.

Why don't we go to our place for a drink?

The five of them went off toward the car, the younger girl trailing behind and looking back regretfully at the beach.

In the condo the two women went into the bedrooms with the men. The younger girl was left in the living room by herself. She touched a nude male statue, trailed her hands over a table, and looked now and then at the two closed doors. The camera, penetrating a door with its x-ray, showed a breast under a hand and then a brief glimpse of a thigh. The girl alone in the living room, still standing, nervously fingered a magazine.

The five of them were grouped in the living room, the men and the two older women with vacuous grins. The men looked at the girl-child.

She's never . . . ?

More laughs. The two women exchanged glances.

No.

The car rolled along a road past palms and glimpses of beach. There was more Hawaiian music from the car radio. In the back seat, one of the women, her bikini top removed, submitted to the caresses of her companion, while the younger girl sat rigidly.

Where are we going?

You'll see.

At the waterfall, the two women flung off their bikinis and the men their bathing trunks. Then they ran around laughing, the men seizing the women and forcing them under the falling water. They were drenched; the women's hair clung to their mouths, and they pushed it away, laughing. The water fell around them like a transparent distorting lens. The details of the bodies could not be made out, only the shapes and gestures, the balletic motions of lust. Through the din of the water there could still be heard the strains of tinny Hawaiian music.

The door opened behind him, and Mrs. Fang (her name was Mei-ling, although people called her Mary) came in with tea. She set the tea tray down and withdrew without a word. Out of the corner of his eye he caught a glimpse of her face, as innocent and wrinkled as Henry Fang's was wily and wrinkled. Like Henry Fang, she too always wore the same thing, in her case a loose flowered muumuu, not very clean, that came to her ankles. He had never seen more of her than such glimpses. The door closed.

☐

The four of them came out of the waterfall soaking wet and ran around, still laughing, until they had caught the younger girl and forced off her bikini. When they pulled away her hands, her breasts were pale and childish, Balinese.

Peter sipped the tea. It was Genmai Cha, weak and yellowish green, tasting of burnt rice, a thing he never had except at this house. The cup had no handle and was small and flowered, exquisite, with a gold rim, a silvery inside. The teapot was to match. On the shelf was a celadon vase from the Sung period, pale green and crazed with darker lines. These things were like the films, which he also saw only in this house, remote and alien, exotic. He finished the tea and set the cup down on the dusty wooden floor next to him.

There were long vines or lianas hanging from the cliff, and the two men used them to tie up the young girl under the waterfall. Her wrists were pulled above her and her legs were spread apart. The water falling over her was like a crystalline garment, translucent, fluctuant, constantly changing, reproducing faithfully every detail of the body under it. The girl's hair danced in the blows of water; her wrists strained at the lianas. The water, rushing down her body, converged in a stream between her legs, where there was a small tuft of hair like the goatee of a stage comedian.

No! Please . . .

The two men approached and worked their will on her. Then it was the turn of the two women. The women's efforts seemed more intended to excite their victim's desire than to gratify their own. There was a convulsive movement inside the falling water; it was difficult to make out the details. Then came a flash of white dots, leaving the screen black again.

Peter sat for a moment in the apathy that is always left at the end of a movie, then he got up from the floor like a lazy tongs, rewound the cassette, and put it back on the shelf with the others. The images of the two men and three women remained in his mind for only a few minutes. They satisfied his curiosity about certain details, but they added very little to what he already knew. The setting of the miniature drama, the remote Hawaiian glade and the waterfall, seemed to him improbable and impractical. The thing did not seem very enjoyable with torrents of cold water pouring down on you. There were the mechanical difficulties of trying to secure the four limbs of the girl with the lianas and persuading her to hold still while you did this. The one thing that might have interested him, the frontal view of the nude girl only a little older than he was, was spoiled by the mantle of crashing water that half concealed her. As he compared what he had seen to the account of Paolo and Francesca in Dante, or to Baudelaire's poem "Hymn to Beauty," it seemed to him that the makers of videos like this suffered from a paucity of imagination and a defective sense of logic. He preferred his own private vision of the transports of the flesh that were to come, which he awaited patiently, as one would a train or the arrival of a friend at a rendezvous.

He left the Fangs' house as he had entered it, through the screened potting shed on the side. When he got home it was a little after five. The house was silent and deserted. From the distance, filtered through the trees, he could hear the rhythmic splashing of surf. A child called; there was the sound of a car starting up and driving away from the house next door. He climbed up the lawn, opened a gate, and passed into the garden at the side of the house. Crowding over the brick footpath were clouds of shrubbery, spotted with red, orange, and violet flowers. A giant agave the size of a basket lunged beside the kitchen door. Peter opened the door and went in. Then he stopped, transfixed.

In the entry that led to the kitchen there was a brass hook on the wall, and three feet below the hook was a mark, a kind of smudge, where *she* had hung her gardening smock, an arc traced by a thousand brushings of soft substance. He had never noticed it before; now through some trick or slant of light it struck him like a knife. This faint hieroglyphic reminded him of what he had felt in his mother's bedroom and forgotten; it filled him with a great empty pain and dread, as though he were on the edge of a cliff and another step would fling him into the void. Abruptly he was made aware of the passage of time and the reality of death; these things became concrete presences, as though he were suddenly gripped by the living hand of something he had only heard about before. The idea of his own mortality struck him for the first time in his life. He clearly saw the pitiless formula of the generations: *As I am, so she once was; as she is, so shall I become.* He passed the empty hook and went on into the house.

six

Harry and Velda went across the road in the dark, he leading the way and she following a step or two after. The Gilberts' house loomed ahead of them in the sea mist like an improbable Byzantine palace. The lower parts of it were illuminated by the pink and green landscaping lights; the Mogul dome on the top was floodlighted. Velda was wearing an outfit she evidently thought suitable for the occasion: polyester pants and an orangy-pink sweatshirt with swirls of silver and gold. Across the front of it, in black letters, were the words HOLLYWOOD NITES. He had told her to dress informally; he was afraid she would show up in a gown with flounces or something décolleté or strapless. For a party at Wolfie and Dawn's, she hadn't done badly. She had, it was true, put on heels, but he didn't feel like telling her to go back and change her shoes. And the little spikes she was walking on did throw her body into a new and unexpected stance, as though she were leaning forward into life, breasting into it with the orange-and-pink sweatshirt bearing its legend about the city of dreams. Her eyes were made up a little too heavily, with eyeliner and green lids.

The dome with its luminous tiles hung over their heads like a floating spaceship. Also illuminated, standing out in the mist, was a giant Japanese paper fish at the top of a mast. More lights were concealed in the shrubbery and under the herbaceous borders; Harry and Velda passed through a faery atmosphere tinged with violet, pink, orange, and blue, as though the particles of the air itself had taken color. Ahead of them they could hear the sounds of the party, still in the early stages of taking birth.

"*Très nouveau riche,*" she commented cheerfully.

"As a matter of fact, the Gilberts are not new money. They are old money. Wolfie is a very fine, serious, unassuming person, in spite of the house and in spite of his name. He inherited this house from his parents. It's the one he grew up in. A lot of houses in Orange Bay have belonged to the same families for generations."

"Well, for heaven's sake. It was just a chance remark that I dropped."

"Just use your sense, Velda. Tell Wolfie you think it's a nice house."

There had been the initial awkwardness about names. Of course, there was never any doubt about its outcome; he would call her Velda and she would call him Harry. But for a while, there was a flurry of Mr. De Spains from her side and awkward yous on his. He still leading, they passed through a grape arbor tingling with tiny white lights and onto the terrace at the back of the house. The presence of the sea below the cliff made itself felt by a low rhythmic grumble and a clasp of tepid moisture in the air.

At the edge of the terrace was a pond with lily pads and enormous speckled Japanese fish, the reflections in real life of the paper fish on the mast. Velda stopped to bend over them, with her hands on her knees. The koi, illuminated from below, looked like ominous zeppelins streaked with the pink of the fires they had started.

"I'll bet they're expensive."

"Come on. You've got to meet everyone."

He had two ghastly monsters of dread sitting on his shoulders: that people would be amused about his hiring a young woman to live in his house, and that she would make some horrible blunder, like asking Wolfie if he was *nouveau riche* or how much the koi had cost. Of course, the jokes would have been a thousand times worse if he had hired

Sylvia Jacquemort. As for Mrs. Bream, there would have
been no question of her coming to the party. Probably he
had done the right thing. If only she would not go on chattering like a pink-and-yellow cockatoo.

There were a dozen or so people scattered around the
terrace, in clumps of two and three. He saw Wolfie talking to
Henry and Mary Fang, and Dawn Gilbert with Tony Pack,
the Gilberts' stockbroker. Standing morosely by himself
with a drink was white-haired old George Grinspoon, a wid-
ower who collected classic cars. Now came the difficult part
of this business, explaining Velda to these people or passing
her off in some way. It would be best to start with Wolfie
and Dawn, basically goodhearted people. But through the
crowd he saw Golo headed toward them, with a broad grin.

Until his wedding day, Harry didn't even know that
Killian had an elder brother. Golo showed up at the wedding
and launched himself at Harry with a vigorous intimacy,
calling him *mon vieux* and clapping him on the back before
Harry even knew who he was: a large man, beak-nosed and
dark-eyed, with a shaven head as wrinkled as a Chinese dog,
great rings on his fingers, and thick eyeglasses that reflected
the light as he moved his head. It was hard for Harry to
remember sometimes that he and Killian were brother and
sister, they were so unlike in many ways. But they shared
their Shrodinger noses, their queer first names, and their
religious conviction of their own specialness, as people to
whom the ordinary rules didn't apply. The difference between them, it occurred to Harry once, was that Killian was
a woman and Golo was a man. This was one of those sim-
plistic insights that seem stupid until you realize how profound they are.

At the wedding Golo wore a pistachio-colored sports
jacket and white shoes, even though it was winter. Harry
stared at him with curiosity. He seemed a queer bird. The
clothes were expensive, but he wore them with negligence,
the tabs of the button-down shirt left unbuttoned and his
socks falling over his shoes. Still gripping Harry by the

elbow, he asked him what he did, and when he said he owned a frame shop (it was a frame shop in those days), Golo revealed that on his part he was a rare-coin dealer. Just a boiler-room operation. A little office with a telephone. But he did all right for himself, he said, the light gleaming in his goggles. His ironic, self-deprecating, taking-you-in-on-the-joke smile indicated that it was all blague, that tomorrow he might say that he was an importer of inflatable sex dolls or a narcotics king; and yet the smile also suggested that it wasn't blague at all, that he was only pretending to be ironic and self-deprecating and that he made a lot of money in ways that he didn't intend to reveal to you. It later became clear that he was very wealthy. In fact, there was some doubt that he was really a coin dealer. When Harry said in a burst of fraternal goodwill, half an hour after he was married, "Maybe I could buy coins from you as an investment," he told him, "Don't think of it, Francis." In some way he had found out that Harry's real name was Francis. At the wedding dinner he made a speech extolling the delights of Hymen and emphasizing the necessity of chastity, loyalty, and tenderness in the conjugal relation, to the accompaniment of repressed laughter from those in the company who knew him. Harry didn't know at this point whether Golo was married or not.

He wasn't married, of course. He lived alone in a tiny house tucked away at the far end of the beach, the smallest house in Orange Bay, a kind of Gauguin cottage with palm trees around it, suitable for his bachelor existence. But he was an expert in real estate. (Perhaps that was where his money had come from.) It was he who had found the house in Orange Bay for Harry and Killian when they came back from their honeymoon in Puerto Vallarta. Up to that time, Harry had lived in a small apartment over a garage in Playa del Mar. Oddly enough, although Harry owned the house in Orange Bay, he was not quite sure where the money for it had come from: from Golo, from Killian, or a little from both?

☐

In fifteen years Golo hadn't changed much, except for his clothes. The pistachio jacket and white shoes were gone. Possibly they had only been rented for the wedding. They never showed up again. In their place, his customary rig was a pair of khaki pants and a calico shirt; sometimes he added a shabby blue blazer. Because he had arthritis and his feet hurt, he went around barefoot for the most part. For special occasions, like the party tonight, he put on an old pair of loafers but no socks. He slit the shoes with a razor to make them easier on his feet. Here he came, arms raised in a what-have-we-here gesture, shaved dome wrinkled, thick glasses glinting.

"Hallo, Francis. Who's your charming companion?"

It was even worse than he'd thought.

"This is Velda Venn. She's going to be taking care of the house for us." This was the formula he had decided on.

To his surprise, Golo dropped his bantering manner and became courtly and ceremonious as he pressed her hand. He seemed almost modest. His smile was warm and sincere. Just another one of his protean guises, thought Harry, who had known him for a long time. He was probably preparing some elaborate joke to blow up the both of them.

"Taking care of the house! Well, well. It's a beautiful house, isn't it? And Harry is such a wonderful person. And charming Peter! I'm sure you'll be happy there."

"I expect to be."

"I can tell by looking at you that you'll do a capable job of it."

There were possibly some innuendoes here, but Harry decided to let them pass.

"Taking care of the house!" repeated Golo in his stately baritone. He suppressed any trace of humor. He looked solemnly first at Velda, then at Harry.

Harry looked around desperately for someone to rescue him. Wolfie and Dawn were headed their way, followed by George Grinspoon, who noticed the activity and drifted across the terrace toward them with the slowness of a crustacean. Wolfie reached them first, followed by the others. He was a chubby pink-faced man, a little smaller than normal, dressed neatly, in a slightly old-fashioned way, like a boy in the Cruikshank illustrations of Dickens. Dawn, tall and queenly, followed in a flowing shapeless gown of chiffon.

"Velda is going to be taking care of the house for us," Harry explained again.

"I didn't catch the name." Wolfie, with a shy smile at Velda, bent his head to offer an ear with a tiny cashew fitted into it.

"Velda."

"And the last name?"

"Venn." She spelled it for them. "Vee, ee, en, en."

"Welcome, welcome," said Wolfie. "Have you met the others?"

He introduced her to George Grinspoon and to the Fangs, who had moved up to the edge of the circle.

"I like your house," Velda told him, exactly as she had been coached. So far so good, thought Harry. Wolfie had rescued them from the danger of a malicious and unpredictable Golo.

"The house! Oh, it's nothing much. Our little hut by the sea. It's a simple life we live, lulled by the soft rhythm of the surf, eating lush tropical fruit that falls into our mouths from the trees." He broke off a small bunch of grapes from the buffet and offered it to her.

Velda took the grapes and nibbled at them. "It looks like the Taj Mahal to me."

"Well, as a matter of fact, that's what some of our friends call it." He chuckled. "On account of the dome. Have you seen the peacocks?"

"I just got here."

"I beg pardon?" He bent his ear toward her again.

"No I haven't."

"Come along. I'll show you."

Lightly holding his hand an inch from her elbow, as though he were afraid to touch her, as though she too were some large rare bird, a fragile creature he was shepherding toward its nest, he led her down the path into the garden,

while the others followed. The little procession stopped at a
kind of pergola with a view of the sea.

Wolfie vanished into the darkness and reappeared after
a moment, driving the three birds before him, not quite
touching them, with the delicacy and tact he had used on
Velda only a moment before. Two of them were electric
blue; the third was an albino, with no color to it at all except
for its dark eyes and its pink bill. They pricked the ground
delicately with their three-toed feet, looking around them
suspiciously.

"Do you have any peahens?"

"Beg pardon? Oh! Yes, they're off in there somewhere,
but they're rather drab and not much to look at. I don't
bother to show them to people."

"The poor creatures."

"You may say so, but look at what beautiful boyfriends
they have. Any woman would consider herself lucky."

The three birds minced out into the light near the pergola so they could be seen more clearly. They stepped around
carefully, lifting their feet as though they were walking on
a hot iron plate. They had small, stupid heads and curved
beaks that looked very sharp. On top of each head was a little
crest on matchsticks.

"Can you make them spread their tails?"

"It's very difficult."

"You have to make them feel sexy," offered Golo, fon-
dling his drink.

"Feel how? Oh, sexy. No, that's not quite it. You have
to make them feel like showing off."

"Why don't you go get the hens and see if that would
do it?" said Velda. This quirk of hers about the peahens was
curious, thought Harry. Perhaps it came from some kind of
feminism. He also noted Wolfie's remark about their having
beautiful boyfriends. All of these people were full of innuendoes, in spite of their friendliness; they were as dangerous
as serpents.

"Oh, the hens are so boring. I can do it myself."

He shepherded the three large birds up the path to-

ward the terrace, while the people followed behind. It was
a difficult business; the peacocks strayed and dawdled,
turned and tried to go back the other way, bumped into
each other and glared irately. Finally they clambered up
onto the terrace and plodded around flat-footed among the
guests, who ignored them; they were a familiar sight at
the Gilberts'.

Dawn's woman Marta was passing around crab canapés.
At the buffet table there were tiny meatballs in a chafing
dish, a basket of fruit, brie, rye wafers, caviar, and oysters on
a bed of ice.

"*Pavo christatus*," said Wolfie. "They come from Pa-
kistan, Nepal, and India."

"The old Romans used to eat 'em," said George Grinspoon. "It's in Petronius."

"Oh, what a shame. Such beautiful creatures," Velda
said.

Wolfie managed to bring them to a halt before the buffet table. He offered them each a grape, and they stabbed
them up off the bricks.

"Try caviar," suggested George Grinspoon.

"Why? Oh, I see. To get them to open their tails."

"Anybody would open their tails for caviar," Golo told
her. "Wouldn't you?"

Harry watched covertly to see what her reaction would
be. She laughed and touched Golo on the elbow.

Wolfie got three small china plates from the buffet and
put a chilled oyster on each one. He squeezed a little lemon
on them. Then he set the plates down one by one on the
bricks. The peacocks ignored them at first. The albino stalked
away, and Wolfie didn't bother to go after it. The other two
shifted from leg to leg and looked at the oysters suspiciously.
In the bright light of the terrace, they appeared even larger
and stranger than they had in the shadows.

"Do peacocks eat oysters? I didn't know that."

"These do. Wolfie has trained them to his bizarre stan-
dards of luxury."

"Conspicuous consumption. Veblen." George Grinspoon cackled.

The first peacock began making gestures of his beak
toward the oysters, like a golfer practicing his stroke. Then
he stabbed abruptly at the blob of plasm on its nacreous
shell. The oyster disappeared, and in the same instant the
blue neck made a cranking motion.

"Sss," Wolfie said. "Gaa. Ah, *bello*." He waved his
hands toward the bird like an orchestra conductor.

The tail opened slowly, with a rustle of quills. Extended
in a circle, it was like green fireworks with blue stars bursting in them. The round decorations were pictures of blue
and green eyes. The bird strutted away among the guests,
who moved to make room for him. He was so encumbered
by this secondary sexual apparatus that he could hardly
walk; he staggered around underneath it like a man carrying
an oversized sign in a parade.

Harry was talking to Henry Fang in the dark pergola
overlooking the sea. Henry made being Chinese a hobby, a
kind of joke he played on the world, a Halloween costume he
went around in to amuse himself and others. In reality he
was born in San Francisco and made a lot of money in the
banking business before he retired at an advanced age, when
everybody thought he should be dead, and moved to Orange
Bay. In his silk suit and silk shirt without a necktie, he gazed
at Harry out of his raisin eyes. He had a way of moving his
head as someone else told a story, not a negative shake but
a slow, persistent motion of incredulity. Yes, I know that
what you're telling me is true, that's the way people are, but
land sakes, I can hardly believe what you're telling me.

"So this woman, this Velda, is going to keep your
house?"

"That's right."

"And what does that expression mean exactly?"

"Just that. She's going to keep the house. Pay the bills,
see to the shopping, and so on."

Henry shook his head.

"And take care of Peter's needs."

"You know, Harry, Peter is an extraordinary boy. I wonder if you realize that."

"Of course I do."

"What plans do you have for him?"

"Plans?"

"Education, his future career, and so on."

"He goes to a very good school."

"Pointz Hall. He's told me about it."

"When did you talk to him?" Harry didn't even know that Peter and Henry were acquainted.

"He comes to see me now and then. We talk about Dante. He could be a professor. A scholar or a critic."

This was a side of Peter's life that Harry knew nothing about. It could only be in the late afternoon, when Peter came home from school. "I don't know what he wants to do. You say Dante?"

"He's reading him in school."

"I didn't know that either." Harry was seized with a sudden attack of guilt. Others knew more about Peter than he did. Perhaps he should talk to him about Dante. He didn't know what he could say to him about it, and Peter was sure to take it as patronizing.

"Reads a good deal," Henry went on. "Too much, perhaps. Things too old for him. At his age he's easily influenced. It's child's play to turn him this way or that. Set evil in his path, and he consumes it unthinkingly." Henry's head wove back and forth. "You should guide him, Harry, with a gentle hand. Set his feet in the direction he should go."

"Graduate school? It's a little early for that."

"Above all," said Henry, blinking, scratching his jaw, "you should stamp out in him any desire for private happiness. The happiness of body and soul. That is his pitfall. He bears in him the sign of his own destruction. His bad angel."

Harry suspected he meant Peter's good looks. Henry Fang, he thought, might have been good-looking himself in his youth.

"Have you stamped out private happiness in yourself?"

"No, unfortunately I didn't. That's what's caused all my troubles."

"How's Mary these days?"

"Old."

"And what have you been doing lately, Henry?"

"In the morning I arise, eat a rusk, sip a little tea, and sit under a tree, listening to the sea. In the afternoon I write down my thoughts. Mary serves me dinner, but she doesn't eat anything. When it gets dark I drink a little French brandy, then I recommend myself to sleep, death's elder brother."

"That's all bosh, Henry. It's dark now and you're not sleeping. You're standing at a party holding a drink in your hand."

"I do feel sleepy."

"It's all fake Chinese poetry, Henry. Death's elder brother. Sitting under a tree drinking tea. Why don't you knock it off?"

"You're hard, Harry. Cruel, good-looking Harry. Why don't we go up and join the others? Now that those *cauchemar* birds are gone. I'm afraid of them."

"Think of them as a Chinese screen."

Velda helped herself at the buffet table, while the others watched her. She had a number of the crab canapés, then switched to the brie on rye wafers. She eyed the miniature Swedish meatballs, but couldn't see any way to eat them with decorum. Then she noticed the small plates and took one. After the meatballs she went back to the canapés.

"What's in these things?"

"Marta makes them. You take crab, a little cream cheese, parmesan, and basil and put it on crackers. A drop of Tabasco, and you put them under the broiler. You must make them for Harry, to have at cocktail time."

Golo told her, "Harry deserves a little pampering. I'll dive and get the crabs for you."

"Dive?"

"Yes, there are crabs right here in Orange Bay, if you know where to look."

Wolfie said, "When I was a kid, there were abalones here in the bay. We'd dive for them holding our noses. Used a tire iron to pry them off."

"The abalones are all gone now," said Golo. "The Inlanders came and took them all. There are still a few crabs."

"Inlanders?"

"That's what we call 'em. Characters who don't even live around here. They come down the freeway and make themselves at home. Go diving right off our beach."

"But isn't it a private beach?"

"Only to the tideline. Beyond that they can swim around and take what they want."

"And they stare at us," said George Grinspoon plaintively. "There we are sitting on our beach, and they stare at us through their face masks."

"Well, my goodness," said Velda. "Here you are all sitting behind your wall in your private enclosure, enjoying things other people can't have. You're like those old French aristocrats. After you the deluge, I imagine."

"What do you think we should do, dear?" Dawn asked her. "Tear down the wall?"

"I think you should publish the recipe for the crab things in the newspaper. Then everyone could make them. The Inlanders could come down the freeway for the crabs. After all, it's their ocean too."

There was a silence. Somebody laughed.

"Legally you're right," said Golo. "Maybe even morally."

Dawn with a smile told her, "You're not like *anyone* we've ever had here before, dear."

She pretty much held her own against the pack of them, Harry was pleased to see. He was in a curious mood, placid, drowsy, content to be a spectator, yet keen and alert. His state of mind was that of a convalescent. Killian's death was a disease that he himself had, one that he was just beginning to recover from. The image of a train coming out of a tunnel occurred to him, and he thought instead that he was a train leaving the harsh pain of reality and entering a warm and dark, comforting tunnel of illusion where he would be safe.

Dawn's woman Marta appeared in the doorway. "Ladies and gentlemen, dinner."

"Oh, I thought this was dinner," said Velda.

Harry and Velda walked the short distance up the road in the dark. The stars were burning fuzzily in a haze that soaked up a milky fluid from them. The whole sky leaked a pale grayish light, a light without shadows. The asphalt of the road sparkled like anthracite.

"We were the first to leave. I would have liked to stay a little longer. I love parties."

"I don't."

He felt like telling her that she had to get up early to fix Peter's breakfast before he went to school. But in the first place Peter fixed it himself, and in the second place it was a Saturday night and tomorrow was Sunday. He knew that the rest of them at the party would probably stay up all night. They had nothing to do except enjoy themselves, and there was no reason for them to get up early. Of course, the same was true of him.

"There were some fascinating people. Not that I liked them all. Who is Golo exactly?"

"My brother-in-law. Killian's brother."

"He's rather rude, isn't he?"

"Eccentric may be the word you're groping for."

"It's rude, really."

"But you laughed when he made the joke about peacocks opening their tails for caviar."

"Oh, you have to be a good sport."

"So you didn't like Golo?"

"Oh, it isn't that I didn't like him. He just needs somebody to brush him up and teach him some manners. Is he married?"

"Oh, no. He's an inveterate bachelor."

"You can see why. He would set any woman's teeth on edge."

"Maybe we could get him to move into the house with us, and then you could brush him up and teach him some manners."

"I'm finding out that a great deal of what you say is jokes."

"Yes, you should engrave that fact on your heart. It will save you a lot of mistakes."

"Oh, I have a sense of humor. It's just that you and these other people tell jokes and don't smile."

"That's our way."

"Why did Golo call you Francis?"

"That's my name."

"I thought your name was Harry."

"It's Francis Xavier de Spain."

"Don't you think Francis is a sissy name?"

"I don't know."

"I mean, a girl could be named Francis, but I never heard of a boy."

"That's Frances with an *e*. I'm Francis with an *i*."

"It doesn't make much difference when you say it."

(Exasperated) "So you think I'm a sissy."

"No, of course not. It's just the name."

"Suppose my name was Violet, or Gwyneth. Would that make me a sissy?"

"I don't know what you're getting at."

"Lots of Englishmen are named Evelyn."

"Well, I never met one."

"What on earth are we quarreling about anyhow? How did we get into this?"

"I don't know whether we're quarreling. I just asked you whether Francis wasn't a sissy name."

"Well, it's not."

"What's Xavier? I can't even say it."

"Saint Francis Xavier was a missionary who went to India to convert the heathen in the sixteenth century. A lot of Catholics are named after him."

"Are you Catholic?"

"My parents were, more or less. They wanted me to be."

"Do you believe in God?"

"Oh, good heavens, Velda. It's late at night. We can discuss that some other time."

"I've always thought that late at night was the time to discuss such things."

"Maybe, but not this particular night."

"Are you cross with me?"

"About what?"

"I don't know. You seem cross."

"It's the farthest thing in the world from my mind. Your performance at the party was a marvel. Now let's go home and go to sleep, shall we?"

They entered the unlocked door of the house like thieves, in silence. It was dark except for a night light at the foot of the stairs. Peter was asleep behind his closed door. Harry went to his room and she to hers. The faint murmur of the sea could be heard through the shutters, and now and then a cackle or a fragment of laughter from the Gilberts' across the road.

Velda lay in her bed for a long time, but she wasn't able to go to sleep. She wasn't sure how long it was; an hour or two, maybe more. Perhaps she drowsed a little. When she woke she could still hear the sounds from the Gilberts'. Now along with the laughter and conversation there was a thin thread of music, something like a flute. She felt restless, excited, and light of weight, like a snake that has shed its old skin. She got out of bed, took off her nightgown, and put on her clothes again, the same ones except that she substituted flat shoes for the heels.

When she got back to the party, Wolfie caught sight of her first. "Look, it's Velda. Where's Harry, Velda?"

"Sound asleep."

"What a poop."

"That's what I told him; he's a sissy."

The nature of the party had changed. It was less twittering and talkative now, more intimate somehow. People seemed more at their ease. Maybe it was because they had all been drinking while she was gone. Dawn was sitting on a barstool playing Handel's *Water Music* on a recorder, while Golo accompanied her on a guitar. This was the music she had heard, lying in her bed. Someone thrust a drink into her hands. It was a large balloon glass of Spanish brandy, fruity, with a sting of wasps. The time went by in a pleasant blur while she sipped her drink. She sat on the edge of a wall and nobody paid much attention to her, although Wolfie smiled in her direction now and then. Perhaps because she had taken an interest in his peacocks, which were old stuff to the others. When Dawn finished her recital, George Grinspoon sang "Pale Hands I Loved Beside the Shalimar" in a quavering but resolute voice, and Tony Pack, badgered to contribute something, did "The Road to Mandalay." Somebody put the "Toreador Song" from *Carmen* on the stereo, and Golo did a flamenco dance in a sombrero he had found somewhere, stamping his feet and, since he didn't have castanets, imitating the sound with his mouth. Even Henry Fang did some *tai chi* figures, holding his arms at different angles and stepping back and forth.

Wolfie turned to her. "How about you, Velda? It's amateur night. Can you do comic monologues? Soft-shoe routine? Isadora Duncan dance?"

Velda looked at him for a moment. She hesitated, then she smiled and took the guitar from Golo. She sat down on the stool, with one leg crossed over the other, and plucked and sang. She had a thin, sweet voice with a country-music catch in it, and perfect pitch; she always had since she was a child.

> *Trumbo Jane was my old pal*
> *She was a down-right honest gal*
> *She wore a pink hat*
> *And she had a pink cat*
> *And she sat a-round singing in the old cor-ral.*

Here came four bars of chords on the guitar. Somebody refilled her glass. She sipped a little, set it by her feet, and went on.

> As she sat on the fence of the old cor-ral
> With her cat on her knee
> And she smiled at me
> Sitting on the fence
> Of the old cor-ral.

More chords. They had all stopped what they were doing and were watching her. She saw Mary Fang's eyes fixed on her, the rest of the old woman's face expressionless.

> Guitar on her knee
> She smiled at me
> Back in fifty-seven when we both were young
> On the fence of the old cor-ral.

Applause and laughter. Golo grinned.
"Where did you learn to do that?"
"Oh, I've always sung."
"Love that song," said Dawn. "And you do have a lovely voice."
"Drink your medicine, Velda."
She picked up the glass and sipped a little, shuddering. It *was* medicine. An hour had passed since she came back to the party. Maybe more. In fact, she had the dim impression that the sky was getting light to the east. She stuck her tongue into the bottom of the glass to reach the last of the brandy. Then she noticed that the others were clustered at the side of the terrace, calling to each other.
"Are you coming?"
"We're all coming. Are you coming, Velda?"
"All right. Where are we going?"
"Velda's coming too. Hurrah! Shhh, everybody, the neighbors."

Wolfie made an exaggerated stage gesture, with finger at mouth. They stole furtively out of the terrace and went down the road in a procession, Dawn bringing up the rear with a bundle of towels. Still without speaking, they crossed the park, vaulted over the low seawall, and came to the beach. The surf glowed white in the darkness; a chill air wafted toward them from the water. The others began taking off their clothes, and Velda followed their example, piling her gilded sweatshirt, her polyester pants, and her underwear on a rock. Only Dawn didn't disrobe; she sat placidly on a ledge of sandstone like a Sibyl, guarding her pile of towels. Mary Fang had disappeared; she hadn't come to the beach.

There was still only a pale stain of light over the hills behind the highway. Velda could scarcely see anything; her own hands before her face were dim aquarium creatures with indistinct outlines. She felt a lust for the coldness of the water. She was still overheated from her singing and from the brandy.

Golo plunged into the sea and then Wolfie; she saw their oddly bifurcated rears, their shadowy outlines breasting into the waves with arms raised. She ran in a crouch and plunged in after them. The shock of the cold water was electric, making her breasts shrivel and gripping her loins like a clutching hand.

Ahead of her, Wolfie and Golo had disappeared into the waves. She began swimming with large inept strokes. The others followed: Henry Fang, Tony Pack, and George Grinspoon. Each of them was funny-looking in his own way; Tony Pack had profuse hair on his back, then below it a patch of fishy white, continuing on down to the place where he split. Men were not really made to be seen with their clothes off. Velda paddled around like a seal, ignoring the cold that gripped every inch of her skin like a large chilly tongue and seemed determined to penetrate her body through its orifices. A wave slapped her on the head, and she sank under. She recovered quickly; it was only a small wave. Everything in Orange Bay seemed dimensioned to the moderate, to the

mild and comfortable, to the convenience of the rich. Even
the mist that hung over the party earlier served to enhance
the effect of the lights in the garden. Orange Bay seemed a
place made not by human hands but by an act of nature, an
alternative world accessible only to those who possessed the
key of this private fantasy machine. That people died here
she had no doubt, but it would be a strange kind of dying,
odorless and illuminated by pastel lights. She didn't believe
for a minute that Harry's wife had died. Not in the way she
thought of dying. She was still lingering around somewhere,
pestering Harry to give her more things and advising against
hiring a housekeeper. A piece of kelp twined itself around
Velda's neck. Instead of pulling it off she kept it, tied it in a
loop around her neck, and swam on with it snaking back and
forth between her legs.

George Grinspoon—she recognized him by his elfin tuft
of white hair and his white mustache—swam by her in a
slow breaststroke, shuddering from the cold. Tony Pack went
by in the distance, in an impressive Olympic crawl. Golo
wafted up to her and said something she didn't catch. He
sputtered and sank under; when he came up again the current had pulled him out of earshot.

Back and forth went Velda, just behind the surfline. The
same current that had swept away Golo displaced her down
the beach; she swam until she was even with Dawn on her
rock again. When she decided she could absolutely not take
the cold anymore, she reached for the bottom with her feet.
The air seemed warm after the water. With one hand in
front of each of her two private places, she came up the sand
to where she had left her clothes, pulling off her necklace of
kelp.

Dawn threw her a towel. Velda had gone into the sea in
the dark and came out in the dawn, with rose-colored tints
on the undersides of the clouds. The others came out after
her one by one, each going to his own pile of clothing. They
barked like seals and chattered their teeth to show how cold
they were. Henry Fang, too chilled to speak, tottered on one
foot to pull on his underpants. His member, in the light

from the pink clouds, was a reddish-brown octopus no larger than a thumb. It disappeared into his old-fashioned drawers. Golo and Wolfie chattered and tittered. She didn't pay any attention to the naked men, although she had the impression they were all eyeing her secretly.

Dawn told them, "You should have seen Velda coming out of the sea. You were all in the water and you missed it. Exactly like Botticelli's *Venus*. Wearing kelp for the golden hair."

"Ah, Venus on the half shell. My favorite picture."

"It's everybody's favorite."

Henry Fang, having pulled on his drawers and his shirt, was too tired to go on and sat down on a rock with the towel around him. The others sat down too, although they finished dressing before they took their places on the rocks. Golo folded a towel under him for a seat pad. It was quite light now; a leak of molten iron appeared at the crest of the hill to the east and grew rapidly until it hurt the eyes to look at it. When Velda turned from it, the details of the beach, the rocky point, the five dressing men and the woman on the rock, were bathed in a pink light the color of wine dissolved in water. It was a picture that was fixed in her mind for a long time, a vision of Arcadian peace and voluptuousness. There was nothing like this in the world she had come from. These people were blessed of the gods.

seven

"My car has a dead battery."

Velda had been in the house now for a month. Harry was getting used to her presence, but it still startled him sometimes when he came into a room and found her there. Her scent of spiced apples and drugstore perfume, the sound of her voice talking to Peter in another room, the kind of aura that any person emits who lives and breathes in a house, had gradually become familiar. Her old Toyota was parked in the road in front of the house. There was no room for it in the garage, where Killian's car, undriven for a year, sat next to his own.

"Maybe you could help me push it."

He saw himself out in the road, pushing her car from behind while she worked the gears.

"I'll bet it has automatic."

"It does."

"You can't start a car with automatic transmission by pushing it."

"Maybe we could jump-start it with your car."

"I don't know how to do that."

"Neither do I."

He sat at the study desk, glanced at the work he had been trying to do when she came into the room, and looked back at her without replying. There was a silence.

"What'll I do, then?"

"I don't know."

"What would you do?"

"I'd call the auto club."

"I don't belong to the auto club."

When he made no comment on this either, she said after a while, "There are some jumper cables in the back of my car."

Exasperated, he went to the garage and backed out his Mercedes. He drove it up nose-to-nose with the disabled car, opened both hoods, and looked into the engine compartments. Velda handed him the jumper cables, which were old and greasy. The engine of the Toyota was covered with a thick layer of muck. In some way, he had to connect up the batteries of the two cars with the cables. This was a thing he would never have dreamed of doing with his own car. He didn't understand machinery, he disliked the grease and grime on the engine of the old Toyota, and he didn't like the violent snapping and abrupt bright flashes that electricity made when you didn't know what you were doing with it. He was embarrassed to be out on the road in full view of the neighbors, looking into the open hood of the car, getting his hands greasy, while Velda stood watching him with a happy smile, confident that he would find out what was wrong and fix it. For Harry the world was divided into two classes of people: those who fixed their own cars and those who hired somebody else to fix them. He had never shared the vanity of most men over knowing about cars and being able to fix cars. He didn't see that it meant you had any more testosterone if you could crawl under a car with oil falling into your eye and figure out why the brakes weren't working.

He uncoiled the two cables and tried to puzzle out how to connect them up to the cars. One of them had red ends, so he connected it to the red post of the battery on his own car and to a post of her battery on which he thought he could detect traces of red paint. The other cable was too dirty to tell what color its ends were. He clamped it onto the other two posts of the batteries, getting grease on the cuffs of his shirt and some kind of white crud on his thumb that made it sting. When Velda tried to start her car, it just groaned.

She said, "Maybe you have to start up the engine of your car."

He did this; it worked and her car started. He had a sense of male accomplishment that made him feel a little sexy, even though this sensation was annoying and made him angry at her.

It was another day, ten o'clock in the morning. Harry was out in the patio reading a French art magazine when the phone rang. He waited for Velda to answer it, but she didn't. Then he remembered that he had told her not to answer the phone when he was in the house. With a sigh, he put down his magazine, went into the study, and picked it up.

"Hello?"

"Day Espain."

"This is Mr. De Spain."

"Dotty."

It was a voice he had never heard before, one that might be male or female. It sounded ambiguous, or vaguely ominous.

"Dotty? What do you mean? Is that your name?"

"Dotty no come."

"No come where?"

"Art store. *Ya no viene.*"

"Dotty is not coming to the art store?"

"*Sí. No viene.*"

"Who is Dotty?"

There was an interval of silence. The voice mumbled something, perhaps "Goodbye," and hung up.

Harry thought for a while, looking at the phone with its buttons and its glowing ruby, a mechanism that suddenly seemed mysterious to him. Then he got his keys and his wallet and went out to the garage, saying nothing to Velda, who gazed at him quizzically as he left.

He drove out through the gate, with its kiosk and its guard, and down the highway to Playa del Mar, where he parked in his usual place behind the bank. It was a pleasant morning; the air was crisp, and the sky was an even blue down to the horizon. In the hanging planters along Paseo, hummingbirds were stabbing the scarlet trumpets of the fuchsias.

When he walked into the gallery he found Mordecai Steiglitz sitting on a stool near the window, looking out into the street. He was wearing a small black Greek fisherman's cap, shiny with grime and paint-stained. His jeans were cleaner than the ones he usually wore, and there were only a few spots of paint on his shirt.

"Hello, Harry."

"Hello, Mordecai. Why did you change your pants?"

"Important new responsibility. Acting manager of the place."

"What's going on anyhow?"

"Dotty called me up and said she wasn't coming in. Asked me if I could tend the store for a couple of days."

"Who's Dotty?"

"Dorothy. You know who Dorothy is."

"Yes, but why is everyone suddenly calling her Dotty?"

"I've always called her Dotty."

"You say someone called and said she wasn't coming in?"

"Yes. She called."

"Are you sure it wasn't another voice, that didn't speak English very well?"

"Sure."

"Why isn't she coming in?"

"She didn't say."

"This doesn't sound like Dorothy at all. She hasn't missed a day of work for years. Then suddenly she sends mysterious phone messages to say she isn't coming in."

"It wasn't a mysterious phone message. She called herself."

"Why didn't she call me?"

"I don't know."

He would have to go around to Dorothy's place, he thought, to find out what was going on. He was curious to see what her house was like anyhow. He could call her from here at the gallery, but he didn't want Mordecai listening in.

"What have you been up to lately, Mordecai?"

"Oh, the usual. Paint all day, drink half the night, sleep the other half."

"What sort of thing are you painting these days?"

"A new period. I've been in it now for about a year. Post-expressionist fauvism with cobalt. There's one right there, to give you an idea."

Without rising from the stool, he pointed his thumb at the wall.

Harry saw a new picture on the wall facing the window. It was a blur of blue and green with large white zigzags rising up from the bottom, like a yucca tree. The impasto was thick. He must have used several tubes of cobalt blue on it.

"Where's the Kati Modane that used to be here?"

"I don't know. I guess Dotty sold it."

"We don't do nonrepresentational art, Mordecai."

"It's not nonrepresentational. It's called 'Sunburst, Alternate World.' "

"You can leave it up while you're working here. Then take it away. How long is that going to be, by the way?"

"I don't know. Dotty didn't say."

"What are you asking for it?"

"Two thousand."

"You know how the place works, Mordecai. We take forty percent. Don't use the phone for long-distance calls, and don't sell anything big. If anyone's interested in a big painting, tell me and I'll make an appointment to talk to them."

"Okay."

"Help yourself to the coffee."

"Okay."

"Did Dorothy sound all right?"

"No, she didn't."

☐

Harry drove slowly up Shadow Lane looking for the house. It was a narrow street lined with pepper trees, mounting at a slight slope up into the hills. When he found the house, it was exactly as he had imagined it, a small bungalow overhung with bougainvillea. It wasn't shingled, however, but was finished in weathered gray clapboards. The trim had once been white but was now peeling and showed more gray than white paint. There was a big weeping willow in the front yard. He parked the car and approached the house cautiously.

It was very quiet on the street. From across the way an old man supported on two legs and a cane, like a tripod, watched him without moving. He went up the walk, made of broken fragments of concrete set in the scraggly lawn, and brushed aside a bee that plunged at him out of the bougain-villea. At the side of the house a brown face appeared momentarily in the flowers. He couldn't tell whether it was man, woman, or child. It had a shock of black hair on top of it.

He stopped halfway up the walk. The door was open, and in front of it was a screen door, an old-fashioned wooden one. He thought he caught a glimpse of something inside the screen, another face, or the same one. There was still no sound. It was eerily quiet.

There was something ominous about all this. The silent house, the voice on the phone, the appearing and disappearing face. He felt a sense of uneasiness about Dorothy and what was going on, but he was going to do something about it, and this, like jump-starting Velda's car, gave him a slight sexual jig. He was a knight riding in to save Dorothy from whatever it was. It was a very primitive feeling, and not unpleasant. He looked around for something, a stick or a weighty stone, in case he had to deal with the owner of the face. He went on up the walk and looked in through the screen. Inside the shadowy room he saw a strange woman in a white dress with her hair tied in the back. She fled without a word.

He pulled open the screen door and went in. The house

was deserted. The living room was clean and neat, decorated in a kind of Pre-Raphaelite simplicity, without rugs on the worn but polished wooden floor. On one side was the doorway of the kitchen, with an old-fashioned breakfast nook, and on the other a hallway leading to the back of the house. There was a kind of alcove off the living room, enclosed with drapes. Harry went into the bedroom and found Dorothy lying in bed, looking wan. She smiled.

Her face was the curious grayish color that an olive complexion turns when its owner is sick. She lay in bed wearing a loose dressing gown with tiny flowers all over it and a large rose embroidered at the neck. In this garment her compact and efficient body seemed lost. She seemed a doll that is all clothing, a large, elaborate dress of colored felt with a small china head attached to it. The covers were drawn up to her waist.

"What's the matter with you, Dorothy?"

"It's just the flu. I'm sorry to bother you." She could hardly talk; it was as though she had a mouthful of thistles. "You needn't have come."

"Do you have a fever?"

"Oh, yes." There was a thermometer balanced on a saucer at the bedside. "I called Mordecai. He's taking care of the store."

"Do you know about his cobalt period?"

"Yes. It's awful, isn't it?"

"Dorothy, what is going on around here?"

"Going on?"

"Somebody called me on the phone. I don't know who it was. And Mordecai said he didn't know why you weren't coming in. And there are people lurking about this place. Who are they?"

"People?"

"Dorothy, you know very well what I mean. Are you in their power in some way?"

She laughed. "Yes, I suppose I am. They touched the right spring in me."

"But who are they? You told me you lived alone."

"No I didn't. *You* told me I lived by myself. I told you why I'd never married."

"You haven't told me yet who these people are."

"Oh, some poor unfortunates. . . . Juana!" she called, in a rasp of a voice that must have been painful with her sore throat.

The woman appeared in the doorway.

"*Ve a buscar a los niños. Traelos aquí.*"

The woman disappeared, without expression and without a sound.

"She's as shy as a wombat," said Dorothy. "She keeps house for me, and in return I give them a little to eat. She goes away and works somewhere now and then. They're illegals, of course. They don't speak anything but Spanish and hardly that. They don't know how to do anything. They're afraid of the Migras. I found them one day wandering in the street. It was like something out of the Bible, except they didn't have a donkey."

The woman appeared again, shyly leading in two boys, who were petrified with terror. She was about thirty, a lean and pinched woman with a furtive look; she always seemed to be staring sideways. Her dress she had evidently brought with her from where she came from. It was simple white cotton, with embroidery on the square neck. It gave her a kind of Grecian dignity; no, Dorothy was right: biblical was it. The boys were perhaps twelve and fourteen. They had a look of numb suffering, a kind of cheek-sucking stoicism that seemed to strike them dumb. But they were keen and watchful; they were aware of everything that was going on. They were not very different from Peter, he thought. It was the older boy who had served as lookout and caught sight of him coming up the walk.

"Juana, Rafael, and Segundo. *Basta ya! Váyanse! Vaya a preparar el almuerzo!*" she called after the woman, still in her scratchy rasp. "Would you like to stay for lunch?"

"No. Dorothy, what do you have besides a fever?"

"Oh, I have a headache, the flux, and I'm weak all over.

Except for that, I'm fine. I'm sorry I couldn't come to work. I would probably throw up all over the pictures."

"Why didn't you call me instead of Mordecai?"

"Oh, I didn't want to bother you." Harry was about to ask why she had told Rafael to call him, but she went on in her hoarse gasp. "No, that's not it. Shall I confess? It's because I wanted you to come here. And you have, haven't you? Perhaps my subconscious mind made me sick and then made all these complicated arrangements, just so you'd come here. When I heard the screen door open, my heart leaped. I thought, He's under this roof! Here in my house!"

"You're feverish, Dorothy."

"Oh, I'm sure I am! I'm rambling, delirious. Don't pay any attention to what I'm saying. I'm not asking you to climb in bed with me. Or even to stay for lunch. I'm just a relic now, a look-under-the-bed old maid, and there's no question of anything more. Just being together here in the bedroom, with our hands on the covers!" Harry withdrew his hand as if it were burned. "The two of us in this room! For years I've dreamed of this happening. When I first caught sight of you, Harry, I fell in love and my life took a new turn. Isn't it crazy my telling you all this?"

"You told me you had decided to live a life in art."

"It was life in you, Harry. You're art."

When Dorothy came back to work, she was exactly the same as before: efficient, pleasant, shy, and a little aloof. There was no embarrassment over her dithyrambic declaration in the bedroom. She showed no sign that she remembered it.

eight

Peter was still ambivalent about the presence of Velda in the house. He hadn't seen any need to hire a housekeeper, and he suspected his father's motives, although he didn't quite know which wrong motive to charge him with. It was true that all the practical things in the house were now getting done again. The clothes were washed, the menus were planned, she went out in her Toyota and came back with the trunk full of groceries. In the long nightmare of his mother's illness and the months of numb emptiness that followed it, both he and Harry had forgotten what a well-organized household was like. They had lived like a pair of bachelors who were strangers to each other and for some reason sharing a house. Now when Peter came downstairs in the morning his breakfast was waiting for him. When the washing machine broke down, she phoned a repairman. A finch got into the kitchen, and she trapped it in a wastebasket and set it free. She replaced burned-out light bulbs and bought school supplies for Peter. In all these things, in the outward semblances of their life in the house, it was just like—Peter hardly dared to think this thought even to himself—it was just like before the Bad Thing had happened.

On the other hand, it was disconcerting to come into his own room and find someone who didn't belong there, a stranger, invading his private male sanctuary, down on her knees pulling socks from under the bed. The rear she pointed

at him as she did this summarized everything he disliked and
feared about women: their weighty authority, their sanctity
as the custodians of reproduction, which in some way gave
them a moral advantage over men. She got up from under the
bed and pointed out to him that there was a hamper in the
room for his dirty clothes, and if he would just put them in
it she would take them away once a day and wash them. "You
look so nice in your school clothes," she told him (the de-
tested Pointz Hall uniform). "I don't know why you go
around in that crummy rig" (his tee-shirt and shorts, with
bare feet). "It's the kind of thing that little kids wear, you
know, in the fourth or fifth grade, the ones who ride around
on those little bikes with tiny wheels. You're just about a
man," she told him, "and besides, I can see right up those
shorts when you sit on the sofa reading, with your feet up."
Like all women, she was harping constantly on sex.

This led to another matter that he ruminated on. He
suspected in a part of his mind that Harry was setting about
to acquire a mistress, or at least he suspected that his father
had this idea in the back of his mind. He had no objection to
this in principle. It had nothing to do with his mother, who
didn't exist anymore. As a child, he didn't have enough
experience to judge such things. In the books he read, a lot
of respectable gentlemen had mistresses. Perhaps it was all
right if you were rich enough. How rich were they? To judge
from the stories of the other boys at Pointz Hall, not excep-
tionally so. To Peter, it was not the rich who were mythical,
it was the poor, the boys who lived in ghettos, didn't go to
school, took drugs, and killed each other in drive-by shoot-
ings. They existed for him as a form of art, a mythology, as
real and yet as intangible as the myths of the westerns or the
myths of the Arthurian court; they were visible in the images on the TV screen, yet so many other improbable and
upsetting things were visible in that rounded rectangle of
moving light that it was safer not to believe in them as you
believed in the things you could touch. That was Peter's
great watershed: between the things you could touch and the
things you only read about or saw on TV. Himself he could

touch; girls were on the screen. There were no girls at Pointz Hall, and none his age in Orange Bay. As he considered the possibilities of his father's reasons for bringing Velda into the house, his mind teemed with a rich gamut of motives, yet he was free from any sense of moral opprobrium. (His English class was focusing on Latin vocabulary just now: *ob*, against; *probrum*, reproach. With relish, he tongued over the fine joining of the words.) Harry, as he now thought of him, was free to do anything he wanted, just as he, Peter, was free to do anything he wanted. He was free to watch the videos at Henry Fang's, and Harry was free to conduct his private life as he wanted. It was no business of his. Harry was half a stranger to him anyhow and always had been. But (this thought crept in stealthily, like a worm into a corpse) it was a stranger he loved at a distance, one whose intimacy and grace he longed for in his secret mind. And if he left off calling him Harry and thought of him as Father, then that word immediately gave birth to another word that hung beside it in his thoughts in letters of fire. Here Peter felt a sharp ache just under the ribs and left off thinking about these things. Mother—father—these words led him to a cave full of sharp dagger points, which he preferred not to explore. He was happier about the whole thing since Harry told him to call him Harry.

Although he pretended to himself that Velda's presence in the house had nothing to do with him and that her relations with Harry were Harry's business and not his own, he still had a secret curiosity about this woman and her ways, which were perhaps the ways of all women and perhaps not. Velda of course could not be touched. Therefore she fell into the second category of things in Peter's mind: those that were only imaginary, or fictional, mere husks of light impinging on the concave screens inside his eyeballs. But was this so? As soon as he thought of it he doubted it. She *was* a real person, and right there in the house; she hardly fitted into the same category as the girls in the videos or the mythical boy gangsters in the ghettos. If she were my mother, he thought, I could touch her, she might put her

arm around me or kiss me good night. (As *she* used to, he
thought, then turned away from this memory in fright.) Or
if he were older and she weren't the housekeeper in the
house (but what difference did that make?), he might touch
her in another way. The videos and the books he read had
taught him how to do this, and the technique of it presented
no difficulty to him. Of course, he didn't want to; on the
contrary, he shrank from the very idea of it. He would go a
long way around in the house to avoid touching her, or being
touched by her. Still, curiosity overcame this lack of desire,
or this repulsion, and Peter decided in a fit of recklessness
that he had to touch her, that he would touch her, but in
some way that wouldn't arouse her hostility or even her
curiosity, in a way perhaps that she wouldn't even notice.
Perhaps when she was asleep; he could steal into her room
in the middle of the night and— He saw immediately what
a rotten idea this was and didn't even finish the thought. Just
bump against her accidentally. Contrive that the two of them
should brush together by the laundry hamper. Pretend to be
sick and call for her to bring him something in bed. Request
that she adjust the pillow under his head. Et cetera. This
scene progressed in his mind until the details became blurry
and it faded.

Just bump up against her. Finding her alone in the
kitchen, he stole up silently and surveyed the situation from
behind her back. She was wearing her emerald jersey and
polyester pants, and she was shaking flour into a bowl and
stirring it into something. It was four o'clock in the afternoon, a time of day when Peter had the habit of dangerous
experiments. He got the step stool, set it beside her, and
climbed up it to look for something in the top cupboard. He
found a china teapot, an old egg timer, and decided that
neither of these was it.

"What are you looking for?"

"Something for an experiment."

Climbing down, he missed his footing, the step stool
tottered, and he fell heavily against her. For an instant, the
instant that a struck tennis ball lingers on the backboard, the

softness of her ample hip fitted into his waist and his ear touched her shoulder. Then he was crumpled on the floor.

"Clumsy oaf!"

He picked himself up, not looking at her.

"Are you okay?"

Peter said nothing and slunk off to his room. He burned with shame when he remembered his inadvertent word *experiment*. Surely she would have understood what he meant. As an experiment it had not been a success, or rather it had been only too successful. What he had felt as the tennis ball bounced was something warm, padded, and comforting. It was nothing at all like what the girl in the Hawaiian video would feel like, as he imagined it. It was what *she* had felt like. It made him a small child again, lonely and abandoned, yearning to be enclosed in an understanding embrace, to be given something warm to drink, to be spoken to in a soft, consoling, intimate voice that only he and *she* could understand. It was a cruel mockery that some other person could give him this darkling facsimile of the feeling he had almost forgotten and now remembered.

He understood now what Velda was. She was a Wicked Stepmother.

nine

Velda put on her blue-and-white running suit and zipped it to her neck. The shoes were blue and white to match, with rubber tongues that came up over the heels and toes. Over her ears she fitted her Heady Song, with its tiny antenna at one side, no longer than a matchstick. She twisted the knob and got first a voice speaking rapid Spanish, then a thump of rock, then a Beethoven symphony, and finally her country-western station. She went downstairs, left the house through the kitchen door, and jogged down the lawn to the road.

Peter wasn't home from school yet, and Harry was away at the gallery or somewhere. He never told her where he was going. Orange Bay had a queer arrangement, and it was a while before she understood it. The houses were on the sea side of the highway, clustered around the cove at the water's edge, but the entrance kiosk was across the highway on the land side. When you went out, you crossed under the highway in a miniature tunnel like something in a toy train set, only wide enough for one car at a time, then the road turned back on itself, mounted a slope, and came up to the entrance kiosk. In this way the residents weren't offended by seeing the kiosk, the living emblem of their isolation and security, when they looked out their windows; it was across the highway, hidden in the trees. Velda jogged through the tunnel, around the curve, and up the slope to the kiosk, a

small structure with glass walls and an overhanging roof.
Here the guard sat all day long, deciding who was to be let
into Orange Bay and who was not. The guard was a bluff and
sternly smiling young man with a scar on his face, a kind of
cheerful Frankenstein monster. Velda had already made his
acquaintance; his name was Frank Woyzeck, and he was
taking college classes in a night school. Right now he was
reading a paperback book. Velda dog-trotted out past the
kiosk and came back in on the other side, dodging around the
red-and-white barrier. This was the end of her jog. Frank
waved at her.

A blue van turned off the highway, made its way up the
short entrance road, and slowed by the gatehouse. Frank
waved it through and raised the barrier. It was the van from
Pointz Hall; as it passed her she could see that Peter was the
only passenger, sitting on her side by the window but staring
fixedly to the front, not seeing her. That poor child, she
thought. It was enough to make a stone weep. He didn't
have a moment in his life that was natural or human. He was
thirteen, almost a man, but he did nothing but moon around
the house with his nose in a book. The school he went to was
apparently some kind of monastery. He sadly needed a female influence in his life. But Harry had made it clear that
she was not to get involved with the quagmires and pitfalls
of human emotion, just to take care of the house. She didn't
have time anyhow. That kid should be down at the beach
with the girls, she concluded.

Thinking this and listening with another part of her
mind to the twangy music in her ears, she jogged back
through the tunnel and came out in the grove of eucalyptus
trees sloping down to the sea. The road was downhill here,
and her pace picked up. She passed Harry's house, the
Gilberts' with its Oriental dome, and a Mediterranean villa
with massive eaves and a flaring coral tree in front. Up ahead
she saw the park and the beach opening out.

Here she stopped, standing on the low seawall. It was
the scene of her nocturnal escapade with Golo, Henry Fang,
and the others, but it seemed very different now in the

daytime. She tried to reconstruct that night in her mind; for an instant, like the flash of a single frame of film, she evoked the darkness, the indistinct shapes of the men calling to each other in the sea, the sting of cold foam, the necklace of kelp, the placid figure of Dawn presiding over the towels in the starlight. In this picture, through some hallucination, she saw the naked figure of Harry charging up out of the sea with the others, a black patch gleaming in his white body, but in the next instant this vision was driven away by the glare of sunshine.

She turned impulsively from the sea, as if in sudden fright, and loped back up the road. She passed the Italian villa and came to the Gilberts'. With the picture of that magic and indistinct night on the beach still lurking in her mind, she left the road and ran without breaking her stride up the path through the flowers to the house.

Continuing on around the path, she came out onto the terrace. Here, too, everything was transformed; she could hardly believe that this was the place where the peacock had spread his tail, where she had drunk the Spanish brandy, where she had sat on the stool and sung "Trumbo Jane." In the pond, the koi were still nosing against the lily pads, but they seemed pallid and listless. The buffet table, the champagne bucket, and the stools were gone. A solitary bird hopped on the flagstones. At the far end of the terrace, a very old lady in a canvas beach chair was basking her limbs in the sun under the south wall, like an espalier. She opened her eyes and stared at Velda, then closed them again.

Velda turned off her Heady Song and pulled it down from her ears. The old lady in the canvas chair had opened and closed her eyes twice now. She opened them a third time and looked at Velda. When she didn't speak, Velda asked her, "Who are you?"

"I'm Grace."

"Do you live here?"

She smiled at Velda in the most gracious way in the world. "This is my house, dear. I'm Wolfie's mother."

She seemed at least ninety. Her face was like an old

redwood burl, and her few strings of silver hair were gathered into a knot on top of her head.

"My dear," she asked Velda, "would you like a drink? Go in the house and find some Scotch for yourself. There should be some Chivas Regal in there somewhere. While you're at it, bring one for me too."

The sliding door was open. Velda went into the house half expecting to find Wolfie or Dawn, but it seemed deserted. From the terrace she passed through a kind of vestibule, then into a large living room the exact proportions of a cube, with the dome soaring over it, covered on the inside with mosaic tiles. Around the rim of the dome was a stone cornice with letters in some unknown alphabet. Exploring the labyrinthine hallways off the living room, she found a kitchen, a pantry, a game room with a telescope on a tripod pointed out to sea, a library, a guest bath, and an office with a computer. Through an open door she saw Dawn's woman Marta stitching the hem of an elaborate appliqué skirt on a sewing machine.

Marta stopped the sewing machine, looked at her, then turned back to her work. The machine started up again. Velda was struck with a sudden curiosity about who Marta was, about *what* she was. Was she a servant? Was she a member of the family? Or something in between? She had no idea how people like this organized their households. She compared Marta to her own situation in Harry's house. Marta probably didn't go to parties. That is, not with Wolfie and Dawn to other people's parties. At the Gilberts' own party, she had passed around canapés like a servant. But now she seemed to be making this skirt for herself. Perhaps her job right now was that she was taking care of the old lady. A companion, that was the word that struck Velda. She wondered if she ought to fraternize with Marta—that is, speak to her. She decided not to. Marta might presume on it and offer herself as her friend, her equal. She, Velda, went to parties with Harry, therefore she was not a servant. And she was not Harry's companion. This last idea made her particularly thoughtful, or rather meditative. It was a queer

business on the whole, she thought. It struck her suddenly
that she didn't know what she was in Harry's house.

She went away and explored the rest of the house. The
stairs, at the side of the blocky living room, evidently led up
to the bedrooms. She didn't go up them for fear she might
encounter Wolfie and Dawn in a private moment. Through
the window facing the garden she heard the cry of a peacock,
a squawk like an old lady being strangled. This reminded her
of Grace, and she began looking around for her drink. There
was nothing in the kitchen, as far as she could see, or in the
pantry or the game room. She stooped to look through the
telescope and saw only a blue blur and a gray smudge of
island. In the living room she discovered that what looked
like a buffet was actually a wet bar if you lifted the lid. In it
was every kind of liquor you could imagine. She found the
Chivas Regal, splashed some into two glasses, and added
some ice.

Outside, the old lady had closed her eyes again. She
opened them when she heard Velda coming and took the
glass with gratitude. Velda sat down on a brick planter and
set her drink on the flagstone.

"They won't let me have it. They say it's bad for me.
And I'm too lazy to get it myself. Don't worry, they're both
gone. They've gone off to L.A. for the day. Won't be back
until nightfall. What harm could it do me, I'd like to know,
when I've got this far and I'm still kicking?"

"Why didn't you ask Marta to get it?"

"If I'm going to get up from this chair I might as well
get it myself. That woman is deaf and dumb when she
chooses to be. Anyhow you came along."

She sipped at her drink and closed her eyes again, then
opened them. "You didn't say who you are."

"I'm Velda."

Grace didn't inquire further. "What's that funny thing
around your neck?"

"Earphones. It's called a Heady Song." She demonstrated, fitting the knobs to her ears.

"So you run, and you listen to that."

"That's right."

"I don't run. And I don't need earphones. I sit here and listen to what's inside my head."

"Your head?"

"This old head right here."

"You mean you hear voices?"

"Thoughts, Velda. I've got lots of thoughts. More than I can ever think about. It's like an enormous library full of books. I can't possibly get to half of them now. And they're all fascinating."

She gazed at Velda as if expecting her to answer. Velda dutifully said, "Tell me just one of them."

She closed her eyes again. "This is my house. Curt built it for me. He read me the Song of Solomon when he was courting me. He called me his Rose of Sharon. So when we married I had him build me the Temple of Jerusalem."

"What are the words around the dome in the living room?"

" 'Thy two breasts are like two young roes that are twins, which feed among the lilies. Until the day break, and the shadows flee away, I will get me to the mountains of myrrh, and to the hill of frankincense.' "

"Are the words in Greek?"

"No, in Hebrew."

"Are you Jewish?"

"Oh, good heavens no, dear. I'm just like you. Like two young roes! Now they're more like two old cows."

Velda took a sip of her drink and set it back on the flagstone. Grace had finished half of hers. With her eyes closed, she mused in a low hum, " 'His left hand is under my head, and his right hand doth embrace me.' "

"I didn't know there were such interesting things in the Bible."

"There aren't. Just the Song of Solomon. I don't know why they let it in. The rest of it is a bore."

"Is your husband still living?"

"Do I look like a woman whose husband is still living, dear? He's gone years ago. He left me all this. The whole

house, everything. They have to do what I say. But of
course, they don't. They're such shits. They're young now,
and they don't understand. When they do, it'll be too late."

"Wolfie and Dawn?" As far as Velda could judge, they
were in their sixties.

"All of them. You too, I imagine. I know who you are
now. You're Harry de Spain's woman."

"I am *not*," said Velda firmly.

"They've told me about you. Or rather, I've overheard
them talking."

"They've got it all wrong. I just take care of the house."

"Harry is very good-looking. I might have a go at him
myself if I were younger. But you have to give up so many
things."

"I don't think that drink is good for you. I shouldn't
have given it to you."

"It was very nice of you. I'll try to see if I can't do
something nice for you in return. Maybe you'd like to have
the house when I die."

Her eyes were closed. Then she opened them and stared
straight at Velda for a long moment. She didn't seem to be
crazy, Velda thought. She had been poking fun at her ever
since she came. She was a wily old creature who knew perfectly well what she was doing. Velda felt a certain kinship
with her. Not a sympathy exactly, but she knew all at once
what it would be like to be Grace.

"Can I help you in any other way?"

"You could bring me another drink."

"No, I don't think I will. You've had enough. Did you
have any lunch?"

"Oh, yes. They gave me my pot of gruel. Then they
went off in their car and left me here to dry out in the sun,
like an old prune."

"Gruel? I don't believe you."

"Actually Marta made me a club sandwich. She's quite
a good cook."

"Yes. Dawn gave me her recipe for crab canapés."

"I'm fairly lucky, I imagine," said the old lady, "when

I think of all the other shits I could have ended up with."

"You do have a family. I don't have one."

"If Harry doesn't have you, what *does* he do about women?"

"I don't know," said Velda.

Their conversation died after this. Grace had closed her eyes and seemed sunk in profound thought, no doubt reviewing again her youth and her poetic husband, who built a temple for her to live in. Velda sipped a little more of her own drink, then left it unfinished and went off to explore around in the garden for the peacocks. She had a conviction that if she could only find them she could make them spread their tails, although she didn't know quite how. She heard their cries, now from one direction, now from another, but they remained hidden in the complicated landscaping. Without knowing where she was, she came to the pergola with its view out over the sea. From here she could see the island on the horizon, and the lighthouse up the coast on Heron Point, a pyramidal white box on three legs. A gull drifted along the surfline; it seemed odd to see it flying below her. The aspect of everything changed according to where you were standing to look at it. Gulls from above, Harry as seen by Grace, herself as seen by Marta. Or by the old lady. The world—this hadn't struck her before—was a network of crisscrossing viewpoints, like a cat's cradle you made with string on your hands. She herself was four or five different persons to these various people. Still circling through the garden, having half forgotten what she was looking for (the peacocks), she came to a gate out onto a road, an exit from the property she hadn't noticed before.

She went out through the gate, closed it behind her, fitted the plastic knobs onto her head, and began jogging again, feeling a little floaty after the liquor she had drunk. She was still undecided whether alcohol was good for her or not. It had been bad for most of the other people she had known in her life, especially Vivian and Max, but maybe they had been setting about it the wrong way. It didn't seem to do any harm to Harry, or to Golo and the others. Maybe it made a difference whether you drank Spanish brandy or six-packs. However, it probably wasn't a good idea in the middle of your jogging. Her legs felt watery and wobbly. She labored up the curving road past Harry's house (as she still called it in her mind for want of a better name for it), past the flat-roofed stone house of the Fangs, and along a road that mounted up through the trees past the last of the houses. Where this road came to an end there was a thicket of junipers and a fence with razor wire at the top. She stopped and sat down on a rock to pant, pulling the Heady Song down onto her neck.

At her back, behind the fence, was the heron refuge, where forty grayish-blue lumps hung like fruit in the branches of the eucalyptus trees. Now and then a few of them would flap away in slow motion, lurch through the green air, soar over the cliffs, and come back to collapse into their nests in an awkward flurry, as though they were doing it for the first time. These forty birds lived like kings in this choice stretch of coastline, behind their fence with plenty of food, while there were people inland who slept in the streets.

From here at the top of the hill she had a view of most of Orange Bay, stretched out in its half-bowl facing the sea. The Gilberts' dome stuck up out of the trees like a child's blue marble. Harry's house was almost hidden in the trees; she caught a glimpse of its roof and a fragment of garden no bigger than a handkerchief. On the other side of the cove there was a mansion with a porch of white columns that looked like the White House, and a zigzag glass house with steel beams painted green. Orange Bay, with its spooky cliffs and its bizarre houses, had a slightly unreal and nightmarish quality for Velda; she hadn't got used to it yet. Directly below her, she saw now, was the Fangs' house. Although she hadn't realized it, the hairpin turns of the road had brought her to a point above it so close that she could have thrown a pebble down onto it. She could see the top of the flat roof, the hump-shaped front lawn, and an old Cadillac the color of verdigris sitting in the drive. There was no sign of Henry or Mary, whom she imagined as inside-the-house creatures who only came out at night; she couldn't visualize them in the sunlight. Across the road a Mexican gardener was going up and down the steep lawn with a lawn mower. Somebody came up the side of the road under the trees; she saw a fragment of white garment moving under the foliage. When it emerged, it was Peter, in the jeans and white shirt that he now put on when he came home from school. He mounted up the lawn to the Fangs' house, turning once to look behind him. She could tell from his stance, from the way he floated along looking to one side, from the way he moved his long sticklike legs, that he wished to make himself invisible. He disappeared into the screened porch at the side of the house. From the tree over Velda's head a black crow let out a caw and flapped away clumsily into the still air. When it was gone, there was silence, except for the buzzing of a bee.

Velda put the Heady Song back on her ears and jogged back down the road. As she passed the Fangs' house she took a more careful look at the place. The screened porch at the side, where Peter disappeared, had green plants inside; it was wooden, and the unpainted boards were weathered with age. The rest of the house was built of water-rounded stones. Velda had a peculiar gift that enabled her to tell when people were looking at her from concealed places, from behind curtains, for example, and now she detected no such waves. She jogged on down the road and entered Harry's house (*the* house, she decided she would call it) through the unlocked kitchen door. Nobody locked their doors in Orange Bay. In the places where she had lived, every house was a fortress, with double locks on the doors and sometimes bars on the windows.

From the kitchen she opened the door to the garage and found that Harry's Mercedes was still gone. In the other space in the garage, covered with a thin film of dust, was his wife's silver-gray BMW, which had been sitting there for more than a year, or probably longer, since she wouldn't have driven it much after she got sick. It was a kind of gravestone to her memory, reminding him every time he got into his own car that she was gone. If it were left to Velda, she would push the thing over a cliff and put her own Toyota in the garage. It would be good for his mental hygiene. It would remind him that things had changed and the house was now arranged in a different way. After a long drink of water in the kitchen, she went upstairs and emptied the laundry hampers in Harry's and Peter's rooms. With her arms full of dirty clothes, she went downstairs to the laundry room, behind the garage. She could clearly detect two odors in the bundle she was carrying: Peter's sour eucalyptus smell and Harry's scent, like hickory smoke—like the musk of deer—like Madeira wine. She dumped the clothes into the washer and turned it on.

Then she went upstairs again, to her own room with its cherrywood bed and dresser, its cool russet shutters, and its orange-and-white prints of tennis players. She took off her clothes and dropped them in the hamper. Everything in the room was neatly arranged: clothes in the dresser, others hanging in the spacious closet, her knickknacks and souvenirs in the pigeonholes of the cherrywood wall unit. Never before had she had a place to put away all her possessions so neatly. In fact, there was room for even more possessions; all she had to do was go out and buy them. She thought for a moment longer, then went into her bath to take a shower.

Her private bath. The steamy blows of the water washed away every trace of the mortal from her body, every speck of dust and molecule of the finite. It left her feeling like a fish, washed clean of all the smuts and curses of animals with legs. All the shower stalls in her life had had mildew, but this one was scrubbed clean every week by Mrs. Manresa or her mute brown assistant. She came out and rubbed herself dry in an enormous white towel with a nap like a polar bear.

The mirror in the bathroom was steamed over; she wiped it until she could see, through the lacework of drops, her own form working the towel and looking back at her. She dropped the towel and frowned fixedly into the glass.

Her own body had always seemed to her not beautiful but familiar and normal, the basic notion of the female form. If its hips were rounder than those of the models in maga-

zines, it was they who were the emaciated freaks. Greek was
the word she had devised for her body. Not boyish, not like
a fashion model, not slim and athletic, not gamine. Greek
like a statue. The shoulders sloped, the hands and feet were
small, everything tapered away at the ends and curved out in
the middle. Her stomach, half hidden by the veil of steam
that still clung to the mirror, was a creamy basin, and above
it were the two young roes that were twins. Her face was a
face. That was all that could be said for it. It was not dis-
figured, marred, or disproportionate in any way. Her sorrel
hair didn't look much different when it was wet than when
it was dry. It was crinkled and stuck out in back. Her nose
was slightly pink around the nostrils.

Of all the creatures of the earth, good-looking people
were the strangest and most remote to her. She understood
them less than she understood pygmies in Africa or mon-
keys at the zoo. They seemed to live charmed lives but not
to be aware of it; or, if they were aware of it, like movie
stars, princesses, and models in magazines, to accept it as an
axiom that they were thus privileged and not to be grateful
for it, or beholden in any way to those who weren't so lucky.
Harry didn't seem to be able to take advantage of this privilege, or didn't know what to do with it; he sat in the patio
half the day, staring at the cat, wrapped in his thistly sorrow.
He didn't seem to be aware that for people like her, for
ordinary mortals, he was a constant reminder of the ordi-
nariness, the pathetic hopelessness, of their own bodies.
Someone should make him pay for it. But they already had,
she supposed, by making his wife die.

Velda rubbed the polar bear over her hair, changing it
from wet to damp but leaving it looking much the same. She
attacked it with a brush and pulled out a snarl or two. Then
she went back into the bedroom and dressed. She had bought
a few new clothes now that she had a job, mostly from
discount stores, but they gave her pleasure. She selected a
loose sleeveless dress in light gray with flecks of gold. When
she tried it before the mirror, the loose part of it flared out
behind her body as she pirouetted and turned. Gold slippers,

gold earrings, eye shadow with tiny specks of gold. Probably he wouldn't even notice this, since he never looked her in the face. A dab of scent under her chin and on her elbows. No lipstick. Velda went downstairs to fix dinner, the gray-and-gold skirt twitching behind her on the landing like a flag.

ten

She was still harping on his name.

"Are you called Xavier because you're Spanish?"

"No, I'm called Xavier because my parents were devout Catholics."

"You look a little Spanish."

"Well, I'm not."

"And then there's your last name, De Spain."

"It's possible that a long way back we were Spanish."

"If your parents were devout Catholics, why were you an only child?"

"That's always been a mystery to me. Perhaps they didn't get on together after they had me."

"That seems very likely."

He had no idea what she meant by this.

"And Peter too is an only child," she said.

He was eating his breakfast at the kitchen table while she cleaned up after Peter, who had gone off to school. Then she brought her own breakfast to the table and sat down with him. He had toast with black coffee, and she had orange juice, scrambled eggs with sausage, a sticky bun from the bakery, and coffee with a substitute for cream in it. This last was an effort to balance her diet after all the calories in other things. She wasn't overweight exactly, but her hips could have been reduced a little without any harm to her appearance. As for the rest of her, the breasts were just the right size. Why in the world was he thinking about these things? He kicked himself in his mind.

"Didn't your wife—"

"Let's stop calling her my wife, shall we? It makes it sound as though you're interviewing me. Her name was Killian."

"Didn't Killian"—she said the name unwillingly, as though it were wrenched out of her—"want more children?"

"I have no idea. We never talked about it."

"Peter is such a wonderful child. It's a shame you didn't have more."

He thought of asking her, Why didn't you have children? But this excessively personal question would be keeping up his end of a conversation he didn't want to encourage; it would be entering into a tacit understanding that whenever they were in a room together they talked; it would involve an implication that they were friends, intimates, equals. He wasn't a talkative person, and he didn't always feel like chatting just because there was somebody else in the room. But you really couldn't *not* talk to a person when you were sitting at a table eating with her. Even a stranger. Maybe it would be better if he and Peter took their meals in the dining room and left her to eat here in the kitchen. But when he thought of this, he couldn't picture it in his mind— she standing to serve them, then going off to eat by herself. It would be reducing her to a servant, something he had no right to ask of her. He had to observe the protocol that he had established even before he hired her, that she was to be a member of the family and do everything a wife did, except for the personal part. But wasn't conversation a personal part? He really didn't see that he had any obligation to talk to her about Killian's sexual proclivities, any need to explain that in spite of their deep attachment to each other, he and Killian had been physically intimate only rarely, and less after Peter was born; to explain to her that Killian was not beautiful, not sensual, just a bizarre, original, wonderful person, so that it had been enough for him simply to know that he possessed her, as you would take pleasure in the possession of a rare work of art, an antique crown in filigreed gold, a strange and valuable tropical bird. Here he felt another stab of the old pain and fell into a gloom, staring across the room and ignoring her.

Velda still wore the emerald jersey with engineering contours and the orangy-pink sweatshirt with swirls, but she had acquired some other clothes too. She came to dinner wearing a flimsy sleeveless dress in shot silk or something; he was not an expert on women's clothes. Along with this she wore specks of gold around her eyes; it made her look like a child dressed for Halloween. She also had a running suit, and a leotard arrangement that she wore for some kind of exercise in her room involving thumping and subdued groans; she shut the door so he couldn't see what she was doing. She had a fondness for scarves with one end thrown over her shoulder, or tied around her frizzled hair so that her face looked stretched back and ratlike, not an attractive effect. Once, she turned up in a man's double-breasted jacket, gray with fine brown pinstripes, much too large for her and obviously not new; she said it belonged to her brother.

"I didn't know you had a brother."

"Oh, yes," she said noncommittally, and didn't explain.

Some of the things she bought were obviously expensive, and not necessarily in bad taste. A Portuguese cameo made its appearance at her throat; she explained negligently that it was an antique. He observed it from across the room, wary of the trap that invited him to bend over her and inspect it more carefully. He restrained an impulse to ask her how much it had cost.

The way the money worked was this: When she moved into the house, he set up a checking account for the household expenses, and paid her salary out of it every month, or rather he simply told her to write herself a check. She was also allowed a sum for the daily expenditures; she wrote checks for this and put handfuls of money for groceries in a crock in the kitchen. Out of the crock she bought a cookbook

called *Southwest Californiental*, with large glossy photo-
graphs in it so you could see the effects you were trying to
achieve. With this propped up in front of her, she began
improving her cooking skills. He remembered the macaroni
and cheese she had made as a test at her interview. Now she
did vegetable stir fries in a wok, quesadillas, broiled shiitake
mushrooms, polenta made with blue corn, and prawns with
peppers in three different colors. Harry and Peter ate these
things without comment; sometimes they exchanged a
glance. Tacitly they entered into a male conspiracy not to
praise the food, lest she vaunt herself on it too much and use
it as a trap or bait to weave her net about them. At least this
is what Harry felt and he imagined Peter felt the same; these
tactics were evidently a matter of male instinct and not
things you learned. Along with the *crevettes aux trois
poivrons* she offered them fresh green beans tossed with
olive oil and garlic; Peter ate most of his, but Harry pushed
them to the side of his plate.

"Is it because of the garlic?"

"No; I'm not hungry, that's all."

"Next time," she said, "I won't be so fancy. I'll just
open a box of frozen beans and boil them in a pan."

He dropped it there.

As she took away the plates she said, "Would you like
some ice cream?"

"Yes."

"You could imagine what an adult would say," she told
him, "if a child didn't eat his vegetables and then wanted ice
cream."

"Yes, isn't it nice that we're not children."

Peter sat with his eyes fixed on the table, waiting for his
ice cream.

Killian's BMW was still sitting in the garage next to
Harry's car. It had been there now for a year and a half; it
was covered with dust, and one of the tires was soft. He came
home from the gallery, got out of his own car, and stood
looking at the BMW for a moment, then he touched it with

his finger to clean a spot of the glowing silver-gray surface.
A line of poetry occurred to him: *And thy quaint honour
turn to dust, and into ashes all my lust.* After he had stood
for a while, contemplating the silver stripe that his finger
had made on the car, he went into the house to look for the
keys.

He found them in the drawer of her dresser in the
bedroom, along with her souvenirs and keepsakes. In the
garage, after another spell of standing bemused, looking at
the car, he opened the door and got in behind the wheel. The
inside of the car was spotlessly clean; the tightly closed
windows had kept out the dust. Everything was immaculate;
the carpets were clean, the shift lever with its white diagram
glowed in the half light, the neatly folded maps were tucked
into the door. There was a handful of quarters in the ashtray
for parking meters. The Italian kidskin gloves she wore for
driving were lying on the passenger's seat where she had left
them. In the corner of his eye was the mirror; he half expected to catch a glimpse of her turban of auburn hair, her
skeptical and amused glance, the long toucan elegance of her
nose. After a while he slowly raised his hands and set them
on the steering wheel. It felt strange, as though he were
touching something forbidden, as though he were stealing
something that was not his own. He had never driven this
car; when they went out together it was always in the Mercedes. She used her car only for shopping and for visits to
friends. The mileage on the odometer was low. It was hardly
even broken in. Only the dusty windshield spoke of the
months that had elapsed since she had walked and spoken.

He raised his hand and turned the key, even though his
mind had hardly willed to do this. The engine started immediately and settled into the subdued whir of its idling. He
backed the car out of the garage and drove it into Playa del
Mar to the car wash, then went by the station to fill the tank
and fix the soft tire. On the highway going back to Orange
Bay it purred along with almost no sound but the wind,
responsive to his hand and foot, like a slave that accepts its
new master. He drove it into the garage and left it exactly on

the four marks the tires had made when they stood for so long on the concrete. Instead of putting the keys back in the bedroom, he left them in the flat bowl with its Pompeiian design in the entry by the garage door, where he kept the keys of his own car and Velda the keys of her Toyota.

This episode left an odd mixture of emotions in him. It gave him pleasure to know that the car was there in the garage and unused; it was a kind of emblem in proof of his love for her, his faithfulness to her, like the drawer in the bedroom with its museum of knickknacks and ribbons. But touching the car, or thinking about it, gave him the same pain as the contact with anything else that had belonged to her, even accidentally stumbling across some memory in his mind, the recollection of a shared joke or a quarrel that had ended in an embrace. These feelings were no doubt morbid. He was in a morbid state. But he did not want to be cured of his disease; he nourished it in his soul as though he were defending a last brilliant but fragile image of her that might disappear forever if he forgot to breathe life into it day by day.

By one of those tricks of chance that seemed to him unconvincingly theatrical and clumsy in their symbolism but are probably only coincidental, Velda came to him shortly after this to report that the battery in her car was dead again. He had come to dislike this old Toyota, faded and gray, with a spot of red primer on the fender, almost as he might dislike a person. It was a permanent feature in front of the house now, although it was against the association rules to leave cars in the road overnight. The last time the battery had gone flat, he had gone out and made a fool of himself jump-starting it for her, and got his clothes dirty. He also remembered the crude male satisfaction he had felt in doing it, the erection of the caveman who has clubbed a mammoth. This time he called a tow-truck service and they came and started it for her. The bill was forty dollars, which she paid.

"Why don't you get a new battery?"

"I can't afford it."

"It would cost about the same as the tow truck."

"I can't afford it," she said, "now that I've paid for the tow truck."

This exasperated him, but he made a particular effort not to let her see it. He remained calm, reasonable, and friendly, but he didn't offer to do any more greasy car work for her or lend her money. The next day she told him, "I got a new battery for my car." He nodded and said nothing. But she seemed determined to use this car and its ills as a way to get him to perform services for her, to pay some attention to her, to maneuver him into a situation where they would be in some way equals instead of the ambiguous relation they now had.

A week later: "Harry, I don't know what to do about my car. It makes a steaming noise when I drive it, and it drips this green stuff on the street."

"The radiator is leaking. Any idiot would know that."

"Could you come out and look at it?"

In answer he went for the classified phone book, set it down in front of her, and said, "Look under 'Automobiles, Repairing.' "

He felt a little guilty about this. She was doing the best she could, given her limited background, and she didn't have much money. He found it hard to account for the lurking hostility, or irritation, that he felt for her under the surface. Perhaps it was because she was constantly pleasant and he was morose by nature. But finally—he put his finger on it—it was the way she made him feel at certain times. When he helped her start her car. When she sashayed into dinner in her filmy dress, with gold spots on her eyes. He had brought a woman into the house, no doubt about it. Of course, he had always known that this was what he was doing. He was just lucky he hadn't hired Sylvia Jacquemort. Taking Velda as a person, he was neither interested nor uninterested in her, although he took a mild amusement at some of her antics. Taking her as a woman, the inchoate stirring he sometimes felt in her presence was purely mechanical. It wasn't his fault. It wasn't her fault either. It was like turning a page in a magazine and encountering a sexy photo. You couldn't blame a magazine photo for anything. Besides, he wasn't really attracted to her. She wasn't his type. It was just that these little twitches she caused in him now and then made him feel unfaithful to Killian and thus guilty and irritated. So the thoughts of Harry, sitting at his desk in the study, trying to concentrate on an art catalog.

A morning or two later he got up late, went to the kitchen, and found that Peter had already eaten his breakfast and gone to school. There was no sign of his own breakfast. Usually it was waiting for him on the kitchen table when he came out, the coffee in a thermos jug, the toast in a napkin, and the butter and jam on a plate. If the weather was fine he would take it out in the patio and spend a leisurely hour in the chaise longue under the ficus tree—not the wicker chair with its yellow pad, which stood empty and unused—with his coffee and newspaper. Sometimes he asked Velda to bring the breakfast out to the patio for him. This was a part of the day that he particularly enjoyed.

This morning the kitchen was deserted and the house seemed empty. He started to look for the bread, the coffee, the butter, and the jam—Velda kept these things in different places now that she was in charge of the kitchen—then changed his mind and decided to go and find out what she was doing and why she hadn't fixed his breakfast herself.

The door to her room was open about an inch. He never went in there, either when she was home or when she wasn't; he was used to the kind of house where bedrooms were private places. He knocked.

"Velda?"

"Mmm."

He pushed open the door and entered. She was lying in bed in a quilted bed jacket, and her own breakfast was on the table beside the bed, her usual scrambled eggs, sausage, and sticky bun, to judge by the remains on the plate.

She said, "Breakfast in bed," in a muffled tone; evidently her nose was stopped up.

"Is something the matter with you?"

"Oh, no, not particularly. I just don't feel up to snuff."

"It sounds to me as though you've got a cold."

"I don't know what it is."

"What are your symptoms?"

"Oh, Harry, I don't want to go into all my symptoms for you. I'm just not feeling very well, that's all."

There were round spots of pink on her cheeks that might have been makeup or the effects of illness. He had never seen the bed jacket before; it was pink quilt, embroidered with tiny roses, and it looked like a relic of her old life rather than the new image she was constructing of herself. Her hair was tied in a large red-and-blue scarf, which streamed down in folds over the pillow. The covers were pulled up to her waist, so that all that was visible of her was the better-shaped part of her body, the upper half in the bed jacket. Through the opening of this garment he could see the bodice of a lace nightgown. Her nose was always a little pink at the nostrils, but now the pinkness extended around the wings of the nose and down the ridges of her upper lip. Her eyes were rimmed in this same pink, and her cheekbones glowed. In some way these naive efforts of her body in its illness to simulate cosmetics made her seem more feminine and mysterious. Her wholesomeness had almost entirely disappeared; she looked like an actress playing Camille.

"Do you have a fever?"

"I haven't looked at the thermometer. You can get it for me if you want. It's in the medicine cabinet."

"You seem to be able to get out of your bed and fix your breakfast all right. Or did Peter fix it for you?"

She smiled as though all this gave her pleasure. She didn't answer the question. She said, "It's so nice living in this house. Even when I'm sick. I love everything about it." She finished off the last of the sticky bun, set down the plate, and sipped her coffee.

He saw now there was a rosebud on the tray. It was highly unlikely that Peter had put it there. If he had, it was a new development that provoked thought. More probably, she had put it here herself to impress him when she fixed her own breakfast.

"You're perfectly all right," he told her. "You've just got a cold. Everybody has them. You needn't make such a fuss about it. You fixed your own breakfast" (she didn't deny this) "so you ought to be well enough to get up and do another couple of things. If not, we'll have to bring in somebody to take care of the house for a few days. But you're all right. If you get up and put your clothes on you'll feel better. I'm going to have lunch at home" (this was her chance to say that she wasn't well enough to fix it) "then I'm going to the gallery in the afternoon. Is there something in the house for dinner? I don't know why I should have to think about these things. That's what I have you for."

She looked at him, solemn and woebegone, like a mistreated child. She was silent for a moment as she tried to control her voice. "You want me to get up and work? Fix your lunch, and then dinner?"

"If you feel well enough. If not, we'll get in a temp."

"There's nothing in the house for dinner. I'll have to go out."

"Well, I leave these things to you."

"Harry, why are you so mean to me? As though you were being deliberately cruel. I've never met anyone like you. I mean, I've known lots of men who were bastards, but they didn't go around behaving normally with other people and pretending they were nice guys, and just being mean to one person. It seems so . . . unusual—I don't know how to say it—so unnecessary. My self-esteem is not all that good sometimes, and you don't help."

"Cruel and unusual Harry."

"That's what I mean!" she broke out, on the edge of tears. "Sarcasm! Mocking! Insults! It's all a joke to you! You make fun of my cooking too! And my clothes!"

He had never said a word to her about her clothes. She seemed to have a keen intuition about what other people were thinking; privately he thought her attempts to transform her wardrobe a little silly. "Velda, let's get something

straight. As I understand it, according to the contract you do
everything in the house except the personal things. And that
means that I don't have to be personal with you either! It's
not in the contract! I'm busy! I have some reading to do this
morning—I don't know whether you think reading is work,
but it is—and in the afternoon I'm going to the gallery to
take care of some things. If you can't do your work, we'll
bring in someone else. It's as simple as that."

Her face worked, and her eyes welled up. Then she sat
up in bed, and the coffee cup tipped over onto the bedclothes.
She seemed not to notice. "Harry, who do you think I am
anyhow? I'm not a human being to you at all! I'm just a . . .
just a . . ." It seemed important to her to find the word, to
say exactly what it was that she was to him, but she couldn't
do it; her face collapsed like a piece of crumpled paper, and
she began sobbing. A moist glister streamed down her
cheeks. She was still sitting bolt upright in bed, with her
arms at her sides; he wished she would cover her face with
her hands, as other people did when they cried. Finally she
flopped over and buried her face in the pillow.

"Tears, idle tears! It's your final weapon, isn't it? When
all else fails. And we're not allowed to do it! We can hit you,
but we can't cry."

Her muffled voice from the pillow said, "Go ahead,
hit me."

"I don't feel like hitting you! That sort of thing has to
come out of genuine emotion. If you do it coldly and intel-
lectually, it doesn't work. Shall I call the temp agency or
not? Let me know."

Her weeping rose several notes in the musical scale. Her
face was still hidden in the pillow; her body heaved spas-
modically. He left her and went to the kitchen and fixed his
own breakfast and took it out to the patio. After he had eaten
the toast, he settled down with his coffee and his paper. He
wondered if he had done the right thing with Velda. Sickness
and tears. Powerful weapons; they called for powerful de-
fenses. He compared her in his mind to Dorothy, the time
she had the flu and he had gone to her house and found her

there with her retinue of spooky silent Guatemalans. Dorothy had not complained or demanded his sympathy. Dorothy had not even let him know she was sick. She had lain there stoically in bed ignoring her body and its ills, like a saint, thinking only of others; but wasn't (the cynical thought struck him) her very not complaining, her saintliness, itself a form of self-indulgence, a plea for special treatment, a call for a sympathy that would be all the more ardent and solicitous since she had not called for it? And of course Dorothy *had* sent him a message that she was sick, even though in a cryptic and roundabout way that made it seem that she had not wanted him to know she was sick. At least Velda was straightforward about it. She was a downright flaming nuisance; she didn't put so many fine points on it. Both women, he concluded, were in love with him, but that wasn't his fault.

After a while Velda got up and put on jeans and a blouse; out of the corner of his eye he was aware of her through the open glass sliding door of the living room. Evidently she wasn't so sick after all. She was setting busily about her work, rearranging the magazines on the table in the living room and throwing out the old ones. It was the idea that he might bring another woman into the house to take over her duties, even temporarily, that had sprung her out of bed like a jack-in-the-box. If he kept on like this, in time he might begin to understand a little something about women.

"Velda, could you bring me a sandwich?"

It was about one o'clock, and Harry had moved into the study. He had decided not to go to the gallery after all; there was nothing for him to do there. He sat at the table looking over catalogs and art magazines and making notes about new painters he hadn't heard of before, a form of activity that looked professional to others but was really unnecessary, since he always got his pictures from the same half-dozen artists he had handled for years. Probably, he thought, he was doing this to impress Velda. She was paying no attention to him and had gone off to another part of the house. Perhaps she hadn't heard him ask for the sandwich.

After a long time, a half hour or more, she came into the study with the sandwich and a glass of wine and set them on the desk by his elbow. Without looking up, he said "Thank you," and she went away.

As soon as she was out of the room he looked at the sandwich. She had split a croissant in two and filled it with chicken salad, lettuce, tomato, mayonnaise, and capers, and the whole thing was on a small china plate with a carved radish like a rosebud at the side. The third thing on the plate was a small jar of ant paste. It said "Poison" on it in red letters, and there was also a skull and crossbones, for the benefit of the illiterate.

Through the door he thought he caught a glimpse of her at the edge of his peripheral vision. Obviously she wanted to see his reaction to this symbolic gesture, but he refused to allow her this satisfaction. He went on looking at his catalog while he ate the sandwich and from time to time sipped at the glass of wine. It was an excellent sandwich, and there was no ant paste in it.

After a while he found that the reading and the wine had made him drowsy. He leaned back in the chair and closed his eyes. He often slept a little after lunch; he ought to lie down on the couch across the room and do it properly, but he was aware of Velda's reproaching presence in the house: *If I have to work, why don't you?* As long as he was sitting at the desk he had some claim to be working, even if his eyes were closed. Pleasant thoughts, sensations, and images trickled through his mind, pictures he hardly bothered to analyze. His catnap was like a warm, soft garment, a mantle of contentment that settled slowly over his limbs. He opened his eyes, saw there was still a little wine in the glass, drank it off, and closed his eyes again.

The next time he opened them he saw through the open sliding glass door that Velda had come out onto the patio in her jeans and was sitting down on the flagstones in the lotus

position, with a ray of sun glinting on her through the ficus
tree. With her she had a bottle of some clear liquid with a
blue-and-silver label. She seemed to be lazily, as though
unconsciously, unbuttoning the buttons of her blouse. He
went on in this way for some time, half following her curious behavior and half enjoying his nap. It was only necessary to open his eyelids a bare crack to see, through the veil
of his lashes, what she was doing. He slept some more. The
next time he looked, she had removed the blouse entirely
and was working on the jeans. She didn't seem to have
anything on underneath either garment. When the jeans
were off she resumed the lotus position and began applying
the liquid to her body, raising her elbows to put it under her
arms and pouring it over her breasts and back.

Harry didn't open his eyes, but he didn't close them
fully anymore. In a revelation that partook generously of
dream, he saw the secret of Velda's lack of attraction up to
the present time: *her body was not made for clothes.* She
became her true and authentic self only when nude. The
bottle shape that was ludicrous when she was clothed was
transformed into an artistic masterpiece, perfect and un-
changeable in any of its details: an Ingres odalisque. Images
from the history of art he knew so well raced through his
mind. Her posture with raised arms had a piercing grace; her
fan-shaped hair was that of a Flemish matron in a portrait by
Hans Memling. He sat stunned by this discovery, even
though he wasn't fully awake and his eyes were still half
closed.

Velda played with a little stick she had found on the
ground, scratching it on the stones. A blue flame sprang up
around her body and played from its angles, her elbows and
knees. It crawled to the bottle on the flagstone and electrified
it too. She held her arms high, like a swimmer entering cold
water, while the blue light climbed up them to her fingertips.
Her eyes were closed, and her hair crawled slowly as though
made of worms. She fell over sideways onto the flagstones
and lay there with the flames still playing over her. In the
sunshine, the veil of blue was almost invisible.

He bolted out through the glass door, still torpid from sleep. When his hand touched her she didn't open her eyes, but she murmured and felt for him. Feverishly he removed his shirt and pressed it over her to extinguish the flames, but they sprang up through his fingers as though he were trying to stifle a running fountain. The blue fire licking at his hands felt only warm, not particularly painful. He threw his still-clothed legs, his arms and elbows, and the writhing center of his torso over her as though, with the gift of his body, the total commitment of all that was mortal in him, he could save her from this fantastic immolation. He didn't remember removing the rest of his clothing.

"Oh, I'm so ugly. Don't look at me. It's so awful."

"Don't talk."

"It's so awful. You can't love me. Not like this."

"It's all right. I do love you."

"I'm too ugly. Cover me up. Get something to cover me up."

"Velda. Velda."

He knew that what he was doing was insane, but he couldn't stop. He was like a fly buzzing at a window, trying to push through it into the light, when another part of the window, only a few inches away, was open. It was easy enough to turn and escape through the open part of the window, unless you were a fly. What he felt was a pure and simple animal ecstasy, free from all the complexities of thought; it stunned his mind and reduced him to a grateful idiocy. He didn't know how to express this to her. She felt she was ugly, but he couldn't bring himself to tell her that she was beautiful. She wouldn't believe that. That she was an Ingres odalisque. A portrait by Hans Memling.

"How did you . . ."

"Harry."

"What was that stuff that you . . ."

"Harry!"

His leg, roaming around over her with the slowness of a clock, bumped against something, which he recognized as an aquavit bottle with its silver-and-blue label. A small blue feather still played from its mouth. For the rest, the fire was out. Along with the musk of his own armpits, he was aware of a thin brownish scent, a whiff of horn, and he identified it as the smell of burned hair. Something orange and white was moving dizzily at the edge of his vision, appearing and disappearing. Everything was happening in numb silence, as though his ears were stopped. After the moving shape had gone past him several times he realized it was Solange, who was coiling and springing around the patio like a jungle animal, or a cat in a circus doing an elaborate trick.

"Harry. Please, please. Now, now, now!"

The burning smell penetrated his nostrils, seeped down his veins, and exploded in his loins. The flagstones under him vibrated with the shocks. He became aware that his own hair was on fire; he felt the prick of its touch on his temple. Instead of reaching to it, he buried his head in her throat to snuff it. The tumult that shook both of them gradually subsided.

"Harry, Harry."

He lay exhausted in her arms like a spent swimmer on the shore. Finally he managed to disengage himself from her, which produced another "Harry!" and coaxed her too into a sitting position. He was terrified that Peter might unexpectedly come home. He was not due for another two hours yet, but somehow he might: they might close the school or send him home sick. Solange, after a final antic leap, settled onto her haunches, then came and sniffed at the unfamiliar odor. She stalked away, looked over her shoulder, and settled down warily at the edge of the patio to regard the two of them.

"Velda, I'm sorry. I . . ."

"Don't look at me. Get something to cover me up."

"Does it hurt?"

"No."

"We'd better call an ambulance and take you to the hospital."

"No, no! Please. I'm fine."

She folded her arms over her breasts and wouldn't meet

his glance. Her hair was blackened at the ends, but not much of it was really burned away. Her eyebrows and lashes were gone. For the rest, her skin was only lightly reddened, as though she had lain in the sun too long. The pinkness of her nostrils had disappeared, swallowed up in this new Red Indian disguise.

"Aquavit is half water. The flame isn't really hot. You're lucky you didn't try it with gasoline."

"Harry! Don't say that."

"I'll help you to your room."

"Get me a robe or something."

Instead he pulled her to her feet and led her off, his arm around her to support her. He deliberately didn't look between her legs, a part of her he had never seen and still hadn't seen. He imagined the crinkly hair there, blackened at the ends like that on her head, and it almost made him weep. Up the stairs they went, in a grotesque silent march. In her room he found her nightgown, fitted it over her head, and pulled it down. She allowed this to be done to her as though she were a doll being dressed. There were tears in her eyes, and mechanically she touched the side of her finger to them. Once she was in bed, she rolled over and seemed to fall asleep instantly.

He went back to the patio, realized that he too was still naked, and put on his clothes. They smelled of burnt hair, but except for that they were unscathed. The aquavit bottle lay where he had kicked it. There was no other sign on the flagstones of what had taken place, no ashes, no scorched stone, no trace of his own concupiscence or her despair. He threw the bottle into the wastebasket, went to his room, and flung himself onto the bed. He felt arid, sterile, exhausted of every emotion, with the tingling of pleasure still taunting him in his limbs. He wanted to weep as she had, but his eyes were hot and dry. He tried to injure himself by pressing his nails into his palms until the blood came. Finally he burst out in sobs that seemed to go on forever, like the convulsions of his body as he had lain on the stones with Velda. *Killian, Killian,* said a voice. It was not his own but came from

somewhere else, perhaps from the shadow of past time that
hung like a nightmare in the room. He pressed his hands
over his ears to stop it.

He caught her cold, of course. After three days he had
the same stuffed-up nose, sepulchral voice, and sore nostrils.
Hers was gone now. Neither of them mentioned what had
happened. She went on as before, chattering away cheerfully
at the dinner table. There was only a slight air that she
emitted—he groped for the words to describe it—a patient
irony, or an injured innocence. Peter didn't seem to notice
anything, or if he did, he didn't comment on it, either on
Harry's stiff gloom or on the odor that lingered in the patio,
as though somebody had set fire to a comb. Velda's missing
eyebrows gave her a very odd look, like a partly finished doll
in a factory. She replaced them with arched lines drawn with
a cosmetic pencil. Harry's scars were not in the body but in
the soul. He woke up in the middle of the night shot through
with remorse and shame, and in the daytime longed desperately for somebody to tell his troubles to; there was nobody
but Velda and Peter. And the ghost of Killian, who lingered
in the air and smiled cryptically, in a way that was far worse
than if he had heard her voice aloud. And what struck him
as most grotesque was that in the middle of his remorse, in
the middle of the deep grief he still felt for Killian, he could
not get his desire for Velda out of his body. Now that she
had cut off the ends of her frizzled locks, she had a very odd
hairdo that gave her a boyish or somehow mistreated look
that excited him every time he caught sight of her. He mentally unclothed her, again and again, and saw her enveloped
in the gown of transparent fire. It lent her an insubstantial
quality, like a saint in a medieval painting, and yet it made
him lust to crush out the blue veil in his arms. He felt like
taking off his own clothes and setting himself on fire.

He mulled over the deep and, for him at least, impen-
etrable enigma of why she had done what she had done. Was
the whole thing an elaborate contrivance on her part? He
couldn't believe this. At least he couldn't believe it was a

consciously planned contrivance. Perhaps a contrivance of her subconscious, or her instincts. But it wasn't fashionable to speak of women's instincts anymore. It was a way of saying that they weren't intelligent. Was Velda intelligent? The question seemed to him perfectly meaningless and futile.

Had she known what he would do when he caught sight of her wrapped in the witching fire? He could hardly believe she had enough imagination for this. Perhaps she had really intended to kill herself. Perhaps she had simply meant to say: Here you see me, naked and dying in torment. Had read some silly thing in the paper about a Buddhist priest or a Korean student. But she seemed too sensible for that, and too cheerful. What then? What had she thought in the moment when she scratched the match on the flagstone and touched it to her body? He had no idea. She was a total mystery to him. She who had seemed so naive, so gauche, so utterly obvious in all of her qualities when she had first come into his life.

After a few days of this, tormented by remorse in the daytime and troubled dreams at night, he tried to make it up to her. Brooding over what he was going to say, in the morning before lunch he made his way to the kitchen and stood for a moment watching her work.

"Velda."

She turned.

"I'm sorry about what happened."

She stopped what she was doing and stared back at him. There was a new astringency about her, a new toughness. He was a little afraid of her, although he didn't know what harm she could possibly do him.

"What happened? What do you mean, what happened? Do you mean that your wife died, which was unfortunate, so you mooned around about it for a year or so, then you went to an agency that specializes in this kind of thing, and you had a whole string of women come to your house and parade before you in their best clothes while you examined all their qualities and asked them embarrassing questions, and when you picked the one you wanted you treated her like dirt and went around hanging your good looks in front of her and taking them away again and wouldn't even help her when her car broke down? Is that what you're sorry for? No, I imagine you're sorry that when she—I'm talking about me, of course—finally reached her wits' end and tried to do away with herself with the only means at hand, you were overcome by a momentary lust and took advantage of her in a way that, although I have to admit it was a memorable experience, was painful and embarrassing for both of us and gave a severe setback to my looks, although you came out just as beautiful as before."

"I can't believe you're saying all this. You don't seem to be the same person. You've turned into some kind of virago. I don't know what you want."

"Women want the right to be bastards just like men. They're tired of being nice."

"Can't I . . . do something to make it right? I've said I was sorry. Isn't there something I can do or say that would make you feel—"

"Oh, you've *made* me feel. God, how you've made me feel. You made me feel like taking my clothes off and setting myself on fire. What's a woman supposed to do? It's easy for you. You've got everything going for you. First of all you look like a movie star, and then you've got all this money. Money is sexy, did you know that? And you bring me to this house, which would make any woman think she had died and gone to heaven, and you sashay around the place weaving in and out with me as though we were two bottleflies trying to mate in the air. And fine wines, and new clothes, and any luxury food I want from the supermarket. You don't have to have balls to know that would make a person horny. And what do *you* do? When I'm in bed with a cold, feeling rotten, you come in and tell me to get up and fix the dinner. I'm sure it feels great for a man to come in and humiliate a woman who's lying in bed helpless. It probably gave you a gigantic hard-on, but you weren't sensible enough to do something about it at the time, in spite of the gown I had on and my new bed jacket. No, you had to wait till I suffered even more, until I had walked through fire and humiliated myself to the utmost and burned off my eyebrows. Then you *really* got excited, enough to do something about it. You did it quite well, I have to admit, although I wouldn't care to have to go through all that every time. You may even have felt sorry for me—who knows what is going on in your mind?—but you were certainly feeling an enormous desire to put that thing in me, I could tell that even though I wasn't feeling all that well. Men are really quite simple. When their anatomy is all on the outside, it's easy to see what they want. And you're feeling it right now. You want me right now. Don't you? *Don't you!"*

He looked at her dumbly, and they went away to her room.

eleven

Velda emptied the drawers of the dresser in her room and carried their contents into the master bedroom. Then she began taking Killian's clothes out of the drawers of the long sandalwood dresser, one by one, and dropping them on the floor. She stowed away her own clothes in the drawers, neatly putting folded jeans, sweaters, slips, and underwear in places she had decided for them. Harry sat on the bed and watched her. When she came to the last of the drawers, the one at the top on the right, he said with a sudden urgency, "Not that one! Leave it alone."

She turned, startled.

"Just don't touch that drawer. I'll do something about it later."

She reached in anyhow and took out some things and set them on top of the dresser: a Russian lacquer box, a seagull feather, a foreign coin, a sachet, a faded ribbon.

He got up from the bed and moved toward her. "*I told you not to touch those things!*"

She looked up, turning the feather absently in her fingers. Their glances met in a way that seemed to him too intimate, too painfully revealing of his feelings. After a while she said, "They should be put away somewhere."

"No."

"You won't have to do it. I'll take care of it for you."

He whirled toward her. "No! I told you no! Don't touch them."

"Harry, look at me. Listen to what I'm saying to you."

"I don't want to hear about it! From you or anybody else."

She turned pale, and her voice rose. "She's dead, Harry, don't you understand? She's dead! She's not coming back! She doesn't exist anymore! She is not conscious! She is not aware of what you're doing! She is not looking down on you from heaven! She is dead!"

"Stop that! Shut up! *Shut up!*"

For a moment it seemed to him that he might strike her; he anticipated the enormous bleak satisfaction that the blow would give him. Then the moment passed, and he stood there in wrenching misery. He crossed the room to put the trinkets back in the drawer, but she stood blocking his way.

"You're going to leave those things in there? For the rest of your life?"

He couldn't bring himself to say that this was so.

After a silence, in which he could hear the sound of the sea in the distance, she said in a calm voice, apologetic, tender, as though she were explaining some necessity to a child, "That won't work, Harry. If I'm going to be here."

He saw now that this was true: that moving Velda's own person into the room, the presence that had become necessary to him and crucial to his happiness, would also mean moving her possessions into it, and therefore violating the things that had stood undisturbed in it for over a year, as though they were a kind of Eucharist for his own secret rite of communion with the dead.

"You thought you could be a bigamist, didn't you? You thought you could live with two women at once. Me, and a ghost. Well, that won't work."

"I forbid you to mention her."

"I wonder if you know what you're asking. You want to go on thinking about her night and day, every moment of your life, but you're asking me not to notice this. You want

to be unfaithful to her in your body, and unfaithful to me in
your mind."

"Please stop this."

"It's what every man wants, whether he knows it or
not. A chaste wife to worship, in your case a ghost, and a
maidservant to lie with."

"I don't want to hear this. *Stop, stop, stop!*"

"But that won't work. It'll make your mind come apart
in the middle. You've got to break loose of her. I'll help you
if you want. I was hired," she said, "as you keep saying, to
do everything in the house except the personal things. But it
seems that a part of my job is to help you bury this zombie
that's walking around poisoning your mind."

His face flamed. It seemed to him that he became momentarily insane. He understood very clearly what insanity
was. He stepped up to her and seized her arm. She lurched
backward, his grip tightened, and there was a confused strug-
gle; he raised his arm, and although he hadn't intended it,
his elbow struck her breast heavily. Wrenching to free herself, she stumbled back against the dresser and almost fell.
The lacquer box and the coin slid onto the floor. She pushed
herself up trembling and set her hand on her breast where
the elbow had struck it. They were still an arm's length apart
and both breathing hard. He realized he was still gripping
her arm; he released it, and his hands fell to his sides.

When she recovered her breath she said quietly, "Are
there some cardboard boxes somewhere?"

"There are some cartons in the garage, I think. I'll go
get them."

He went away and came back up the stairs with a tower
of cartons in his arms. He set them down by the bed, and
they bent over together to pick up Killian's clothes from the
floor. Harry felt a blackness come over him; he could hardly
see what he was doing. He blindly stuffed underwear, ho-
siery, and scarves into a box. Out of the corner of his eye he
saw that Velda had come to the top drawer on the right. He
turned away and sat down on the bed, not looking.

When he turned back a few moments later, the clothes were gone and the five cartons stood in a row on the floor.

She pointed to the carton at the end. "This is the one with . . . what do you call them? The souvenirs."

"All right."

"Shall we put them away in the garage?"

He nodded.

"I'll take care of the clothes in the closet too. There's some hanger space in the spare room."

She went away with the boxes, then came back. Without turning his head, he heard her taking the things in the closet and carrying them away on their hangers. This took a long time. When she came back again he was still sitting on the bed, facing the shuttered windows, with the dresser behind him. She opened the shutters and sat down beside him.

"You can see the sea here, even sitting on the bed. I don't know why you keep the place closed up like this. Imagine making love in a place where you can lift your head from the bed and see the sea. Do you want . . . ?"

"Not now. Peter's due any minute."

"Tonight, then."

He nodded.

The Embrys, visiting from southern France, came to dinner at the house. Golo, who knew David and Giselle slightly, was also invited. Peter and Velda made up the rest of the table. Although Harry was nervous about this dinner, it turned out fairly well. Velda deftly put on and took off her apron as she moved from dining room to kitchen. Peter helped with the serving. It was the custom now in the house that he set the table and cleared away after dinner. The menu was from Velda's cookbook, duck with honey and cilantro, followed by radicchio salad. The dessert was miniature profiteroles with Belgian chocolate. It all had a slight air of the inauthentic about it, but perhaps this was only Harry's imagination.

David seemed to have aged since Harry had seen him last. His mustache, which had always been salt-and-pepper, was now more salt than pepper. His pink face was speckled from the Provençal sunlight, and his cheerful, cynical, drawling voice with its Oxbridge accent seemed to linger more between sentences, as though it was searching for the exact fragment of flat wit to express. In honor of the occasion Harry had hung a big Embry facing the dining table, a new one that had just arrived, and David gazed at it placidly as he ate. Giselle was a small gray ferretlike woman whose English was not very good; it was not clear how much she understood of what was going on. Golo tried his French on her, and she had to ask him twice what he was saying; after that all the conversation during the evening was in English.

No one showed any sign that they found anything odd about the new arrangement in the house. Harry introduced Velda to the Embrys with his usual formula: "This is Velda Venn, who is taking care of the house for us."

"Miss Venn?" inquired David with his usual punctilio for titles and conventions.

"Velda."

"And do you have anyone?" Giselle asked her.

"Anyone?"

"Do you have anyone in the world," she went on with her gooselike persistence. "As, a husband?"

"No. I just have Harry and Peter."

This eloquent ambiguity was all they could get out of her. Harry was able to steer the conversation away from what it was exactly that she took care of in the house. "I find your new pictures very nice," he told David. "A little fuzzier than the ones before. More soft-edged. A kind of late Matisse thing. An indefiniteness to the line. A new verve. A nudge away from the edge of convention."

"Fuzzier?" said David.

"David is not fuzzy," said Giselle.

"That was the wrong word. A verve. A kind of slapdash sense of fun. An element of self-parody."

"David is not slapdash," said Giselle.

The conversation had taken an unfortunate direction. David had always been a somewhat nervous person under his British aplomb; now, as he heard his work called fuzzy, his fingers tremored like telegraph keys or the wings of beetles. "I daresay Harry means it as a compliment," he said. "He means my work is getting freer and more expressive."

David was impeccably dressed as usual, in what he imagined was the proper costume of a British visitor to California: a houndstooth jacket, a shirt with French cuffs, and a crimson ascot. Perhaps it was what he wore in Cassis as well. The speckled flesh of his hands, beef-colored and patchy, contrasted sharply with the gleaming white of his shirt cuffs. His hands and his head were real; the rest of him was glossy paper cut out of a fashion magazine for men. Yet David was hardly old; he might be fifty. At dinner Harry thought he detected something different about him since the last time they had met, a slight hesitation of speech, a slurring, a difficulty in picking up his fork; he noticed that Giselle was watching him intently.

Golo showed David how you really dressed in California: khaki pants, moccasins without socks, and an old blazer. To these he had added tonight a bolo tie with a turquoise slide, perhaps to amuse the visitors from Europe. Giselle stared curiously at the moccasins slit with a razor to make them easier on the feet. Golo dominated the conversation at any affair where he was present. Harry had hoped the dinner would lead to some serious talk with David about his work, but instead it turned to Noel Coward repartee led genially by Golo as though he were conducting a chamber orchestra. For some reason he picked on Peter first, although the child held his end up well enough.

"What are you studying in school now, Peter?"

"Fossils. French poetry. The laws of probability."

"Probability, eh? What's the probability that I'm going to die in the next minute?"

"I don't know. I'd have to calculate it."

"But you could?"

"Oh, yes."

David grinned. "The probabilities are probably very

tiny. Golo is such a healthy brute. Couldn't you speed up his mortality a bit? Fudge the figures."

"I'm not the Greek fates. I'm just taking a probability class."

"Oh, my heavens, he knows about the Greek fates," exclaimed Giselle. "And what are their names, pray me?"

"Atropos, Clotho, and Lachesis."

Golo said, "Well, I'm sure that we should all fall at the feet of this prodigy."

"A Marvelous Boy, as Dr. Johnson called Chatterton," said David.

This embarrassed Peter, and he got up to clear off the table. When he was gone David said, "Does he miss his mother much?"

"I don't know. He doesn't talk about it."

"Of course he misses her," said Velda. "Harry and Peter are a gloomy pair, I can tell you. I do what I can to cheer them up."

Harry stiffened. The others stared at her, as though noticing her penciled-in eyebrows for the first time. A little fine stubble was now beginning to appear underneath them, not quite on the same lines.

"Harry has always been gloomy," said Golo. "As long as I've known him. It has nothing to do with Killian's death."

The mention of this taboo name caused Giselle to stare at Velda again, a little more intently this time. At that moment Peter returned from the kitchen for more plates. They all fell silent. When he had gone away again Giselle said, "Perhaps it consoles him to read about the Greek fates. It makes everything in the life seem inevitable."

"I don't know how he would find that consoling," said David.

"The sense of tragedy."

"A person dying is not a tragedy. It's just rotten luck."

Peter had excellent senses, and he could easily hear what they were saying when he was in the kitchen, Harry thought. He came back for the dessert dishes and went away again to get the coffee.

"He reads too many books," said Velda. "It fills his head with nonsense."

David exchanged an amused look with Giselle. "Surely not."

"Well, the school costs a hell of a lot of money and it ought to be doing him some good," said Harry.

David said, "I'm sure it does." They all looked at Velda to see what she would say next.

"Well, I don't agree. He leads an unhealthy life. He needs to be outdoors more. He spends all of his time indoors poring over books. At his age he should be interested in other things. Sports, and music."

"Oh, he does have his own stereo. He enjoys music. I'm afraid he doesn't have very good taste though. He likes Tchaikovsky and Rachmaninoff."

Golo said, "Ah, well, he's young yet."

Velda looked from one of them to the other, feeling her way warily. Her eyes stopped on Harry. "What are you talking about? Are you serious? He's an American boy, he's thirteen, in perfect health, and he likes classical music? Is that normal? And you say he has bad taste. He doesn't have bad taste; he's a freak."

"Tchaikovsky and Rachmaninoff are postromantic, not classical."

"When I said music, I meant the music that kids his age listen to. I didn't mean these old Russians with beards."

"Rachmaninoff was clean-shaven, I believe. Tchaikovsky may have had a beard," said Golo.

They were all enjoying the game except Harry, who was nervous and wished they would knock it off. Or if they wouldn't, that Velda would come to her senses and realize they were making fun of her. She plunged on undaunted. "He spends too much time by himself, shut up in the house. At his age he ought to be getting interested in girls."

"Sure he would. What would any normal American boy do if he were offered a choice between girls and old Russians with beards? Didn't you have girls when you were thirteen, Harry?"

"I didn't have girls. I talked to girls."

"Well, maybe that's what Velda means."

Peter came back into the room at this point, and they went on talking in front of him. Golo said, "Surely there are girls for him to talk to at school."

"It's an all-boy school."

"The lycée I have gone to in France was an all-girl lycée. It's a very good plan. No distractions. Without boys, we have read very many books."

"That's why he's so odd. He doesn't know any girls, and he reads too many books."

"What else is there for him to do?"

"Volleyball, that's the thing. When I was his age, I met loads of boys playing volleyball at the beach."

"We play volleyball at school," said Peter.

"Not with girls. Go to the beach and find some."

"There are no girls my age in Orange Bay."

"Well, for heaven's sake, Orange Bay isn't the whole world. Go somewhere else now and then. Go to the public beach at Playa del Mar. I go running down there sometimes. It's just a mile down the highway. Lots of kids playing volleyball."

Golo, with a smirk at Harry, said, "I'm not sure that volleyball at the beach is all that wholesome for a boy Peter's age. All those nymphets with budding breasts, straining upwards to hit the ball."

"Nymphets, eh? Don't you call them lolitas in America?"

"We do if we have dirty minds."

"Well, you do have a dirty mind, Golo, so that's what you ought to call them," said Harry a little crossly.

"So you run?" David asked Velda with what seemed a friendly curiosity.

"Just about every day."

"And do you have a special costume?"

"Oh, yes. A running suit and shoes. Also a Heady Song."

Glances between the Embrys and Golo. "What's that?"

"It's a radio that fits on your head. I listen to music while I run."

"What kind of music? Since we're on the subject."

"Country western, mostly."

"Splendid, splendid."

She examined their expressions. Nobody smiled. "Well, what kind of music *is* best?"

Golo interrogated the others silently. "I like Baroque myself. Bach and Vivaldi. There's nothing wrong with Beethoven."

"I can't see Beethoven for running, though."

"Well, you're right, David. Maybe the 'Goldberg Variations.' "

"Who's that by?"

"Bach," David told her.

She seemed to be making a mental note.

"Here's coffee," said Peter. He set the tray with the espresso, sugar, and lemon twists on the table, for them to serve themselves. He lingered, attentive, with his hands behind him, like a professional waiter. "Would anyone like brandy with it?"

"After," said Golo. "First coffee, then brandy, Peter."

Velda said, "Do we have any Spanish brandy? Go and see, Peter."

Golo drew Harry out into the patio by the elbow. It was a chill, misty night; the leaves of the trees were silver with dew. Harry shivered in his light seersucker suit.

"How's art, Harry? Contemporary representational, as you call it."

"Very well, thank you."

"What's it representing these days?"

"Nightmares. Tennis players. Girls in white dresses."

"I heard the other day of an artist you should handle. Saw him in an art magazine. The reproductions were tremendous. One of them was in color. The heads in terrific details, glowing, luminous. Vital, you know, like old masters. The rest of it just pasted on, collage, like gilded wallpaper, very ornate, so you couldn't tell the costumes from the background, it all just blended together. Except for the faces. Fascinated me."

"That's Ioann Vlach," Harry told him. "A Romanian. Died a few years ago. Well known to critics. If you knew anything about art you'd know who he is. Mainly known for his drawings. He did only seven or eight major paintings in his life. Most of them are in big collections. One in Munich, one in the Rijksmuseum, a couple in a private collection in Enghien, and so on."

"None in America?"

"Not that I know of."

"You should take him up."

"I told you," said Harry, annoyed, "that there are only seven or eight in the world, and they're all in big collections. They're not for sale. If they were, they'd be worth millions. Why don't you stick to coins, Golo? Something you know about."

"Are you always going to handle those same six artists, Harry?"

"As long as they keep the place going."

"Yes, but going where? Nothing new has happened in the gallery for ten years. Now that you're entering into this new phase in your life, Harry," he told him in a lightly pontifical tone, making it unclear whether he was kidding him or making a serious speech, "you ought to leave old things behind and strike out for new frontiers."

"Leave what old things?"

"Your whole life. The life you've been living. You were lucky to have Killian, Harry." Harry attempted to suppress the flinch that came, like a reflex, whenever her name was mentioned. "You only had her for a few years, but you were lucky to have that. Then there was a bad time, in which you, I think, took your troubles a little too much to heart. And now you're coming out of that. Coming out of the tunnel. And what lies ahead? Eh?" He took Harry's elbow and tweaked it in the friendliest way imaginable.

"What are you getting at?"

Harry was cold; the night air seeped into his thin clothes. He looked through the glass into the living room, where the others were talking in pantomime. Peter was gesturing about something.

"When you were married to Killian, for all those years, your life went in a certain direction. Now it can't go in that direction anymore. It was Killian's money that bought the gallery, Harry, do you remember that? And the house. Before you met her, you were living in a tiny apartment in town, up a flight of outside stairs. Now look at you. You've got a new girlfriend." Harry opened his mouth to speak but he went on. "You entertain artists from France and wealthy coin dealers." A jovial smile. "And this"—he spread his arms in a theatrical gesture to indicate the house, the Mercedes in the garage, the invisible sea beyond—"could be just the start. You've got to take your destiny in your hands, Harry! Wrench the future out of it!"

"Is there some point to all this? Otherwise I'd just as soon go inside."

"Suppose a painting by this Vlach turned up, Harry?"

"I've told you there aren't any for sale. Anyhow I couldn't afford to handle it. I'd be competing with the museums and wealthy collectors."

"Suppose it came up in some way that it might be a bargain?"

"What do you mean?"

"Suppose that when the Romanians changed their government recently, a certain number of works of art came to light. Suppose that one of them were one of Vlach's paintings. I don't say that this is so; just suppose it."

"You're talking about stolen goods."

"Not necessarily. Under the previous Romanian government, as I understand it, a lot of works of art found their way into private hands. Government officials and so on, or their friends, or girlfriends. It was all perfectly legal under the laws of that time. And it would also be perfectly legal for these people, or their heirs—some of them unfortunately perished in the excitement of the change of government, I'm afraid—to sell these things to raise a little cash. At the same time they might not want to do this in a way that was right out in the open, so to speak. People might be incensed against them for being so rich in the past. There's a lot of feeling in Romania now against the former government. So they might be looking for ways to put these valuable things on the market in ways that didn't attract too much publicity."

"And that's legal?"

"Of course it is. These people have bills of sale for these things."

"It's a shady business. I don't like the sound of it. It's too big for me anyhow."

"How much would a Vlach fetch on the market?"

"It would depend on the quality. Eight or ten million, probably."

"Suppose you could get it for a fourth of that."

Harry looked at him. "That's crazy, Golo."

"Just as you say."

He felt in the pocket of his old blazer and produced a rumpled slip of paper with a telephone number on it. It began with 01. Harry recognized it as a London number.

"Where did you get this?"

"From a friend. He passed it along to me. He said it was a way to make a lot of money quickly. I told him I couldn't handle it. I'm a coin dealer, not an art broker."

"Why didn't he do it himself?"

"He's a coin dealer too."

"Then why did he give it to you?"

"I don't know. Maybe he thought I was interested in diversifying. Or maybe," Golo said, "he remembered that I had a connection with you."

"I'm not interested, Golo."

"Just as you like. I'm just a selfless intermediary here. It's just a slip of paper. You can do whatever you like with it."

"Why were you reading an art magazine, Golo? I've never known you to be interested in art."

"It was in a dentist's office."

"But then you say somebody gave you this slip of paper."

"Throw it away if you like. Do whatever you want."

"What were you two talking about out there for so long?"

"What were you all talking about in here?"

"We were talking about France. David and Giselle asked me to come and visit them," said Velda.

"Unfortunately you can't do that, because you have to stay here and take care of the house and Peter."

"Oh, Peter could come with me."

"How about me?"

"I imagine you're invited too. Isn't Harry invited too, David and Giselle?"

"Oh, absolutely," said David.

Harry said, "David and Giselle have a very nice place in France. It's in Cassis, on the coast near Marseille. I've visited them several times."

David seemed to be getting along particularly well with Velda. He was sitting next to her and talking as though she were an old friend. He said, "The house is very nice. It's all due to Harry. If he hadn't sold so many of my pictures we wouldn't be able to afford it."

"And they have no children, David says."

"My pictures are my children, my dear."

"Yes, but how does Giselle feel about that? Maybe she'd like to have children." Velda prattled on.

They all stared at her again.

Giselle told her with a trace of hauteur, "We have no children. Instead David makes pictures." Harry could see that if these two women were left together for any time they might fight like cats. Luckily there was no chance of their being left together for any time. He still hadn't had a chance to talk to David seriously about his new pictures, except to say that they were fuzzy, which had plunged David into gloom and made Giselle irritable.

About ten the Embrys got up to leave. They were staying at an airport hotel and they were going to fly to New York in the morning, and they wanted to get a good night's sleep. Everybody had had quite a lot of cognac, except for David, who was going to drive to the airport. Even Peter looked a little glassy-eyed. Harry wondered if he had been drinking too, when he was out in the kitchen. Harry himself had had two or three drinks, more than he should; it really wasn't good for him.

David seemed to be very shaky. He stumbled at the doorsill, and instead of expressing annoyance he looked around to see if anybody had noticed. When he raised his hand in farewell, it tremored a little. The gallery would really be in trouble, Harry thought, if David turned out to have Parkinson's or something. He didn't like it when Harry said his paintings were getting fuzzy. Maybe he should tell him that he would be able to sell them no matter how fuzzy they got; people liked lots of color and cheerful scenes in a sunny climate. Instead he said, "Nice to see you, David. Maybe I'll be dropping in on you one of these days." He didn't say he would bring Velda or Peter. He added, "Bye, Giselle." Behind him Velda chimed in *"Au revoir."* It was one of her four French expressions, along with *nouveau riche, beaucoup* (used in English sentences, as in "He has *beaucoup* money"), and *Toujours gai,* kid.

"If you come, let us know first," said David.

The door closed, and they were left with Golo, who seemed to be in no hurry to leave. He hung around for another half hour, exchanging suggestive badinage with Velda, inspecting Harry's books, and setting his hand paternally on Peter's head. Finally he finished his drink, set the glass down on the rare books, and took Harry's hand, pressing his elbow with the other hand.

"You have a lovely house here, Harry. A home, I should say. I envy you. Brings a tear of nostalgia to my eye.

Well, enough sentiment for one night. I can't take much more of it. *Ciao.* Thanks for a lovely evening. Harry, think about that piece of paper. And Velda, if you go to France to visit the Embrys, don't take Harry. He's an awful sourpuss. He'll spoil it all."

Velda said, "He's nice when you know him better."

Golo stared one last time at her ample figure, her burnt hair, and her childishly drawn eyebrows. "It's so nice," he told her, "having somebody like you in Orange Bay. There hasn't been anyone quite like you before."

"Good night," Harry told him.

Velda put her arm around his waist, and they stood there with their sides pressed together, facing the open door. In the chill air from outside, Harry was conscious of the warmth of her body, which seemed to be without bones; it pressed softly against his side and adjusted to its contours, the angularity of shoulder and convexity of hip, as though it were made for it. Her fingers, winding around his waist, ended in the front just below his ribs. The pleasure he felt at this touch was not erotic, or if it was, then erotic in a chaste and comforting way, a consoling way, as though after all the months of misery he had finally recaptured the recollection of what it was like to be happy. Killian was still there in his mind, but she had become someone he was once married to; her excruciating picture inside him was gradually losing its solidity and assuming the transparency of a dream that fades upon awakening. *I must not forget,* he told himself at the same time that he flowed warmly with gratitude for the touch of the body next to him. The door closed, excluding Golo's knowing smile.

twelve

About a week after the visit of the Embrys there was a brush fire in the hills across the highway from Orange Bay. This happened once a year or so after a long drought. Harry was not aware of it until several hours after it had started. About five in the afternoon, when he noticed the smell of burning chaparral in the house, he went out to look. There was a patch of grayish smoke in the hills, drifting slowly upward and dissolving into the sea mist. Now and then there was the sound of a siren going up the highway, hidden behind the trees. From a point on the lawn by the kitchen door he could see tiny figures in yellow raincoats dragging hoses up the hill. A helicopter went by over the column of smoke, coughing a shower of reddish sputum that seemed to evaporate even before it reached the ground. The light wind was from the sea, and the fire was creeping slowly up the hill, following the course of a canyon and spreading out onto a ridge above. There was no danger to the houses in Orange Bay, as far as he could see. The wind would have to change, and the fire would have to cross the highway. It was still a long way away. That was what you paid firemen for. He watched the moving yellow figures for a while and went back into the house.

At seven he had dinner with Velda and Peter as usual. Velda chattered away about the dish she had fixed for dinner and all the things she had put into it. "I got it out of two cookbooks. I put the two recipes together." Essentially it was her old macaroni and cheese baked in a mold and turned out in a pastry crust. When she finished rambling on about this she went on to quiz Peter about what was happening in school. She never left an interval of ten seconds without finding something to say.

None of them mentioned the fire, which seemed odd to Harry, because the cinnamonlike smell was clearly detectable in the house. Or it was an odor like apple pie. Or it was like the pieces of crust that fall from the pie tin and burn in the oven. These culinary images occurred to Harry because of Velda's prattling on about the cooking. The three of them seemed to have entered into a conspiracy about the brush fire. If neither of the others would mention it, he was damned if he would.

About eight o'clock, as they were finishing dinner, the wind changed and began blowing from the northeast, down from the hills toward the sea. There was a new force to it; it hummed in the trees around the house. It was a dry wind, a santana, driving away the sea mist and making the air crisp and astringent. Without saying anything to the others, Harry went out onto the lawn again and saw a haze of moving sparks on the ridge, sifting up and falling down slowly toward the highway. It seemed to him that the center of the fire was a little up the coast from Orange Bay, so that if it crossed the highway it would be into the heron sanctuary and the open bluffs along the sea and not into the houses.

After watching it for a while he went down the lawn and started up the road toward the Fangs' house. It was dark now. The wind was warm, and he was wearing only a shirt and a pair of slacks. He still had on the old slippers he wore around the house, and he was sockless, a habit he had picked up from Golo. After he passed the Fangs'—the house looked empty, and there was only a single light burning in Henry's study—he mounted up the curving road through the hollow, past a house where people were standing out on their lawn looking at the pink glow across the highway. He couldn't hear what they were saying but the tone of their voices was blasé, amused, as though the fire was something entertaining that had brought them out of their houses onto the lawn to look, rather than a danger to them.

At the end of the road there was a thick row of junipers, with a chain-link fence behind them that marked the limits of Orange Bay and the beginning of the heron sanctuary. Pushing through the branches, he stopped and laced his fingers into the wire of the fence. From here he could see the fire clearly for the first time. It shed a pinkish glow over the hills, and it sent up slow spirals of sparks that hissed out now and then with a greater intensity. As he watched, the flames vomited in a new place up on the hill, closer to him, illuminating his hands clutching the fence and staining the sea pink on his left. Directly in front of him, through the fence, small red flares appared in the branches of the eucalyptus and dropped embers to the ground. For the first time he could hear the fire, a crackle like bacon frying. The eucalyptus grove, dark only a moment before, was filled now with a thin pink phosphorescence. Over his head there was a fluster and a rush; the shadows of two herons, then another, rose up out of the trees and floated noiselessly down toward the sea. Now he saw that others were leaving the trees and undulating away in slow motion, without a sound, until the air was full of large silent clumsy shapes circling through the darkness, weaving past the branches, passing like wraiths through the night air over his head, now flapping slowly, now gliding, visible in the thin pinkish light that seeped through the trees. There was no sound but the insistent and lazy, almost meditative, crepitation of the fire.

Harry turned and went back down the road, forcing himself not to run, going on at a walking pace. He ought to go back to his house and turn the hose on his roof, but for some reason he couldn't take this duty seriously. There was something else on his mind, preoccupying him; it was about the fire, but it wasn't the danger to his house. As he passed the house in the hollow, the same people were still out on the lawn, chattering in the same tone, amused and bantering. Some of them, he saw, were holding drinks while they watched the fire. He lifted his hand to them, and they waved back. Then he broke into a run.

Since Velda had become his lover (an odd term to apply to it; it hadn't occurred to him before), he was the victim of a compulsion he had never known before in his life: the need to know where someone else was at all times. He hadn't felt this for Killian at all. They were companions, friends of the opposite sex, and their love was most typical not when they were in bed but when they were walking together on the beach without speaking, or at dinner with a candle on the table, or when he simply admired her from across the room as an expensive and valuable possession. When they were apart they had gone their separate ways and not worried about each other. His desire for Velda (love was not the word for it) was like a kind of madness. When he needed her he had to have her immediately, or he was flung into the pangs of a most exquisite torture. When she was not in his immediate presence, he needed to know where she was at every moment. He was never really comfortable when she was out in her car shopping in Playa del Mar or on the freeway going to the city; he imagined a careening oil truck out of control, a crazed rapist who appeared out of the dark when she had a flat tire, a tree falling on her, some other vague disaster that was all the more vivid and piercing for being unknown. None of these things would really happen. They were simply expressions of his sexual need for her. But this intelligent thought didn't help. She dominated his thoughts at every moment, as Killian never had. In the secret cupboard of his obsession, she had replaced Killian. Now the incubus that dogged him night and day was not a ghost but a creature of flesh and blood. The fire drove this anxiety out of his secret thoughts into his very nerve ends. He passed the flat bulk of the Fangs' roof, outlined now in orange, and loped up the lawn to his house.

In the kitchen he stopped and found that he was panting. Everything was exactly as usual. The dinner dishes were

washed and put away, and the coffeemaker was filled, ready
for breakfast in the morning. There was no sign of Velda.
Her car was standing in front of the house in its usual place.
In the dining room the vase of flowers had been put back on
the polished table, with a shawl under it. His book was set
out on the table by his chair; next to Velda's chair was a
magazine. He looked into the patio, where the smell of fire
hung in the air, remembering the other fire, where he had
first lost his wits over her. The laundry, the study, the
garage.

He went upstairs, taking the steps two at a time. He half
imagined that he would find her in bed, although it was only
nine o'clock. This idea excited him, in a way that trampled
over his reason and his emotions. If he had found her in bed,
with the idea of enticing him into making love with the pink
light of the fire filtering through the shutters, he would
quickly have fallen. She was not in the bedroom. The bed
was neatly made up, with the checkerboard spread pulled up
over the pillows. After a moment he saw that Solange was
curled up on Velda's side of the bed. He had never seen the
cat there before. In his feverish state of mind, he wondered
if this was somehow significant and would give him some
clue as to where Velda had gone. He looked in the bathroom,
even opening the glass door of the shower to look in the stall,
and hurriedly checked her closet. Which of her clothes were
gone? He didn't remember them well enough to tell. He
couldn't remember what she had been wearing at dinner.

Peter's door was shut, with a bar of light showing under
it. He thought of knocking on the door to see if he knew
where Velda had gone, but he was unwilling to reveal his
anxiety to him so obviously. He imagined Peter at his desk
doing his schoolwork, a boy calmly studying French poetry
or calculating probabilities and entering them in a notebook
while the world took fire around him. He would push the
door open. Peter would enter something in his notebook and
look up.

Have you seen Velda?
Isn't she in the house?

No.

Maybe she's gone to the neighbors.

Who?

I don't know. Maybe the Gilberts.

Why would she do that?

Peter would stare at him. *To borrow a cup of sugar.*

He stood at the door for another moment. There was no sound from inside. He went downstairs and left the house again, still in his thin shirt and slippers. At the Gilberts' he stole up the path and walked around the house through the herbaceous borders and onto the terrace.

Wolfie and Dawn were out on the terrace having their after-dinner coffee. The old lady, Wolfie's mother, was curled up in a chaise longue, holding the coffee cup like a chalice on her chest.

"Hullo, Harry. Short time no see. Just yesterday, I think."

They looked at his slippers. Neither Wolfie nor Dawn got up, nor did they offer him coffee. Perhaps they detected the air of urgency that he was doing his best to conceal.

"What do you think about the fire?"

"Oh, we've gone to look at it. It doesn't seem to be doing much."

"It's across the highway into the sanctuary now," Harry told them.

"Are you going to hose down your roof?"

"What about you?"

"Oh, ours is tile," said Wolfie.

"You haven't seen Velda, have you?"

"She hasn't been here. Do you mean when we were out looking at the fire?"

"No, I mean here."

"Was she *supposed* to be here?" inquired Dawn brightly.

The old lady spoke up unexpectedly. "I saw her. She came here. We had quite a talk."

"No you didn't, Mama," said Wolfie genially. "You've never met her."

"We talked about how good-looking Harry is." The old woman gazed at him now with a particular intensity.

"You just imagined that, Grace," Dawn told her. "Although Harry *is* very good-looking. You probably heard us talking about it."

"You talk about my good looks when I'm not here?"

"They never tell me anything," said Grace.

"Velda's not at your place, you say?" Wolfie asked him.

"She may have come back. I'd better go and see. In any case, I ought to hose down the roof."

"Yours is shakes. Bad stuff," said Wolfie, still perfectly cheerful.

Grace said, "She was wearing her Mind Song."

"Her what?"

"It's a thing that she wears on her head. It makes music for her."

"Don't talk nonsense, Mama."

"I just thought she might be here."

Harry left the terrace like a Chinese courtier, backing away until he was out of sight and then hurrying down the path.

He loped down through the small canyon and came out in the park. It was deserted. Probably everyone was away at the top of the hill, watching the fire. There was nobody but a dog sitting on the grass in the lamplight, watching him as he passed. He went on and vaulted over the low seawall onto the beach.

There was no sign of anyone here either. From the rocks at the edge of the beach he could see the fire a little way up the coast, burning down through the heron sanctuary to the sea. A red glow reflected from the undersides of the clouds, and the white lines of surf moving in across the sea were tinged with pink. He was too far from the fire to be able to hear it; the only sound was the crushing of the waves as they foamed around the rocks and the soft hiss as they withdrew. He stood for a moment staring out at the dark horizon. He could see nothing because of the light behind him. To a watcher out at sea, he thought, he would be a black silhouette outlined in the glow from the fire.

"Harry!"

Startled, he stared out to sea. The thin transparent voice seemed to come from a point in the dark a little to his left. The bands of white surf moved evenly in toward him, and beyond that was blackness. He could barely make out the line where the sea ended and the dark sky began. His heart pounded.

"Harry!"

"Harry!"

The voice seemed a little fainter each time, as though it were losing strength. It was thin and plaintive, yet somehow pert, free of fear, with an upswing on the end, a voice that in its tone *expected* that he would know what to do, that he would prevail over the situation with his wisdom and his superior strength, that there was no reason to panic as long as he was there and heard. He couldn't decide if it was Velda's voice or not. It was unmistakably feminine and youthful; it resembled her voice, and yet it was distorted by distance and by the effort of yelling.

"Harr-ee!"

He kicked away his slippers, threw off his shirt and pants, and plunged into the sea. The chill hit him like a blow. At first he stumbled in the shallow water, splaying out his hands as the breaking waves surged over him. Then his feet left the bottom and he was swimming. He tried to orient himself by looking over his shoulder at the land behind him. From the beach, each time he heard the voice it had been a little farther to the left, as though it was drifting down the coast with the current. A breaking wave, a large one, smashed over him. He struggled aimlessly under water for a few seconds; when he came up he was outside the surfline. The sea rose and fell under him like a slowly breathing animal. When he swam on his back for a moment he could clearly see the fire, which had crept down the bluff under the knees of the eucalyptus and stopped at the edge of the sea.

He rolled over, put his face in the water again, and doggedly forced one arm and then the other through the black liquid, which seemed to grow heavier by the minute. He was not a strong swimmer. His underpants slipped down from his waist and impeded the motion of his legs; he kicked them off and they sank away into the dark water under him.

He didn't hear the voice again. The sea was empty and dark; only the necklace of lights along the coast behind him reassured him that he was still in a world of people, of fellow intelligences, of houses, rooms, and warm beds. He went on swimming in the direction he thought the voice had come from. After what seemed to him a long time he stopped and circled. If the voice belonged to a swimmer in difficulty, surely she would call again, or splash to attract attention (he imagined the small fire-colored flutter in the darkness), or do something that would lead him to her. She would not simply sink under the water without a sound. And the voice, as he tried to reconstruct it in his fatigued mind, had not really been a call for help; it had a lilt at the end, a playful note, that seemed to say *come and join me.* He was not sure now that he had heard it at all, that there had really been a voice, that it had called his name. Over the sound of the sea, muffled by the night, he had perhaps misheard. It might have been someone calling from another point on the beach; the sound might have been bent by the cliffs. Or it could have been a voice from his own imagination, where odd things had been happening lately. It might have been the voice of the sea, luring him to his death. He became aware now that the current had moved him steadily down the coast as he swam. The cove with its small beach was no longer directly inshore from him; instead he was facing the headland that sheltered Orange Cove on the south. Farther along, down the coast, he could see the lights of Playa del Mar against the loom of the hills.

Harry decided that the voice was imaginary and that it was he who was in danger now, not Velda or some other person. He swam against the current for a while but exhausted himself and made no progress; the small headland was still in the same place. Treading water for a moment to recover his breath, he began swimming directly toward the point.

After another ten minutes it seemed to him that the point of land was still the same distance away but was moving by to his left. Then he saw that, trying to keep the point ahead of him, he had been drifting in a long curve around it. There was something different on the sea ahead, a dim white band with lights behind it. Fatigue gripped his limbs like bands of iron. He gasped in the rhythm of his arm strokes. His fluttering ankles ached; when he stopped, his legs sank in the water, and it was an almost insuperable effort to raise them again. In the exertion of swimming he hadn't been aware of the coldness of the water for a while, but now the icy numbness sank in to his bones. The headland was behind him now; the white beach with its lights was ahead. It was still a long distance away, too far for him to reach, he thought. He swam with greater difficulty and without opening his eyes to see where he was; he stared into the blackness inside his lids, turning his head up now and then to grasp a mouthful of air. He felt the wash of a wave over his back and a lift that pulled him forward; then another. He lowered his feet to reach for the sand, but it wasn't there and he sank under, pulling himself to the surface again only with the effort of desperation. He went on swimming weakly, his face in the water, until his knees bumped against the sandy bottom. He half swam, half crawled until he came to the last foaming plate of surf, and there he lay on the wet sand and panted. The pain stabbed in his lungs, and his arms and legs felt as though they were paralyzed. He did not have the strength to raise his head.

When he was able to push himself up from the sand, he saw that he had come ashore at the north end of the Playa del Mar beach, a half mile or so from the town. Behind him was the rocky point he had swum for and missed. The beach was deserted. He could see cars passing on the highway, and the lights of the town, with the white bulk of the hotel in its center. The beach ended a little to his left, at the feet of a sandstone cliff draped in iceplant. He managed to make the effort to stand up, and moving still with his hands touching the sand like an orangutan, he reached the shelter of the cliff, where its shadow hid him from the lights of the town.

He had changed his mind about the voice. He was pretty sure now it came from Velda. It might have been only a hallucination, but if it didn't come from the real Velda, it came from a Velda inside his head. He had to find out; the doubt in his mind was like the sharp pain in his lungs. Meanwhile he was naked, cold, and exhausted. His obsession with knowing whether the voice had been Velda's merged with an enormous desire to be home inside the shelter of his own house.

The entrance to Orange Bay was only a mile up the highway. If he ran he could be there in a few minutes. But this would entail running along the highway in the head-lights of the cars. He set out to climb the sandstone cliff. The soft stone crumbled under his fingers; he wedged his foot into a crevice and pushed upward. Twice he fell and had to start over. When he got into the iceplant it was easier; he pulled himself up with the soft slimy ropes that broke in his hands and seeped a sticky fluid onto his body. At the top of the cliff there were more lights, a small café with tables outside it, and beyond it houses with lighted windows.

Luckily there was nobody sitting at the tables outside the café. Inside he could see a waitress moving behind the curtain and the silhouetted heads of people at the tables. Staying behind the shrubbery as well as he could, he stole along past the café and into the suburban street.

Almost immediately he met a middle-aged gentleman walking his dog. He was portly, with a mustache and a tweed jacket with patches, and his dog was a doberman. Harry ran by them without turning his head. Out of the corner of his eye he was aware of man and dog turning like two search-lights to watch him pass. He dodged on down the street, at-tempting to stay behind trees and in the cover of hedges as much as he could. In spite of his exertion he shivered with cold. He was in a maze of curving streets intersecting at various angles. He lost his way once and found himself in the same street he had passed before, going back toward the café. The houses were all alike, and the cloudy sky hid the stars and moon. He guided himself by the sound of the highway on his right and occasional glimpses of cars through the bushes. At one house he attracted the attention of a face looking out from a window; he ran on. He crossed the street in the full light of the streetlamp and disappeared into the bushes on the other side. The sensible thing, he thought, would be to ring at the door of a house and tell them that Velda had drowned, that someone had drowned, that he himself had lost his clothes and was suffering from hallucinations, or simply to present himself in his obvious predicament and leave it to someone else to decide what to do. He would hardly be arrested for indecency if he told frankly what had happened, exactly as it had happened. *I thought I heard a voice from the sea . . .* He ran on down the street, ducking under the shadow of a large oak with low-lying branches and narrowly missing its trunk, and came to the last of the houses. Beyond this was a stretch of open country, chaparral with scattered pines, and on the other side of it was Orange Bay.

With the houses behind, it was dark except for the headlights of the cars on the highway to his right. He blundered his way along through the scratchy brush, fending it out of the way with his hands, and came to the chain-link fence. There he stopped, panting. Through the trees he could see the lighted entrance kiosk across the highway, with the guard sitting in it like a doll in a dollhouse. As he watched, a car passed through the gate, waved on by the guard, ascended the short slope, made an abrupt turn into the tunnel under the highway, and appeared a moment later directly in front of him, on the road that wound its way through the eucalyptus grove with its scattered houses. He crouched low in the brush as the headlights passed.

When the glare was gone he turned his attention to the fence. As well as he could tell by feeling in the dark, it was a tough chain-link fence of heavy wire, supported by galvanized-iron posts set in concrete. It was possible to fit his bare toes into the diamond-shaped openings, although this was painful. He climbed a foot or two and found that there was a coil of razor wire along the top; he explored it with his fingers, but he could hardly touch it without cutting himself. They certainly didn't make it easy for cold, naked people without identification to get into this place. As an alternative, he imagined himself crossing the highway in the stream of headlights and explaining himself to the guard with gesticulations, pointing to the sea, to the fence, and to his own unclothed state. In a single hour he had become one of the excluded, the people for whom the fence and the kiosk had been erected. Getting over the razor wire was only a matter of a little pain, he thought. Other people did things like that all the time. It was probably not half as bad as bearing a child. He reached the top of the fence and tested the razor wire gingerly with his hands. After some hesitation he lowered his chest onto the wire and rolled himself over. He felt a shock of many little stabbing pains, which he ignored. As he went on, the razor wire cut his legs now and then, but he kept his private parts carefully away from it. Once he was over the top, it was easier going down the other side. He dropped to the ground. His chest and the fronts of his legs stung as though they had been attacked by pygmy swordsmen. Stupefied and a little giddy from pain, he limped away in the dark toward the backs of the houses.

If he stayed in backyards and made as little noise as possible, it wasn't likely that anyone would notice him at this time of night. He crossed from garden to garden behind the houses, squeezing through hedges and climbing fences. After five or six yards he came to a house, where he heard people talking in the garden in the rear. He thought it was the Maccabees. They were young people who had no children and did a lot of entertaining. He crept along the hedge to the front of the house, where he found the cars of the guests on the road and the garage door open. He ducked into the garage; it was almost pitch dark inside, except for the lights from the windows of the houses across the road.

There were two cars in the garage, the nearer one a black

Jaguar. As his eyes adjusted, he made out other objects: gardening tools, a trash barrel on a dolly, a pair of skis, yellow-and-blue sailbags from a boat. Hanging on a hook at the front of the Jaguar was an old raincoat. He slipped it on, feeling a warm slime on his chest as he fastened it. He could smell the blood now that he was standing quietly in the dark. Shuddering from the cold, he left the shelter of the garage and stole cautiously up the road. The rough pavement was painful; he suspected that he had cut the soles of his feet climbing over the fence. He came at last to his own house. From the lawn he could see that the fire in the hills was almost out; a few orange pinpoints glowed here and there, illuminating the pall of smoke that still clung over the highway.

He entered the house through the kitchen door. The lights were on in the kitchen and the living room, as they had been when he left, although there was no one downstairs. He saw that he was leaving tracks of blood on the kitchen floor and turned around to look; the prints made a curious effect, like the steps left by the criminal in a drawing of a crime.

He went upstairs, leaving more red tracks on the carpeted steps. Peter's door was still closed, with a bar of light under it. The door to the bedroom was open. He went in and found Velda in the bathroom in a dressing gown, brushing her stubbly crinkly hair. There was a damp towel on the floor at her feet.

"Why is your hair wet?"

She turned to look at him over her shoulder. She scarcely seemed to notice his bizarre garment or the blood on his body.

"I've been taking a shower."

"Where were you earlier?"

"When?"

"A couple of hours ago. I looked for you, but I couldn't find you."

"I stepped out to look at the fire."

"Where?"

"On the back lawn."

"You haven't been to the beach?"

"Of course not. I told you I was looking at the fire."

He didn't know whether to believe her or not. He knew that she had swum in the sea the night after the party at the Gilberts', because he had peered out through the crack of the bedroom door and seen her come back in her wet clothes. He didn't know where she had gone or what she had done, either that night or this one, and he didn't know what she was thinking now. The idea that we "possess" a woman by taking her to bed seemed to him one of the greatest naïvetés of the male sex. The fear and terror he had felt when he was searching for her in the sea turned to anger. And then, as he pierced through the dressing gown to imagine the form underneath, the classic Greek *kore* with swelling hips, narrow bosom, sloping shoulders, grooved nape of neck, the anger was swept away in his awareness of the preciousness of this creature he had somehow enticed into his house, into his bed. His anger dissolved and was replaced by a vast fear of saying or doing anything that might alienate or anger her, that might drive her from his presence even for a moment, even into another room. And yet he still felt traces of the old hostility, if it was not she, then it was her ghost, her projected voice, her perverse and crudely complicated willpower that had somehow bewitched him into enacting this humiliating and painful farce. He took off the raincoat and dropped it on the floor. For the first time she turned from the mirror and looked at him directly.

"You'd better take a shower too if you expect to go to bed with me," she told him.

thirteen

Y ou say she has no eyebrows?"

"They're growing back in now. For a while she drew them in with a pencil."

"And how did it happen?"

"I don't know. She said she was lighting the oven and it blew up."

"Do you think that's what happened?"

"The oven is electric."

"Then what do you think happened?"

Peter had an explanation that was really only a childish and silly one, a kind of picture in his head, in which Velda's missing eyebrows and frizzled hair were connected with the fact that from the time it happened she had moved into Harry's room and shared his bed, thus taking the place of his mother, which Harry had promised him she would never do. In various societies, as he knew from his reading, they practiced different rites of defloration. It wasn't a question of Velda being deflowered, of course; still, the changes in her eyebrows and hair were connected in some way with the change in living arrangements and her admission into a special and private place in the house, in the life of Harry, into which Peter was not admitted. The fire that had touched her was in some way a *rite de passage*. This was a totally crazy idea and not a correct explanation of the facts, as he knew very well, and he had no intention of telling Henry Fang about it. Yet he couldn't get the picture out of his head. He saw Harry and Velda sitting on the bed and Harry burning off her eyebrows with the little blue flame of a cigarette lighter, while she sat perfectly still in the lotus position. In this picture, they were both naked and Harry had an erection, which was ritual rather than physical; he was caparisoned with the hieratic trappings of Priapus, and she was crowned with a wreath of leaves and draped with garlands. Peter banished this from his mind and came back to the present scene.

Henry Fang was sitting as usual at the table in the large room at the front of the house. The notebook was open at his elbow, with a fountain pen lying on it, but for the moment he didn't write in it. He leaned back and contemplated Peter with interest. Peter was in the big black lacquer armchair facing the table; he was wearing a white shirt, faded jeans, and loafers. It was dark outside, and the only light came from the reading lamp on the table. From the windows, which faced west toward the sea, there was a dim reflected glow of the fire from the hills behind the house.

Henry Fang smiled. "And now, you say, she sleeps in his room?"

"I didn't say that. You asked me if it was true."

"And is it?"

"The door is shut. I don't know what goes on in there."

"But surely you can see her going in and out."

"I keep my own door shut. I don't pay attention to such things."

Henry Fang reflected. "It's curious that this business of the eyebrows and her moving into his room took place at about the same time. Surely they're connected."

Peter said nothing. He rankled a little, in his secret mind, against Henry Fang's probing him in this lightly mocking, playful way to reveal the secrets of Harry's life. When he did this, Peter felt a smoldering loyalty to his father and regarded Henry Fang as an antagonist who needed to be dealt with skillfully and warily. But in other ways his father was the antagonist. Henry Fang was a strange kind of surrogate father, one who saw deeper into him than Harry did. He saw things that Peter knew were there, even though he didn't want to admit it even to himself. He would have to decide in time, he thought, which father he wanted to have. He couldn't have both of them. Perhaps he could get along without either. He had two impulses: one to be loved, to have a companion, a friend; the other to be independent.

"Maybe," said Henry Fang, "she burned her eyebrows in an accident, and he felt sorry for her and took her to bed. Or he might have been applying some unguent to her burns and got carried away. Or maybe she burned herself deliberately to get his sympathy. Many women would like to go to bed with Harry. He's a very good-looking man." Here he paused and smiled at Peter, bringing to bear his mask of benevolent wisdom. "And you will be too, in time."

"Everybody tells me that. I'm getting tired of hearing it."

"Would you rather be ugly?"

"I'd rather be nobody. I'd rather that people left me alone. I'd like to be invisible, so that I could pass through the world and go wherever I wanted and see everything, but nobody would notice me."

"Maybe you will change your mind when you become a man and find ways of using your good looks to get things that you want."

"I have everything I want now."

"Perhaps you are already a man," Henry Fang offered suggestively.

"I don't know what you mean."

"When you become one, life will tell you so in unmistakable ways."

Peter met his glance steadily without replying.

"And has it yet?"

"I'm just myself. Nothing has happened. I'm thirteen years old. I'm like the other boys at school."

"You know, you're not very candid, Peter. You're not very honest with me. You come here night and day and make yourself at home, just as though you were a relative or a member of the household; Mary gives you tea, I let you watch my valuable collection of videos, and yet you won't tell me anything about yourself. You won't tell me what's happening in your secret life. You won't tell me what's happening in your house." He seemed perfectly genial, as though this were an amusing story he was telling. "I thought you were my friend. If you were my friend, I could help you in many ways. I could tell you about things you have not even discovered or thought of yet, things that are very beautiful."

Here he paused and seemed to reflect on what to say next. "You see, these things that are happening in your house are bound to make things difficult for you. You've lost your mother, and now you lack a father too. Harry is preoccupied with other things. It's very unfortunate for you. These things are not your fault, and yet you suffer from them. You have a great deal of talent and many other valuable attributes."

It was clear that he was about to make another reference to Peter's good looks; when he saw Peter's annoyance, he passed on quickly to another subject.

"Ah, by the way. I had forgotten. Our habitual *cérémonie de fumerie,* our little vice. Since you are a man now, perhaps you would like a man's cigarette."

"A Gauloise."

"No, not a Gauloise. Those are for *poseurs.* Francophiles. People who use French phrases." Peter thought, He smokes Gauloises himself. But Henry Fang, anticipating him, said with his confidential smile, "I too pose for you, Peter. Everyone poses."

From the drawer of the table he drew an enameled tin box of Turkish tobacco with a maiden in houri costume on the lid, a pack of cigarette papers, and a miniature glass cruet with a stopper. Setting out two cigarette papers on the table, he shook the tobacco carefully into them and spread it around with his finger. In the cruet, which was no bigger than his thumb, was a brownish fluid with an oily consistency. He looked at Peter narrowly. With the stopper he applied a drop or two of the oil to the tobacco on the papers.

"What is that?"

"Just a little flavoring."

Without taking his eyes off Peter, he rolled the cigarettes up and sealed them with his tongue. He passed one to Peter and lit them both.

He went on. "Things are difficult for you just now at home. I can't defend Harry's conduct. Still, it's very human. That is what you have not learned yet, Peter, what it is to be human. You judge people too severely. You live a life of privilege. You imagine that you are invulnerable to the troubles that come inevitably to all men. All people. All human beings." He corrected himself with the precision of a stylist.

"The human condition. I've read all about it. Camus, Pascal, *Oedipus*. Aristotle on tragedy."

"Books." Henry Fang smiled. *"La vie est autre chose.* Life is what is not art, art is what is not life. Yet the relation between life and art is very complex."

The cigarette was strong and sweet; it had an oily taste. Peter coughed. This made him blush; he set the cigarette in the ashtray, leaned back in the chair, and coughed once or twice more.

Henry Fang, gazing at him placidly, wrote something in his book. Peter could imagine what it was. *Peter de Spain came to see me again tonight. He is reticent about the secrets of his house, but he is angry at his father. I gave him a new kind of cigarette, one for men, and when he smoked it he coughed.* Peter picked up the cigarette and drew on it again, more carefully. No more coughs. The smoke coated the inside of his mouth and gave it a medicinal taste like camphor. His body began to buzz.

"I have some new videos," said Henry Fang, looking up from his book. "Some you haven't seen."

"It doesn't make any difference. They're all the same. People do the same things."

"These aren't. These are different."

"They all end the same way."

"That's because the thing they depict always ends the same way. But some people find it interesting."

"The people in the videos aren't real people. They're only actors. They only do things that are done in other videos, not in real life."

"How can you know?"

Their eyes met, and the old man almost laughed at him. Peter smiled too.

"Nature copies art. Didn't they teach you that in school? If things appear in art, then sooner or later they will appear in the real world too." The old man seemed to be enjoying himself. "Your father is telling himself a story about a governess. And now it is coming to life."

"I don't know what you mean."

"Yes you do. You don't want to understand. You don't want to believe it. But the story is coming true."

"What story?"

"*Jane Eyre*, perhaps. The mad wife in the attic upstairs. But the wife is upstairs in his head, and it is he who is going mad."

"Harry is not mad."

"He has just lost his head a little, let's say."

"I don't care to talk to you about Harry. He's my father. What happens at our house is our business."

"Just as you like. Look on the right end of the shelf. The new ones are in yellow boxes."

Peter selected *A Spartan Idyll*, took it out of its yellow box, and slipped it into the VCR. Then he settled into the armchair to watch. The screen made its usual flicks and flutters, then it steadied and a picture appeared, in slightly exaggerated color. Boys his age or a little older were sitting on the steps of a marble temple, clad in short tunics that left one shoulder bare. Behind them was an olive grove and a peasant with a donkey. An older boy seemed to be in charge, or to be their leader. He had a shock of reddish-blond hair, and his skin was as pale as the marble of the temple. When

he leaned forward to speak to the others his tunic fell open
to reveal his muscled chest. Unlike the voices in the other
videos, which were reedy and scratchy, these were as clear as
though they were the voices of real people.

If we wish to be Spartans, we must be brave.

And what does it mean to be brave?

Brave in battle. Generous. Loving. Loyal to one's com-
panions.

To be brave is to love?

Love is the greatest bravery.

The older boy struck one of the others playfully. The
two rose and wrestled. A man of fifty appeared in the background. Instead of the short tunic he wore a longer toga that
covered his body but left his arms free. He had a short beard,
but his hair was clipped in the back to leave his nape bare.

Phidias, you will do well. You will be a general. One
day you may be our king.

Peter took a drag from the cigarette and set it back in
the ashtray. His body was filled with a pleasant swarm of
warmth; he floated a little above the seat of the chair, his
arms not touching it either.

On the screen the napes of all the boys were shaved. As
the two boys wrestled, the tendons of Phidias' neck swelled
like two columns of a temple, with a shadow in the groove
between them. He threw the other boy to the ground and
pinned his arms. The tunic of the fallen boy rose up his legs,
offering a brief glimpse of the rosebud in his hairless groin.

You have won, Phidias! Now, generosity to the de-
feated! You must offer him the kiss of the conqueror.

The two boys embraced. The bearded man laughed,
noticing the swelling in the front of Phidias' tunic.

A true Spartan is never without his sword.

There was a noise in the room, the sound of a door
opening and a rustle. Peter imagined it was Mary coming in
with his tea; instead, when he glanced around he saw it was
Henry Fang himself, a shadowy figure in his brocaded robe,
still smoking the stub of his cigarette. Driven by some cur-

rent of air, perhaps from the opened door, the smoke sifted around the room and sank down slowly in front of Peter's chair, hanging like a thin veil between him and the video.

On the screen, the bearded man sat on the steps of the temple with his hand on the knee of the boy next to him.

As you have said, Phidias, a Spartan is brave and loyal to his companions. And to be brave is to be clean. In our country, we do not bathe in water, which washes away our manhood and weakens the body. We anoint ourselves with oil, and then we scrape ourselves with fine implements made of ivory.

He stood up and slipped off his toga, facing away so that he was seen at an angle from the rear. Unlike the bodies of the boys, his body was brown except for a paler zone around his groin and buttocks. The boys disrobed too. A younger boy produced a ceremonial vase, an amphora decorated with scenes of athletic contests.

Take, Leonidas. The rare scented oil.

Henry Fang did not appear to be watching the video. Standing behind Peter, he smoked and talked in a low tone, ignoring the voices from the screen, which sometimes almost drowned out his own. "The mystery of age. The last of all mysteries, the most devious and reticent, the one that reveals its secret only at the end. At first I took old age for a reflection of myself, an alter ego, a Rembrandt self-portrait, one that gradually grew older along with me. One that would counsel and console me as the years went by. Then I saw that it was an implacable and relentless enemy. Now in the morning I wake up and think for a few minutes that all this may be a mistake, an illusion, an illness from which I'm about to recover. That I'll walk around on the earth again with the young body that I still remember. That I will make love to women, deal in millions, write books, and travel to Tibet and Patagonia. Then I wake up fully, and I know that it's the same. I'm myself, and I'm an old man."

Peter scarcely heard the voice behind him. He watched the screen detachedly, with a mixture of fascinated interest and repulsion. He felt as though insects were crawling on his body, or as though he himself were an insect stirring and on the point of crawling upward.

Leonidas poured the oil from the amphora into the boys' hands. They separated into pairs, and one boy rubbed the oil into the other, beginning with the head, the neck, and the throat and continuing down the chest and legs. When he was finished the process was reversed, and his partner anointed his body. The bearded man spoke to them.

This is the finest pressing of our groves, sacred to Adonis and scented with myrrh.

And you, Leonidas?

Formerly it was your hands that cleansed and purified me, Phidias. Now you are a man, and it is for you to instruct another in the rite. As for me, I will select the youngest of your friends.

Phidias and another boy anointed each other and began scraping away the oil with ivory implements, and Leonidas selected the youngest of the boys. Drawing him close with gentle fingers, he applied the oil with long, slow strokes to his chest. The boy stood solemnly while Leonidas rubbed it into every corner of his body. Then Leonidas took the ivory knife, like a comb without teeth and curved to fit the body, and passed it down the boy's neck, his arms, his chest, and his legs. A golden film of oil curved away under the blade, leaving the skin behind it pale and glowing.

Now, Adonais, you must do the same for me.

The boy began rubbing the oil into the body of Leonidas.

Henry Fang reached around Peter to crush out his cigarette in the ashtray. A small wisp of smoke curled up from it into the still air. His arm disappeared again.

"I am reminded by these classical scenes of a painting I love every much. On the porch of a temple in the antique world, an adolescent girl is on the point of waking from sleep. She is lying on her back, with one knee raised and her hand resting on her brow to shield her eyes from the rising sun. The other arm is curved about her head. There is a simple Doric column at one side, an inland sea, and craggy mountains in the background, dimmed by the fine mist of morning. The violet shadows are just beginning to be gilded by the sun's rays. The branches of flowering trees overhang the porch. Bending over the adolescent, with his hands on his knees, is a naked child of indescribable beauty, a golden body, soft bronze hair, patrician features. He or she—it is impossible to tell the sex—looks down on the awakening adolescent with a playful and questioning, an affectionate, a placid expression, and she, opening her eyes to find him watching, smiles with a blush. The two children are of a beauty more than human, and their souls are as refined and pure as those of the classic gods. For the adolescent, to be awakened by the naked child, under the flowers on the porch, in the violet and golden light, is the consummation of the heart's bliss, pure and unalloyed happiness, the final sublimation of the sensual into the rapture of the soul. The picture is called 'Daybreak,' and it is by Maxfield Parrish. It was painted in the time of my youth. I have a reproduction of it somewhere. I ought to look for it. I believe that Mary may have put it away."

As he stopped, the voice on the screen spoke again.

Take, Adonais, and purify my body as I have purified yours.

The older man handed the ivory knife to the boy, and he began scraping the oil from his body with the sacred instrument. Leonidas raised his arms to allow the knife to pass down his sides. His armpits were as clean and complex as pale seashells. The rest of his body too was hairless, except for the short beard, the stiff mane on his head, and the tuft at his genitals. Now and then he helped the boy, showing him how to hold the ivory implement and correcting him when he passed it over the areas of the body in the wrong order.

The chest is the Temple of the Divine Afflatus. The arms are warriors. The abdomen is where Courage dwells.

Adonais finished the ritual cleansing. He handed the ivory knife to Leonidas, who set it down on the porch of the temple next to the decorated amphora. Then, at a sign from

Leonidas, the boy fell to his knees, and his head descended toward the groin of the man. Leonidas remained grave and hieratic. He gazed fixedly at a point in the sky. The other young Spartans had disappeared into the grove of olives. The image on the screen gave way to a logo of olive leaves, then this too faded; there were some white flashes, and the screen went dead.

Henry Fang seemed not to have noticed that the video had ended. "But sometimes I think—I know for certainty in a dream—that the picture by Parrish is not a myth, not a mere fragment of the artist's imagination. It portrays a world that exists, not only in art, but in our minds, and it is a world that we can bring into being. Youth and age exist together, side by side, in the daily fabric of our lives. But we misunderstand one another, we grope in the dark, our eyes are veiled, our bodies trick and betray us. What we desire, the gift of immortality, is lurking there always at the edge of our vision, just beyond our grasp. The frailty of the body, its pains and torments, are as ephemeral as the air we breathe. The shadow that menaces us is as fragile as a nightmare; we need only to awaken in the roseate light of morning, with a Beloved Questioner bending over us, to know the happiness we have groped for in vain in the world, the moment of bliss that obliterates time and becomes eternal. Do you know what I am speaking of, Peter? There is beauty all about us; we fail to see it only because our eyes are blinded by the ephemera of the senses. The Philosopher said that the Good, the True, and the Beautiful are one. He said that we are like creatures bound to a rock in a cave, unable to see things as they are and forced to look only at their shadows on the rock. And how may we free ourselves from those chains, how may we turn and face the light, how may we see things as they really are, how may we pass through the shadow and emerge shining and young, alive, exultant in our knowledge of the One? Through Love, the Philosopher says. Just as the appearances of things are illusions and their true nature can be known only through the Ideal, so are the imperfections and frailties of our bodies illusions, which fall away from us in the true knowledge of Love.''

Now that the sounds from the screen had stopped, his voice was gentle and methodical, with pauses like a walker stopping now and then to reflect on the beauty of the landscape he is passing.

''In Love there is no youth or age, no imperfection or corruption, no sickness or death. The souls are as immaculate as on the first day of the world, the moment of Daybreak. We must trust to Love, we must put our faith in it as the foolish of the world put their trust in images of themselves which they have named gods and elevated to the clouds. In Love each of us may be that adolescent awakening on the porch of the temple with the angelic child bending over her, inviting her to the blissful moment of youth.''

Peter felt the slow and soft touch of the old man's hand on his shoulder. He leaped to his feet and turned, upsetting the chair. Henry Fang had fallen to his knees.

Peter shouted, ''I don't care if you're old! Everybody gets old sometime. I will too someday! You're trying to steal something from me! You're trying to make me old so you will be young!''

''Peter!''

''You're an evil old man! If you weren't, I might do what you want. But you are full of lies and untruth. You lie even to yourself. I've known all along that you were not my friend. When you believed you were deceiving me, it was I who was deceiving you. For a while I was in your power. Now you've touched me, and the charm is broken. I'm free of you. And you too are free. Now you can turn from the Cave and look into the sun. You can see what you really are. An old man whose wits are leaving him. An old man who doesn't want to die. I'm young! That's the only thing worth having, and I'm not going to give any of it to you. You imagine that love is a boy kneeling before you. I know what you want me to do. You don't have to show me the video. They have it all wrong anyhow. I've read about the Spartans in Pausanias. For them love was for warriors, not for senile old men and schoolboys. You think you've tricked me, but you've only tricked yourself."

Henry Fang still knelt on the floor. His eyes were closed. "Peter. Stop."

"You are evil," Peter told him.

He ran from the house, outside into the garden, where the reflection from the fire still glittered in the blood-red flowers of the bougainvillea.

On the beach he flung off his clothes with the agility of a quick-change artist and hid them in a crevice in the rocks. Then he plunged into the water, stamping through the surf with lifted knees. When it reached his shoulders he pushed forward and swam. The water was icy cold and as refreshing as a draft from a forest spring. His body was still humming from the hashish. He swam with twisting motions as though flicking something away from his body, washing away the taint of the video and the old man's touch. He felt good, vigorous, clean; the darkness and the luminescent surf, the pink reflections in the sky, exhilarated him and drove him to a frenzied wish to strive, to tire himself, to kick at the sparkling pinpoints of water that followed his feet and drive them away in silver fountains that sank into the darkness of the sea. He took mouthfuls of water and spewed them out like a porpoise; he buried his head in the water and swam with rapid motions of his arms until his lungs ached and he shot to the surface again. Behind him, up the coast, he could see the fire burning in the heron refuge. He wondered where the herons would go. Out to sea, probably; he imagined them gliding noiselessly in the dark, looking for another eucalyptus grove far out on the water, sinking finally into the sea to drown. The thought of the great birds wandering lost in the air made his heart ache but, paradoxically, in a way that was pleasurable. In this instant everything about him seemed fitting, and proper, natural, vibrant, chill, suffused with energy, sparkling in tiny silver points. The cold sea with its waves that lifted and lowered his body in the slow rhythm of a dance, the lights twinkling on the shore, the pink loom of the fire. Directly inshore was the short stretch of sand between the two rocky points, and above it the lights of the houses. Silhouetted in the glow, a figure in light clothing appeared on the point to the left.

He recognized it instantly as his father, not so much from the details he could make out in the poor light, with the brine stinging in his eyes, but from the stance of the body, the skeptical angle of the head, the nervous alertness that was the mirror image of his own.

He cried out, "Harry!"

In the figure on the rock he saw all at once not a figure of authority, a biblical father whose commands were to be obeyed or evaded, but a friend like himself who had suffered from grief and, seeking solace for it, had fallen under the spell of a tender enemy. He himself had escaped from Henry Fang, but Harry was still in the clutches of another adversary, equally ruthless and far cleverer. He felt a strong impulse to entice his father into the sea, into a bath of innocence that would free him from the taint of his defilement and unite the two of them in this nocturnal adventure.

"Harry!"

"Harry!"

The figure moved down from the rocks onto the sand and turned toward him. If he had any doubts before, he was sure now it was his father. With the passion of a lover he wished for the two of them to be together in the sea.

"Harr-ee!"

He heard his own voice echoing thinly from the cliffs. The figure on the beach bent to do something he couldn't make out in the dark, and when it straightened he saw that it was naked except for a scrap of underwear. It plunged forward into the sea and disappeared. The dark head bobbed up for an instant in the foam, then Peter lost sight of it.

He was beginning to be assailed by confused thoughts now. He had not expected his father to take off his clothes before he came into the sea, but he had not expected him to swim in his clothes either. He had not thought this out. It struck him now that Harry perhaps did not know who he was, that he had simply swum out to sea after a voice. He had made a muddle of it, Peter thought. It was a crazy idea. What did he expect of it, how would it end, when the two of them were united in the dark water offshore? What would they say to each other? *I've saved you from her.* . . . He must have been out of his mind. Peter was seized with an acute embarrassment.

He swam slowly to keep himself in position off the cove, against the current that bore him steadily down to the south. He knew the currents thoroughly; he had observed them from the beach, and he had swum in them many times. Harry didn't seem to be aware of them. When his head surfaced again it was farther out than Peter and drifting slowly south. Peter thought of calling again and decided not to. He swam in a diagonal line across the current until he reached a point inshore of Harry, off the cliff south of the cove. Here under the rocks the current was weaker, or turned in an eddy and flowed back up the coast. Harry was farther offshore, barely visible in the waves that tossed him and hid him from sight. Each time Peter caught sight of him he had drifted a little farther down toward Playa del Mar, the lights of which were visible around the edge of the cliff. Peter saw now that he was moving in weakly toward the Playa del Mar beach. He swam slowly along after him until he was sure his father was close enough to the beach to make it. Then he turned and made his way easily under the rocks, aided by the eddy, until he reached the cove of Orange Bay.

On the beach he retrieved his clothes from the crevice in the rocks and put them on over his wet body. He was not tired at all and only a little cold. Scattered on the sand he saw Harry's own clothes, as though flung off hastily by someone because they were on fire. They looked pitifully small and vulnerable; a pair of rags, here a slipper, there another. Turning to look past the point where his father had disappeared, he changed his mind again. Perhaps he should have swum to meet him in the water. The two of them might have said *something* that would make things different. But he was not quite sure what the thing was that they would have said, or how things would be different after they had said it.

The wind sighed in the trees as he crossed the park. The last sparks of the fire were still glowing in the heron sanctuary; he could smell a trace of smoke in the air, acrid and not unpleasant. The thought struck him that of these two elements, water and fire, water had always been his familiar, but now he was entering into a time when fire too would be his friend, or his adversary. He was not the same person who had set out for Henry Fang's earlier in the evening, leaving the light on in his room so they would not know he was gone. He felt keener, more powerful, invulnerable to the complicated dangers of the world that he had feared so much. If he could not be burnt by fire, if he could not be drowned by water, then the elements of evil were powerless over him.

He entered the house through the unlocked kitchen door. He could hear Velda taking a shower upstairs. Finding that he had left muddy tracks on the floor, he got a paper towel and wiped them up, and threw away the paper in the wastebasket. Then he went upstairs to his room, where he took off his clothes with the fervor of a new convert to nudism. He was in bed with the door shut, reading, when Harry came home.

fourteen

Here are your pants and your shirt and your slippers."

"Where did you find them?"

"I went down to the beach and got them this morning. You came back stark naked and looking as though you'd had a fight with a cat, soaking wet. Where else would they be?"

"You might take the raincoat back to the Maccabees."

"Who are they?"

"The house at the bend of the road, on the way to the kiosk. With the Jaguar in the garage."

"The one with the big tree in front with the red flowers on it?"

"That's right."

"What's the tree called?"

"A coral tree. A naked coral, in case you're interested in botany. Because it flowers before the leaves come out."

"I never know whether to believe you. Did they lend you the raincoat?"

"Just take it back, will you? Tell them you found it in the street."

"If I found it in the street how would I know it was theirs?"

"All right, we'll just throw the raincoat away with the trash."

"All in all it was an eventful night."

"Is the fire out?"

"All the fire engines are gone except one little one. I guess they have to leave a couple of firemen in case it breaks out again."

"No doubt."

The pants and shirt, with the slippers on top of them, were piled on the kitchen counter opposite him so that he had to look at them with every sip of coffee he took. Instead of coming down to breakfast in a dressing gown, he had dressed completely, including shoes and socks, so that no trace of his wounds from the night before was visible. They turned out to be minor scratches anyhow, less serious than he had thought.

She had resurrected the jersey with the fine lines curving around her breasts that she had worn when he first interviewed her. Somehow it didn't look the same. Her body seemed to have contracted and become more svelte since then, as though she had lost some weight. Along with the jersey she wore a flowered skirt, a kind of wraparound sarong. He saw that her skin had begun to peel a little at the points of her cheeks from the touch of the blue flames, exactly as though she had been sunburned. Something, either this or the lines around the jersey, made his desire come back with a rush.

It was only nine o'clock in the morning. Peter had just left for school. His plate and cup were still sitting on the table.

"I thought," she prattled on, "that maybe you were off fighting the fire. But I don't see why you'd have to take off your clothes to do that."

"Do you really want to know?"

"Yes."

"The neighbors formed a bucket brigade to pass up seawater to the fire. I took off my clothes to fill the buckets in the sea, then later I scratched myself in the chaparral, throwing water at the fire."

She looked at him, not smiling.

"You're quite a strange person, Harry. You're much

stranger than I thought you'd be when I first met you. I don't know why a person like you, who has every advantage in the world and is good-looking in the bargain, has to behave so strangely."

"Let's leave my good looks out of it, shall we?"

"When I went out to look at the fire, one of the neighbors said that if the wind changed it might cross the highway and burn the houses."

"It didn't, though. The wind changed and the fire crossed the highway, but it went into the heron refuge instead."

"Weren't you afraid?"

"Afraid?"

"That the house might burn down."

"It's insured. Everything in it is replaceable. Except the paintings, perhaps. We could have carried them out if the fire got closer. Anyhow they're insured too."

"Are they really valuable?"

"The paintings? Of course. They're worth a lot of money."

"How much?"

"An Embry is worth enough to buy a car. A very good car. As a matter of fact," he went on, not understanding why it was necessary for him to explain all this to her, "I don't own the paintings. I take them on consignment from the artists."

She sipped her coffee. From the remains of her breakfast he could see she had had eggs, sausage, and French toast with syrup. It was difficult to see how she could lose weight on this diet. She ate heartily for lunch and dinner too. He had his usual coffee and toast.

"Have you always had a gallery?"

"Before I was married I had a frame shop in Playa del Mar."

"And then you got married?"

"Yes."

"And opened the gallery?"

"That's right."

"How were you suddenly able to open a gallery when you'd only had a frame shop before?"

"Killian had some money. We went into it together."

"You mean it was Killian's gallery too?"

"No; she just helped out with the money."

"And now does the gallery make a lot of money?"

"It's what we live on. I have some investments too."

"Where did the investments come from?"

"Killian had them before she was married."

"Oh."

She seemed to grow very keen and thoughtful at this information.

He said, "Why are we talking about money so much, at breakfast before the day has even started? I don't remember your talking about money before. You never seemed to be interested in it. Suddenly it's all you can talk about."

"Just curious, that's all. We can change the subject if you like. I mean, in some ways I know you very well, but this is a part of you that I don't know anything about. When a person knows a person well, it's funny when you realize that there's another part of his life that you don't know anything about."

"The gallery makes a little money. Not as much as you might think. The rent is high on Paseo. We don't sell an Embry every week. I have to pay Dorothy's salary. Still, we do all right."

"Dorothy?"

"Dorothy Gaspar. She's the manager of the gallery."

"I've never heard you mention her before."

"Surely you have. You've been living here now for four months."

"What's she like?"

"Just a woman. About my age. She's very nice."

"Can I have a look at her sometime?"

"If you want."

"What is your age, Harry?"

He set his coffee cup down. She seemed just the same as always, chatting away about anything that came into her head. She had never asked such questions before, but perhaps she was entitled to them. He was desperately afraid of having a quarrel with her.

"I'm forty-one."

She considered this.

"I would have taken you for older. Or younger, in some ways." A pause. "You know, Harry, I had the wrong idea about you when I first came here. I mean, here is this fabulous house and a Mercedes and a BMW and a private school for Peter and all these things, and I imagined that you made all this money at the gallery. Now it turns out that the money all came from your first wife."

That was a very strange expression. His first wife. Just a slip, probably.

"I wouldn't say that. It takes capital to start up a business. But I've worked hard at it since then."

"You only go to the gallery a couple of hours a day."

"I do a lot of work here at home in the study."

"What is the work you do? I don't understand."

"I look at catalogs and art magazines and keep up with what's going on in the gallery world."

"It seems to me," she said, "that the gallery is a hobby. You couldn't afford it if it weren't for the money you got by marrying *her.*"

She took the breakfast dishes away to the sink. He got up and followed her and slipped his arms around her from behind. Against his body he felt a soft bifurcation.

She turned and looked at him, shaking the water off her hands.

"No, Harry, I don't feel like it. It's not the right time. It's too early in the morning. I've got these old clothes on and I'm ugly. Besides, my breast still hurts where you hit me. Do you remember when you hit me? It was in the bedroom, and we were arguing about clearing out the dresser."

"My elbow hit your chest. It was an accident."

"You were *trying* to hit me. That was the best you could do."

"Why don't you hit me sometime? Then we'll be square."

"Women are not violent."

"Your breast didn't hurt last night."

"That was last night. Once a day is enough, don't you think?"

"Velda, do you really care for me? Tell me what you feel for me."

She looked at him queerly, then she slipped out of his grasp and left the kitchen. He didn't know where she went. Perhaps she had something to do in another part of the house. It was the first time she had refused him. He lingered awhile longer over his coffee, thinking that after her remark about having old clothes on, she had perhaps gone off to put on lingerie or something. But she didn't come back. He felt an ominous little vacuum in his chest. Something was wrong, but he couldn't tell exactly what it was. Something had slipped in the set of gears that held them in their relationship to each other; now, in this subtle *engrenage*, it was her wheel that was beginning to drive the others. He hadn't even known that he had any secrets, least of all secrets that would put him at a disadvantage to her. But this thing about his money had been a secret.

Harry sat at the desk in his study, looking for something in the drawer. The drawer was full of things and hadn't been cleared out for a long time. He was basically a neat person, and it bothered him that the drawer was so untidy. It was because he had been distracted by other things lately. Finally he found what he was looking for. It was a slip of paper with a telephone number on it, a London number, beginning with 01.

It was not a propitious time to call. The difference in time was eight hours; it was eleven o'clock in the morning now, so it would be seven in the evening there. In his impatience, however, he couldn't imagine waiting until late at night, when it would be the next day there.

He dialed 011 for international access, then 44 for En-

gland, then 01, then the rest of the number. There was a
series of clicks interspersed with silences, then the phone at
the other end began trilling in the two-burst English way he
had almost forgotten. After the third pair of rings a voice
answered. It was a man's voice, but it didn't seem to be
British, as well as he could tell from the single word hello. It
was soft and breathy, with a cautious, insinuating quality.

"I'm calling about the Vlach painting."

"The what?"

"I think you know what I'm talking about."

"Who is this?"

"My name is De Spain. I was referred to you by my
brother-in-law, Golo Shrodinger."

"I never heard of him." After a pause he asked, "Are
you a dealer?"

"I own a small gallery in California."

"A gallery?"

"Xavier Gallery."

"Ah. And you're Xavier?"

"That's right."

The Voice must know something about him, if he knew
that there was a Xavier Gallery and that it was owned by
someone named Xavier. In fact, it was highly unusual for
anyone to know that this was his real name. Only a few
people knew it. Golo for example. And Velda.

"All this has to be highly confidential," said the Voice,
which struck him now as having a light German or Middle
European accent.

"I'm aware of that."

"You are interested in buying the piece of art?"

"I'm interested in finding out something about it."

"It has come to light in Romania."

"So I understand."

"It is highly valuable."

"It is if it's a real Vlach. And if you really own it."

"If you care to insult me, we might as well terminate
the conversation."

"So it's not stolen?"

"I can show you perfectly authentic papers. It happens that certain persons have decided to put it on the market because of recent political events in Romania."

Exactly what Golo had said. Of course, it was perfectly clear that it wasn't stolen. Had any Vlachs been reported as stolen? Of course not. Why hadn't he thought to ask himself that? If there had been such a theft, it would have been reported in every art magazine, every bulletin, every newsletter for dealers across the world. There had been no such report.

"What are you asking for it?"

At this the Voice fell silent. Then it said, "Who told you of this piece of art? You say Godo, but we don't know a Godo."

"Golo. My brother-in-law. His name doesn't matter. He just passed the information along to me."

"Do you have some way of proving that you are not an authority?"

"An authority?"

"A policeman or something of the kind."

"No, I don't. You mean a password or something?"

"I mean are you not a policeman."

"No, I'm not."

"We are talking about an artwork that will not come cheap."

"I know that."

"There are only a few of these pieces of art by Vlach in the world. This one is not in the catalogs. It is so far unknown, except to private persons who have had it in their possession."

He pronounced the name queerly. It was almost like Wallach. Perhaps this was the way it was pronounced in Romanian.

"I'm interested in the painting. Can you send me a reproduction of it?"

"A reproduction? No." A pause. "I can send you a picture of it."

"A Kodachrome slide?"

"Kodak?" Another pause. "No, I have the Polaroid apparatus."

"I see. Well, that will be better than nothing."

"I will speak to Mr. Silvio."

"Who is Mr. Silvio?"

"He is the one who is in charge of the artwork. If he says good, I will send you the Polaroid picture."

"Of course, I will want to come to London to look at the original."

"To buy it?"

"That depends."

"You come to London now?"

"No," said Harry patiently. "Only after I've seen the Polaroid. Then perhaps I'll come over to look at it."

"How much money do you have?"

This question was so blunt and naive that it sounded like something Velda would say.

"I don't know what you mean. It's not for me to tell you how much money I've got. It's for you to tell me how much you're asking for the painting."

"Asking?"

"Yes."

"Not asking. We are telling."

"Well, what are you telling?"

The Voice mentioned a figure that was so high it made Harry wince. It was at least twice what he had imagined. He abandoned the whole idea in his mind, although this gave him a wrench of disappointment. Perhaps they would come down to something more reasonable if they went on talking about it.

"Send the Polaroid. Let me give you my address."

He dictated it to him: the gallery, not the house. For some reason he had an irrational fear of this soft-spoken movie villain showing up at the house and talking to Peter, or to Velda.

"Can you give me your address in London?"

"No. Not now. Later. To talk to me, call this number. Which you already have."

"All right. I'll expect the Polaroid."

Harry was reluctant to hang up and cut this tenuous filament of the telephone line, the only link he had with the painting in London.

The Voice said, "Goodbye."

A few days after this phone call, Harry woke up late one morning and thought he heard voices downstairs. One of them was Velda, but the other wasn't Peter; he would have gone off to school. Anyhow it didn't sound like Peter. When he got dressed and went down to breakfast he found a strange person in the kitchen, not sitting at the table but leaning in the doorway with his ankles crossed. He was wearing faded jeans and a western shirt with button-down flaps on the pockets.

Velda was sitting at the table, with the remains of her breakfast before her. She told him, "This is Cory."

She seemed a little flustered. He had never seen her this way before, even when he first interviewed her. Harry didn't know whether to offer his hand to the man in the jeans or not. He might have been somebody who had come to fix the plumbing. Still, Velda would hardly have called him by his first name.

Harry saw now that Cory had a cup of coffee, which he had set on the kitchen counter. He was smoking an unfiltered Camel, and it gave Harry a choking sensation whenever he caught a whiff of it. Out of some delicacy the man had not sat down at the table. He too seemed a little awkward in his manner. He said, "Pleased to meet you, Harry." He waited until Harry had sat down to his breakfast, then he said, "Well, I guess I'll go see to my stuff."

"Your stuff?" Harry stared at him curiously.

"Got some things to wash."

He disappeared up the stairs.

Harry buttered the hot toast waiting for him on his plate, put some marmalade on it, and poured his coffee. He was damned if he was going to ask Velda who he was.

After a minute or so she said, "Cory is my brother."

"You never told me you had a brother."

"Yes I did. When you asked me where I got that man's coat, I told you it belonged to my brother. You see," she said after drinking some coffee, "he stayed here last night. He needed a place to crash. He's got some clothes he needs to wash. He's no trouble. He said he didn't need any breakfast."

"I don't see a car out in front. How did he get here?"

"On the bus. No, a friend brought him."

"Where did he sleep?"

"In the guest room."

"The guest room?"

"Oh, for heaven's sake, Harry. The room where I slept when I first came here. Nobody's using it, so what's the harm?"

"How long will he stay?"

"I don't know. Just a day or two. He's down on his luck right now. He needs some money to buy a car."

"Did he ask you for money?"

"He didn't *ask* me. He does need a car. He doesn't need a very good one. He says he knows where he can get one for eight hundred dollars."

"I see."

"The trouble is, I'm a little short myself right now."

After he had put his clothes in the washer, Cory came and sat down at the kitchen table. Harry had finished his breakfast by this time, and he was sitting talking to Velda. So far, Harry had not got a good look at him. He seemed to be younger than Velda, perhaps twenty-five. He was friendly, slow-speaking, and lanky, with scarcely any hips. His hair was curly, but it wasn't crinkly in the way that Velda's was and it wasn't the same color; his was a speckled blond, and hers was the color of a cocker spaniel. His narrow hips were the opposite of hers, but of course he wasn't a woman. Harry didn't know whether to believe he was her brother or not.

Later in the morning, Cory was out in the road under Velda's car, which he jacked up and lowered onto some pieces of firewood he found stacked in the patio. Only his jeans were visible, sticking out from under the front bumper.

Velda said he was fixing the brakes.

"They really need it," she said.

"Doesn't he need to buy new brake shoes?"

"I don't know. Not the way he does it, I guess."

When he was finished he came into the house and washed his greasy hands in the kitchen sink, drying them considerately on paper towels so he wouldn't soil the dish towel.

"It was the master cylinder," he told Harry.

"It's all fixed now?"

"Yep."

"Didn't you need some parts?"

"Brought them with me."

"Velda said a friend brought you last night."

"Nope. Hitched. Lot of nice people on the road."

"How did you get in the gate?"

"Guard called Velda. She told him to let me in."

Harry hadn't heard any phone call. He might have been asleep. "What time was that?"

" 'Bout midnight."

He seemed very friendly, cheerful, and ready to answer any number of questions. Because he had got his jeans and shirt dirty lying on the road under the car, he had to wash them too. This was the second wash he had done during the morning. Harry was not clear on what he had washed the first time. He didn't seem to have any other clothes. While he was washing the jeans and shirt he wore Velda's bathrobe.

Wearing this garment and carrying the clean clothes in his arms, he stopped by the door of the study, where Harry was sitting at the table.

"Don't you have to go to work, Harry?"

"No. I work here at home."

"What line of work are you in?"

"I have an art gallery."

"And you don't have to go to it?"

"No, there's a woman who manages it for me."

"Nice deal."

After a pause he said, "I like art."

He turned to go away with the clothes, then he said, "Velda says you're a real nice person."

Cory spent most of his time fixing up Velda's car. He belonged to the other half of men in the world, those who worked on cars themselves. He rotated the tires, tightened up something to fix an oil leak, and adjusted the windshield wipers. Harry hoped that he would paint over the spot of primer on the front fender, but instead he found another dent on the rear of the car, pounded it out with a hammer, sanded it by hand, and painted it with more red primer from a spray can. Shortly after he finished this, Harry looked out the window and saw him driving away.

"Where's Cory going?"

"He said he had to buy a gasket."

"A gasket?" He knew what this was, but he doubted she did.

"A manifold gasket. It fits between the manifold and the header. If it's worn out, it makes a noise, and exhaust gas gets in the car."

"Did he explain that to you?"

"Cory knows all about cars."

"Is he a mechanic?"

"He's had a lot of different jobs. He's worked as a mechanic."

She was fussing about in the kitchen, trying to find things to do that would make her seem busy, while he stood in the doorway watching her.

"Also he worked in a body shop, so that's how he knew how to fix the fender."

"What other jobs has he had?"

"For a while he was in the merchant marine."

"He doesn't look old enough to have done all these things."

"He worked in a sheet metal shop too. And he drove a truck for a bakery."

"How long does he plan to stay here?"

"I don't know. Right now he's out of a job, so he can't come up with rent. He's gone now to see somebody about a job in L.A."

"I thought you said he had gone to buy a manifold gasket."

"He's going to do both. Harry, I've got to go out and do the shopping. There's nothing for dinner, and we're all out of detergent for the washer. Cory used it all up washing his clothes."

"Well, go ahead."

"But you see, he's got my car."

She had a look of absolute innocence, as though it had occurred to her just at this moment that Cory was gone out with her car and there was nothing in the house for dinner and they were out of laundry detergent. She brushed past him to get something in the other room, and he felt the soft touch of her hip.

"Well, take one of the other cars."

"Which one?"

The Mercedes was his car, and if he told her to take it it would just be lending it to her this once, because Cory had gone off in her own car. The BMW was Killian's. No one had touched it since she died, except for the one time he had driven it into town to get it washed and filled with gas. He had been making a fetish of it, a monument to the grief that was almost dead in him now and which he could revive only with effort.

"Take the BMW."

He got the key from the bowl and gave it to her. She went out to the garage with it, and through the wall he heard her trying several times to start the unfamiliar car, which had to have its pedal pushed in a particular way when you started it. Finally she got it started and backed out of the garage. He watched her through the window as she drove away. He had expected her to look odd in it, like a circus animal, or like a confident but wary car thief, but she looked perfectly natural, as though the car had always been hers. A trace of her odor of scented apples still hung in the room. He looked at his watch and calculated how long it would be before she came back.

When he heard the rumble of the car coming into the garage he went out and helped her carry in the groceries. He had never done this before. She showed no sign that she noticed anything different about his behavior. She fixed lunch for the two of them, and they sat down and ate it.

"It's a nice car," she said.

He let her rattle on about it, hardly listening.

"Cory says it's the best car made."

"I'm partial to the Mercedes myself."

"He says the Mercedes is a businessman's car. The BMW is a car enthusiast's car."

He wondered if he could entice her into bed after lunch. The idea of making love in the daytime excited Harry, because it was unconventional and illicit, and because he had never done it with Killian. Also because it took Velda away from her work and thus demonstrated his power over her. Anyhow, morning, noon, and night was not too much for him. He was driven temporarily insane by his need for her. He planned rapidly, with the concentration of a stalking predator. Was this perhaps the day that Mrs. Manresa came with her helper to clean the house? No, that was Thursday. He managed a furtive glance at his watch. It was a little after two. Still two hours before Peter came home.

He heard the Toyota stopping in the road outside and he felt a dagger-stab of disappointment and frustration. Cory came in through the kitchen door, carrying a baby. It seemed to be a child about a year old, a strong-jawed baby with a pink face, two dark eyes like raisins, and a cap of dark hair on its head. Cory carried it with expertness, one hand under its bottom.

"Hi," he said.

Velda asked him, "Did you get the gasket?"

Still holding the baby, he reached into his back pocket, took out the gasket, and set it on the table. Then he reached into another pocket for a couple of dollar bills and a handful of coins.

"There's your change."

"What about the job?"

"Nope. Man wants a vet. Told him I could handle animals, but he said he wants a vet."

Harry asked him, "What kind of a job was it?"

"Pet store."

"I didn't know you had to be a vet to work in a pet store."

"This one you do."

"Too bad," said Velda. "Well, that's life."

"I'd better take her upstairs and change her," said Cory.

He disappeared up the stairs with the baby. Harry waited until he heard the door of the bedroom upstairs shut, and then he turned on Velda. He was still suffering in the throes of his frustrated lust.

"Well?"

"Well, what?"

"What is this anyhow?"

"He can hear you here. Come out in the yard."

They went out into the rear garden, on the opposite side of the house from the bedrooms. "See, it's not his fault. Cory has to take care of the baby because nobody else will."

"Is it his baby?"

"Not exactly."

"You know, you say Cory is your brother, but he doesn't look like you." Harry was beginning to be filled with a strong suspicion, or terror, that Cory was really Max or Vivian, one of the former men in her life.

"He's not exactly my brother. He was married to my sister. Or not married to her exactly, but he was living with her for a while. And the baby is his, but not from my sister, but from another woman he was involved with, just for a short time. This other woman is crazy, Harry. She is irresponsible, she takes drugs, she drinks, she leaves the baby alone when she goes out at night with men. Most likely the baby is not Cory's at all. But he feels responsible because there's nobody else to take care of it."

"There are public agencies to take care of these things."

"Caseworkers! You wouldn't turn a little baby over to them."

After Cory had his lunch he left the baby in Velda's charge, went out and fitted the gasket onto the Toyota, and then he got into it again and drove it off somewhere. He came back in an hour with an unassembled crib in a large cardboard box. He took it into his room, the former guest room, and he and Velda began assembling it. Harry passed the door and found them down on their knees in front of it, Cory with a red-handled screwdriver Harry recognized as one of his own tools from the garage, and Velda passing him the nuts and bolts. There was also a plastic pad with pink flamingos on it, which Cory put into the crib when he got it assembled. He put the baby in the crib, and then he closed the door while both he and the baby had a nap.

Harry stared at Velda. "He was only gone for three hours. He was interviewed for a job, bought this gasket, and then came home with a baby."

"He just went by the apartment. This woman had gone out and left the baby alone. She's really a horrible woman, Harry. She's been in trouble with the law several times. They should never have let her have the baby."

"I've never heard that there was a they who let you have babies or told you you couldn't have them."

"Well, somebody should have told her."

"The baby doesn't sound as though it has very good genetics."

"Well, you shouldn't be prejudiced against a little tiny baby. Give it a chance first. The father is a very nice person. That is, the person that everybody thinks is the father."

"You said it might be Cory."

"It might be Cory. But the person that everybody

thinks is the father is somebody else. He's a quite intelligent person. He's just not very well organized, that's all. He's not ready to live up to his responsibilities. He is around a lot at the place where this woman lives. That's another reason why you can't leave the baby there, because this person is not only irresponsible but sometimes he loses his temper and hits people."

"You mean he hits the woman who is the mother of the baby?"

"Her and other people."

"You said he was a nice person."

"He is. He just loses his temper. That can happen to anyone. You hit me once, you know."

"I don't really know that I care to know all these things."

"Well, just suit yourself. You asked me where the baby came from."

She seemed a little cross, although he himself, Harry felt, was the one who had a right to be cross. He took a book and went out to the patio and sat in the chaise longue under the tree. When Velda stuck her head out the door he asked her to bring him a Calistoga with a twist. She brought it and then she came out herself with her magazine and sat down in the wicker chair that had always been Killian's. It still gave Harry a twinge to see her sitting in that chair. He told himself that he was over Killian and that was all in the past, but he hadn't quite retrained his nerves to the new situation. Sometimes a reflection from a mirror, a forgotten garment in a drawer, or an old letter would still give him a pinprick of pain. Of course, he had never told Velda that the chair she was sitting in was the one where Killian always sat.

"Don't you have any work to do?" he asked her.

"Nope. Don't you?"

"Today too many things are happening around here to get much work done."

Through the glass door he saw Peter coming home from school with his book bag, sloping across the hall, and going up the stairs to his room. Harry counted the hours until ten o'clock, when Peter would be asleep. His blood was still singing with his desire for Velda, and it probably showed in his face; he had the feeling that it was red and burning. He thought she had noticed. She seemed to be amused at something.

It was now four. Six more hours. The baby, it occurred to him, was a possible new hitch in these plans of his.

"I hope the little monster doesn't make a lot of noise."

"It's a sweet baby."

Solange stalked out of the house into the patio, slunk around the tree, froze as she saw a bug floating in the air over the azaleas, and lay on her side for a while, licking her paw. Then, getting up, she leaped softly into Velda's lap, coiled around, and settled down with her tail suspended at one side.

fifteen

A man and a woman were embracing on their knees. There was little that was real about them except their heads and hands, which were painstakingly delineated, almost photographic. The man's head was bent down and visible mostly from the rear; every hair was carefully worked in a technique that nevertheless suggested impetuosity and abandon. The woman's head was tilted sharply to the side in an anatomically impossible position. Her hair was done in the same brush technique as the man's, but mahogany in color. Their four hands, hers small, his large, groped on different parts of their upper bodies. The flesh was done in a parchmentlike ivory with shades of blue, except for touches of red on the woman's lips and cheeks. The rest of the picture was decoration that might have been done with very expensive wallpaper. The two gold costumes, intricately filigreed like the halo of an icon, merged together in a burst of radiance in the center of the picture. The background was golden brown spotted with brighter gold (perhaps only flecks snapped from the paintbrush), and the foreground was a wallpaper of green meadow with flowers. Everything seemed to have been pasted onto the picture—gold leaf, rare paper, rococo cigarette wrappers, lozenges of black and gray silk, circles of Indian calico—except for the luminous heads and hands that protruded from the gilt of the costumes. In spite of its stiff Byzantine artificiality, the painting projected a stunning vibrance and power, a feverish passion. Everything drew the eye to the flushed cheeks and red lips of the woman with her head tilted sideways and her eyes closed—a head that Harry seemed to recognize as a memory out of his own past, perhaps from the obscure world of his dreams, where he had generated this image in preparation for encountering it in the real world. It was difficult to make out the details on the small Polaroid with its sticky plastic surface. The colors were pallid, and everything seemed cast over with a veil of green. The surface of the paper was blurred here and there. Held to a strong light, it reflected only a glare. The rhetoric of the painting had to be inferred from this imperfect imitation. But even as it was represented on the oblong of tacky paper it struck the mind with the force of an angelic visitation.

He examined the envelope. It had a London postmark but no return address. His own address was written with the clumsy upright precision of an inmate of a home for the mentally retarded, as though with the tongue held in the corner of the mouth.

Golo said, "Are you sure they really have the picture?"

"Somehow they've got their hands on a photo of it. The painting in the Polaroid is unmistakably a Vlach. A previously unknown one. This doesn't mean, of course, that they really have the original and can deliver it to me. The only way to tell that is to go over to London and see."

"Maybe you should get on the phone and talk to other people. Critics. Dealers. Find out if anybody else has heard about it. Get an outside appraisal."

"There's no time. If the word gets around that this picture is on the market, there will be a lot of other people after it. The big museums. Wealthy collectors. People who have more money than I do."

They were sitting in Golo's tiny garden, tucked away behind his house under the hill. Harry had been in this garden, and in the house itself, only a half-dozen times in fifteen years. Golo never gave parties and didn't seem to want to have people in the house, which was small and only designed for one person. The place was untidy, the windows dusty and the floors unswept, and it was filled with stacks of books, old magazines, empty bottles, and clothes draped on chairs. But Harry hadn't wanted to talk about this business in his own house with Velda and Cory there. Golo poured them brandies; Harry scarcely touched his.

"Big museums. Wealthy collectors," said Golo reflectively.

He was dressed in faded madras pajamas, expensive but rumpled, and his feet were bare. He sat in a round basket chair and massaged the feet with one hand while he held his glass with the other.

He sighed and said, "My, my. Our Harry. Launching into the big-time art business."

"It's a risky thing to do. Too risky, really. I'm doing fine as I am. I don't need a lot of money. I have everything I want."

"Maybe you have some deep reason inside yourself."

"What do you mean?"

"Oh, nothing special. If there are all kinds of reasons not to do a thing but you can't decide whether to do it or not, then maybe there are strong reasons why you want to do it but you're not aware of them. Not in your conscious mind."

Harry was silent for a moment. Golo glinted back at him through his glasses. His brow was furrowed with seriousness, like that of a rare Chinese dog. He was unable to remove entirely the look of mischievous fun that was a permanent part of his physiognomy.

"You've been a lot of help to me over the years, Golo. You helped me through the bad business of Killian's sickness and death. You helped me find Velda." Here he blushed, finding Golo's optical mechanism still fixed on him, then went on. "You're the one who gave me the tip that this Vlach might be on the market. You're the closest thing to a friend that I've got, I suppose. But I don't know if you can possibly understand what I'm going to say."

"It's Velda, isn't it?"

Harry stared at him dumbfounded. This short blunt phrase was far too crude a way to put it. He had imagined that this secret was concealed in the most private part of his mind, to be revealed to Golo with intricacy and eloquence and with respect for its mystery. He had already rehearsed in his mind the rather long speech in which he would explain it all to Golo modestly, earnestly, with humility and candor. He felt that Golo had tricked his dream out of him, so that it became *his* possession, Golo's, whereas Harry had planned to divulge it to him as a gift, a mark of intimacy and trust.

But, crassly as Golo put it, it *was* Velda. He would never have thought of doing this thing if he were still married to Killian, or if he were living by himself. It was because Velda had discovered that all of his money had come from Killian. It was a rude truth that he had never really faced himself, that if it weren't for Killian he would still be running a hole-and-corner frame shop and living over a garage in a small beach town. Now for the first time in his life he saw what the point of his good looks was. Killian, who had a great deal of panache and was a clever woman but was ugly, had a lot of money, and she bought him because he was beautiful. Yes, they had been in love, in their way, but she had bought that too; she had bought their life together. She had paid for the whole thing, and he provided the beauty. Nobody had ever said this to his face, but Velda had seen it right away, and she had got it out of him with a half-dozen questions.

Golo broke in on his thoughts, serious for once and speaking in a reflective, musing way. "Everything is for the women, isn't that right? We conquer empires for them, paint great paintings, slay dragons, rob banks, and we lay it all at their feet. And do they appreciate it?"

He groped for his glass, found it was empty, and poured himself another half inch of amber fluid out of the bottle.

"They may give us a little token for our pains now and then. Some little tidbit. I don't mean the going-to-bed thing. I don't mean *only* that. We need their esteem. Their admiration. We need their praise when we drag the mammoth home to the cave. We need them, to be really sure we're important."

"You seem to get along without it all right."

"I'm talking about life, Harry. Not about me."

"Then you think I ought to do this thing?"

"You've never taken a chance in your life, Harry. Why don't you try it once?"

"I don't know where I'd get the money. It would take quite a bit."

"You shouldn't hesitate over little things like that, Harry. Money isn't important."

"It is if you don't have it."

"Don't you have something in the stock market? Some mutual funds?"

"How did you know that?"

"Killian had some investments before she married. I assume they ended up with you."

"It's not enough. Not nearly enough."

"You've got the house and the gallery."

"I thought of that. But I'd hate to borrow money on them from the bank. I might lose them."

"There's no need to go to the bank, Harry. You have friends. You know a lot of people who have money like that."

"I wouldn't want to borrow from a friend. If it didn't go right it would cause hard feelings."

"It could be perfectly businesslike. The house would be the security. The house is worth a hell of a lot, Harry, in case you didn't know it."

"Who could I go to?"

"I'd be glad to help you."

Harry looked at him. He seemed to be more interested in massaging his feet than in what he was saying.

"I'm not sure that would be a good idea, Golo."

"Keep the business in the family. It was really Killian's house anyhow. I mean, the money that bought it was hers."

"I wish you wouldn't keep reminding me of that."

"It's just that I have a kind of proprietary interest in the

house. I think of it as Killian's house. Yours too, of course.
I've always been fond of the house. I like to go there. It's
such a nice place. It's a change from this dump."

"This would be a nice place too if you'd clean out the
junk."

"That's woman's work. I don't have a woman."

"So you'd lend me something on the house?"

"And on the investments. Look, I'm no altruist, Harry.
I wouldn't do this if it didn't make good business sense. Just
a swing loan. Say thirty days. Then when you get the painting you can borrow on it to pay me back."

There was a silence. Golo had stopped massaging his
feet and was sitting in the chair looking at him with an odd,
friendly, somehow conspiratorial smile. In this posture the
fly of his pajamas occasionally fell open and Harry caught a
glimpse of a hairy pink bud inside.

"Why would you do this, Golo?"

"I'd like to help you out. You're a good friend of mine,
and a relative of sorts. I've always been fond of you, Harry.
And in a way, it's sort of doing something for Killian."

"I don't see that."

"I thought maybe you wouldn't. It's just that I was
very fond of her, and she was fond of you, so I'm very fond
of you too."

Harry checked around the house, found there was nobody downstairs, and went into the study and shut the door.
Unfortunately there was no lock on it. He dialed the number
in London and told the mysterious Voice that he would be
there at the end of the week.

"Very good, Mr. De Spain. With the sum of funds that
we mentioned?"

Harry didn't feel like bargaining. He was like a little
boy who wants a toy dirigible. As long as he could get his
hands on the money it didn't matter how much it was.

"That's right."

"Very good, Mr. De Spain. The work of art will be at
your disposal, as soon as we have verified the sum of funds."

"What mode of payment will you accept?"

Here the Voice made one of its pauses, as if to examine something in its vest pocket, or to cover the phone to speak to another person.

"Mode? Why, money, Mr. De Spain."

"My check, then?"

"A check, Mr. De Spain?" A pause. "Ah, no, Mr. De Spain. That's not money. That's only a piece of paper signed by you saying that you have some money."

"How about a certified bank check?"

"That is not money either, Mr. De Spain. I imagine you would not want us to give you a piece of paper with a written description of this work of art by Wallach? No, you would insist on the work of art in its own self." A pause. "The *Ding an sich*, as the philosophers call it, Mr. De Spain. In the same way, we ask not a piece of paper but the thing itself. Valuta. *Espèces*. If I make myself clear, Mr. De Spain."

The Voice was perfectly friendly, insofar as it was possible for a robot or a talking ape to be friendly. Harry was sure now that the pauses were times when the owner of the Voice covered the phone with his hand to talk to somebody else. It was this other invisible presence, no doubt, who supplied him with technical terms from German Idealism.

"Very good." (He was picking up this expression from the Voice.) "How will I contact you when I arrive in London?"

"Contact?"

"How will I find you? I don't have your address."

"Call this same number. From your hotel."

"I don't even know your name."

"I am Mr. Silvio's friend."

Harry was left staring at the dead phone. The house was silent. From upstairs he heard the baby make a faint caw, like a bird in a nest.

After he met Golo at the bank to sign the papers for the trust deed on the house, the loan on the investments, and the lien on his savings account, he left with the well-being of a man who has just had a good bowel movement. He had signed away just about everything he had. This idea exhilarated him, and he thought he deserved a little reward for this audacious new turn in his life. He stopped by the travel agency for his London tickets, and then he went to the Trois Magots, on Ramblas a block over from the gallery, and ordered a cappuccino with brandy and whipped cream.

He was sitting with it on the terrace, half hidden behind the miniature hedge in boxes, and had just dipped his spoon into it, when he saw a woman come in who looked familiar. All the tables on the terrace were occupied, although there were some like his, with only one person at them. She surveyed the situation. After a moment he recognized her as Sylvia Jacquemort. She was dressed in a mannish suit with trousers, a derby, and a Byronic black tie. The large tortoiseshell glasses were the same. Their glances met, and he smiled. She showed no change in her expression, but she came directly to his table and sat down.

"Nice to see you again."

"Yes."

"What a surprise."

"Yes, isn't it."

"Are you still living here in town?"

"Yes. The same place."

"I still have your card somewhere."

"I see you found somebody else for the job."

"How did you find that out?"

The waiter came, and she ordered a cappuccino exactly like his. "Oh, your affairs are not as secret as all that, Mr. De Spain. Playa del Mar is a small town. Everybody pretty much knows what everyone else is doing."

"I don't live in Playa del Mar. I live in Orange Bay."

"I think perhaps your gate and your fence give you an unrealistic idea of how private your life is. The air," she said, "moves freely in and out through the fence. You have your gallery here in town. It's right there on Paseo. I see that things are going a little slowly in the gallery lately, although you did sell a nice Embry."

"Have you been talking to Dorothy?"

"Who? Oh, the woman in the gallery. No, I just drop in now and then to look at the pictures. The Embry came in, in a slightly different style from the others, it seemed to me, and then in about two weeks it disappeared."

"A different style how?"

"More fuzzy."

He thought, Maybe I should have hired her to manage the gallery and brought Dorothy home to run the house. But what then about Velda? He would still have her as a lover. This insane scheme, he thought, was a proof of how disorderly his mind had become recently.

"I notice you're going on a trip, Mr. De Spain."

"A trip?"

"Otherwise why would you stop by the travel agency after you went to the bank?"

"Have you been following me?"

"It *is* a small town, isn't it, Mr. De Spain? It's just these two little streets here. This café, and the shops on Paseo, and the hotel, and a few restaurants. It's as though we were on a ship together. We can't help passing each other now and then as we do our promenades around the deck. We walk up Paseo, and down Ramblas, and back to Paseo again. That we will meet now and then is a certainty."

He was struck even more now with her thinness and the fragile, deluxe elegance of her bones. After the months of living with Velda, her angularity now seemed a sharpness that might cut the body if you embraced it. Her attraction was all externals, all effect; her body gave the impression that it was a system of expensive coat hangers on which to display clothes. Velda's body was not made for clothes. Sylvia's was made for nothing else. Seeing her without them would probably be a disappointment.

"You don't have to call me Mr. De Spain. You're not being interviewed anymore. I'm Harry."

"Have you thought of calling yourself Xavier instead?"

"Why do you say that?"

"It's your real name. You'd do much better to use it instead of Harry. It makes you sound like a Spanish grandee, which is much closer to your real character. If you were called Xavier, you could sign your name X. People could leave notes for you addressed to X. That would be very dramatic. Harry sounds like the hero of a musical comedy." To his consternation, she broke into song. " 'I'm just wild about Harry . . .' " People in the café turned their heads and looked. She laughed. He had never heard her laugh before. She had an unexpectedly hoarse laugh, which was not in accordance with the rest of her person. "But you're not like that at all. You're not a happy, likable hero in a comedy. You're deep and remote, aristocratic. You sign your name X. You're a Spanish grandee. A person with deep thoughts, a brooder. You brood over the tragedy of your life. You hire a woman to take care of your house, and as soon as she moves in, you—"

"Careful."

She laughed again. "And you make mysterious trips to London, wrapped in a black cloak."

He changed the subject. "How are you getting by these days? Do you have another job?"

"I don't know that that's any of your business."

"Just as you like."

The top half of her face was shaded by the derby. Through the amber glasses she surveyed him with the calm of a large cat. Her cappuccino came, and she ignored it.

"You asked me what I'm doing. My concerns are still the same as the last time we talked."

"What do you mean?"

"My life is much the same as it was then." After a small pause, she looked straight at him and said, "I am still interested in the same things."

"I don't think you ever really imagined washing my clothes and going to the market for me."

"I didn't. That's why you ended up not hiring me. But if you had, things would have worked out much the same way, wouldn't they? Except with a different person."

He was determined to ignore all references to Velda. "The idea did cross my mind of offering you another job."

"What was that?"

"Running the gallery."

"I don't have any head for business. I wouldn't put myself out for the customers. I can only put myself out for one person at a time. I'm bored sitting in one place for very long. Besides, Dorothy Gaspar is very good at the job."

"Is there anything about my life you don't know?"

"What you're really like. What you think about when you're alone. What you really want."

He stood up. "It was nice to see you again."

"London is a lovely place. I'm sure you'll have a good time there. You might enjoy it even more if you went with somebody else. You know, the airlines have a special rate in which you can take along a second person at half fare. You could go right back to the travel agency now. They're open till six."

"It's a business trip."

"Regrets, then. Goodbye, Xavier."

He left her at the table with her still untouched cappuccino. As he made his way down the sidewalk he heard her voice behind him singing again. " 'And he's just wild about me. . . .' "

The last thing he heard was her laughter.

Harry showed up at Golo's carrying a black leather attaché case, brand new, with a combination lock on it.

"What's that for?"

"That's for what you're going to give me."

"That's your carry-on baggage?"

"That's right."

"Then where are you going to carry your tickets and

your passport and your paperback book to read on the plane?
Every time you want something you'll have to open up that
attaché and show everything that's inside it. You really
haven't thought this out, Harry."

"What do you suggest, then?"

Reaching painfully over to the sofa, without unspring-
ing his legs, Golo managed to capture a gray tweed flight bag
with a leather strap. It was not new; it was worn at the edges
and the tweed was faded.

"I've had this for years. I'll make you a present of it. It
has four pockets with zippers. Nothing is going to fall out.
You put your tickets here, your passport here, your paperback book here. And in this big compartment in the middle
you put the valuta."

"Why do you call it that?"

"Just a funny word. It's what they call dollars in Eastern Europe."

"Are you sure it will all go in there?"

Reaching again with his expression of a martyr coura-
geously undergoing torture, which was perhaps only an affectation, a mock play for sympathy, Golo managed to pull
a cardboard carton out from the clutter under the table. It
too was not new; it was dented and discolored and covered
with a thin film of dust. In it were lying neat packets of
brand-new hundred-dollar bills. Each packet had a paper
strip around it stamped 100 in red ink. There were a great
many of them in the carton. Harry was ready to believe that
they came to the right sum.

"I'll put them in, and you count."

Golo packed them away in the flight bag, one by one.
Harry lost count somewhere, but he didn't mention it. When
Golo was finished, he zipped shut the middle compartment
of the bag and handed the bag to Harry. It was surprisingly
heavy. You wouldn't have believed that mere paper could
weigh so much.

"Of course, it's illegal to take this much cash through
customs."

Golo looked at him. "Of course it is. They don't ever

let you make this much money in one deal if they find out about it."

"They?"

"They."

"Quite an adventure, isn't it?" said Harry cheerfully. He really felt quite cheerful.

"No one's going to look into your flight bag unless you call attention to yourself. Affect an air of nonchalance."

"I don't have to affect an air, Golo. I *am* nonchalant. I'm the person the term nonchalant was originally invented for."

"If you say so."

Harry left the attaché case with Golo and walked back up the hill in the dark with the flight bag on its strap over his shoulder. It seemed to him now to derive its weight, about that of a small dog, not only from its material contents but from its portent in his life; it was a burden that was in one sense his house, in another the Vlach painting, and in a third the heavy and erotic premonition of the new life he would live with Velda once the painting had passed through his hands and won him instant riches and fame in the world of art dealing. He felt a coziness, an intimacy, toward the flight bag; it seemed a natural and familiar part of his body, even though it had belonged to Golo only half an hour before. He wasn't afraid of losing the bag to some malefactor in the dark. For one thing, Orange Bay was a gated community. And second, how could anyone steal from him his arm, his leg, the dark and rudimentary mass of his lust for Velda? He wasn't afraid of the word lust. It was only a word. What he felt was real, the weight of the strap of the flight bag cutting into his shoulder.

It was arranged that Cory would take him to the airport. The flight left at noon; he would be in London the next morning. He brought his suitcase downstairs and checked to be sure his ticket and his passport were in the flight bag. He had slept with the flight bag next to his bed, and after he got up in the morning he carried it around with him on his shoulder. He even took it with him for a final trip to the bathroom. It was still just as heavy as it had been; it seemed to have gained weight in the night.

The farewells were brief. Peter had already gone to school; Velda kissed him, and he picked up the suitcase.

Cory told her, "I'll be back in a couple of hours. You'll have to fix Rochelle some lunch."

"All right."

"Who is Rochelle?"

"The baby."

"Oh, the baby."

Cory said, "We might as well take Velda's car."

He led the way to the garage and opened the trunk of the BMW. Harry tossed in the suitcase and kept the flight bag over his shoulder. They got into the car, Cory behind the wheel and Harry in the passenger's seat. When he went anywhere in a car, he almost always drove, and it felt queer to be sitting in the right-hand seat, the woman's seat, as he always thought of it, although he was probably a little old-fashioned on this point. Cory backed out and drove down the road through the tunnel to the entrance kiosk, raising his hand to Frank the guard as though they were old friends. He shifted down and accelerated onto the highway.

"Nice car."

"I've always liked it," said Harry.

"It used to be your wife's."

"Yes."

"She must have been a lady who understood cars."

"She didn't know much about them. She wanted the best. I got it for her."

"She must have been some lady."

Now, in the car, when Cory had to keep his eyes on the road, Harry could inspect him at leisure. In the house he didn't want to seem to be staring or to catch his eye. He was a little older than he seemed at first; there was a light trace-work of lines around his eyes. His knuckles were scarred, and grease was embedded in the lines of his hands from his mechanic work. He always wore the same clothes, jeans and

a western shirt with flaps on the pockets. He extracted a
Camel from the pocket and lit it with the lighter on the dash
of the car. Harry didn't know anybody who smoked anymore except old Henry Fang. He had forgotten the smell of
it. If Cory did it in the house, he must have done it in his
room with the door shut. Everything about Cory was lean,
wiry, and flexible. He might have been a rodeo performer in
his street clothes. He had an assurance about him, a sinu-
osity, as though he was adept at coiling through life without
attracting attention and finding the minimum sustenance he
needed for survival. He picked pieces of tobacco from his lip
and dropped them absentmindedly.

"You going to Europe?"

"That's right."

"Never been there myself. Would like to go."

"Cory, where did this baby come from anyhow?"

Cory looked at him, then grinned. "It belongs to a crazy
lady that I got mixed up with somehow. Don't ask me how.
Sweet little tyke. I'm not all that hot on babies generally, but
this one is a sweetheart. Her mother is the most mixed-up
lady I ever met. She's very religious, and she takes every
kind of dope in the store. She once tried to poison a policeman."

"She did?"

"Yep. Caseworker lady came for the baby and brought
a policeman with her. Eugenia offered him a cup of coffee
and broke up a light bulb in it. He didn't drink much of it
before he found out. He was going to take her in on a felony,
but she told him the glass was put in the cup by evil spirits.
Violent too. Takes a swat at just about anybody. Tried it on
me once, and I swatted her back."

"How did you get involved with her?"

"Well, you know how it is, Harry. Sometimes when
you first meet people, they're on their best behavior. You
don't know what you're really getting into until it's too late.
Where this baby came from I don't know, if that's what
you're asking. It could have been a number of different
people."

"Who named it Rochelle?"

"Velda, as I remember. It's a name in her family."

"Was Velda involved with Eugenia too? Or just you?"

"They were a bunch of people we were all in. I wouldn't say involved. Velda has more sense than to get mixed up with somebody like Eugenia."

"And Velda is your sister?"

"Half-sister. Like, my mom and her dad were married at one time, but they broke up after Velda was born. Then she went one way and I went another."

"Did you know Max and Vivian?"

"Oh, sure. We were all in the same bunch."

"What were they like? For example, Max, the one she married."

"I always thought it was Vivian she married." He looked at Harry dubiously. "I don't know how much Velda wants me to talk about them. You'd better ask her."

"Just curious. It's not important. Did you ever date Velda?"

"Date her?"

He looked at Harry warily, then turned his attention back to the road.

"She's my sister, Harry."

"Then the baby is not hers?"

Cory turned to him with a look of shock. "Harry, what are you talking about? I told you the baby belongs to Eugenia, that crazy lady. Velda had nothing to do with it. I was the one who went to Eugenia's and took the baby. It's true that it was Velda who named it Rochelle."

"What was its name before that?"

"I don't know, Harry."

"You know, I don't like leaving Velda. It's the first time we've been apart. I hope you'll take good care of her while I'm away."

"She can take care of herself, Harry."

sixteen

As soon as Harry arrived in London he checked in at the Hotel Russell, went to his room, locked the door, and called the number on the slip of paper, sitting on the bed with the flight bag still over his shoulder. The phone rang only twice before it was answered by the Mitteleuropean Voice."

"Hallo. Who is on the wire?"

"Harry de Spain."

"Ah. Mr. De Spain."

"I've just arrived in London."

"Very good."

"I'm staying at the Russell."

"Ah, yes. A very good hotel. A traditional hotel. Of the older sort. I had an uncle who always stayed at the Russell when he visited London."

"What do I do now?"

"Do now? Enjoy yourself, Mr. De Spain. Take a walk through the town. Do you know London well? There are many things to see. At the Russell, you are only the throw of a stone from the British Museum."

"I know where the British Museum is. What about our business? The thing I've come to London to see."

"If you are speaking of the piece of art by Wallach" (his way of saying Vlach) "you need not be so reticent, Mr. De Spain. I doubt if anyone has tapped our telephone line. Buggèd, as I believe you say in America. You can see the artwork at any time."

"Immediately, then."

"Ah, well, Mr. De Spain, immediately is another matter. Arrangements will have to be made. Mr. Silvio has a calendar with many other things on it. Do you have with you the necessary, Mr. De Spain?"

"The necessary?"

"If we give you something, you will have to give us something."

"I have what you are speaking of in my bag. If the phone isn't bugged, then why are we talking in this cryptic way?"

"Cryptic?"

"Never mind. I have with me the sum agreed upon. Now I want to see the painting."

"You shall, Mr. De Spain, you shall. Mr. De Spain, can you be at the door of your hotel at two?"

"Two o'clock?"

"Two o'clock local time; that is, London time."

Harry had imagined it might be a day or two before he could set up an appointment to see the painting. He hadn't yet reset his watch. He made a mental calculation. "That's three hours from now."

"As I said, it will take a little time, Mr. De Spain. I will have to see if Mr. Silvio is available. And I will have to arrange for a car. Let us say two o'clock, just to be safe."

Harry thought it might be possible that he was talking about two o'clock the next day, or two o'clock in the morning (he imagined a rendezvous after midnight at the London docks, with footfalls echoing in the fog), but it was impossible to get anything entirely clear when he was talking to the Voice. He would have to take it on faith that the car would come for him at two o'clock.

"And will you yourself be coming in the car?"

"The car will be driven by a driver, Mr. De Spain."

"Very good. Until two o'clock, then."

"The two o'clock is London time, Mr. De Spain. Not the same as your American time."

Harry hung up and sat on the hotel bed with his heart doing ballet leaps.

He ordered a light lunch at the hotel grill and ate a third of it; he was too nervous to have an appetite. Then, with an hour to spare, he went for a walk, not to the British Museum as recommended by the Voice but to a small gallery on Coptic Street that he and Killian had discovered one summer when they were on their vacation, to a certain Greek restaurant (he looked in through the greasy window, saw the table where they had sat and the waiter wearing a napkin for an apron), to Bedford Square, where they had kissed under the trees at midnight. All this had been years ago. These old places from the past, the sights and sounds, even the smells, filled him with a mild sense of dislocation, as though nothing had changed, as though he could shut his eyes and open them again and find Killian beside him and walk with her back to the Hotel Russell, but at the same time as though something *had* changed, as though the simulacrum of London he was seeing now was in another time warp or made of a different set of molecules, a metaphysical stage set meant to trick him into thinking that it was still possible for him to be happy and live a life like other people, free from ghosts and grief. The one thing that assured him that it was a new world was the weight of the flight bag over his shoulder. It occurred to him that he was no longer inside a gated community in California and that here in London somebody might snatch the bag from him; he imagined a quartet of Rastafarians with dreadlocks, or a boy with pimples on a motor scooter. But nobody knew what was in the bag. It was old and worn. Only he could lose it, by leaving it in the Tube or on the chair of a café.

Passing a red telephone box, he had an impulse to enter it and call America. In his slightly delirious state (he was still suffering from the effects of the long plane trip) it seemed to him that if this was a transformed London made out of different molecules, then it was possible that the phone box too was an object from an alternate world and might put him in touch with people he imagined to be phantoms but had only undergone a similar transformation in their molecular makeup. It seemed to him that he was only a step from Killian's voice; it lurked in the red box, thrumming expectantly, clearing its throat before speaking. But the phone box when he touched it was hard and gritty, covered with a thin film of dust, and was only capable of connecting him with the voices of real people, as he should have known all along.

He entered the box, put in an international call to the house in Orange Bay, and waited while the three phones rang in unison, one in his study, one in the hall downstairs, and one in the master bedroom. After several rings he heard her voice, somewhat blurred by the distance.

"Hell-o?"

"This is Harry."

"Oh, Harry. How are you? Where are you calling from?"

"I'm in London."

"What are you doing?"

"I've just had lunch, and I'm going to see a picture."

"What's the picture?"

"Not a movie. A painting."

"Marvelous."

"What are you doing?"

"Doing? It's five-thirty in the morning. You woke me up."

He had forgotten about the time difference.

"Well, just forget I called. Imagine the phone rang in a dream. Go to sleep again."

"But what did you call about?"

"Just to say I love you."

"Oh, Harry. You never say that, even when you're here. Is something wrong? Is everything going all right?"

Yes, something was wrong. That was the reason he had

called her. He was suffering from sexual deprivation, and it was beginning to hurt.

"Everything is fine. I'm sorry I called so early. I didn't think about the time. Go back to bed. If you do it quickly you may be able to fall sleep again."

"All right."

He was a little shocked when she hung up. He had expected her to hang on for at least a sentence or two. He imagined her flopping back into the warm bed and pulling up the black-and-white checkerboard spread so that only a snatch of her dog-colored hair showed, her rear pushed up so that it made a mound under the covers. He felt that with a particular and tremendous effort of the will he could squeeze himself through the wire and slip into the bed with her; imagined the mound in the covers disappearing as she turned on her side to clasp him. At this point he developed an enormous erection. It was the all-time champion of his life, he thought. He had never thought that he could love such a person in such a way. Love was not the word, of course. Love was not in it. It was just lust, pure and simple. He remembered then that there was a connection between all this and the reason he had come to London. The Vlach!

He left the phone box and found himself in a grayish and dematerialized Bedford Square. Tiny globules of something black dangled in the fluid of his eyeballs, floating slowly after his vision as he looked to left or right. His body felt sticky; he hadn't had a chance to have a bath yet, and he was undoubtedly dehydrated after the long plane trip. He went back to the hotel and had an ale in the bar, used the W.C. adjoining, and was out the door of the hotel at exactly a minute after two. The strap of the bag had not left his shoulder since he had slipped it into place there in the house in Orange Bay.

In only a short time the car drew up. It was an old Daimler, black like all Daimlers, polished and in good condition. The driver's door opened, and a man got out who was so nondescript and unremarkable that Harry had difficulty focusing his eyes on him. He was a little less than normal height, dressed in gray. His hair was gray, and his face was white with a grayish cast. He wore a suit that looked as though he had slept in it, even that he had been born in it. The suit had no qualities except that it covered his body and was gray. The only touch of color in his person was a flowered necktie, knotted wrongly so that it lopped to one side. His hair was cut short, except for a tuft in front that came down over his forehead like the visor of a helmet. He resembled one of those performers on the streets who pretend to be robots or wax figures but by subtle motions of eyelids, a bend of fingers, or a cast of complexion reveal that they are actually human beings in heavy makeup with a talent for jerky motions.

"Mr. De Spain?"

"Yes."

"I am Kaspar. I have been given the job of driving you in this car. I am at your service."

He was so obviously the owner of the Voice that Harry could hardly keep from smiling, in spite of his nervousness.

"Are you Mr. Silvio's friend?"

"Mr. Silvio was not able to come here to the hotel. He will meet us at the warehouse."

The Voice, mysterious and reticent on the phone, had changed character now that it was attached to someone in real life. It was not so intimate and it was more formal. It was chatty but subservient, with the manner of an ill-trained chauffeur.

"If you will please to get in the car, we will be on our way."

The Daimler was essentially a limousine. There was room in the capacious rear for four or more passengers. Harry tried the rear door and found it locked. He opened the front door on the left and got in; Kaspar, in some way, had floated his way into the driver's seat without opening the door, as far as Harry could tell. The hotel doorman, a stony-faced giant in Napoleonic uniform, closed Harry's door, and the car moved off into Russell Square. For all Harry knew, there was a person behind him in the large gloom of the back seat. He had not turned his head to look. It struck him that he was in the passenger's seat again, but that since all the molecules were different in London this was the left-hand seat. He knew the real reason for this, but this was the way it struck him.

Kaspar had a curious driving style. Both arms worked in unison. When he wished to turn, his two hands rotated the steering wheel a few inches, then let it go for a split second to grab it at another place; the steering wheel lost most of what it had gained but not all. Several of these spasmodic two-armed assaults were necessary to get the car around a corner. Because he was short, he had to tilt his head up to see out the windshield.

He turned his head halfway to Harry.

"You are familiar with London, Mr. De Spain?"

"Somewhat."

Kaspar looked to see what was going on in the street ahead, then turned to Harry again.

"We are driving now to the east part of the town. This is Charterhouse Street, which farther along turns to Chiswell Street, and then Houndsditch. It is all the same street, you see, but takes different names."

Liverpool Station went by. After that they entered a part of east London that Harry didn't know very well, and things became successively more gray and squalid. He had no idea where they were going. The flight bag was on the seat beside him, with its strap over his right shoulder, and since the car was right-hand drive, this meant that it was resting on the seat between him and Kaspar. He hadn't told the hotel where he was going or who he was going there with, and nobody else in the world knew about this thing. In a half hour, he thought, he might very well be dead, or kicked unconscious in an alley, while the bag sailed off into the immense slums of London. He was not at all suited for this role that fate had flung him into. He was a mild man, an intellectual, artistic in his tastes, fond of comfort, with a horror of violence, who suddenly found himself playing a part in a rather dangerous thriller. That "rather," he thought, was typical of his thinking processes; he always qualified everything. It was not *rather* dangerous; it was dangerous.

He felt a little giddy; when the Daimler turned, it rocked like a ship in a running sea, and the street ahead tipped with it. It had been a mistake to drink that strong English ale at the hotel, especially when he was tired from the plane trip. He tried to get his bearings by looking out through his window at the city revolving and gliding by. They were somewhere in Whitechapel or Stepney, perhaps Limehouse, although he had only a vague idea where Limehouse was. The car entered a street of Dickensian warehouses, grimy with age, and drew to a stop before a concrete dock.

Harry got out on the gritty pavement with the flight bag and saw another car drawing up to the loading dock. It was an Alfa Romeo, white in contrast to the black Daimler. Coming to a stop with a swerve of its wheels, it cut him off in the triangle between the two cars, as in a crime film.

A man got out on the other side of the Alfa and looked at Harry over its roof.

"How do you do, Mr. De Spain. I am Silvio."

He was nothing at all like Kaspar. He was young, pale, lean, dapper, and in spite of his name apparently English. He was wearing a dark suit with fine, almost invisible lines and a striped waistcoat like that of a waiter or a butler. His necktie was violet with pale-yellow spots. Instead of coming around the car he stood behind it as if waiting for Harry to speak. Kaspar got out of the Daimler and stood waiting.

"A pleasant day," said Silvio, still talking over the top of the car. "We were able to produce some good weather for you, in spite of the season. But," he said as if suddenly remembering, "you have come to look at the picture."

He left his car standing exactly where it was, blocking the approach to the loading dock, and came to Harry and shook his hand lightly with the ends of his fingers. He had the engaging smile of a long-forgotten friend who recognizes

you when you have not yet recognized him. There was
intimacy in the smile, warmth and generosity, the suppressed good humor of someone who is secretly acting as a
benefactor. He didn't seem to notice the bag that Harry was
carrying over his shoulder. If he did, he made no comment
on it. Neither had Kaspar.

"Here," he said, "is where we enter the building."

He didn't so much as turn his head to acknowledge the
presence of Kaspar. Kaspar, for his part, had changed from a
chatty robot to a store mannequin who was capable of walking but not much else. They approached the warehouse and
entered through a dusty glass door. Inside was a room with
a bureaucratic air about it, like a tax office or a police station.
A middle-aged woman, a clerk or the manager of the warehouse, was sitting behind a glass partition, looking at some
papers through her Franklin glasses.

Silvio led Harry through another door, at the far side of
the office. All the walls in the warehouse were made of
galvanized iron, and all the doors had locks on them. Halfway down the corridor Silvio unlocked a door, and they
passed into a vast metal room with a high ceiling. Here a
warehouseman in a shabby blue duster was pushing around
some boxes on a dolly. Silvio made a sign to him, and he
disappeared into a vault at one side of the room, leaving the
vault door open. Silvio and Harry waited. Kaspar stood a few
feet to the rear with his hands clasped behind his back, inspecting the ceiling.

The warehouseman came out with a large easel, which
he set up in front of Silvio and Harry. Then he beckoned to
Kaspar. The two of them went into the vault and emerged
with something draped in a white cloth, one of them carrying each end, even though it was not very large, about five
feet square. With care they set it on the easel. Since it was
square, it was hard to tell where the top was. Kaspar peeked
under the cloth, and he and the warehouseman rotated it
ninety degrees on the easel. Then they stood back respectfully.

After a pregnant pause Silvio whipped off the cloth like

a stage conjuror. He stood holding the end of it for a moment, then dropped it to the floor, staring at Harry.

Harry had studied the Polaroid carefully in California. But it was as though what he had seen was a small and tacky effigy of the Blessed Virgin in a church, which now exploded into a full-scale blinding manifestation of the Divine. He could scarcely understand how Silvio, Kaspar, and the warehouseman could stand there looking at it so calmly. It was the gold appliqué of the two costumes that caught the eye first. In the gloom of the warehouse they glowed as though burning. Then the eye rose to the heads of the two figures and what was visible of their limbs: in the Polaroid a metallic, oily, slightly bluish ivory, now in the virginal shock of the original a luminescent surface that might be polished silver. The odd bent angle of the woman's head, which had seemed gauche on the Polaroid, now sprang out as the posture of willing and ecstatic torture. Her chin was pressed into her lover's face like a weapon, as though seeking to penetrate him. Her lips and cheeks were so feverish that Harry felt they might exude warmth if he held his hand to them. Below the golden garments the woman's feet appeared, bent like those of a kneeling supplicant. The garments were inlaid with hieratic decorations, rectangular and black and white on his, oval and flowerlike, concave like vaginas, on hers. Where the two garments met, a power rippled and melted their edges so that they merged into a single burst of gold.

Harry realized that he had been standing for some time staring dumbly at the painting, while the three men watched him. He moved forward to examine it at closer range; it was not on canvas but on a stiff panel of some kind, enclosed in an unpainted frameboard of white pine. He stepped back again. His mouth was dry, and he touched his tongue to his lips. In a part of his mind, the rational part, he knew he was held in the spell of the painting; he was not quite in his right mind. On the other hand, he had no desire whatsoever to free himself from this spell. It seemed to him that he desired the painting more than anything on earth, more than any woman, and he almost forgot for the moment that he wanted to possess the painting in order to secure his possession of Velda.

"Does it have a title?"

Silvio looked at him as though he didn't understand. He took a cigarette from his pocket and lit it. In the silence of the vast room Harry was startled by the yelp of the match. Silvio drew at the cigarette for some time. Then he took a tiny silver pot with a lid on it from his pocket, broke the match and put it inside, and replaced the pot in his pocket.

"It's something in Romanian which is very difficult to translate."

He thought some more and said, " 'The Kiss.' "

" 'The Embrace,' " suggested Kaspar.

"No. 'The Lovers.' "

Silvio seemed satisfied with this. He drew at his cigarette, tapped some ashes into his little pot, and put it away in his pocket again. He seemed to be waiting for Harry to comment on this title, as though he had just invented it and hoped to be praised for it.

"Is it signed?"

"Oh, yes."

Instead of moving from his position he made a gesture to Kaspar, who came forward and indicated with a stubby finger something in the lower-right-hand corner, which might have been taken as part of the gold decoration of the painting but which when examined more carefully, like a figure in one of those puzzling charts to test for color blindness, spelled the word Ioann, with a complex rococo initial.

Harry felt he ought to say something, make some comment, but he hardly knew what to say without revealing his overwhelming covetousness of the painting.

"It's something like Khnopff. Or Jean Delville. Or Félician Rops."

"It's a Vlach, Mr. De Spain."

"The Byzantine influence is obvious. It has many of the qualities of an icon. The use of gold leaf. The bright enamel of the lozenges in the garments."

"No doubt."

His lecture in art history had been futile. It occurred to him that Silvio was not an art expert and had perhaps never heard of Khnopff, or of icons.

"Naturally I'd have to have an independent appraisal."

Silvio smiled in his friendly and engaging way, a little regretful this time.

"My dear Mr. De Spain, absolutely nobody must know of the existence of this painting before this transaction is concluded. Absolutely nobody. In any case, I am leaving London this afternoon and will be out of town for a week, so the earliest I could show it to anyone would be toward the end of the month. And in the meantime, there are other persons that are interested. Isn't that so, Mr. Kaspar? That there are other persons that are interested?"

"That is so."

These other persons were probably only the figment of a sales technique. But Harry couldn't wait a week, because he was drawn to the painting the way a lover is drawn to the body of the beloved. His urge for it came not from his mind or his artistic sense but from the very particles of his blood itself. An obsession—very well, he knew that; he was a little crazy. He thought: I was created and put on earth to possess this painting. It only pretended to be a portrait of two lovers; it was a portrait of his own innermost and hidden desire. But, he told himself, he had forgotten Velda. It was only on account of Velda that he had wanted the painting in the first place. He imagined himself at home in California with these two precious objects in his possession, one in the house in Orange Bay and the other in the gallery. He pressed ahead recklessly.

"Would you give me a certified bill of sale?"

"Of course."

"Who would sign it?"

"This painting doesn't belong to me, Mr. De Spain. I am empowered to act on behalf of the owners."

"You have documents to show that?"

"Naturally. But of course, these documents don't show the names of the owners of the painting. For obvious reasons, they can't be revealed."

"Has the painting been cleared through customs?"

Silvio smiled. His smile was capable of infinite variations. This time it was the smile of a child playing games.

"The customs service, Mr. De Spain, has broken down in Romania."

Harry meant to ask whether it had been cleared through British customs, but he didn't inquire again.

He returned to his gloating and prurient lover's examination of the painting in a state of excitement which he attempted to conceal as best he could from Silvio. Golo had said that the heads in Vlach portraits were like old masters. This was an unerringly keen observation; they were like Goya or El Greco. But how could Golo, who was not an art expert, have seen this in a tiny reproduction in a dentist's office? The thought struck him that somehow Golo had seen the painting itself. This would account for his knowing it was available. But, he remembered, getting a grasp on his imperfectly functioning mind, it was another Vlach that Golo had seen in the magazine, a catalogued Vlach. Nobody outside of Romania knew about the existence of the painting he was now looking at.

Then another revelation burst on him in the churchlike gloom of the warehouse, which was perhaps contributing to the abnormal state of his mind. Twice, when he had first seen the Polaroid and a moment ago when Silvio had whipped the cloth off the painting, he had felt a twinge of the sensation well known to critics as the shock of recognition. Now he knew there was more to this than a simple déjà vu, a banal psychological phenomenon. He knew one of the two figures. It was the one whose face was fully visible, the woman. In the painting she was much younger than his memory of her. The face with its feverish coloring, which gave the effect of rouge, the passionately closed eyes, the actressy exaggeration of features, was a purification, an idealization, of a person he knew well from a brief encounter that, nevertheless, had stamped an indelible impression on his hidden mind. As he stared at it the figure in the painting aged a decade or two, turned shabby and flashy, and became a middle-aged neurotic with dyed hair, clad in layers of paisley and covered with pins.

Edna Colchis-Wincroft.

Under the stimulus of this visual epiphany he remembered his conversation with her in its last detail. Along with her tales of having served as companion in the best houses of Europe, she had coyly confessed to a relationship with Ioann Vlach, who had used her and then betrayed her. He had used her, it was clear now, as a model, along with other things. The hot flush of the face in the painting came from the endocrines, not the paintbox. If Vlach had bent her head in making his composition, it was because he had first installed himself into the picture and then added her, of secondary importance because she was only the outlet for a momentary lust. Like all artists, Vlach was a monumental egotist. He was not capable of love, only of lust, and of the reception of adulation. Miss Colchis-Wincroft had attempted to push herself into his soul, but she had not succeeded. Vlach had betrayed her, she had said, just as the Simons had. But Vlach had not betrayed his painting. That was what was important to him. He had caught the concupiscence of this silly woman, her willingness to assume the postures of a contortionist in order to copulate with a celebrity, her gilded exterior, which shabbily resembled his own, and out of it he created the masterpiece of a gifted career. Miss Colchis-Wincroft had told the absolute truth about herself. She had known Vlach, he had taken what he wanted from her, and then he betrayed her. For all his interest in her, the male figure in the painting might have been sucking a brilliant and gilded orange.

☐

What came next was awkward. Harry had never engaged in such a business before and would probably never do it again. He was unsure of the gestures. Under the eyes of the two men, he set the flight bag on the small metal table with wheels next to the painting and unzipped the middle compartment. He took out a stiff bundle of bank notes and set it on the table, then another.

"That won't be necessary, Mr. De Spain."

"Don't you want to count it?"

Silvio's eyes flicked in the direction of the warehouseman. He was fussing away doing something with his dolly at the other end of the bay and seemed to be paying no attention. Silvio smiled in the most friendly and genuine way imaginable.

"No; we trust you, Mr. De Spain."

Without seeming to hurry, he deftly slipped the two bundles back into the bag and zipped it shut.

"We are among friends here. We do things with a handshake." (Evidently the fingertips he had offered to Harry on the pavement outside.) "That's the best way for both of us, I'm sure you'll agree." His manner, without changing a particle, suggested that there was an element of the clandestine in what was taking place and that they both knew it.

"But I have some things of my own in the bag."

"Put them in your pockets, Mr. De Spain."

Harry distributed his passport, his air ticket, his checkbook, a small address book, and some other objects into the various pockets of his clothing. The flight bag sat on the table between them, having changed ownership by the alchemy of their common agreement.

"And now the painting is yours, Mr. De Spain."

Kaspar showed the first expression that Harry had seen on his face. He smiled and nodded, a single abrupt jerk of his chin. Silvio took a stiff envelope from his pocket and handed it to Harry. Harry examined the bill of sale. There were names on it that were indisputably Romanian, ending in *escu* like all Romanian names, and he was quite ready to believe that these were the people who had had custody of the painting, whether or not they were the owners.

"About shipping."

"Yes."

"Is there a crate?"

Silvio seemed bemused by this question. He frowned lightly.

"Is there a crate, Mr. Kaspar?"

"I don't know of a crate. There might be a crate. I never saw a crate."

This seemed to exhaust the various ways that Kaspar could use the word "crate."

"How did it get here from Romania?"

"It flew on angel wings, Mr. De Spain."

"I can't just carry it away in my hands, you know."

Silvio had finished his cigarette. He took the miniature silver pot out of his pocket, crushed out the stub in it, pushed the remains inside, and put the pot away in his pocket.

He said to Kaspar, "Mr. De Spain can't just carry it away in his hands. Do it up for him somehow."

Kaspar went off to the warehouseman at the other end of the bay and explained the matter to him. The two of them disappeared into the storeroom and were gone for some time. When they reappeared they had with them a large roll of black paper and some twine. It was the ordinary kind of tarred paper used in the construction of buildings. First, with great care, they wrapped the painting in the square of white cloth and fixed it into place with some tape. The warehouseman unrolled the black paper onto the floor and cut off fifteen feet or so of it with his pocket knife. He and Kaspar set the painting carefully onto the black paper and folded it into a package, tucking the ends in neatly. Then the two of them tied the twine around it, with two pieces of twine going each way, so that it looked like a pattern for a tic-tac-toe game. The warehouseman cut off some more black paper, folded it into little pads several layers thick, and worked them under the twine at places where it might chafe, glancing at Harry every so often as if to be sure of his approval before going on to the next step. He got up from his knees, and he and Kaspar set the black package back on the easel.

Kaspar and Silvio smiled at Harry. They seemed to believe seriously that this was an adequate way of wrapping up a valuable painting to be shipped to America. One of the little folded pads of paper slipped out from the twine, and Kaspar pushed it back, still smiling. Nothing in this clumsy dumb show bothered Harry in the least; in the exhilaration of his possession of the painting, everything seemed to him entertaining and amusing. Silvio and Kaspar were clowns who had found a treasure in the palace of a tyrant. Through the working out of this fairy tale, Harry had come into the possession of his heart's desire. He felt only charity at their ineptitude and their ill-concealed dishonesty. He could hardly keep from smiling himself.

Nobody seemed to know what to do now.

"Suppose we carry it out to the car," Harry suggested.

Silvio took the flight bag and slung the strap over his shoulder. Kaspar and the warehouseman picked up the black package and headed for the exit with it. Another folded paper pad fell off, and Harry picked it up. They went out past the glass cubicle of the warehouse manager, who didn't look up from her work.

Outside on the pavement the two men set the package down and Kaspar opened the door of the car. Harry saw immediately that the painting wouldn't go into the Daimler, at any angle or diagonal. Although it seemed like a large car, it had the low swooping profile of a fox. Harry induced Kaspar and the warehouseman to try various ingenious solutions to this problem in solid geometry, turning and inverting the package in various ways, but shook his head. Silvio looked at his watch.

"It won't go in."

"Y' might hire a lorry," said the warehouseman. These were the first words he had pronounced. Up to now he might have been taken for a deaf-mute.

"It will not go in the other car either," said Kaspar. He

glanced morosely at the Alfa. Silvio seemed not even to have heard this suggestion.

"Or it c'd go atop the car. Lashed firmly with a cord."

"You'd better ring a cab, Mr. De Spain," Kaspar told him.

"Would it go in a cab?"

"Anything will go in a London cab, Mr. De Spain."

"M' sister moved three rooms o' furniture t' Bermondsey in one."

"Where is there a phone?"

Kaspar motioned toward the office of the warehouse. Harry started in that direction, then he reflected that he would be leaving the painting standing on the pavement and the flight bag on Silvio's shoulder. He thought of asking Silvio to give him back the bag while he went into the warehouse to phone, but this would be silly and would imply a lack of trust.

From this impasse he was saved by Kaspar. "Let me ring for you, Mr. De Spain. Do you have ten p, Mr. De Spain?"

Harry gave him the coin, and he went off toward the warehouse. The rest of them waited. Silvio had stopped looking at his watch and was examining the points of his polished shoes.

"A vurry pretty picture," said the warehouseman.

Kaspar came back and joined them without a word. In only a few minutes the cab appeared. When the driver opened the door it was apparent that the black package would go in nicely, provided the front of it rested against the folded-up jump seats and the rest of it slanted back to be held by Harry, with his hands over his head like a caryatid. The cab drove off. In the last glimpse that he had of Silvio, he was bending his leg to slip under the wheel of his low sleek car without removing the flight bag from his shoulder.

seventeen

Harry took the painting to a shipping agency in Poland Street, where the cabman helped him carry it into the office. He knew this firm and had used its services before; it was absolutely reliable and confidential. He arranged to have a crate made, paid for the shipping and the transit insurance out of his rapidly shrinking checkbook, and received a certified invoice as receipt for the painting. Before he left he saw the Vlach locked in a vault. Then, with a feeling of exultant release that he was free of the thing and it was safely in the hands of a bonded firm, he went on foot to the travel agency in Russell Square across from his hotel, enjoying the brisk fifteen-minute walk. It was typical London weather, the sky gray and the air bracing. It was a Saturday afternoon, and he was lucky to find the travel agency open. He hoped to get a plane back to California in the evening, but there were no seats available; the first flight he could get left Heathrow on Monday morning.

He had thirty-six hours to spend in London. Thinking about this, he had an impulse and bought a ticket to Marseille for the next day. No problem on money for this; he was still short of the limit on his credit card. There was some other pleasure he had denied himself and could now indulge in. He methodically sorted out his mind, in which too many exciting things had been happening recently, and remembered what it was. Sucking his cheeks with anticipation, as he had often seen Peter doing, he went back to the hotel to phone Velda.

He felt funny. He thought it was good-funny, not bad-funny, but he still felt funny. Something was missing. Finally, standing in his room looking out at the square, he realized that the flight bag was no longer over his shoulder, as it had been night and day since he left California. He vividly imagined the bag, now in Silvio's possession, as an odd animal, its double proboscis attached at two places on its body, its zipper mouth clamped shut, and in its bowels the gleaming moist entrails of green paper. He felt as though he had got rid of something corrupt and menacing in his soul, as though a dangerous tumor had been cut out of him. The place where it had come out was a little tender, like the wound left after skillful and restorative surgery. A strange inchoate pleasure filled him; he felt light and pure. Smiling, he sat down on the bed and picked up the phone.

This time she answered almost immediately.

"Velda! How are you? It's so good to talk to you." There was a silence, and he told her, "I'll be home on Monday."

"Oh, good," came her matter-of-fact, unexcited voice.

"It's Harry. Are you sure you know who I am?"

"Of course. I was asleep when you called before. I'm awake now. It's nine o'clock in the morning. What time is it there?"

"Five in the evening."

"Is the time difference always the same, or does it change?"

"It's always the same."

"I thought it might change with the moon or something."

"No, it doesn't. Velda, I bought a painting," he told her.

"Is that so?"

"It's a tremendous painting." He was at a loss how to describe it to her in nontechnical terms. "It's the most beautiful painting in the world."

"Have you been drinking, Harry?"

"No; I'm drunk on this painting. Wait till you see it."

He waited, but she made no comment. "How is everything at your end?"

"Just fine."

"Have you missed me?"

"Of course."

"What have you been doing?"

"We took Rochelle to have her picture taken. We saw the proofs. They came out just beautifully."

"We? Oh, you and Cory."

"And yesterday we took her to the beach. She had never seen a beach. When the wave reached her feet, she laughed."

"How is Peter?"

"Just fine, I guess. Haven't seen much of him."

These banal family details and anecdotes of babies seemed curiously flat to Harry after his exciting afternoon with Kaspar and Silvio. It seemed to him that they were repeating formulas that both of them had memorized, while the heavy portent of their conversation remained hidden under the words. Vividly in his mind's eye he saw her splayed-out brown hair, her Grecian-urn form, her dress with gold flecks, and her golden eyelids.

"Don't take a bath."

"What?"

"When Napoleon was coming back from the wars, he sent a message ahead to Josephine saying, *'J'arrive. Ne te lave pas.'* "

"Oh, Harry."

When he finished the phone call he left the hotel and had something to eat in a Greek place on Wardour Street. Now that he was coming home to Velda, he carefully avoided places where he and Killian had gone together or anything that would provoke any memory of her. After dinner he took a walk in Soho, looking in through the windows of closed art galleries, and then went to a movie in Leicester Square. When he came out it was still only ten o'clock. In Covent Garden he

caught the eye of a trollop and looked away. Instead he
bought a paperback novel in a news shop and took it back to
the hotel. It was *Vile Bodies*, by Evelyn Waugh.

At Marseille he rented a car (credit card again) and
drove from the airport at Marignane through the center of
the city and out the other side of it on Départementale 559,
a road he knew well from his travels with Killian and his
previous visits to the Embrys. The road rose steeply to the
col, then wound down through the hills to Cassis. In the tiny
port he drove down a street lined with shops and cafés and
out onto the seafront promenade. To his right was the prom-
ontory of Cap Canaille and the emerald sea sparkling with
sailboats. His memory was shaky, and he made several
wrong turns, but finally he found himself in the familiar
narrow lane up the ravine, wide enough for only one car to
pass. The lane was lined with prickly pears, and there was a
strong smell of lavender.

He left his car in a little alcove cut into the hill, where
he had parked many times before. The car was a small
Renault and exactly the size and shape of the hole in the hill.
He crossed the lane and climbed up the steep path of lime-
stone steps through the pines.

Twenty years ago David had been an unknown and
unsuccessful painter, living in the single room of a studio in
Richmond and supported by Giselle's work as a translator.
He had bought the villa with his paintings, most of them
sold by Harry. The path came out onto the level under a
large umbrella pine with a rustic bench next to it, a place
where he had had many conversations with David. From
here the villa itself was visible, surrounded with oleanders
and lavender. It was a rambling stone house in the local
style, with a tile roof and a massive chimney at one end to
heat the place when the mistrals blew. There was a small
terrasse paved with flagstones, and across it Harry could see
directly through the open door into the studio. There was
something not quite right about the scene. He stopped in the
shade of the pine, half hidden by its trunk.

The easel was set up in the studio with a large unfinished Embry on it. The colors were as usual, white and blue
with flashes of red. He made out a tricolor flag, a sailboat, a
girl in a white dress, with hands and face not yet painted in.
David sat in an armchair facing the painting, trembling
slightly in every limb like a leaf at the approach of a storm.
Giselle was standing at the easel in a paint-stained smock,
holding a brush. By her elbow was a table with brushes in a
jar of tap water and dabs of color on a sheet of glass with
white paper taped under it, the paraphernalia of acrylics
familiar to Harry from his previous visits to the villa.

She dabbed with a brush of pale pink paint at the unfinished face of the girl. David shook his head. She wiped it
away and tried again. Again he shook his head. The gesture
only enhanced the side-to-side tremor of his head that appeared to have become permanent, so that even when he was
trying to hold himself steady he seemed to be constantly
saying nay, nay, nay. He raised an oscillating hand and
spoke a few words in French that Harry didn't catch. Finally
he got up and snatched the brush from her hand, with the
imperfect and violent motions of a robot out of control. He
attempted to jab at the face on the painting. Then he threw
the brush down and retreated to his chair. Giselle took up
the brush again and touched its very tip to the picture. David
watched her. Nay, nay. Nay, nay, nay. The scene before
Harry flickered like a maladjusted movie projector.

He stole away from the pine tree and went down the
path, careful not to make a noise on the flagstones. He started
up his car, cringing at the brief snarl of the engine, and then
spent five minutes carefully turning it around on the lane,
no wider than the car was long. There was no sign of life
from the villa above. Only when he was out of the lane and
onto the road did he increase his speed. As he left the small
seaport he looked at his watch. *Velda.* He had plenty of time
to be with her on Monday if he made his London connection.
He sped toward Marseille.

eighteen

Velda sat in the white wicker armchair under the ficus tree in the patio, lazing and surrendering herself to her thoughts. She knew it was the chair where his wife always sat but she didn't care a snap for that. She rejected several attempts on the part of the cat to climb into her lap. The house was silent and deserted. Peter was at school, and Cory had gone off with Rochelle to the beach. She pictured him sitting spraddle-legged at the water's edge, with the baby between his knees. A white-and-yellow butterfly floated through the shade of the tree, emerged into the sunlight, and alighted to bend its wings for a moment on the paving stones.

In her mind's eye, by analogy with the butterfly, glimmered an airplane that winged westward over the Atlantic—she saw it with propellers for some reason, even though she knew that airplanes didn't have propellers anymore, but this was the way she had drawn them in pictures when she was a child, and she couldn't remember very well what jet engines looked like—torpedoes, probably, or silver bananas. Inside the plane was Harry; his lean, cavelike, judgmental face was visible at a window.

In this moment she felt, with a kind of lazy and sensual stretch of her soul, that she was perfectly happy, sitting in the wicker chair in the sunlight with the cat wandering around like a spooky spirit on the flagstones—finally she allowed it to spring onto her lap and settle there with one leg

hanging down and its tail twitching. By another process of
association, cats this time, she was led to a fragment of song.

> *She wore a pink hat*
> *And she had a pink cat*
> *And she sat a-round singing in the old cor-ral.*

Never had she felt so free, so wise, so virginal and pure, as
she had that morning when she emerged naked from the sea
and they had compared her to Botticelli's Venus. (All in a
joking vein, of course, but that was the way men were; they
could never be serious when talking to women.) That was
the picture of life that she had sought, that she had been
seeking all along without knowing it: the rediscovery of
nature, of happiness, at the edge of the fundamental and
all-forgiving sea. And that was where Cory was right at this
minute: sitting in the sun with the sea washing gently up to
him, and a baby between his legs. Harry, why haven't you
seen this? Why must you chase over the world in search of
this or that, seeking to buy more pictures when you already
have plenty, mourning for your dead wife (a strange creature, a tropical bird with a menacing caw, for whom Velda
was now beginning to feel a certain sympathy), brooding
over the deep problem of how to love your son when it was
really all very simple? But perhaps, she thought, there was
a time when Harry too had sat at the edge of the sea with a
baby between his legs. With this, she felt a great heart attack
of love for both of them. A distant whir of machinery ended,
and there was silence. Scatting the cat, she got up and went
to take the clothes out of the washer.

Cory and Rochelle came home from the beach with sand
all over them, and the two of them got into the shower
together. For lunch they had warmed-up pizza and Cokes
with ice cream in them. Coke floats were one of the best
things there were in the world to eat; Rochelle liked them
too and advertised it to the world by getting most of hers on
her face. After lunch Cory went away to get Harry at the

airport, and Velda set the baby to bounce and crawl around on the big bed in the bedroom while she busied herself with sorting the laundry. Women were supposed to be good at matching socks, but she failed in this category; she could never tell one faint shade of color from another. All of Harry's socks were black or dark blue, and she had to line them up on the bedspread with a strong lamp shining on them, while she juxtaposed a sock with one and then another to try to make a pair out of them. There were various patterns of ribs, some had clocks and some not, some were thicker than others, and the number of shades of dark blue you wouldn't believe. Peter seldom wore socks at all, but when he went to school he wore his uniform socks, which were all pale blue, so this made things easier. In an ideal household, either the men would be required to wear identical socks so that any of them could be matched with any others, or the socks would be so different that the pairs would leap to the eye—chartreuse, scarlet, black with red stripes, electric green, white with red circles the size of coins. Such an infusion of color into his life might cheer Harry up a little, although she hardly imagined that he could be persuaded to do it. Rochelle, crawling around on the bed, disarranged the socks that had not yet been matched and decided to try eating one. She sped around on the bed on her hands and knees, with the sock dangling from her mouth like an entrail from the jaw of a crocodile. "Oh, you nuisance!" Velda picked her up, kissed her, and took the sock away from her.

As she was puzzling over a pair of socks that were probably not mates, Velda heard the garage door opening and the sound of the car pulling into the garage. Harry and Cory came up the stairs, Cory chattering away about something and Harry not saying much. He appeared in the doorway of the bedroom with his suitcase in one hand. He seemed tired but radiant, as though suffused with some kind of inner fire. Cory followed behind him, still talking.

"So I tuned it a little while you were gone. But the injectors need working on. I haven't got the tools for that. It needs to be done in the shop. There's the ECU too. Probably they'll just pull that out and put in a new one."

Harry set down his suitcase.

"Why don't you just drive your own car? Velda's old Toyota."

"I thought maybe you'd want the Beemer tuned up. So it wouldn't break down with Velda on the freeway."

Harry kissed Velda with the stiffness of one ambassador embracing another. He glanced sideways at Cory. Cory sat down on the bed and began playing with Rochelle, attempting to lift her up like a trapeze artist on his two forefingers. Rochelle fell off the trapeze and laughed. She had never realized before what fun adult beds were. You could fall on them and it didn't hurt. The wet sock fell out of her mouth. Cory tossed it onto the floor.

"What's the ECU?" Velda asked him.

"That's the Electronic Control Unit. It's the whole heart of the engine."

"Then why don't they call it the Whole Heart of the Engine? That's so much nicer."

"Well, maybe it is."

"Then you could say it needed a heart transplant."

He laughed. "I'll try that on the shop when I take it in."

Rochelle, joining in the hilarity, scuttled away on the bed; Cory caught her by one foot, dangled her upside down, and finally lifted her into the air to kiss her inverted face. Then he slithered her down his body like a toboggan until she reached the bed again. She found another sock to carry around in her mouth.

Cory said, "Cute little tyke."

After a while he said, "Anything happen to her while I was gone?"

"You've only been away a couple of hours. Harry's been gone even longer."

She looked at Harry. He was sucking in his cheeks the way Peter did when he was embarrassed or wanted something and didn't want to ask for it. He walked back and forth in front of his suitcase and picked up the wet sock from the floor and threw it back on the bed.

"You're probably tired from the plane. Maybe you should take a nap."

"Maybe."

"Do you have anything particular planned for tonight?" she went on, enjoying herself curiously and unexpectedly in this malicious little game.

"Not particularly."

"You look a little sleepy now."

"I am."

Harry went to the window, tilted a shutter-vane to look out across the road at the Gilberts' blue dome visible through the trees, and turned around and stared at Cory. He was throwing socks at Rochelle to see how many he could pile on her before she brushed them off and freed herself. Rochelle flapped her arms, and the socks flew away to the four corners of the bed.

"What's the idea of covering the bed with socks exactly when I'm coming home?"

"I was matching them. You have to lay them out on something."

"Surely there's somewhere else than the bed."

Velda gathered them up and threw them back in the laundry cart. She could match them later.

"Harry said he had a nice time in London. Didn't you, Harry?"

"Very nice."

"Wish I could go there. Never had a chance to travel at all myself."

Cory sat down and put the baby on his knees. Now that the socks were gone, there was plenty of room for the two of them to roll around chortling and chuckling, a game that took them from one end of the black-and-white chessboard to the other and then back again.

"Maybe the baby needs changing," said Velda.

"Looks fine to me."

"Why don't you go and see?"

"Did you pee, Rochelle? You wouldn't do that, would you? Not on Harry and Velda's bed."

Velda sat down on the bed and forked the baby over her knee. "This is the way the lady rides, trip trap, trip trap. This is the way the gentleman rides, gallop-a-trot, gallop-a-trot. This is the way the farmer rides, hobble-de-hoy, hobble-de-hoy."

Rochelle rolled off her knee, giggling insanely. Cory picked her up and went off to his room with her.

"Velda, are you sure you've never had a baby?"

"Not one of my own."

"You seem to know how to handle them."

"Oh, any woman knows that."

"What about Eugenia?"

"Oh, Harry, she's crazy. I told you that."

Velda heard the van from Pointz Hall stopping in front of the house. After a moment the kitchen door opened and Peter came up the stairs. He disappeared into his own room and shut the door without coming to greet his father. The little barbarian, Velda thought. He could at least come in and say hello. She knew that Harry heard these sounds too and that he would never close the bedroom door in the daytime when Peter was at home. She could imagine his state of mind and felt sympathy, and at the same time amusement, and at the same time annoyance. The people she knew didn't do it in the daytime anyhow. Not even perpetually unemployed Max, or smirking Vivian. They did it at night, like everybody else. Then she thought about the time she set herself on fire with aquavit in the patio. But that wasn't doing it in the daytime. That was just setting herself on fire. Doing it was his idea. Oh, was it? said a voice. She knew in a part of her mind that this was not entirely true, but she had revised her memory just a little on this point. Everybody did this. Revised their memory, that is. If you talk to two people that the same thing has happened to, you always get a different version. That was the way people were; they fooled around with their memories, and added little bits, and pulled off the unwanted parts and threw them away, until they got the story just the way they wanted it. Well, here was Harry, pacing back and forth and staring at her. These days he seemed to be constantly in a priapic state. (A word for horny she had found in the dictionary.) Of course, now he had come home from a trip, sending ahead messages about Napoleon. If he wanted to shut the door, let him shut the door! She didn't care one way or the other.

"Velda, how long are Cory and the baby going to stay here?"

"How long? I don't know. I haven't talked to him about it."

"Well, talk to him about it, will you?"

"The thing is, he doesn't have any other place to go. Unless he goes back to that crazy woman and takes Rochelle back to her."

"He could get a job. Then he could have his own place."

"He's tried. He went to talk about a job at a pet store."

"He knows all about cars. Surely he could get a job as a mechanic."

"But you see, Harry, nobody likes to live all by themself. And nobody's living in the guest room. We have this great big house. It seems a shame to let it all go to waste. When there are people that don't have a home at all."

"Now don't throw that up to me. I'm not responsible for homeless people. I just know this is my house."

"What harm is he doing by staying here?"

Their eyes met. He seemed feverish, with a tendency to twitch.

"It's just that . . . I've been looking forward to getting home, Velda."

"Well, me too. I mean, I've been looking forward to your getting home."

"I bought a painting in London."

"So you said on the phone."

"I carried it off, Velda. I did it."

"Well, what's so special about that? It's what you do all the time."

"This one is different."

"Good. Maybe you can show it to me sometime."

"I hope to. It'll arrive in a few days. Then tremendous things will start happening."

"What kind of tremendous things?"

"You'll see."

"Why wait for the painting to get here?"

"What do you mean?"

"You're funny, Harry. You're so priapic."

He stared at her, hard-jawed.

nineteen

Isaac Saint-Germain was a round, well-padded man who somehow gave the impression of a dwarf, an immaculate dresser in a slightly old-fashioned style. His small, neat feet were encased in shiny black shoes. He looked out of place in Playa del Mar, where people went around in beach clothes and were tanned like Aztecs. He carried with him a black leather traveling case like that of a salesman; Harry wondered what was in it.

"So you have a new job now, Isaac."

"Yes. I've been an appraiser for TransCo for about a year now."

"Do you like it?"

"It beats being a curator in a museum. I make more money, and I don't have to go to work in an office. I get outside once in a while. I had a pleasant drive down the coast this morning, for example."

They walked around the gallery and looked at the pictures.

"I see you still have a lot of Embrys."

"They do well."

"When I was at the Norton Simon I tried to get them to buy a couple. But I wasn't in acquisitions, you know. They said they were magazine illustrations, and overpriced. I don't think that's fair. Embry typifies a certain movement in modern painting. Goes back to Dufy and then to Manet. In these new ones you have he seems to be going into his Impressionist period. Weaker drawing. Those blurry edges. I haven't seen that before. Getting a little old, maybe." He smiled at Harry in a friendly, suggestive way. "Eh?"

"Maybe he just wants to try something different."

"Have you seen him lately?"

"I saw him briefly when I was in France last month."

Harry was afraid Isaac would pursue this. He knew that David was *foutu* and would never paint another picture. But Isaac went on down the wall.

"Now, the Nagamotos are something else."

He stopped before *Cormorant Fisherman.* "Genuine originality. He uses *dark* as a color, not black but dark. Those colored threads. Faultless composition, at just the right angle. And those serigraph appliqués. In this case, the spooky birds. If I could select a picture I'd like to have in my own house, it would be this."

"I like them. Especially this one."

Isaac moved on to another Nagamoto. This was not what he had come to see, but Harry had butterflies in his stomach about the Vlach and would just as soon delay showing it to him. He was like a man with an abscess in a tooth that hurt like hell. The dentist was here with his forceps to take it out and make him feel better in a twinkling, but not quite yet. Dorothy appeared with the coffee—decaf for Isaac—and they sipped it as they moved around the gallery. Dorothy offered Isaac a miniature Danish pastry with a dot of apricot glaze in the center, and he declined. He was an expert at taking refreshment while looking at pictures; he held the cup and saucer on the flat of his left hand, braced against his chest, while he used his right hand to point. No thick coffee mugs at the Xavier; the china was Royal Doulton.

"Ah, Giagiù. We do have a couple of them at the Norton Simon, did you know that? Or I should say they have, since I'm not there anymore."

"Yes, I sold them to you. I think you bought four."

"I'd forgotten that. I never knew whether to put them

in Sardinian folk art or contemporary sculpture. They cost a hell of a lot too pound for pound."

"So do pearls."

"So do authentic nuraghi figures. That's where he got the idea, of course. These things are a collision between prehistory and Giacometti."

"You turn a neat phrase, Isaac. You ought to write for the art magazines."

"That's even worse than being a curator. Less money, and no security at all. And that sickening jargon they have to write. I'd rather paste labels on vases at the County Museum. Hm. The Modane tennis players. Why do you handle these things, Harry?"

"People like them. Not everyone can afford an Embry or a Nagamoto."

"Bright primary colors. They could make their own with a silk-screen kit from the art store. You too can do work like the professionals. Six easy steps. Try two colors at first. Then add a third."

"They're not that bad, Isaac."

"Oh, I don't knock it, Harry. It's a business like any other. Maybe I should have gone into making serigraphs instead of the racket I'm in. Easy to do, and I'd make a hell of a lot of money."

"If you had a silk-screen outfit you could make tee-shirts too."

"Make even more money." He moved on. "Now, Nelson Kell. He's good. But he does an awful lot of these things, doesn't he?"

"Hundreds. They don't sell as well as the tennis players."

Isaac turned back to the other wall. "I'm really puzzled why Embry changed his style like that. I don't like it as well. Do you get as much for these as you did for the others?"

Harry shrugged. He reminded himself that it really didn't matter whether David painted any more pictures. The Vlach was going to change everything.

"It's like a new-model car, I guess," said Isaac. "Makes

the previous ones obsolete. Thank you, no, Dorothy," he
said, declining a refill. "Your name is Dorothy, isn't it? I
don't think I've ever really met you."

"Dorothy Gaspar," said Harry.

"I try to be inconspicuous."

"Well, you don't succeed. You're really quite pictur-
esque. You remind me," he told her, "of Rembrandt's wife
Saskia when she was about your age. She wore her hair the
same way."

"Did you know her personally?" asked Dorothy,
matching his playfulness, drawn in by his charm.

"Yes, I did, but I'm thinking of the 1641 portrait, the
one at Dresden. Almost got blown up in the war. They hid
it in a salt mine. That was his first wife. In his later life he
took a mistress."

Harry felt a touch of warmth on his cheek. But Isaac
knew nothing of his private life.

Isaac asked Dorothy, "Do you paint or do something
clever?"

"I do something very clever. I help Harry here at the
gallery."

The two of them grinned at each other with a mutually
pleased air. Harry was afraid that Isaac was about to ask her
to go out to lunch. Like a fool, he felt a twitch of something
he recognized as jealousy. Isaac smoothed the sparse lacework of hair on his cranium and looked first at Dorothy,
then, after a moment's thought, at the Mona Lisa parody he
had just noticed by the door.

"I'll buy that, Harry, if it's for sale."

"It's not. Do you want to get to work? Or if you like we
can chat all day."

"Well, where is this Romanian masterpiece?"

He handed his empty coffee cup to Dorothy, who, instead of putting it away, walked around with him for the rest
of his visit carrying it, perhaps in case he should want it
refilled. More probably she was simply distracted by the
excitement and charmed by the roly-poly dwarf with his
impeccable but seductive manner.

▢   Harry led the way into the back room. He had gone out
of his way to avoid a repetition of the drama staged by Silvio
in the warehouse in London: the painting brought out of the
vault with solemn pomp, set up on the easel still under
cover, then the cloth whipped off with a flourish: *Ecce!* Instead he had got the picture out of the vault before Isaac
arrived and set it on a massive easel too large for it. It sat
there dominating the small cluttered room, all gold and
black, with the decorations on the costumes flaring like jewels, illuminated in the strong but milky light of the clere-
stories at the top of the wall.

Isaac reverted instantly from playfulness to his serious
art-appraiser manner. "I would . . . Hm." After a pause he
said, "A very gilded whore of a painting, that's certain. From
the walls of Babylon."

Harry was not sure how to take this. He should probably keep up the light badinage with Isaac, but he was too
nervous.

Isaac said "Hm" again.

He stepped up and fingered the frameboard, walked
around the picture and looked at the back, and came to the
front to stand by Harry again.

"This is something all right that you've got here,
Harry."

Next to the easel was a table with a gooseneck lamp on
it and a collection of materials for packing paintings: tape,
cord, labels, and marker pens. Isaac set his sample case down
on this and opened it. Inside, fitted into green baize depres-
sions like those in a flute case, were a scalpel, pincers, a
jeweler's loupe, a small tack hammer, and other tools, along
with various vials of clear and colored liquids. He twisted up
the gooseneck lamp to shine it on the painting. Then he took
out the scalpel, which looked shiny and sharp enough to
work on the brain, and went straight to a section of the
glued-on collage that he seemed to have selected in advance.
He pricked up a tiny triangle of it, no larger than a grain of
sand, bent to examine it through his loupe, and pressed it

back into place with a dot of transparent cement. He put the tools away and squinted at the painting again, playing the lamp on various parts of it.

"Hm. Hm."

He turned the lamp off and, stepping back, contemplated the general effect of the painting, absentmindedly allowing his mouth to open and twist from side to side. "Huh. Huh." He resembled a goldfish examining a floating crumb: the same dispassionate eye, the same slowly pulsing mouth. Then he sighed and rubbed his head.

"It's a pretty good job."

"What do you mean?"

"How much do you want to insure this for, Harry?"

"Say ten?"

He examined Harry too now with this goldfish look, as he had the painting. Even though he didn't wear glasses, his eyes seemed somehow magnified, like anatomically complex and polished optical instruments.

"Ten thousand?"

They were both silent.

"You mean ten million, don't you, Harry?"

Dorothy was still hovering at his elbow with the Royal Doulton cup. He glanced at her briefly. "Yes, thanks; I would as a matter of fact." She went off to refill it.

"This stuff that's glued to it"—he poked with his finger at the place where he had pried up a fragment of it—"is authentic European wallpaper. Probably made in Austria around the turn of the century. Art Nouveau stuff. It's quite common all over Europe. There's a nice collection of it in the Victoria and Albert.

"This frameboard," he said, walking around the painting to repeat his inspection of it, as though he were doing the same scene over in a play, "has never been in Romania. It's not a metric board, Harry. It's an ordinary one-by-two, white pine, planed and sanded."

Dorothy came with his coffee refill. He sipped it, set the cup down on the table, and turned his attention to the corner of the frame, where the two boards came together. He seemed to enjoy his work. As a professional he knew what he was about and exactly how to do it. With his pincers he dug at the head of a nail and scrutinized it. Then he clutched the nail in the twin tails of his tack hammer and pulled it out half an inch. The nail made a little squeak as it came out of the wood. Harry's nerves jumped.

"See that? That's an English nail. See how shiny it is? Cadmium-plated. Eastern European nails are not shiny like that, and they don't have these little cleats so they won't slip. They're just pieces of iron wire."

Harry said, "Maybe the frameboard was put on after the picture was brought to England."

"Maybe."

He got out his scalpel again and scraped a microscopic fragment from the back surface of the painting. This he put on the table, then he twisted down the gooseneck lamp and examined the sample with his loupe, bending over it like a Dutch jeweler with a diamond.

"Do you think they had Masonite in Romania under the Communists, Harry?" He looked at him and shook his head.

Harry felt a sinking inside. "The female model is a woman named Edna Colchis-Wincroft. She's known to have been a friend of Vlach."

"Now, I didn't know that. You could write a monograph on it, Harry." He looked at the painting again. "Anybody can paint a picture of a woman."

"What are you going to tell TransCo?"

He rubbed his head and did a calculation inside it.

"Maybe four or five thousand, as a curiosity. There are people that collect such things."

"So it's not authentic?"

"How many Vlachs are there in the world, Harry? Six or seven? You should know. Well, there are still the same number."

He shut up his sample case and took it from the table. Then he contemplated the painting again. "To think of all the work that somebody put in to do this thing."

"Maybe I could get somebody else to look at it. Maybe I could get another opinion."

"You can if you want, Harry. Vlach has been dead for ten years. This thing was made in England, and not more than a year ago. The glue on the paper appliqué is not even hard yet." He gave him another look: "Harry, you're looking a little green. What's the matter with you? You haven't paid for this thing, have you? Surely you took it subject to authentication?"

"It's authentic. It's got to be."

"Too bad. If it were, it would be the art event of the year. See you again soon, Harry, when you've got another one."

He offered his hand. Harry pretended he hadn't seen it.

"Goodbye, Saskia. Thanks for the coffee."

He was gone.

There was a silence. Harry wondered whether he was going to be sick. He looked around for someplace to sit down. There was only the chair at the table, with the microscopic brown crumb of Masonite bathed in the yellow circle of the lamp. Instead he went out the door and walked to his car in the lot behind the bank. As in a nightmare, he fingered for his keys. Yes, he had them.

Dorothy cleared away the coffee things and ran water into them in the sink. While she worked, moving about in the kitchenette, as neat as a galley on a yacht, she nibbled at one of the Danish pastries, circling around the coin of apricot in the center and leaving it to the last. When she was finished she took the chair from the table and moved it to a position in front of the easel. She sat down on it and looked at the painting. It struck her as very nice. Very erotic. It seemed odd to her that neither of them had mentioned this. Perhaps it was because she was there in the room. She didn't see why there was such a fuss about whether it was authentic or not. Mr. Saint-Germain said it was worth four or five thousand in any case. She was sure Harry could sell it for a lot more than that. She was in an ebullient mood, and she had enough insight into her feelings to realize that it was because of the compliments that this funny-looking little bald man had paid her. Life was very strange, Dorothy concluded.

Harry came in through the door from the garage to the kitchen, ignored Velda, and went straight to his study. He shut the door and sat down at the table. He punched out one by one the buttons of the London number and waited.

There was what he thought at first was a ring, but it was only the buzz of the international connection. A silence. Clicks. Then after a few seconds a sepulchral black box spoke, imitating a young Englishman with a good accent. *The number you have dialed is no longer in service.*

He placed the telephone gently back on its cradle. He felt cold and empty. He felt that the world was hostile, that people around him were hostile and menacing, that he was a victim. A voice told him, *Isaac seemed to know the painting. He knew just where to go to find the clues that it was fake.* It was an enticing open door, a temptation to enter a place where everything would be icily clear and simple. With an effort of the will, as though he were a believer rejecting Satan, he turned away from this door. It was stupid of him to accuse Isaac. He probably wasn't in it at all. In fact, nobody was in it. To believe that everyone is in a circle around you, whispering and pointing when your back is turned, is madness.

But the Tempter suggested, If they really are there in a circle, then it is only clarity.

He contemplated in the dusty backdrop of his mind the figure of Edna Colchis-Wincroft, first a mawkish talking doll hung with necklaces and pins, then, stripped of her wrinkles and clad in gold, a feverish nymphomaniac offering herself to his lust, a vision set in his path to undo him and turn him mad. But he had encouraged them, he had begged them to trick him, he had begged them to lend him money he couldn't pay back. Edna and Velda merged into one. The thought struck him now that they really were one, that she had visited him twice to be interviewed in different guises, that she was an actress who was neither of these persons, that she was a demon Killian in a series of deft masks, that she lurked there even now, tempting and taunting him at the edge of his thoughts. Jewels, rings, ceramic pins, golden eyelids, an ostrich with carrot-red hair, a portrait by Hans Memling, an Ingres nude, *The Happy Lovers* of Fragonard. As he watched in the darkness (his eyes were closed) they assembled into a glowing figure in a gown painted with vaginas. *A very gilded whore of a picture.*

twenty

Golo spread himself largely over the pale-beige sofa under the lamp, one hand stretched out over its back, the other nursing his drink, which he set down now and then to massage his feet, crossed on the leather in front of him. He had dropped his slippers to the floor. The light from the lamp caught the great rings on his fingers, gleamed in his thick eyeglasses in radiant needles, and fell over his Shrodinger nose with its knob in the middle, casting the shadow of it on his cheek. As he moved his head, the nose-shadow plunged and leaped as agilely as a bicyclist between the two spoked wheels of the glasses. He seemed to be in an excellent humor. His drink was cold coffee with a lot of cognac in it. He had helped himself from Harry's bar.

"*Pas de hâte, mon vieux.* The end of the week is fine. That gives you a couple of days to find another place. As for all your things, you can leave them here for the time being. Books, records. These pictures"—he indicated them with a sweep of his arm—"which as a matter of fact don't belong to you."

"No; they're on consignment."

"I found that out when I tried to sell them. It struck me you'd been overlooking a good market for all this stuff. Embrys in banks. Giagiùs for corporate boardrooms. Tennis players in dentists' offices. Nagamotos in seafood restaurants. Ha ha!"

A sip of his drink. Suddenly turning confidential and intimate, he lowered his voice as though he were a true friend commiserating on a loss. "Nice pictures. But be frank. They're not the greatest art in the world, are they? They're just worth a lot of money."

"Golo, tell me again how you found out about the Vlach painting."

"I told you. A friend mentioned it to me."

"Who is this friend?"

"Nobody in particular. Just somebody I know. A coin dealer."

Harry stared at him skeptically.

"Who has an interest in the arts. An educated man. A humanist. Has a few nice things of his own in the house. Pictures, Roman fragments, fine bindings."

"And how did he find out about the Vlach?"

"He didn't say."

"Is he Romanian?"

"He doesn't look like it. He looks just like you and me."

"And if I asked you, you'd say you never heard of Silvio and Kaspar, wouldn't you?"

"What do you mean, Harry, old man?"

"It was you who told me I should strike out for new frontiers. You told me I should take more chances in life. You told me money wasn't important. I took your advice. And now Silvio has got my money, you've got my house, and the bank has got the gallery. The painting is fake."

"I told you you ought to get an independent appraisal. But you were in too much of a hurry."

"Do you know a woman named Edna Colchis-Wincroft?"

"I don't think so."

"She's a worn-out old tart with a face like the one in the Vlach painting."

"I can't say I've ever met such a person."

"Then she's not an old girlfriend of yours, and she didn't tell you about the Vlach painting, and you didn't send her here to be interviewed for the home manager job."

Golo looked at him strangely. After a while he said, "All this has been a strain on you, Harry. I'm sorry for it. You're getting a little unhinged, I think. I'm sorry the business didn't go the way you hoped. It would have been very nice if it did. I would have been the first to congratulate you. Yes, I did think you ought to try something new. That your life was in an impasse. That you should take more chances in life. And it might have worked out beautifully. The mistake you made was in thinking that you're an art critic. You're not, Harry. You're just a guy who used to have a frame shop and then moved up. I never believed in the gallery, to tell you the truth. The gallery was a hobby business. Killian bought it for you. Always those same six artists, second-raters all of them, who painted trashy pictures for rich people. I hoped that you would break out of it. The Vlach might have done it. It might have put you in the big league. But I'm not an art critic either, and I had no idea whether the Vlach was authentic or not. That was your decision."

"You mean you've seen it?"

"What do you mean?"

"You said, 'I had no idea whether it was authentic or not,' as though you'd seen it."

"Of course I haven't seen it. It was in London in some warehouse."

"How did you know it was in a warehouse?"

"Where else would you keep a painting?" He looked at Harry reflectively, dispassionately, sympathetically even. "I see you're still blaming me for what happened. That's understandable. It's natural. When such a heavy blow hits you, you have to blame somebody other than yourself. It's perfectly human. But I'm sorry you feel that way. I've always been fond of you. I'm sorry you're holding this grudge on grounds which are totally unfounded. I took time from my busy affairs to lend you the money to buy this painting. I thought I was doing you a favor. Maybe I was. Maybe this will be the beginning of a new life for you. One in which you no longer sell meretricious paintings to people who have more money than sense. One in which you do something useful."

"What are you going to do with this house, Golo?"

"I? Move into it, of course. I've always been fond of it. I've always thought of it as Killian's house—*my* house in a certain sense. The place I have now is too small. I'd like to be able to entertain people more. I'd like to have parties like Wolfie and Dawn."

"What about the furniture?"

"Isn't the furniture included in the trust deed? I think it is. I'd have to get it out and see the exact wording."

"You don't mind if I keep my clothes?"

"Ha ha! Turn you out wearing a barrel, eh? With straps over your shoulders, as in the cartoons. Good heavens, old man. Do you imagine that I'm inhuman? That I'm some kind of a monster? Come on now, Harry, cheer up. It isn't my fault. We entered into an agreement on the house, all fair and square. You knew perfectly well what you were getting into. Your little business venture didn't work out, so the house is mine now. And do you know what I feel?" He rubbed his teeth together. "I'll be candid with you. Why should I conceal it? I feel . . . an exultation! I'm like the peasant in the Chekhov play—what's his name, Lopakhin?— who gets rich and buys the cherry orchard from the aristocrats, the place where his father was a serf."

"Your father wasn't a serf. You've had money all your life."

"The emotions are the same. From my little shack under the hill, clutching my loneliness to myself—yes, my loneliness, Harry; get that ironic smile off your face—I've looked at your life with envy."

He looked around the room, with its rich redwood paneling, its luxurious furniture, its shuttered windows facing the sea, a privileged enclosure shutting out the world outside.

"With envy. Not jealousy, Harry. Jealousy is a mean and low emotion. No, with envy. When Killian was alive, I envied your happiness with her. I wanted to be as happy as you were. And now, if I haven't got that happiness, at least I have the place where it will be possible. Peace. Order. Cleanliness. Light. Be sure to leave me the name of your cleaning woman."

"You'll just be knocking around all alone by yourself in this big place."

Golo seemed to hesitate. He started to say something several times. Then he smiled and said, "I'm going to marry Velda, Harry. She's a fine woman. She's not clever, but she's a good person. She has talent. She's musical." They could hear her humming a tune out in the patio. "She's not dumb. She's had a hard lot in life. I'm deeply fond of her. Sorry I never mentioned this to you before."

Harry was stunned. It took him a minute to grasp what Golo was saying. "But . . . Velda . . . What you're saying is crazy! She and I . . ."

"It's all settled. We've talked about it. We're in agreement. I'm sorry, old man. I know it's a shock to you. But you didn't marry her, so why shouldn't I?" He looked around the house again and scratched his feet. "I hunger for domesticity. For an end to my loneliness. I stretch toward it like a thirsting man toward water! For this house with its soft dark wood and its green light. Its woman. Its cat."

Harry stared at him. "You won't take her. You can't." He stopped, then abruptly burst out, "What have you done to her? What have you said to her? She would never . . ." He felt a bump of panic in his chest, a cool white sweat spreading on his skin under his clothes.

"Because you're such a good-looking fellow, eh? And I'm not. Is that it?" Golo became very kind and friendly, very confidential. "Let me explain to you about women, old man. They're not like us. Sex is not all that important to them. We're poets, Harry, we men. We're romantics. Women are economic animals. They want security. It's a very deep need with them. They want to be inside the cave with the fire burning. There's something primeval about this need of theirs for permanence, for being married and having their own house. You can't just pay them by the month and take them to bed whenever you feel like it. That's what you're doing now. Velda was waiting for you to offer to marry her. That's why she set herself on fire. How could she send you a brighter signal than that?"

"She told you about that?"

"Velda . . ." He stopped. "Velda. How I love that name! I caress it at night when I'm home alone. I close my eyes and say Velda Velda Velda to myself. Velda is an extraordinary woman, Harry. Surely even you have noticed that. Another woman might have been content with her lot, doing your laundry and sharing your bed indefinitely. But she has a dream of a finer life for herself. She reads, do you know that? She gets into your books when you're out of the house. I was talking to her the other day about Swedenborg. It was when you were in London, I think. She has a very good grasp of what she reads, and she asks intelligent questions."

"You mean, you came over to the house and talked about Swedenborg to her while I was gone to London?" Harry remembered those phone calls when she seemed dazed and hardly interested in what he had to tell her.

"She was out jogging, and we happened to meet. She asked me a question about Swedenborg, so we came back here to the house to look up the passage."

Harry got up and strode around the room. He said sarcastically, "The two of you. Like Paolo and Francesca. They fell into sin reading a book. *That day we read no more. A panderer was that book and he who made it.'* "

"She's interested in Dante too. She'd like to learn Italian. And travel. To England and Italy. She was disappointed you didn't take her along to London."

"She had to stay here to take care of Peter."

"All three of you could have gone. If you had, things might have turned out differently. She has more sense than you. She might have talked you out of buying the painting.

Peter's going to be staying with us too. He's a fine lad. You'd
have no place for him, of course."

Harry stared at him glumly without speaking.

"Children," mused Golo. He seemed to have forgotten
Harry. He stared across the room. "They're a part of it.
Maybe Velda would like to have a baby. She's about thirty.
Clock is running out, as they say." He fixed Harry in the
glint of his goggles. "Have you thought of that? No, you
haven't. But I'll bet she has."

He sipped the last of his coffee-and-cognac and looked
around complacently at his new house.

Harry found Velda in the patio, sitting in the white
wicker armchair with Solange in her lap. There was only one
chair and he remained standing. There was the chaise longue
but it didn't seem like an appropriate time for lounging. He
didn't feel like sitting anyhow because he was too restless.
He paced the patio like a ship's captain on the bridge, or a
leopard in a cage. Velda held Solange by the tail and
scratched her under the chin, doing it the wrong way, Harry
saw. She wanted to be scratched at the place right below the
ears. Solange twisted her head and bared her teeth, but Velda
went on holding her in this non-cat-lover's grip, imprison-
ing her in the lap of the dress she was wearing, a garment
that Harry had never seen before, a kind of dashiki with
stripes that came down to her ankles and had no belt at all.
He stopped pacing and confronted her.

"What did he say to you? How did he persuade you?
Don't you feel anything for me at all? I can't believe this is
happening."

"Oh, I feel lots for you, Harry. This is really very sad.
It's made me very cast down when I think how everything
has gone. But I'm not leaving you, you see. You're the one
that's moving out. This is my place here—it's where I live.
I can't go back to living the way I did before I came here. If
you move out, I'll be sorry to see you go."

"And Golo is moving in."

"Well, it's his house now as I understand it. And anyhow, you see Harry, Golo has been very nice to me."

"I know; he came to the house and explained Swedenborg to you."

"Oh, not only that. He's always been nice to me in all kinds of ways."

"I can hardly get you into bed myself these days, with Cory and Peter and the baby wandering in and out of the bedroom all the time. I don't see how he managed."

"Golo is a perfect gentleman, Harry. There was no question of anything of the kind. I'm an old-fashioned person. I wouldn't dream of going to bed with him before I married him."

"You did with me."

"I went to bed with you before I married you? I don't follow that."

"I should never have gone to London."

"Oh, that's your business."

"Golo says I should have taken you with me."

"That would have been nice. I've never been to Europe."

"And then you wouldn't have fallen into the clutches of Golo while I was gone."

"I didn't fall into any clutches. And he's been nice to me for a long time. Since the first night I met him, when we went skinny-dipping at the beach."

"But if you had been with me in London he wouldn't have proposed to you."

"What a funny expression. Proposed to me! It sounds old-fashioned somehow. Anyhow he didn't propose to me when you were in London. It was just this morning. He explained to me that the painting was fake and you've lost all your money and have to move out of the house. So I'd be out of a job. It isn't easy for me either, Harry. Golo says you can take the cars because they're still yours. I don't think that's fair. The BMW is my car."

"It was Killian's. I let you use it."

"You said you were giving it to me."

"I didn't. And you're scratching the cat the wrong way!"

"I'm sorry! I never do anything right in your eyes!" She got up abruptly, spilling Solange onto the flagstones, and stalked around the patio with the creases on the dashiki switching back and forth on her rear. "You're a very nice person, Harry. You've been a friend. You weren't a friend at first, but I made you into a friend. I've always wanted to have good looks. I don't have them myself, so finally I got somebody else who had them. That was almost as good. I could write a song about the love I had with you, Harry. Your Spanish eyes looking out of caves. The bones at your throat. The way your hair hangs over your forehead. You make a girl melt. I'm sure you've melted hundreds of them. And Peter's the same way. He's going to be very successful with the girls too."

"Velda—"

"But I've had all that now, Harry. I've been loved by the most beautiful man in the world. Many times. I know what it's like and I'll always hold it in my memories, as they say. There are so many nice things to remember! All the nice things you've done for me. Gave me a BMW. Put me out when I was on fire and so on. But you see, that's all over now. You're leaving me. We get used to men leaving us. That's what men do. Three of them have done it to me. Max, Vivian, and now you. I'm going to make darned sure that Golo doesn't do it too. If he does, I'll sue him for everything he's got. And that," she said, "is what getting married is all about."

"I can't believe you'd give yourself to a man like Golo."

"Give myself? What an old-fashioned expression."

"He must be twice your age."

"What on earth does that matter?"

"He's disgusting. That great belly. That bald head. Those huge eyes staring at you."

"I've seen him naked. And I expect to see him that way many times again. He's not likely to be impressive in the

bedroom. Not like you." Here she turned away and bit her
lip. "It's not a wedding night that a girl looks forward to
exactly," she said with her back to him. Then she turned
abruptly and faced him. "But I have a plan for that. For our
wedding night. It will be at midnight on the beach and we'll
be naked. Some friend will say a few words over us, and then
we'll fall down on the sand."

"You must be out of your head."

"Oh, I think I am. I've never looked forward to anything so much in my life. I can't believe how excited I am."
She moved in through the glass door to the living room, and
he followed her. She let her hand trail over the leather sofa,
the glass-topped Finnish table, the rosewood buffet. "And to
think that now all these things are going to belong to me."

"Velda, you can't mean these things you're saying."

She picked up Solange and stroked her. Her eyes were
moist, and she bit her lip.

"Oh, Harry . . ."

It seemed to him that she had never been more desirable. With a shock like the flash of a camera he saw all at
once the apparition of her unclothed, down to the tiniest
detail, every curve and shadow, every turn of sinew, every
magnified particle of her secret body. What he felt was a
new kind of desire, a need to *possess* her in the clearest and
simplest, the most unambiguous sense of the word, to claim
her and own her, to keep her to himself in a place with walls
around it and roofed against the elements. She seemed to
him all at once terribly valuable, and her loss a blow from
which he would not recover. He moved toward her, and she
turned to face him, with the alertness of a wary but unafraid
animal. He was desperate to rescue her in this last fleeting
moment, to rescue his own life. If he could touch her, his
instinct shouted, the warm blood-knowledge that ran from
his fingers into her body would make everything all right,
the nightmare would dissolve and it all would not have happened. He pictured the two of them fleeing from Orange Bay
and sharing a rented room, in the squalor of unwashed
clothes and fetid bodies; and with this image his lust was

reborn with the violence of a railroad semaphore. He was only a hand's touch from her.

She told him with her eyes still wet, "No, stop, Harry. Don't touch me." She stretched out her arm like a Melusina, a fierce dominatrix, and pointed to the door. "Go now. Or I might do something foolish."

His tentative gesture halted in midair and faltered. He had never suspected this steely toughness of character in her. It was clear that her desire for him fought a losing battle with something else, and this something else was her marriage, her future, her dignity as a human being. In this new guise even her form, her naive breasts and amphora hips, which before had seemed an invitation to easy conquest, now became the fierce armored chastity of a Viking goddess. Had this strength always been concealed in her, invisible to his eye, or had something changed in her, some metamorphosis? Or was she now being cleverly simulated by a double, a spurious Velda as false as the painting he had coveted in the dark hall of his lust?

He turned for one last look at her glistening eyes. He felt a sentiment that had been a stranger to him for a long time: compassion. "You can keep the BMW," he told her over his shoulder. He went to get his car keys from the bowl in the kitchen.

Harry drove the short distance down the road to the beach, in his purring Mercedes, which was comfortable and solid, just as it always had been, unmistakably real, reassuring him that he too still existed. He circled through the park and stopped the car against the seawall at the edge of the beach. There he was, in his old shorts and tee-shirt, sitting on a rock, staring out to sea. Harry had the feeling that once before he had gone looking for him and found him in this place, and then he remembered: it was the afternoon in December—it seemed terribly long ago now—after he had interviewed Sylvia Jacquemort. Perhaps he came here when events at the house were not to his liking, or something he didn't want to face.

Harry got out of the car and stood tentatively behind the open door. Peter saw him immediately; it was as though he had been waiting for him, or as though he had some occult organ in the back of his head for detecting him. He got up from the rock and looked back at the car. They were perhaps a hundred yards apart. Harry made a come-here wave. He had the idea that Peter would come and sit in the car with him and they would talk for a while.

But Peter only stood looking at him, as though Harry were a stranger who for some reason had driven down to park his car at the beach. Harry shut the car door and walked over the sand to the cliff at the end of the cove, clambering awkwardly over the rocks in his house slippers, which he had forgotten to change. It occurred to him that Peter preferred not to meet him in the car, a miniature power center, but at the edge of the sea, which belonged to him. When he got to him they both sat down. Peter said nothing; he only turned his head briefly and went back to looking at the sea. Harry noticed the shadow of a mustache on his upper lip. He was fourteen now.

"They've told you?"

Peter nodded.

"Golo says you'd rather stay here." Before Peter could speak he went on. "I can't take you anyhow. There won't be any room. I'll be living in some tiny little place. You'd be better off with them."

"I want to go with you."

This short, blunt phrase was totally unexpected. Harry felt a rush of love for his son. It caught him off balance and melted something in him.

"You'll be better off in the house. You'll have books, good food. Someone to take care of your wants. You'll go on going to Pointz Hall. I couldn't afford that."

Peter left off staring at the sea for the first time and turned to him, with something in his eyes like a small but fierce and determined wild animal. "No. I'd rather go with you . . ." He hesitated, and then finished awkwardly:

"Harry." Wild horses could not have dragged the word Father out of him.

"Peter, I'm not who you think I am. You've taken me for someone else. I've made a botch of everything."

"You're very much like me."

Harry had been on the point of saying this himself, but he was afraid that Peter would reject it angrily, or wouldn't understand it.

"Yes." The two of them sat comfortably for a long time, looking at the sea and not saying anything. Harry felt an inchoate sense of privilege, of gratitude, for this moment of intimacy with this child who had been a stranger to him. "We're very much alike." Then, after a pause: "Your job is to live my life over again but do a better job of it."

"I don't know how to do that."

"You don't have to know now. You have plenty of time. When the moment comes—the moment when your happiness is lying at your feet—you must seize it. It won't be something you can buy. It will be something you can only take with your love." He wasn't sure himself what he meant by this. "Velda is right. You shouldn't read so many books. You should get out and meet some girls."

Their glances met, and they both smiled. In the smile was their common opinion of Velda, the recognition of their own sameness, and the basic pessimism that both of them had wryly learned to turn to humor. In the smile was the knowledge that people you love die, that others betray you, and that sex is a cruel and delusory trick.

"Peter . . ."

He stretched out his hand to touch him, just as he had toward another person, who now seemed a distant stranger, only a few minutes before. Peter detected the gesture out of the corner of his eye and stood up abruptly from the rock. He was all at once boy-shy and afraid of sentiment. Without turning his head, he stripped off his shorts and tee-shirt, then he ran down to the sea like a sprinter and splashed through the shallow water to the point where he could fall forward and swim. The first wave struck him; he broke through it, tossed his hair, and went on. He looked back only once; Harry caught a fleeting glimpse of his face as he turned and treaded water, far out beyond the surfline. He knew he would stay out there until the car was gone and the beach was empty again.

By habit he found himself driving up the road to his old house. Only when the redwood-and-glass shape came up in the windshield did he remember that he didn't live there anymore. With a jerk he swerved off and headed up the road to the tunnel. He had no particular plan for where he was going or what he was going to do when he got there. The idea that he might sometime no longer have a house was like the idea that he might sometime no longer have his body, perfectly possible in the natural order of things but not something you thought about a lot. But at least when you were dead other people took care of your problems from then on. When you were evicted from your house you still had all your old problems, plus a lot of new ones.

When he had gone out past the kiosk, with its cheerful guard reading his book, he drove down the highway toward town with the vague idea of going to Dorothy's house on Shadow Lane to see if he could stay there for a few days. It was Sunday, so Dorothy would probably be home. Of course, because it was Sunday the traffic in the small beach town was heavy. The highway was jammed from side to side with Inlanders with beach chairs piled on their vans and their kids panting to get into the water. In the car ahead there seemed to be a half-dozen small blond mops, all trying to get a little air from the windows at once.

The trouble was caused by the single traffic light in town, at the intersection in front of the hotel. Only four or five cars were getting through with each change of the light, and the others just inched along behind them. The car full of blond mops made it through the light just as it turned red, and Harry jammed on the brakes.

He heard a loud clang, and his head jerked back and bumped against the headrest. After a moment of psychic paralysis he opened the door and stepped out onto the pavement in the white sunlight. His limbs felt liquid, and the air around him swam a little. It was just because of the surprise and the loud noise. He wasn't hurt a bit. He looked around to see what had struck him from behind.

It was an old Ford Fairlane with many decals advertising motor oil and additives stuck onto it. The pavement under his rear bumper was strewn with rubies and diamonds, and one headlight of the old Ford was broken. Inside the Ford were two dark young men who seemed to be the shadows of his own bad dreams. Everything happened quite slowly, perhaps so that Harry's slightly numbed wits could take account of it. The young man on the right side of the Ford got out, leaving the driver at the wheel. He was in a pink tank top, and he wore a fine gold chain around his coffee-colored neck. He paid very little attention to Harry. For some reason, instead of inspecting the damage from his side he came around to the left side of the two cars. He stood for a moment impassive, giving the cars a skilled appraisal. Just then the light turned green. Without hurry the young man got into Harry's car and drove it off. The Ford, setting out with a jerk of rubber, followed after it.

The Ford was still moving slowly as it went by him, so Harry got a good look at the driver. He was wearing a black plastic vest, and he too had a gold chain. Everything inside the car was shadowy, and his eyes, his teeth, and the gold chain gleamed. He was not so young after all; he might have been about Harry's age. He stared at Harry with indifference and contempt, without any real interest. It was clear that for him being black conferred on him a kind of immunity. *You think you've got it bad?* said the look. *Well, that's the way it is for me every day.*

The Mercedes slipped adroitly away through the traffic, accelerating up the hill and out of the small town. The Ford followed as best it could, belching blue smoke. Both cars were gone. Harry was standing in the middle of the intersection with pebbles of red and white glass around him on the pavement. Somebody honked. He made his way out of the street through the cars and started walking up the sidewalk in the direction he had been going when he still had a car. There were lots of other people walking. It was a perfectly natural thing. People walked for centuries before cars were even thought of.

twenty-one

Harry was installed in a tiny room in Dorothy's house on Shadow Lane. It was too much to call it a room, really; it was a kind of alcove separated from the living room by a chintz drapery and furnished with a narrow cot, a table, a chair, and a lamp. There was also a miniature bookcase, two feet wide and five feet high, containing an eleventh edition of the *Encyclopaedia Britannica*, published in 1911. Always before in his life he had had something to do. Now there was nothing to do but sit in this room. Boredom. And that, he now saw, was what hell was all about. Anything he did, every cough, could be heard by everybody else in the house.

After two days of this he was almost out of his wits, and he turned to the encyclopedia. There were twenty-eight volumes plus an index, and it would take him years to make his way through it. He opened the first volume and started on Aeroplanes. The crude engravings had all the fascination of a Jules Verne novel read in early youth. It was clear that none of these contraptions would ever get off the ground, but their ingenuity, their complexity, and their sheer impracticality held him in the numb grip of fascination. De la Landelle's Flying Machine was an old-fashioned ship with air screws to lift it from the sea. Moy's Aerial Steamer was nothing but a pair of immense fans on a tricycle. There was Armour's Elastic Aerial Screw, and Henson's Aerostat, a large bat with wings flapped by a steam engine. Sir Hiram Maxim's Flying Machine, also propelled by steam, looked like a grain harvester with two square fans. He lost interest in the aeroplanes as soon as they began to work, around 1906, and went on to Aeschylus, Aesthetics, and Aethel-weard.

"Harry, why don't you come out of there once in a while?" said Dorothy. She pushed her way in through the chintz drape. It was nine o'clock, and she was about to leave for work. "Get out of the house. Get a little fresh air. Take a walk. If you cross the highway, there's a path that leads down through the houses to the beach. It isn't marked; you have to know where to find it. We're just poor people here. We don't have a private beach. Do some gardening; you can trim my roses. The bougainvillea in front is getting out of hand. It's going to cover the house completely if I don't do something. Fool around in the kitchen. You could fix dinner for us some night. Do you like to cook?"

"No, I don't like to cook."

"What do you like to do?"

"I like to read the encyclopedia."

"You've gone a little daffy, I think. It's natural after what's happened."

"How are things going at the gallery?"

"Very well. He's doing a good job of it, I think."

"Who is he?"

"Mordecai. I wouldn't have thought he could. But you never can tell about people. He's not dumb, and he knows a lot about art. It's a change, having an artist in charge of the gallery. He does things differently. Not better than the way you did them, I wouldn't say. Just differently."

Harry went into the bathroom, his second-favorite place in the house. The only bathroom, of course. It was tiny and smelled of damp wood, urine, and the pine-flavored stuff that Dorothy used to cover up these smells. He did his business (the only business he had now), buttoned his pants out of habit, and looked at himself in the mirror, in the light of an overhead lamp that cast exaggerated shadows onto the contours of his face. It looked like the face of a sex criminal in a bad movie. One eye higher than the other, and the mouth on the other side just a hair lower.

He thought of Peter and his skeptical smile, which Killian called his Pirate Smile. We are both sinister, he thought, Peter and I. Before, we seemed sinister to other people; now I seem sinister to myself. I said the wrong thing to him at the beach. I told him to go out and chase some girls. I should have told him to be kinder and think about other people a little more. I must tell him what will happen if he doesn't change.

In the gallery everything seemed exactly as it had been before, except that several of Mordecai's cobalt-period pictures were hanging on the walls. As near as he could tell, they were in places where Modane tennis players had been. Also one of the new Embrys was gone; possibly Mordecai had sold it. Mordecai too, in his Greek fisherman's cap and his paint-stained shirt, was exactly as he had been before. Harry wondered how people like Yasir Arafat and Mordecai managed always to have a week's stubble on their faces, no more and no less.

"Have some coffee? Dotty'll fix it for you."

"No thanks. Tell me again, Mordecai, why it is that I don't have the gallery anymore."

"You borrowed money on it from the bank and then didn't pay them back."

"I don't remember that. If you say so it must be true."

"Dorothy says you've been having a little trouble with your mind."

"I'm sure I am."

"Well, a lot of people do."

"How are things going, Mordecai?"

"Not so bad now. The first couple of weeks were slow. We were fighting the wolf from the door. Then we sold an Embry, and we're okay for a couple of months."

Dorothy was in the back room going over her accounts. When she saw him come in she looked up, waved to him through the open door, and went on working. The Vlach painting was still in the back, leaning against the wall with a canvas over it, like the corpse of an accident victim.

"How could you afford to buy the gallery anyhow, Mordecai?"

"Oh, I might have saved up a little over the years. Maybe an uncle died. I had to hock my back teeth to the bank, I can tell you that. It isn't going to be easy."

"It wasn't easy for me."

"You had a rich wife, as I understand it. I've never even had a girlfriend. Maybe now that I'm a gallery owner some little gal will take an interest in me."

"Money *is* sexy. I've found that out. Lack of money is unsexy."

"Got a lot of it when you ran the gallery, eh?"

"I wouldn't say that. I was married. Then afterward I had somebody else."

"Must of been a nice life."

"Yes, it was."

"Dotty says you came in only a couple of hours a day. That surprises me. I'm always sitting here. Anybody comes in, I pounce on them. Dotty can't do it; she's in the back adding up numbers. That's how I sold the Embry."

"Mordecai, haven't you noticed that the Embrys are changing?"

"Every artist changes as he goes along. Learns new things. Tries new techniques. My cobalt period, for example. It was a real breakout. It happened because I bought the wrong stuff at the art store. I thought I was getting cerulean blue. Got home and started smearing it on, I saw it was terrific. I sold one of them too, right after I sold the Embry."

"The Embrys are getting fuzzy."

"Hard line is out, Harry."

"David has Parkinson's. He can't paint anymore. His wife paints the pictures for him. She's not an artist."

"You don't say so. Well, that may be true. I sold this one without much trouble. It doesn't really matter very much who paints them. Embry signs them. If Picasso drops an egg on the floor when he's cooking breakfast, is it art? It is if he signs it."

"I'm surprised that David can even sign his work."

"Well, the signature was a little wavy, like the rest of it, but the lady bought it."

"So you're making it all right, Mordecai?"

"Making it, I guess. All right would be saying too much. But see, Harry, I don't have a house in Orange Bay. I'm still living in my shack up in the canyon. I live on Dotty's coffee and those pastries she gets me down the street. Don't spend money on clothes. Don't have a car. I don't really need one. You can walk everywhere here in town, and why anyone would want to go anywhere else, I can't see."

Dorothy came out of the back room. "Hello, Harry. So here you are. I told you it would be a good idea for you to go out and take a walk."

"It does make me feel better."

"Would you like some coffee?"

Everyone kept trying to get him to drink coffee, as though that would cure what ailed him. "No, thanks. I'm just leaving."

"On your way home get some tortillas, some salsa, and a pound of hamburger, will you? Juana can fix some tacos."

"I don't have any money."

She gave him a five-dollar bill. "And lettuce."

"Uh oh," said Mordecai. "Somebody's coming in." He stood up from the table and straightened his Greek cap. Two middle-aged women came in through the door, and before it swung closed Harry ducked out onto the street.

He bought the groceries at the Beach Economart and walked home with them. Home, that was a funny expression. It was just the way the language worked. He ought to be grateful that he had a place to lay his head. Dorothy was an intelligent, sensible woman. A very nice person too. In this new life of theirs, he noticed that she had a strange way of shrinking away as the two of them moved about in the tiny house, so that there was no danger of their touching. He had the impression that she had lost a good deal of her

interest in him now that he no longer owned the gallery and
no longer lived in Orange Bay. She could no more separate
her feeling for him from what he owned than Velda could.
Of course, there were his well-known good looks. He still
had those. Maybe he could do something with them. He
tried to imagine what. There was a male stripper club in
L.A.; women came and stuffed dollar bills into their G-
strings. He was a little old for that. It would be ludicrous. He
could get a job selling shoes, maybe. There were all kinds of
possibilities. His life was not over, by any means. He felt
very queer, as though he were an impostor going down the
street wearing his clothes and a Harry-mask. Inside was an
interloper, a stranger even to him. A shoe salesman. A male
stripper. Anyone who encountered him would have the same
reaction: that he was a person who obviously had nothing to
offer the world except his good looks.

As he approached the house on Shadow Lane he met his
neighbor, the old man supported on his cane. They stared at
each other; neither bothered to nod. The tripod man had
quite possibly discovered Harry's secret, that there was nothing inside his clothes or behind his face. He went up the walk
of the house and pushed through the overhanging bougainvillea onto the porch. The two small brown faces flickered
momentarily behind the window, then disappeared. But
when he went through the door into the living room they
floated past him and out the door onto the walk. They reappeared in a moment with Juana behind them. She was just
coming home. She had left the children alone. He didn't
recognize her at first without her white Guatemalan dress
with its square neck. She was in an outfit he had never seen
on her before, jeans with a kind of smock or duster over
them. She took the grocery bag from him, looked into it, and
carried it off into the kitchen. He followed her, and the boys
tagged along. She unwrapped the lettuce, washed it, and got
out a knife to chop it. Then he knew what the clothes were.
She worked as a house cleaner.
    "Juana."

She turned, with the knife still in her hand.

"*Conoce usted mí?*"

"*Sí,*" she said shyly.

"Where?"

She looked at him patiently. The two boys in the doorway were solemn. They had never heard him talking to their mother, or attempting to.

"*Dónde?*"

"*Bahía Naranja.*"

"Orange Bay."

"*Sí.*"

"You're Mrs. Manresa's helper."

"*Señora Manresa. Sí.*"

"You've been coming there for months to the house. And I never noticed you. You scrubbed the floors, washed the woodwork, threw out the intimacies in my wastebasket, scrubbed the urine from the toilet, saw what I did with my woman, saw my child and what we said to each other, and never said a word to me. I never noticed you."

"*Linda casa,*" she said.

"Do you know any English at all? *Inglés?* None? *Ninguno?*"

She shook her head.

The obstacle of language prevented them from communicating at all. It prevented him from doing something foolish, or saintly, he couldn't decide which; for example, apologizing for the way the world was arranged so that some people had to spend their lives serving others who were no better than they were, in fact probably worse. But he was no saint, and he was not much good at apologies. He had never learned the trick of them. He had apologized to Velda by giving her a BMW, but he had nothing more to give; he had only the change from Dorothy's five dollars in his pocket.

"*Lo siento mucho,*" he remembered from his high school Spanish.

She gazed at him uncomprehending, the knife in hand but motionless. The two boys had disappeared from the doorway. He smiled at her as though it hurt his mouth, then he went into his alcove behind the chintz curtain and lay down on the bed. She must have thought I was crazy, he told himself. *El señor es loco. Lo siento mucho.* He closed his eyes and tried to doze. After a while he would get up and read Aether, Affidavit, and Afghanistan. There was a nice map with that one, he had noticed by looking ahead. He could hear Juana in the kitchen, chopping lettuce for his lunch.

twenty-two

In the clutch of the midsummer night, Harry went down the highway toward Orange Bay. It was about ten o'clock. There was no sidewalk, so he had to dodge through the bushes and occasionally circle out around a parked car. When he did this he felt the glare of rushing headlights on his back, an unpleasant sensation. It was the other side of the highway, he remembered, that he had gone down, cold and bedraggled, on the night of his nudist escapade. At least he had his clothes on now, and when he came to the entrance kiosk he would be on the right side of the highway, so he wouldn't have to cross against this murderous stream of headlights tearing by in both directions. It was amazing how being a pedestrian changed your view of cars. Before, he had floated along this same highway in a private living room, sealed in behind the glass, with a pleasant odor of carpets and leather, and a set of tiny colored lights like a Christmas tree just below his angle of vision to cheer things up. In those days, in his former existence, the distance of a mile from the town to the entrance kiosk had seemed only a trifle, hardly enough for him to have a single complicated thought. Now he had time for many different thoughts, some of them knocked flat by the rush of white photons blasting at him from the rear, but others managing to survive and swimming around quite freely in his mind.

At this time of night Frank the cheerful student was

replaced in the kiosk by an older gentleman of Oriental
persuasion, who substituted a Vietnamese newspaper covered with chicken tracks for the paperback novel. He showed
no surprise at seeing Harry come in on foot (maybe he had
heard about his comedown in the world) and hardly looked
up from the paper. Harry was not home safe yet however;
he had to deal with more headlights in the tunnel under the
highway, where a single car shot up behind him and bolted
by with a thump of air. The tunnel had never seemed so
narrow. He leaped up onto the tiny walk at the side of the
pavement, where he had to balance like an acrobat until the
car passed. Worst of all, whoever was in that car, it was
doubtless somebody who knew him. Before, he could have
identified the exact model of car owned by every resident of
Orange Bay, but he seemed to have lost his expertise in cars
now that he no longer had one himself. They all seemed
alike to him, large dark monsters rushing along piercing the
darkness with their two tubes of glare and showing him their
twin red anuses after they passed. He emerged from the
tunnel into the starlight; there was no moon. The Orange
Bay he had known seemed to have turned into one cut out of
black cardboard by a child. It was only a crude approximation
of the real thing, and it had lost all its colors. The windows
were square eyes looking at him. The houses were animated
into presences, blocky animals that had all lined up along the
road in this way for some purpose. Careful! Another speed-
ing monster whizzed up behind him, illuminating the scene
like an explosion and forcing him to leap up on somebody's
lawn. At the side of the road he saw Velda's old Toyota, now
Cory's, and it was by this that he identified the house.

He went cautiously up the sloping walk. The lights
seemed to be on, but they were dim, maybe only by contrast
to the car headlights that had made him jump in his skin.
From the outside the house smelled of flowers, of sawn wood,
and of the faintest possible trace of recent cooking, something like ginger. He went up the redwood steps and in
through the large front door, which was unlocked as always.
The house was silent. The few lamps that were on were

turned to the lowest stroke of their three-way bulbs. Inside there were other odors: perfume (cheap, but in tiny quantities it seemed exotic and provocative), baby shit (also in small traces not offensive), the tang of Cory's unfiltered Camels, and the pleasant musk of Peter's boy-sweat. All of these olfactory mementos convinced him, in some way, that their owners were not in the house. If they had been, they would not have left their scents behind as calling cards.

He prowled in through the door to the study. It was dimly illuminated by the desk lamp. The books were still lined up in their usual order, and the Nagamoto was still on the wall, gleaming like an Oriental lacquer box. The desk was bare except for the telephone and a blank notepad. Golo didn't seem to have moved into the house yet, a delicate tact on his part.

He glanced out into the patio. It was a warm night, and the glass door was open. From a spot on the flagstones under the ficus tree Solange stared back at him, motionless, her back legs sitting down and her front legs like two stiff columns, her turquoise eyes catching the glow from the light inside the house. As its *genius loci*, she had elected to stay home when the others went out. In fact, as he thought about it, he had never known her to leave the house even so much as to explore the limits of the front lawn or the property line at the rear of the garden. Her life was a kind of black hole in which everything converged on a single point, the white wicker armchair under the tree in the patio, and might stray a little from that focus but only a little, drawn back as though by a magnet. He was not sure about her attitude toward him now, and fearing a rebuff, he said nothing to her and didn't attempt to touch her. The jewel eyes stared at him, unwinking.

The dining room. The kitchen. The door to the garage. The notion came to him to open it and see if the BMW was still there, even to get into it and sit there savoring what it smelled like, and open the glove compartment and touch the gloves in it. But he shrank back as though he were in a funeral parlor and somebody was inviting him to see what was in a room behind a closed door. He was struck with the

strangeness of it that people could feel this way about inan-
imate machines that rolled along the pavement on four black
circles and could be bought for a few thousand dollars. He
envisioned himself locked in the embrace of the BMW, dark,
cold, smelling of corrupt roses and cinnamon, knowing that
it belonged to somebody else now and was only a bitter
memory, a sensitive nerve not to be touched. He turned
away from the door without opening it.

He couldn't bring himself to go upstairs. Doubtless the
arrangements of things up there would give him some information about what was going on in the house now, about
how people got along together, whether a fat bald man had
moved in, whether the baby had learned to talk and called
Velda Mama, whether Peter was learning Greek, whether
Cory had got a job. But none of it seemed very important to
him, or rather it was none of his business; he was an interloper in this house, a thief, a prowler, and he would be liable
to arrest by the first policeman who flashed his light in
through the window.

He sat down on the Italian leather sofa, crossed his legs,
and then got up and went to the bar and made himself a
drink. He made a stiff one, a standing column of Scotch with
a single ice cube in it and only a small dollop of water.
Probably the liquor too belonged to Golo now. He was not
sure whether it was included in the trust deed. Anyhow it
was good stuff. That is, alcohol was good stuff. If it was good
alcohol, all the better. This was excellent Scotch; it had cost
. . . but he was no longer good with numbers. As he drank
it he sank into the old familiarity of his years in this house,
and he could hardly remember the details of the tiny place
where he now lived with Dorothy and three Guatemalans,
his chintz-enclosed alcove, the single bathroom where a
prism of green deodorant hung in the bowl, and the encyclopedia in which he had now got to Bimetallism. With his
feet cocked on the coffee table and the glass propped in his
crotch, he swam in a warm and pleasant ocean of self-pity, of
lost beauty, of a complicated but blurry contemplation of the
workings of fate. Through the open windows he could hear

the gruff murmur of waves. Now and then there were distant voices and fragments of music.

When the amber column had been reduced to an empty glass with an emaciated ice cube in it, he got up and made himself another one, trying brandy this time. It made absolutely no difference. They were exactly the same, brownish-gold, pungent, and tingling to the esophagus. He had never been a great fan of drinking, except for a little wine with dinner, but now it seemed to him an attractive form of sensuality. He could take it up as a hobby. Of course, the stuff cost money. But he could always steal here into the house and get some when he wanted it. Evidently the people who lived here now were going to go on leaving the doors unlocked, as he always had. He found that he was facing a Modane on the wall at the other end of the room. White tennis clothes, blue sky, blue wall of the house behind. It struck him now that the orange splotch in the center was really the sun. It was a clever trick of Kati; she pretended it was a face, but nobody's face was that orange or gave off that incandescent glow so that it could be felt like a hot stove. Drinking was good for art criticism too. It threw an entirely different light on things. He got up and made himself another one. There was a wealth of bottles to choose from, some full, some almost empty, some half full, so that the varying heights of the different-colored liquids seemed to play a kind of tune as they jagged up and down in the illuminated cabinet, an interesting phenomenon of synesthesia. He selected some English gin, the very best, and filled up the glass, omitting the ice cube and the water this time.

He decided to get up and look at the rest of the pictures in the house. If the Kati Modane was transformed, then so might the others be too. He wandered around sipping Beefeaters and trying to remember which walls the pictures had been on when he lived in the house. He picked his way through the rooms with caution, since he found that while he had been sitting on the sofa the house had tilted a little to the left, only a few degrees but enough so that it took a special effort to walk around in it upright. In the entry there was a picture he didn't recognize at all. It was the color of midnight, with smudges of green here and there, and someone seemed to have dropped a can of white paint on it near the bottom. He stood studying it for some time in a leisurely way, determined to make sense of it. After a while he decided that it was one of Mordecai's cobalt-blue paintings. At least that was the most sensible explanation; it certainly wasn't anything he remembered ever having in the house. It might, however, be a Nagamoto transmuted by some trick of light, or by the fact that he no longer lived in the house, which made everything in it look different. He tried to move closer to see if there was a signature on the painting and found that it went out of focus entirely. Part of this was due to the fact that the lamp in the room was turned down low. He tried to correct this but found it difficult to locate the switch. You would think that the switch for a lamp would be somewhere on the lamp, either at its base or farther up where the brass socket fitting was, but all his groping was futile. The lamp, an affair shaped like a giant gourd and signed by an Italian designer, fell to the floor, shattered, and went out with a pop.

He couldn't locate his drink either. This was not really important, because the house was full of glasses and he remembered where the bar was. *Mon vieux, la situation est désespérée mais pas sérieuse.* (A French general said that. Stout fellow.) He wandered around through a movie set that cleverly resembled the house he had once lived in. In fact, there were plenty of glasses in the bar. This time he tried aquavit (he had a dim memory that it made a lovely blue flame when ignited) and put some ice in it, but found that for some reason, when he put the ice in, some of the aquavit spilled over the rim at the top of the glass. He picked the ice out with his fingers, dropped it on the floor, and topped off with more aquavit. He congratulated himself on the sensible, forthright way he had solved this problem.

Carrying the glass, he set off now to inspect the rest of the pictures in the house. He hadn't checked the study yet, or had he? Yes, he had gone in and looked at the Nagamoto when he first came, but that was before he started drinking. No doubt the Nagamotos would be different too now, and since they were such beautiful pictures to begin with, the transformation might be something really interesting. Now where was the study exactly? He stood in the living room, with the Italian sofa on his right and the bar behind him, and swayed like a cobra trying to locate the door. Golo had perhaps rearranged the furniture. Or if Golo hadn't moved in yet (Velda said she would never go to bed with a man before she married him), then perhaps Velda was the one who had moved the furniture. But a simple moving of the furniture couldn't account for this complete disappearance of the study. Evidently one of them, or both of them, had moved the doors around too. The study should be right ahead when he was facing in this direction. Finally he located it. It had been hard to see before because it was more shadowy and dim than the rest of the house, illuminated only by the desk lamp. There was a bright red pinpoint hanging in the air over the desk. It was either a small glowing light the size of a matchhead, or there was something wrong with his vision. It took him some time to make up his mind to go into the study and see what it was. It seemed to him that it was probably bad news, about something that was happening in the house, or about his own mind. He went into the study and found it was the light on the answering machine.

He pushed the button and the red jewel went out. A voice said, *You have one message,* in its slightly stiff mechanical way.

There was a hiss, an electronic trill, and a moment of silence.

Hallo. Got your call. Hope I've got your new number right. Golo, there's one thing that bothers me about all this. Do you think he might come over here and try to prance? Of course, we didn't give him an address, but he might be able to trace us through the warehouse. Ring me when you can, eh? Let me know how he's taking it. Ta ta.

There was another hiss and a click as the tape inside the machine rewound itself. Then the shadowy room was silent.

Swaying slightly, holding himself erect with an effort, he went back into the living room. He became aware now—or became aware again—of sounds coming in through the windows. A distant quasi-human murmur that resembled the chanting of oracles, an occasional fragment of laughter, and a thread of music, dying away and then reappearing like a filament of incandescence in a Nagamoto painting. The background of the sound, it seemed to him, was cobalt blue, and the singing voice was electric green.

He thought, *I must go and tell Velda.*

Still carrying the glass of crystal-clear elixir, he made his way out of the house and down the walk. The floodlighted dome bulked large in the darkness across the road. It was probably the source of the bluish background to the green thread of music. The singing became louder after he climbed the lawn and made his way into the pink and green landscaping lights. He turned to the right, bumped into something, and found himself confronted by a wooden fence, almost spilling his drink. He took a long sip of it and contemplated the problem before him.

The first thing was to get over the fence, which Wolfie seemed to have erected since the last time he had been to the house. He could hardly do this carrying his drink. He pondered the problem of getting both himself and the drink over the fence. There were two ways to do it. He could pass the drink over first and then climb the fence himself, or he could climb over the fence and then reach back for the drink. It was pretty difficult when you thought about it. The fence was about six feet high and had no handholds. He was not going to be able to take the drink with him. This was clear now. It was a major difficulty. In the babble of voices from the house he could now make out words, all of them spoken by women for some reason. *Lovely. Banshee. Cuernavaca. Christian Dior.* And laughter. Mostly feminine too, but counterpointed by an occasional gruff ho-ho from the opposite sex. The party smelled like pretty women, whiskey, and Swedish meatballs, along with a circus odor as though of greasepaint.

He finally decided what he would do about the drink.

He could drink it first and carry it over that way. An ingenious solution. He did so and set his foot on the fence; the foot slipped and came back to the ground with a thump. That was understandable, since there was no foothold. He heard the singing voice more clearly now.

> *And that the stars*
> *Above her lied*
> *And that the night*
> *Was in a dream*

He remembered again why he had to climb the fence: *to tell Velda.* He gave a great lunge at the top of it and fell back. Once again. The third time he managed to get his chest up on the thing. He balanced on top of it, swayed, teetered, and fell heavily down on the other side.

He was lying on his back. He could still hear the laughter and voices, but the music had stopped. Every so often there were other sounds around him, the caws of gigantic soprano crows. Harry lay on the grass at the bottom of the garden, one arm on either side of him, legs slightly splayed. He contemplated the night sky, which was its usual black with blue variations. Swishing by went black fringes, oversized blue eyes, green fireworks with blue stars bursting in them. His own eyes stared upward like two blobs resting on the shell of his skull. He saw the shadow of a curved dirk, silhouetted in the pinkish light from the house, ducking and feinting like a boxer. It withdrew and approached again. He felt an excruciating flash of pain, then another, and his mind rushed out with a shriek through the two holes in his head.

twenty-three

Dawn's woman Marta sat on the terrace next to a table with paints, spangles, jars of colored sparkles, makeup creams, and a collection of brushes and cosmetic pencils. One by one the guests came to her to sit down and receive their party faces. Some had colored lines and curlicues, sine or cosine curves, concentric circles like targets, maplike contour lines, extra mouths drawn on their cheeks, third eyes on their foreheads, Rorschachs of primary colors with black Rouault outlines, fine hatchworks of red and blue lines, magenta dots that covered them like fevers, faces half black and half chartreuse or divided into squares like checkerboards, yellow, black-dotted faces with red ears, or white with Vandykes and mustaches, or with moons, Saturns, and constellations. Other faces, coated with white grease, were dusted with glitters of silver, crimson, gold, green, and magenta. Some hands were decorated too: white with drawn-on emerald rings, or white palms with each finger drawn in a different color. Golo had a white face with gold sparkles; his eyelids were pale green and his lips black. In the middle of his bald spot was an eye. Velda too had a white face, with pink lips and pink disks on the cheeks, and sparkles of gold. Her frizzly hair was sprinkled with metallic spangles that caught the glow from the lights. Cory had an American-flag face, with the blue field over his eye. Rochelle in a white party dress, riding on his hip, had a red spiral that began in the center of her nose and circled out until it reached her chin and ears. The only face that was not decorated was Marta's own. She was wearing the appliqué skirt that she had been making for herself for several months, along with a plain white blouse.

Velda, on a stool, sang in a green thread of a voice, barely audible over the chatter and laughter of the others and the clinking of glasses. Plucking the guitar with gilded fingers, she bent her head to the side. Each short line she stretched out like taffy, held up by the guitar chords, until it fell and she went on to the next.

> *A maiden rode*
> *To the valley low*
> *Her face was pale*
> *Her steed was white*
> *The stars above*
> *Were diamonds bright*
> *The forest round*
> *Was black as night.*

Here followed a series of guitar chords, working their way through the same harmony three times. Golo sat watching her, entranced, smiling with his black lips. Velda went on in her thin voice, an exact simulation of a famous folksinger. She was clever at mimicry, at grasping the sounds and stances, the minute nuances of tone in the world about her.

> *And there she found*
> *Her lover true*
> *Beside a lake*
> *Of deepest blue*
> *He took her in*
> *His loving arms*
> *And kissed her lips*
> *And then she knew.*

A pause for more chords. Only Golo, the old woman Grace, and Peter were paying attention; the others were caught up in their chatter and hilarity. Wolfie Gilbert, in a magenta face with white saucers around his eyes, was talking to the red-and-black checkerboard of George Grinspoon; he glanced sideways now and then at Velda on her stool. The song went on.

> That her true love
> Was cold and stark
> And that the stars
> Above her lied
> And that the night
> Was in a dream
> And that she held
> A shadow dark.

"*Beaux sentiments!*" Golo laughed. "Morbid music this, my dear, for a wedding night."

"I didn't make it up. It was on the radio."

"It's her Mind Song," cawed the old lady to no one in particular.

The red-and-black checkerboard floated into view. "What's this all about, Golo? Velda singing this funny song. What's the point of it?"

"She has to demonstrate her talent before she can be married. You know. Like a girl in an old English novel."

"I knew you had to have talent. Not that kind."

Golo socked him playfully. He was in an excellent humor. "What would you know about it, George? You've been a bachelor for so many years, you've probably forgotten how to cock your snoot."

The old woman didn't quite understand what was going on, except that everyone was painted for a gala. She glanced at Golo, then at Velda. Her own face was a Mexican flag, green on one side and red on the other, with a white stripe down the middle.

"Now it seems you've taken up with Golo."

"I haven't taken up with him. I'm going to be married to him."

"Why did you take up with him instead of the other one?"

"The vagaries of a fickle heart, Grace," Golo told her. *"La donna è mobile."* He hugged her too, with one arm still around George. When he laughed, his cupid-bow black mouth parted to show his white teeth and the gleam of his gold inlays.

Grace was holding an empty glass and looking around hopefully. But Wolfie wouldn't let her have liquor. He took the glass out of her hand. "Mama, we're going to eat soon. After the wedding."

"The wedding? Who is getting married?"

"Golo and Velda, Mama. Velda told you just a moment ago. Don't you remember?"

"Velda has to keep house. She can't get married."

"She's going to keep house for Golo, Mama."

"He needs one for the house and one for his bed."

Everybody grinned. Wolfie told her, "Velda is going to do both, Mama."

"Golo has plenty of women. Why does he have to take this one?"

"He likes her, Mama."

"Why does she need a new man? She's got the other one."

"Harry, Mama."

"Yes, Harry. What about him?"

"She doesn't have him anymore."

"I always thought they were a lovely couple. Harry and the other one, who looked like a bird."

"Killian."

"Yes, Killian. What happened to her?"

"Don't be an Ancient Mariner, Mama."

"What's an Ancient Mariner?"

"One who brings up unpleasant things at weddings."

Grace was grinning too. Velda knew now that she understood perfectly everything that was going on. The pretense of a faded mind was a game she played with them. It gave her pleasure to do it. It was the role she had chosen for herself, to play the dim-witted crone. Velda wondered if the others understood this too. She felt a sudden fondness for her, seeing her all at once as an ordinary person, a person like herself, who faced a universal destiny with fortitude and good humor, with courage.

"Why can't I have a drink? Everybody else has one."

"We're going to have champagne in a while, Mama."

Marta carried a drink cooler with the champagne, the ice, and the chilled flute glasses down to the pergola. They all followed her and clustered under the tiny roof. Wolfie began working on the wires of the first bottle, treating it with gingerly care. Golo, laughing, took the bottle from him, shook it violently, then handed it back. When Wolfie had the cork halfway out, it shot the rest of the way like a bullet, followed by a geyser of hissing foam. The cork bounced from the roof of the pergola and struck Grace, who was startled. Golo was delighted when the cork shot out. He seized all the other bottles and shook them, one by one, so that they exploded when opened. There was a din of popping and gushing, and the squeals of the guests when the spray fell on them.

"Is this part of the wedding, Wolfie?"

"We always have champagne at a wedding, Mama."

"But you have it after the wedding."

"We'll do that later. Now we're celebrating the sacrifice of Velda's virginity. And Golo's," he added, to the acclaim of hurrahs and laughter.

"Oh, you must be joking."

There were some comments about Golo's virginity. Suggestions as to obscure and esoteric ways in which he might conceivably still be virgin. Laughter. The chatter became blurred. A peacock shrieked from the bottom of the garden.

Wolfie said to Grace, "You can have just a tiny bit,

Mama." He poured a thimbleful of champagne into a flute and handed it to her. Looking around solemnly at the others, she drained it in a single gulp. Then she sidled away to the cooler, found an open bottle, and disappeared with it into the darkness. Wolfie didn't notice. He was flushed and pleased, playing the host, serving the very best champagne, elated by the heavy nuptial portent in the air and by his own magenta face with its oversized white eyes that made him look like some rare lemur of the jungle.

"Is everybody here? Where's Peter? Peter, will you have some champagne?"

"Thank you."

Wolfie filled his glass. "The lad's a bit young for the sap of the vine, but it won't hurt him just this once, I imagine."

Peter smiled and said nothing. His face was white with red hearts, a large one on each cheek and smaller ones on his chin, his forehead, and each side of his nose. His hair, like Velda's, was dusted with sparkles. He looked like a young love god in a Renaissance pageant. He sipped the champagne thoughtfully, not sharing the hilarity of the others.

"And you," said Wolfie, turning. "I don't even know what your name is."

"Cory."

Wolfie filled a glass for him too. Cory took it in his left hand, since he was balancing Rochelle on his hip with the other arm. He took a long sip, draining half the glass, then he dipped his finger in it and inserted the finger into Rochelle's mouth. Rochelle chortled beatifically.

"To . . . to . . ." Wolfie stammered and looked around for help.

There was a chorus of suggestions.

"To Velda."

"To the bridal pair."

"To Bacchus."

"To those who are not present," said Dawn in a low voice.

Golo shut his silky-green, serpentlike lids and smiled. Everybody drank, but things were too confused for a toast.

The bride and groom drank and kissed. When they separated, a few touches of black clung to Velda's lips, and Golo's were smeared with pink.

He grew suddenly serious. The eye on his shaved head wrinkled with the profundity of his thought. He drew Velda by the elbow, and they turned away toward the sea. The others made way for them, and he led her to the edge of the pergola. The night was deep and calm; the dark surface of the sea turned in the starlight with slow silver wrinkles. The island offshore lay like a sleeping sable on the horizon. He drew her close to him, then intoned in a low voice that shook a little.

> So might I, standing on this pleasant lea,
> Have glimpses that would make me less forlorn;
> Have sight of Proteus rising from the sea;
> Or hear old Triton blow his wreathèd horn.

"Do you think that will happen?" she asked him.
"If you believe it."
His hand clutched her head like an eagle grasping an egg, and sparkles sprang from her hair into the darkness.

The procession left the terrace and wound its way down the road to the beach. It was the precise moment of the solstice, the longest day in the year and the shortest night. The bride and groom were clad in garlands. In the middle of the procession was a bald saffron-clad Irishman from the local Krishna center. Each celebrant, except for the bride and groom, carried a brown paper bag with a lighted votive lamp in it. The line straggled and separated, widened and came together again. Voices called from one end to the other: laughter, hoots, confidential murmurs. There was an air of hilarity mingled with the solemnity of the erotic. The luminarias exuded a dim and moving wavery light, brownish at the edges, white at the top. The decorated faces were underlighted and seemed to float disembodied down the canyon, with the dark bulk of the houses on both sides. Peter followed just behind the priest, carrying his luminaria with care so as not to upset the lamp in the bottom. His eyes were fixed on the saffron robe ahead of him and on the pink neck that protruded from the top of it. In his heightened consciousness he was aware of his own white face with red hearts, which seemed to project itself into the air in front of him. The voices around him chattered and lisped.

"Oh, I feel like getting married myself."

"You've been married for years."

"Yes, but doing this."

". . . pink."

"Let's leave quickly after."

"Why?"

"Are you so dense?"

"Okay."

Old Grace, whose luminaria tipped and almost went out: "Slower, all of you. Oh, I get so exasperated. When people won't . . ."

"Come along, Mama. Don't set fire to yourself."

". . . Peter . . . could just eat him." (Titter.)

"Control yourself; he's just a child."

Peter heard this clearly. And he heard:

"If Wolfie can evoke the peacocks by cooing, maybe Golo can evoke old Proteus from the sea."

"Where are those rare birds anyhow?"

"Never come out Midsummer Night. Have their own ceremonies."

"Wolfie, you must hold my elbow."

"I can't, Mama. I'm carrying this lighted bag."

"But why are we carrying them?"

"*Lux amor est.* Scuse, my Ratin is lusty." (Giggle.) "I mean, my Latin is rusty."

"Why, old Henry Wong is not here. Mary either."

"He's not well, I hear."

"Is that so?"

"A little under the weather. Nothing serious."

(Sung): "I dreamt I dwelt in marble halls, where demons held me by the balls."

"Are we going to take off our clothes?"

"Father McZen will instruct us, no doubt."

"What do you hear . . ."

". . . lives in town."

"What's he doing?"

"Wolfie, is it far now?"

"Just a few steps, Mama."

Peter veered off from the others, then stopped under the shadow of a tree. The rest of them went on. No one noticed him in the dark. He waited until the procession was past and the line of brownish lights had disappeared around the edge of the cliff, then he turned and hurried back up the road. He was still carrying his luminaria, which teetered and dimmed. He tried various ways of carrying it and settled on a hieratic pose with both hands under it held at the level of his navel. He passed the floodlighted dome and his own house with dim yellow outlining the windows. Behind him he heard an eldritch screech, piercing, which fell away with a dying fall. He went on up the hill to the Fangs'.

The house was almost dark. Only the windows of the bedroom upstairs were lit. He made his way with difficulty through the unclipped shrubs of the garden and into the screened porch on the side, where his luminaria cast a subterranean glow on the wooden lattice. He explored the dark downstairs and found no one. In the recreation room the dead video screen reflected the oblong of brown light in his hands. In the front room the large window facing the road was uncurtained as always, transmitting starlight, the lighted eyes of the house across the road, and the transparent reflection of the luminaria with his own valentine face above it. Henry Fang's massive black table was covered with books and papers. There was the armchair with its persimmon cushions where he himself had sat many times. The luminaria, which he had carried up from the beach without quite knowing why, served as a kind of flashlight in the dark house. Everything was dim and transformed in this new papery light he brought to it.

The kitchen, where he had never been in his life. Mary's

domain. It seemed very ordinary except that there were garlands of roots hanging from the ceiling: garlic, ginger, and something twisted like mandrake. A mixer set with its paddles cocked over a bowl; the batter in the bowl had turned brown, and there were cracks on the surface. On the marble counter were a half-dozen shrimp, dry and curling up their tails. Nobody had been in the kitchen for some time.

With the luminaria teetering in his hands, he went up the stairs to the floor above, another voyage of exploration. The walls of the staircase were upholstered in a greenish brocade with a silver thread. At the top was a long hallway in the same decor. The doors on the hall were all shut except for the one at the end, where a dim light wavered.

When he entered the room Mary was standing by the bed with her hands clasped, gazing at him with a placid blankness. She didn't seem to notice that his face was painted white with red hearts and that he was carrying a paper bag with a light in it. It was as though she had been waiting for him. There was something in her motionlessness, in her unblinking stare, in the slackness of her oversized dress, that suggested idiocy. A sprig of her gray hair had come loose and stuck out at an angle from her temple.

The bed was large and ornate, black lacquer like the rest of the furniture in the house. On the nightstands at the sides were two bronze oil-burning lamps of the Shang period, primitive shapes on tripods. Their flickers were the only light in the house. Henry Fang was lying on the bed with the covers pulled up to his waist. He was clothed in his brocaded robe with an undershirt visible under it. His face had changed color and texture; it was bluish gray and seemed waxy and deliquescent, like an underwater plant. He had acquired a pomp and dignity, a seriousness, a power of character that he had lacked in his real life, when he had been merely imposing and wise. His eyes no longer examined Peter with their gentle superiority; instead they were turned within himself to ponder the mystery of his own corruption.

Mary said, "I knew you would come."

She said, "Nobody has forgiven him but you. I have not. It would not make any difference if I did."

She said, "I have known many different sides to this man. He had more different sides than the earth itself. Some of them made him cry like a baby. I could not make him happy by myself. Only devils and demons could do that."

Peter said, "I haven't forgiven him."

"You have, since you came."

He could think of nothing to say to this.

She said, "He could never be satisfied. As soon as he had one thing that he craved, he would start plotting in his heart for another. He did everything with his body and his mind that is forbidden."

She said, "He bought things from bad people, and these people said they would tell on him, and he paid them money. And then he would buy more of the bad things from them. The police found out, and he had to pay them too. It was then that he cried. But he didn't stop."

She said, "He paid men and women."

Peter looked back at her without speaking. She went on with her explanation, leaving long silences in which neither of them spoke.

She said, "He never talked to me, but I could see behind his face into his mind. I was frightened of the things that he did, but he wouldn't talk to me about them. I couldn't speak to him because I was frightened of him, and because I loved him. He loved me because he needed my body too, along with the others', and because I said nothing about the other things he did."

She said, "All the world he brought to this house. All these Chinese things, and he was not Chinese. I was Chinese. He was born in San Francisco. He sucked my Chineseness from me and used it to nourish himself. He lived in a China that he stole from me. I became American. I have no Chinese left."

She said, "All these things he bought with the money he got foreclosing on widows. Cheating old people of their savings. Lending money to buy guns. Investing in bad countries. Countries where they do bad things to their people. These lamps," she said, without moving her hands and indicating with her eyes the Shang bronzes by the bed, "are each enough to feed a child until it is grown."

She said, "He sucked my Chineseness from me, and he wanted to suck your youngness from you. Your innocence."

"But I'm not innocent."

She didn't seem to be listening to him or paying any attention to him. She had scarcely looked at him since he came into the room.

"You were lucky. You escaped. He made a mistake. He got old and he blundered. He couldn't plan so well anymore."

"We talked about books."

"He read many books. But he transformed them into wicked things. Because of the bad things he did, he turned to books, and the books told him more bad things to do. Maybe all books are wicked things. I don't know. He would never let me read them. He said I wasn't smart enough."

She said, "And right now I love him. I still do. He was all there ever was in the world to me. I had nothing else. But for him I was never more than a tiny bit of what there was in the world."

She said, "I could only live by putting on his body and his mind as though they were a garment. And it's still that way. I am his body lying on the bed. I know what is happening to him, I know what is going on inside him. I don't know what is happening to me, because he has taken my will from me. That is what love is, I think, to take somebody else's will from her. And now I can not weep. I can not weep because I have no will. He can not weep, so I can not. Maybe you, a child, can tell me how to weep."

Here she sat down abruptly on the floor and pulled her skirt over her knees. In the dim flicker of the lamplight she seemed a small bundle inside the skirt, a legless dwarf. She stared straight past Peter, her eyes like two bright nuts in the antique map of her face.

□

Peter left the house through the latticed potting shed, still carrying the luminaria, which was beginning to smell of candle wax and scorched paper. After the darkness of the house the starlight burned fiercely. Under his feet he felt the descending slope of the lawn, then the hard grittiness of the road. His feet in their canvas shoes made no noise. Everything was quiet. In the distance was the very faint grumble of the surf. He went down the road more slowly than he had come up it.

He had almost forgotten what he had seen in the house. It was unreal, just as everything was that happened in that house. It was contrived and dramatic, theatrical, unconvincing, like the videos with their Hawaiian palms and their papier-mâché classical temples. It was not the image of the wicked old dead man that he carried with him, but that of the big black table covered with books. He had grown up surrounded by books and talk of books: at home, at Pointz Hall, and at Henry Fang's. Books were his familiars, his intimate companions. They were the thing that set him apart from the others, the sign of his specialness and isolation in the world. A sweep of joy went through him like a sunrise, and he felt a sudden insight and keenness, an ascending step of wisdom; he went on through the dark carrying his hieratic lamp of paper and smiling to himself. He clearly imagined the future he was sure to have—he had no doubt about it—as a professor, an identity which would seem so natural to him as an adult that people would wonder how he could ever have been anything else; in which all the qualities he had now would become natural, suitable, and necessary to his profession—his superior mind, his curiosity, his lack of interest in the opinions of others, his conviction that he was right in most matters and that other matters were not important, his intellectual arrogance, and his invulnerability. Just as he had never known material want as a child, so he would never know it as a tenured professor in a university. Even though these things had just flashed through him now in an instant, alone on the dark road carrying his luminaria, he knew that he had always known them, just as he had always known that he had always known that he would grow taller, that his voice would change, that he would grow pubic hair, that he would eventually know the love of women well enough to become expert in it and then to neglect it with a Casanovan detachment, that he would look back one day on the omniscient, much-admired teachers of Pointz Hall and the encounter with Henry Fang as unimportant incidents of his childhood.

Passing by his own house, he thought *them*. Not the people who lived there now but the others, before. The days when the three of them were together; and he felt a spasm of anguish at what had happened. That night in the sea, when he had called out *Harry*. A chance missed. If he had cried out, *Father! I'm your son!* Then the precariously tottering moment might have swerved, and everything afterward might have been different. But he didn't. Everything had fallen apart without a center to hold it. And the center had been the beaky red-haired woman who was now becoming remote and distant to him, without substance, like something he had seen in a movie. Even his grief for her was distant, something he remembered, and he had to force himself to remember. Why had it all worked out as it did? Because it had to; there was no other way. It was necessary for his mother to die, for his father to suffer, to know the torments of hell, to grasp out blindly in his grief, and to fall to lust. It was necessary for people to suffer from misunderstanding and the failure to speak their hearts. It was necessary for the stars to glow at night and the sun in the daytime. The surf washed at the shores of Orange Bay just as it did at Pondicherry and Vladivostok. Rochelle was a baby. Cory was a man. Velda was a woman. Henry Fang was a corpse. Each had its part and was necessary, just as the waves washed on the shore without thinking about it and the souls of real people paraded the world in hearts, spangles, and flags. He still lived in the same house, but now there were different people in it, Velda, Golo, and Cory. It seemed unreal to him, but perfectly natural, comprehensible, and comfortable. They would be different, but he would be the same, and what they did would not touch him. The house, the people, other faces, the daily squalid and living world, and everything except himself and his seething of desire and thought became unimportant to him. Halfway down the road he met the procession coming up from the beach. Dawn's woman Marta, in her appliqué skirt, ran past him from behind and fled to meet it. Stopping panting before Wolfie, she said, "Here's Mr. De Spain in the garden."

twenty-four

Harry was trying to climb up a cliff. He believed it was the same cliff he had climbed up the night when he went swimming in the buff, but he couldn't be sure. He broke his nails in the soft stone; it crumbled and he fell onto his knees. Once or twice he managed to get as far as the dangling fronds of iceplant, but they snapped and he dropped to the sand again.

A light but crisp autumn breeze chilled his cheeks. Around him, muffled by the surf, he could hear the excited voices of people calling to each other on the beach. The burr and mumble of cars passing on the highway. A distant siren. A church bell. A flutter of pigeons' wings. The pad-pad of someone running in the sand, a thump as a football hit a chest. A smell of popcorn and fried food, of suntan oil, of kelp drying in the sun, of drugstore perfume.

He set his foot into the sandstone again and reared up; it broke with a gritty sound, and he descended the twelve inches to the sand as on a tiny elevator. The trouble was, he decided, that he was trying to climb while holding his cane. He propped it against the cliff, checking with his hand to be sure it was still there and hadn't fallen sideways. Then he tried again.

The last time he had done this, of course, it was dark. Whether or not it was dark now was of very little concern to him. It was dark for him. Of course, the touch of the sun warmed his shoulders and prickled in his hair, but it only made the darkness shimmer a little without lightening it. That was one of his new discoveries, that darkness could resist the light beating on all sides of it, that the sun for all its warmth was unable to redden the dead bulbs under his eyelids.

For weeks he had wandered around the familiar streets of the town, and the beach where he came by preference again and again, drawn by the moving breast of the sea, which he could not see but could hear and smell and feel in the fine nerves of his blood. Dorothy's place was on the land side of town, and he had to cross the highway to get to the beach. At first this was a terrifying obstacle, but in time he mastered it. He would find the corner in the middle of town with the hotel on one side and the ice cream store on the other, and there he would join the cluster of people waiting on the curb for the traffic light. When the light went green he hardly needed to be clued by their footfalls or by the squeak of stopping tires; he was aware in a vestigial organ of his mind of the redness of their waiting, of the greenness of their going. It was as though the pores of his skin transmitted to his mind some signal of the color of the light, which wound its way into the proper lobe even though it came from the wrong messenger. Red: stand stiffly holding cane to locate curb. Green: step forward confidently with the others.

He treasured these moments of standing on the curb in the awareness of the others waiting with him. In shops and doorways he tried to get close to other people, strangers, just to touch them accidentally with his elbow. Men or women, children, old bums, it didn't matter. These brief contacts gave him a deep and innocent satisfaction. So animals huddled together in their dens; so horses stood rump to nose, flicking flies off each other with their tails. Without these touchings and brushings, these battery recharges of the spirit, these totally innocuous transfers of warmth and humanity, he would not have survived. All is touch. People must touch. With a heroic pessimism, a Buster Keaton stoicism, he tried to climb the cliff for the tenth time and failed.

I imagine you think that you're doing it all over again. That it's happening right now.

What?

Climbing the cliff in the nude. Your rather ludicrous escapade.

How could you know about that?

I know a good many things. I've made it my business to know what you're doing.

She picked up his fallen cane and restored it to his hand.

Who are you?

Don't you know who I am? Can't you tell from my voice?

Let me touch you.

She offered her face, and he stretched his free hand toward it. It was cool and metallic, full of concavities, like an artist's charcoal sketch before he fills in the flesh.

How did you find me?

You're quite conspicuous, Xavier. It's broad daylight, and you look funny shambling around with your white cane like that.

I've learned the trick of it. I'm getting along all right.

All by yourself?

There are people. I touch them.

Yes, you do, quite a bit. But sooner or later somebody's going to scream and call a cop.

Warm comradely humanity.

Citizens going about their business. They don't care to be fondled by cripples.

What cruel language you use.

I'm not cruel (she said with just a trace of mockery). I'm here to save you.

What must I do?

Take my arm.

He hung on to her elbow. It felt like a rake handle with a lump in it.

Where are we going?

She didn't answer this. They went along the sidewalk together, he hanging to her arm and dangling his cane.

You're probably curious about the world, said Sylvia. It's quite different from what you remember. Everything is changed. The sea is no longer blue but violet. The surf throws up diamonds and zircons, which anyone can take in his hands. The clouds have gold leaf on them. At night everything is the color of cranberries. People are more beautiful now. They have all had face-lifts and do their hair differently, and their clothes are prettier. There are no more ugly people. The children have beautiful grown-up faces, as though they were wearing little movie-star masks. Even the dogs are more handsome. They have mink fur and they wear silver collars. And the cats are all tiny jaguars and ocelots, with sharp teeth.

It's nice of you to tell me this.

You can't tell if it's true, so what's the difference? You might as well enjoy it.

They were going along the sidewalk toward the traffic light at the hotel.

They have a new kind of cars now; they're made of spun sugar, and they come in pastel colors. Their tires are candy. The trees all have Christmas lights. The flowers, on the other hand, are various shades of gray. This is to enhance their smell; it's a new invention. You wouldn't imagine how this changes everything.

Yes I would. I have a healthy imagination.

They had arrived at the traffic light.

Now do your trick. Show me how it works.

He waited, feeling the red light in his skin. There was the closeness and warmth of other people waiting. When the light turned green he was the first to move from the curb, towing her after him.

Bravo! You manage beautifully. I wonder how you do it.

The traffic lights are the only thing that hasn't changed color.

How clever of you to notice.

You're full of flattery. You never were that way before.

You never gave me a chance. In the interview, you were so wrapped up in your own ego and in your power as the manager of a slave market. You must have done the whole thing with an enormous erection.

I was just looking for a home manager.

Horseshit (she said in what seemed to be a cheerful voice).

And you were too beautiful. That's why I didn't pick you.

Anorexic is another word. It must have occurred to you.

And you were a snappy dresser.

I still am. Watch the curb now.

The one I picked (he said) didn't work out.

She worked out far too well. She wrecked you.

I wrecked myself.

The meaning behind the events eludes us. You got wrecked. And now here you are.

Where are we?

They were somewhere on Paseo.

In front of the gallery. Would you like to go in?

Not particularly.

Mordecai has done very well. He now handles Picasso, Rembrandt, Cézanne, and Jackson Pollock, along with several other famous artists, including himself. Mordecai has become famous. His cobalt-blue period is all the rage; all the other artists imitate it.

Does he wear different clothes?

No, still the same shirt with paint on it and the Greek fisherman's cap. He's adjusted well to riches.

He's a nice chap.

You and your anglicisms. An affectation you'd do well to get rid of. Speaking of clothes, there's spaghetti sauce or something on your shirt.

Salsa. From Juana's cooking.

You need taking care of. Careful now, here's another curb.

Thank you. I can feel them quite well with my third leg.

That cane! The old gentleman who lives across the street from you is nonplussed. He thinks you're making fun of him.

Farthest thing in the world from my mind.

They were going along a sidewalk in the shade, away from the press and ruckus of Paseo. He could smell pepper trees and the rich fertile corruption of a garbage can.

Where are we? We're on Mermaid, aren't we?

There was a silence.

Aren't we?

I'm sorry. I nodded. I forgot you can't see (she said with another slight trace of her mockery, like a touch of spice on food). Yes, we're on Mermaid. This is where I live. It's near where you used to live in the apartment over the garage. It's only two doors down.

And it's Tuesday, isn't it?

How did you know?

The garbage cans are out on the curb.

How clever you are.

It's funny we didn't know each other then.

Oh, that was before my time. So you've come back to the same place, you see. Now we go around to the rear and climb up a spiral staircase, a funny thing made of iron. You won't be able to hold my arm.

He followed her up the staircase, his cane tapping the bars at the side. He heard the scritch of her unlocking the door.

There's not much to the place. Just one room with the bed, and a tiny kitchenette. Most of it's full of my clothes. I do enjoy clothes, even though I can't afford them. It's a mystery to me how I get them. They just appear magically on my body. Maybe you can explain it to me.

They stood together in the middle of the room. He set his cane down on the floor.

Can I feel your face again?

If you want. Why?

I still can't believe it's you. Put on your big glasses and your earrings.

All right.

She disappeared for only a few instants, then he could sense her warmth next to him again. She stood motionless while he felt the oversized horn-rim spectacles and the hard metallic circles that hung from her ears, the size of bracelets. Then, to compare, her breasts. They were exactly the same size, and soft. It was a revelation to find that there were some parts of Sylvia not made of bone and tight-stretched skin, that there were some places where she felt things and was human like other people.

Are you still dressed the same way?

Yes, everything I wear is black. Except that everything that is black now has a light sheen of mauve.

And do you still wear a derby?

When I want to amuse myself. Do you want me to put it on?

No. Let me feel your hair.

It was like a helmet of silk, lightly fragrant.

Is it mauve too?

Black with mauve highlights.

And what color is your room?

The color of twilight. Gray, tangerine, and dark blue.

Is Orange Bay still orange?

Sunsets are cobalt blue now, if that's what you mean. In the morning, it's pale pink there.

And in the afternoon? When you came for the interview it was teatime.

Things are the same color they are at other places.

You had no pockets in your clothes. I was waiting to see where your car key was. You hid it on top of your tire.

Did you see that? I meant you not to.

Sylvia, why have you brought me here?

What better place? You were wandering like a lost soul on the beach.

I knew where I was. I was doing all right.

Yes, climbing up a cliff, making a public spectacle of yourself.

Is that what I was doing?

You need someone to take care of you. Whether you knew it or not, that's why you set out to hire a governess.

He smiled. Then it's you?

If you won't govern yourself, you must be governed by others.

All these months! I wonder at your persistence.

It's characteristic of women, you may have noticed, Xavier, that they don't dash directly at their prey like lions. They cruise around it, like sharks. They have patience. They know there's plenty of time. They survive. They persist. They polish up their fertile store of cruel arts. And when the prey is weak, they strike.

She made her raucous laugh, rather goatlike.

When I first set eyes on you, I knew I had to have you, Xavier. It made me numb with desire. I could just barely totter out to my car. Since then, I haven't been able to get you out of my mind for a single minute. When my blood beats, it throbs *him, him, him.* Constant vision of you hanging before my eyes. Shadow of your hair on forehead. Mouth. Hands. Especially hands! The way you move. The way you smell, like wine and Spanish leather. Your voice—an intimate buzz. I can feel it in my bones.

She took a breath and seemed to calm down.

In short, love in its usual forms. Not that I'm unaware of your faults. You have the body and mind of a Greek god, and the Greek gods were not noted for their wisdom or their unselfishness. Never mind. The rest is enough!

He heard the creak as she turned to walk around the room, the tap-tap of her heels.

This way it'll be nice. You can't see me, so you won't notice as I get older. I can stop smearing all those creams on me to cover up the lines. For you I'll always be the way you saw me for the first time. And the second time, at the café. At my best. Dressed to the teeth. Perfect complexion. Fashion-magazine figure. Sheer white hose. Clothes from the most expensive designers. No pockets for car keys. That's Sylvia. That will always be Sylvia. And you can see me that way right now, can't you?

He nodded.

It will be nice for you. You've got her. The model out of *Vogue*. The perfect governess. The one you thought you couldn't afford. And you couldn't, Xavier, because you didn't know the price. The price is everything, Xavier. Everything.

Her voice was different now. The mockery was gone. She was gentle, intimate, and affectionate. She said things they both knew were true. And it was amusing. It was as though he had never been candid with anyone and nobody had ever been candid with him. And now he would no longer conceal anything, and no one would conceal anything from him. There was nothing to conceal. He realized that it was the first time in his life he had ever trusted anybody completely.

What do you live on here?

I live by licking my paws, Xavier. I get along. I won't need so many clothes now that they've done their trick. We can get by on very little. Neither of us will need clothes if we just stay in this room together.

She laughed again, but in a different way, an offhand way, a confiding way, as though at a shared joke.

And there's only this one room?

That's right.

I need to explore it. I need to feel it and find out where things are. The doors and windows. The cupboards. The kitchen. The groceries. The water faucet. The toilet. The bed.

Would you like to go to bed now? I imagine you would. It's probably been a long time.

All right.

In the darkness where he lived he heard the tinkle of her earrings and the rustle of her dress. Through his mind passed another figure with a friendly and mocking smile: young, pale, dapper, in a black suit with a striped waistcoat, whipping the cloth off the painting with the dexterity of a stage conjuror. Silvio-Sylvia, the twin angels of his destruction, or of his salvation. The two forms merged in a blur of dark clothing, pale white skin, graceful limbs, and magnetic waves provoking desire. Sylvia clad in gold like an icon, Sylvia with head bent back, Sylvia feverish at the twin points of her cheeks, Sylvia luminous and Byzantine. In his blindness the painting merged with the slim presence before him who, in the banal world of the sighted, was the farthest thing possible from it. It was a sample of the bright and imaginative concatenations that lay before him in his new life. He remembered how she had told him at the café (derby, trousers, Byronic tie, a music-hall parody of Silvio the cockney fop) that he was a Spanish grandee. Now it struck him that he had behaved in a truly aristocratic way, staking everything on one throw of the dice and then surrendering himself to a proud and distinguished poverty. And his companion was to be this exiled princess, as poor as he was, whose beauty would illumine the darkness. In a part of his emotions that was still a strange land to him, not yet explored, he felt a warm wave of bliss. In spite of pain and death, the betrayal of friends, the malice that pervaded the world like a tropical fever, in spite of the cynicism of others and his own cynicism, there were good, true, and beautiful people in the world who were capable of love, and he knew now that he could become one of them. Yet this could not have come to him if he had not lost everything, wife, son, cattle, kith and kin, and passed through the cauldron of suffering. Very wise he was getting amid the ruins of his old palace. With the vision of the gilded figure in the painting before him, his nerves erect in warm honey, he surrendered himself with a childlike trust to the Stranger who beckoned to him from the dark.